O9-AIC-534

WITHDRAWN

STEVENS MEMORIAL LIBRARY
NORTH ANDOVER, MA 01845

NIGHT
MOVES

Center Point
Large Print

Also by Randy Wayne White and available from
Center Point Large Print:

Night Vision
Chasing Midnight
Gone

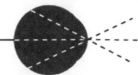

**This Large Print Book carries the
Seal of Approval of N.A.V.H.**

NIGHT MOVES

Randy Wayne White

CENTER POINT LARGE PRINT
THORNDIKE, MAINE

This Center Point Large Print edition
is published in the year 2013 by arrangement with
G. P. Putnam's Sons,
a member of Penguin Group (USA) Inc.

Copyright © 2013 by Randy Wayne White.
All rights reserved.

This is a work of fiction. Names, characters, places,
and incidents either are the product of the author's
imagination or are used fictitiously, and any resemblance
to actual persons, living or dead, businesses, companies,
events, or locales is entirely coincidental.

The text of this Large Print edition is unabridged.
In other aspects, this book may vary
from the original edition.
Printed in the United States of America
on permanent paper.
Set in 16-point Times New Roman type.

ISBN: 978-1-61173-715-8

Library of Congress Cataloging-in-Publication Data

White, Randy Wayne.
Night moves : a Doc Ford novel / Randy Wayne White. — Center Point
Large Print edition.
pages cm
ISBN 978-1-61173-715-8 (Library binding : alk. paper)
1. Ford, Doc (Fictitious character)—Fiction.
    2. Marine biologists—Fiction. 3. Florida—Fiction.
    4. Large type books. I. Title.
PS3573.H47473N48 2013b
813'.54—dc23

2013002140

This book is for my father, Floyd L. White,
member of the 101st Airborne Screaming Eagles
and a generation of men and women
who rescued the world

DISCLAIMER

Sanibel and Captiva Islands are real places, faithfully described but used fictitiously in this novel. The same is true of certain businesses, marinas, bars and other places frequented by Doc Ford, Tomlinson, and pals.

In all other respects, however, this novel is a work of fiction. Names (unless used by permission), characters, places, and incidents are either the product of the author's imagination or are used fictitiously. Any resemblance to actual persons, living or dead, or to actual events or locales is unintentional and coincidental.

Contact Mr. White at WWW.DOCFORD.COM

AUTHOR'S NOTE

One of the joys associated with researching Florida's social and natural history is that the facts often exceed the boundaries of believable fiction, which is why writing about the state also presents its challenges. I've published a number of books that prove this point, but none employ as many factual curiosities as *Night Moves*. For example, the Bone Field exists and is accurately described except for its location. I've walked that ancient place, seen the human bones entwined by roots, and will continue to protect the spot, along with the few others who know about it, until archaeologists agree to investigate.

The disappearance of five Navy torpedo bombers is another Florida mystery that plays a role in this novel, and I've used the most dependable information available to describe the event accurately in each detail—as fantastic as those details may seem to the reader. I relied heavily on the foremost authority on the subject, researcher and author Gian J. Quasar, who was kind enough to reply to my e-mails, and to discuss a theory that the five Avengers ultimately crashed in or near the Gulf of Mexico (a theory that is at odds with Mr. Quasar's own conclusions). As noted by Doc Ford, Mr. Quasar's book, *They Flew Into Oblivion*, contains the most exhaustive original research by far on the subject, and is highly recommended to those who want to learn more about that tragic incident.

There is nothing mysterious about the population boom of exotic snakes in the Everglades, and the situation is portrayed accurately, as are facts regarding the so-called jig-fishing techniques used in Boca Grande Pass tarpon tournaments. Hopefully, lawmakers and Florida's Fish and Wildlife Commission are finally awakening to the fact that jig-fishing is a euphemism for snag-fishing and will put an end to a practice that is detrimental to all but TV production companies that profit from the fast action which snag-fishing guarantees.

I learned long ago, whether writing fiction or nonfiction, that an author loses credibility if he's caught in a factual error. Because of this, I take research seriously, and my research benefits from experts in varied fields. Before recognizing those who provided assistance, though, I would first like to remind the reader that all errors, exaggerations and/or misinterpretations of fact, if any, are entirely the fault of the author.

Much thanks goes to my good friend Captain Mark Futch, a superb floatplane pilot who advised me (sometimes daily) on everything in this novel associated with airplanes, and who was my enthusiastic partner while researching Flight 19. Dr. Marybeth B. Saunders, Dr. Peggy C. Kalkounos, and Dr. Brian Hummel all provided invaluable expert medical advice. Sports psychologist Don Carman, once again, contributed unerring insights into human behavior, aberrant and otherwise, and his advice regarding Marion Ford's fitness routine is much appreciated. Pedro and Hannah Franco also deserve thanks.

Bill Lee, and his orbiting star, Diana, as always, have guided the author—safely, for the most part—into the strange but fun and enlightened world of our mutual friend, the Rev. Sighurdhr M. Tomlinson. Equal thanks go to Kerry and Donna Terwilliger for helping the author to escape, undamaged. Steven Dougherty of New York and California has also provided useful insights into the mind-set of hipsterdom and various modes of übercoolness. My niece Zoe Webb added help as well.

Others who provided help or insights, information, and advice include: young Captain Matthew Hirst of St. Louis, Kenneth Wright of the Florida Fish and Wildlife Commission, Hackensmith Cattle Company (Bull of the Beach), Dr. Pearl D. Miller of Tampa, Florida, Darryl Pottorf, Mark Pace, Gene Routh, and Kirsten Martin of VersaClimber. Special thanks goes to Wendy Webb, my life companion, adviser, and trusted friend, as well as Stephen Grendon, the author's devoted SOB, Mrs. Iris Tanner, guardian angel, and my partners and pals, Mark Marinello, Marty and Brenda Harrity, and my surfing buddy, Gus Landl.

Much of this novel was written at corner tables before and after hours at Doc Ford's Rum Bar and Grille on Sanibel Island and San Carlos Island, where staff were tolerant beyond the call of duty. Thanks go to Raynauld Bentley, Amanda Gardana, Amanda Rodrigues, Ashley Rodehaffer, Amazing Cindy Porter, Desiree Olson, Fernando Garrido, Joey Wilson, Khusan (Sam) Ismatullaev, Kory Delannoy, Mary McBeath, Michelle Madonna Boninsegna, Magic Milita Kennedy, Olga Jerrard, Rachel Songalewski, Tall Sean Lamont, High Shawn Scott, T. J. Grace, Yakh'yo Yakubov, Captain Brian Cunningham, Mojito Greg Barker, Jim Rainville, Nathaniel Buffman, Crystal Burns, Donna Butz, Gabrielle Moschitta, Maria Jimenez, and Sarah Carnithan.

At the Rum Bar on San Carlos Island, Fort Myers Beach, thanks go to Dan Howes, Andrea Aguayo, Corey Allen, Nora Billeimer, Tiffany Forehand, Jessica Foster, Amanda Ganong, Nicole Hinchcliffe, Mathew Johnson, Janell Jambon, C. J. Lawerence, Josie Lombardo, Meredith Martin, Sue Mora, Kerra Pike, Michael Scopel, Heidi Stacy, Danielle Straub, Latoya Trotta, Lee Washington, Katlin Whitaker, Kevin

Boyce, Keil Fuller, Ali Pereira, Kevin Tully, Molly Brewer, Jessica Wozniak, Emily Heath, Nicole English, Ryan Cook, Drew Fensake, Ramon Reyes, Justin Voskuhl, Anthony Howes, Louis Pignatello, and John Goetz.

Finally, I would like to thank Captain J. B. Marlin for his generosity, and my two sons, Rogan and Lee White, for helping me finish, yet again, another book.

—*Randy Wayne White*
Casa de Chico's
Sanibel Island, Florida

Now on the day that John Wayne died
I found myself on the Continental Divide
Tell me where do we go from here?
Think I'll ride into Leadville and have a few
  beers.

—JIMMY BUFFETT,
INCOMMUNICADO"

1

WE WERE HALF A MILE HIGH IN A bright Everglades sky, on the trail of five Navy torpedo bombers that vanished in 1945, yet my friend Tomlinson remained fixated on the fate of our marina's cat, which had gone missing only two days earlier.

The curse of obsession is one of the few qualities my hipster neighbor and I share.

"The problem with cats," he lectured through the plane's intercom, "is they have the ability to block human brain probes whenever they're in the damn mood—hunger and horniness the only exceptions. Otherwise, I would have tracked him down last night. Crunch & Des is always on the prowl, which I used to admire. Not now. Either something bad happened or he's behaving like an ingrate, showing off just to prove he doesn't need us. Doc'll back me up on this one. Won't you, Doc?"

Crunch & Des is the communal cat at Dinkin's Bay Marina, Sanibel Island, west coast of Florida, where I run a small company, Sanibel Biological Supply. When, as a young stray, he appeared at a Friday-night dock party, a friendly debate ensued over a fitting name for an ink black kitten with

15

six toes on each paw. By the time three favorites had emerged—Poe, Sasquatch, and Ernest—many cold beers (and saucers of milk) had been consumed, and debate had become mildly contentious. Fortunately, Mack, who owns the marina, intervened. He had just finished one of the late Philip Wylie's books, so honored the writer by naming the cat after Wylie's two hard-nosed 1940s fishing guides. It seemed an absurd choice at the time, looking at that sleeping, potbellied kitten curled next to a beer keg. Within a year, though, the cat was big enough, and sufficiently scarred from battle, to shoulder two names.

"If a gator grabbed him," Tomlinson continued, "I think I would have sensed the panic vibes. Like, alarm bells, you know? With sentient beings I care about, my subconscious maintains a telepathic link. That's why his disappearance has me so freaked. I think the little bastard's just screwing with my head. Like, when women intentionally try to make us jealous—but, hey, don't get me started on *that* subject."

Beside me, at the controls of his beautiful little Maule M-7 seaplane, Dan Futch, the best pilot I know, glanced at me, his expression asking *You trust this guy?*

I nodded *Usually* before adjusting my headphones and saying, "Shouldn't your mystic powers be focused on Flight 19? Five planes and fourteen men vanish without a trace almost

16

seventy years ago—if you can make a telepathic link with them, I'll be impressed. We'll look for the cat when we get back. If he hasn't turned up already."

Tomlinson was sitting behind me and put a hand on the back of Dan's seat. "Doc gets pissy when dealing with stuff that can't be explained, you ever notice? Same with anything that requires emotion."

I ignored him, my thoughts on the missing planes. Fourteen men lifted off from Lauderdale sixty-eight years ago on a routine flight that should have taken two hours. Instead, their disappearance has baffled generations of searchers—and spawned the myth of the Bermuda Triangle.

I looked out the starboard window and asked Dan, "We're close to Big Cypress Swamp, right?"

The pilot's eyes shifted to the GPS screen mounted above a console of gauges and electronics. "Parks aren't marked on this software version. Everglades City is about fifteen miles off our tail, Tamiami Trail a few miles north. No roads or landmarks for the next thirty miles until we're closer to Miami. So you can see why it'd be easy to get lost without electronics. Or think you're still over water. The more research I do, Doc, the more I'm convinced it could have happened."

Futch, too, was thinking back to that stormy winter night when the five torpedo bombers went

17

missing. It was possible his theory was valid, but I was skeptical despite the fact my pilot pal knows a lot more about aviation and missing planes than I ever will. We were over a sea of sorts—a sea of scud-colored swamp and sawgrass; the horizon a plain of flaxen gold in the late-morning sun. Below, the Earth was pocked with limestone implosions, random as craters on the moon, and there were islands of cypress trees that illustrated isolation, each silver dome set miles apart, alone, eroded into tear shapes by the slow flow of water draining seaward off the Florida plateau. *A river of grass,* Marjory Stoneman Douglas had described it, which is accurate but does not capture the immenseness of the lower forty-eight's largest roadless, unpopulated wilderness— the Everglades.

"We've got some thermals building up ahead," Futch said, "but that's what we're here for, right? And that high-pressure system is still moving toward us from the northeast. So it's looking like we chose the right day." The man was preparing us for the bumpy ride ahead, but his manner said *No need to be concerned.*

I wasn't. Much of my traveling life has been spent in choppers and small planes, and I've done some flying myself. Nowhere near Futch's league, though—he'd logged more than twenty-six thousand hours in the air and was among the most respected seaplane pilots in the country. In my headphones, I heard Tomlinson respond, "So far, the smoothest ride ever." Then added, "You ever think about flying into a waterspout? You know, just to see what would happen? I did it once in my sailboat. Really an interesting experience. Maybe not today, but let your subconscious work on the idea. *I'd* go with you."

In reply to the pilot's questioning look, I nodded, then shook my head: Yes, Tomlinson really had sailed into a waterspout. No, he was not crazy. *Well . . . maybe a little.*

As we communicated, the little plane shuddered, then began bucking at the rim of a thermal, which was not unexpected. But then something in the tail section went *BANG!* For a moment, the seaplane paused in midair, listing mildly to port as if it, too, were surprised, and suddenly undecided about which laws of physics applied. Beside me, I was aware that the steering yolk had lost resistance, moving freely as a trombone slide in Futch's hands.

"Pitch control elevator," he muttered, "it's gone," which is something you never want to hear from a pilot, yet he said it coolly as if he'd anticipated the possibility, maybe even practiced what to do. At the same instant, the plane teetered, nose-heavy, like a roller coaster that has topped a hill, then we dropped from the sky like a dart, the propeller pulling us downward. The sick sensation of my stomach falling slower than my chest plastered me to the seat. I thrust out my hands to stop the Earth from accelerating toward us, but the windshield flooded the cockpit with mushrooming details of where we would soon impact: a prairie of lilies, rock, and sawgrass, a film of black water glittering beneath.

Pilots use the abbreviation *G-LOC* to describe the loss of consciousness that occurs when excessive gravitational force drains blood from the brain. Maybe that's what happened to me because the next few seconds were a blur of images and sensations. I was aware of Dan working feverishly at the controls, his right hand darting between the trim wheel and the throttle, while his left babied the steering yoke. Even wearing headphones, sound was obliterated by engine noise, the airstream howl of chattering aluminum, so those moments passed in a roaring silence. Later, Tomlinson would swear he'd shouted, "Looks like we'll be on the ground early!" before whispering some Sanskrit chant. Maybe it was true. If so, his words didn't register. All I remember clearly is taking comfort in the confident flow of Futch's hands moving among the controls, all the while my eyes fixed, unblinking, on a patch of limestone that was hurtling toward my face.

Gradually, I became aware of the plane's changing angle of descent. We were still plummeting toward the hardpan, but on an incline that suggested we might hit belly first and not auger in like an arrow. Great! Emergency crews would be able to identify us piece by piece instead of scraping us off the ground with shovels. Then, off to starboard, a flooded sinkhole came into view, and I felt hopeful. The pond wasn't large, but at least it would soften our impact when the seaplane's floats made contact. Maybe I pointed, maybe I called out advice, I'm not sure. But it only caused Futch to shake his head and raise his voice above the din, yelling, "No—the grass! Water will kill us!" He stabbed at the trim wheel, then applied throttle. Increase speed while landing? That was a new one. Seconds later, as the Earth rushed up to crush us, the man hollered, "Hold on, guys, we're going in hot!"

Yes, we were.

One hand on the door latch, I moved my eyes to the airspeed indicator while Futch tilted the nose until blue sky filled the windshield. We were doing a hundred knots, and still gaining speed as we ascended. The odds of surviving were plummeting just as fast.

On those rare occasions when imagining how I will deal with the inevitable, I embrace the hope I'll accept my last moments as a rational man, which is to say dispassionately, beyond the reach of panic. Which is pure damn fantasy. I was too numb for panic but did feel a suffocating dread that perhaps is as inevitable as death itself.

Worse, that fear was blended with regret—regret for all the infinite experiences, done and undone, that vanish with the last thump of our own fragile hearts. At the end, in truth, my thought stream was neither detached nor rational, just pitifully human: *Not yet! I don't want to die! Not like this!*

Die in a small plane, on a sunny February morning, searching for something that is synonymous with paranormal weirdos and the UFO lunatic fringe? What a damn ridiculous way for a rational man—a respected marine biologist!—to end his years.

Not that I'm a believer, but Tomlinson had implied a spiritual verity by speaking on behalf of all our sorry asses: God must alternately flood the eons with ironic laughter—or his grieving tears.

2

I WOULD NOT HAVE WASTED A MINUTE searching for the iconic Flight 19, let alone a day flying around Florida, if Dan Futch hadn't asked me to get involved. Dan comes from Old Florida waterman stock, a fourth-generation fishing guide, when he's not flying charters, and he's as solid and smart as they come.

It didn't matter that Futch had convinced me

there was a statistical chance the torpedo bombers had disappeared in the Gulf or the Everglades, not in the Atlantic as most believed. It didn't matter that out of all the so-called experts on Flight 19, few had done enough original research to be credible. And those few, with rare exception, agreed that there were so many variables, so few facts, that it was impossible to reach an unimpeachable conclusion about the fate of those five planes.

I joined the hunt because Dan is Dan *Futch.* True, he'd helped me land a controversial tarpon project in nearby Boca Grande Pass, so I owed him a favor. But he is also among the most competent men I know—a quality that runs in his family.

Between Orlando and Key West, the name Futch has the ring of blue-collar royalty. It is a family that has earned, over the decades, the instant respect accorded by those who appreciate boats, gutsiness, mechanical savvy, and saltwater. Since the 1800s, the family has been associated with the banyan-shaded village of Boca Grande on Gasparilla Island, forty miles south of Sarasota. *World's Tarpon Capital,* as the village is known. But generations of Futches have excelled as fishing guides, boatbuilders, and hardworking innovators throughout the state. The reputation of the patriarch grandfather, Daniel Webster Futch, remains near mythic, even years after his death, and the man's exploits as a rum smuggler and tough-guy fisherman are still a favorite topic around the docks. Dan, the legend's namesake, is Futch to the bone, from his horn-rimmed glasses to his big-shouldered appetite for life.

A month ago, Futch had landed his seaplane in Dinkin's Bay and appeared in the doorway of my laboratory carrying a briefcase. I assumed it had something to do with the tarpon study I had recently completed. Wrong. Nor was it a purely social call, but that was okay. We've been friends for years, and he has arrived carrying all sorts of odd objects—from a small brass cannon he had salvaged to a hydraulic oyster shucker—but a leather briefcase was unexpected.

"Take a look at this, Doc," he'd said, unbuckling the hasps. "One of my nephews found it snorkeling. What do you think?"

I'd been making notes on a gravid stingray penned outside because the animal was too big for the aquaria that line the walls of my lab. But I stopped what I was doing and said, "What'd you find this time?"

On the marble top of the chemical station, Futch placed a triad of levers affixed to a metal plate. Beneath a patina of barnacles, the levers were forged of brass and stainless, still solid but frozen by corrosion. On the plate was die-stamped MIXTURE in military block letters. Enough barnacles had been sanded away that I could also read AUTO LEAN/AUTO RICH/FULL RICH on a tracking rim that guided the levers. In what might have been yellow paint, remnants of numbers were barely visible along the aft edge of the plate. Serial numbers? Possibly. The apparatus had the weight and feel of something that had been precisely machined, engineered to meet demanding specs and tolerances.

"You want those numbers checked under a microscope?" I'd asked. "It won't fit, but I can drop the viewing tray, or maybe we can rig something. At lowest power, we might get more detail. It's from the controls of an old airplane, right?"

What Dan's nephew had found was the throttle assembly from a World War II torpedo bomber, an Avenger. The Avenger, as Dan would explain, was the largest single-engine warplane of that era. The ship carried a crew of three—pilot, radioman, and gunner—plus a single thousand-pound torpedo, along with a lot of clunky radio equipment that today would have been distilled into something the size of an iPod. The plane had a thirty-yard wingspan, a range of a thousand miles, and cruised at one hundred forty knots, or about one hundred sixty mph. Fully fueled, even carrying a payload, the plane could stay aloft at cruising speed for six hours or more.

"That's key to what makes this interesting," Dan had told me. "Six hours of flight time and a range of a thousand miles. Remember that—it'll help you keep an open mind."

The comment piqued my curiosity, yet I failed to make the connection with the fabled Flight 19. No reason I should. Why would Futch be interested in a bomber squadron that, according to who you listened to, had either been abducted by aliens or disappeared into a time warp? For him, it would have been as out of character as expressing an interest in aromatherapy or vampires.

Twenty minutes later, I looked up from my Wolfe Stereomicroscope and said to him, "I'm sure of three numbers—the second, fourth, and fifth. The next number might be a one, or a seven . . . or a letter. But that's unlikely, knowing the military. The rest of the paint is too far gone. There are some high-tech methods of recovery, but that's the best I can do."

I wrote the numbers on a yellow legal pad and slid it in front of Futch, who had been arranging research material and photos of Avengers on my stainless steel dissecting table. He looked at the pad, cleaned his glasses, then opened a book to do a comparison. The book, I noticed, was *They Flew Into Oblivion*, by someone with the unlikely name of Gian J. Quasar. Minutes later, a slow smile told me Futch liked what he'd found.

"It's a stretch, but these could be serial numbers . . . and they *might* match up," he said. "Not with

Taylor's plane . . . but maybe one of the five." He spun the open book around. "Take a look."

That was my first serious introduction to Flight 19's flight instructor, Lt. Charles C. Taylor, and the few verified facts regarding five missing warplanes and a crew of fourteen men. Futch had done so much research that he could have recited the data verbatim, but he's not the sort to lecture. Instead, he had handed me his own written summary and offered comments as I read.

On 5 December 1945, 2:10 p.m., five TBF-1 Avengers left Fort Lauderdale Naval Air Station on a training flight known as Navigation Problem #1.

Their orders: Fly east (91°) for 141 statute miles. Turn northeast (346°) and fly 84 statute miles. Turn southwest (241°) and return to Lauderdale 140 statute miles away.

All aircraft had been checked in preflight and were fully fueled per operational procedure. Weather was reported as "Clear." Wind 15-20 knots out of the southwest. A "perfect" day for flying, one report noted.

The route was to have covered 365 statute miles in approximately two hours and fifteen minutes. But the squadron never returned. No trace of the crew or planes was ever found despite the largest land-and-sea search in the nation's history . . .

I had looked up from my reading long enough to reassure myself by saying, "You're too smart to believe in the Bermuda Triangle thing. What happened to those men might be a mystery. But there's nothing mysterious about planes or ships disappearing at sea, which no one knows better than—"

"You're preaching to the choir," Futch had interrupted. "Even in shallow water, there's nothing harder than finding a small chunk of anything in a big chunk of ocean. Doc, the only reason those planes haven't been found is because no one's found them. Sounds simple-minded, I know, but there you go. At least, no one *realizes* they found them."

The emphasis implied an interesting possibility. Modern fishermen use electronics to scan the ocean's bottom for what they call "structure." It is a generic term that applies to any rock, hole, ledge, or three-dimensional object that provides shelter and prey for fish. Fishermen don't much care what constitutes the structure, and the locations are kept secret, always logged by precise GPS coordinates. These coordinates are known as numbers.

Every offshore fisherman accumulates a list of

known structures, and those numbers are hard currency in fishing circles. Numbers are jealously guarded, although sometimes traded and occasionally sold. The lucky few who stumble onto an undiscovered piece of structure, however, keep their mouths shut. They trust no one. The smart ones use all sorts of trickery to disguise their true destination when they head offshore. Rather than be seen fishing a new number, the smart ones will drift the site, engine cowling open as if they've broken down. A virgin chunk of structure is a fishing gold mine to its discoverer—and also its claim jumpers.

"I see what you're getting at," I said. "Particularly over the last ten years. Digital sonar is a dozen times better than the old white-line recorders, and GPS is more accurate than ever. Could be that one, maybe all five Avengers have been found, but no one's bothered to dive the numbers and see what's down there. That's what you're thinking?"

"The odds are even better if they went down in less than two or three hundred feet of water," he'd responded. "Back in the seventies, when Mel Fisher's bunch finally found the *Atocha*, divers had to dodge all sorts of fishhooks and lures snagged on stacks of silver bars. Wouldn't be the first time an important wreck has been found but not identified."

I nodded, familiar with the story. I told Dan I'd

had a similar experience a few years back when Tomlinson and I formed a little salvage company to recover the manifest of a wreck we'd found off Sanibel Island. Anglers had been working the spot for years—lots of broken leaders and hooks—but we were the first to actually see what was on the bottom.

"It's kind of funny when you picture it," Futch had observed. "Some poor fisherman cussing his bad luck, pissed off 'cause he's lost a three-dollar lure, not a clue in the world he's just snagged a fortune in Spanish treasure. Whole time, it was right there under his feet." Futch had paused, anticipating my reaction to what he said next. "But that's only *if* the planes ditched at sea. Which has never been proven."

It was a pet theory of his, I could tell. So I motioned to the throttle plate. "But you said your nephew found this thing snorkeling. Even if he was close to land, it couldn't have been that deep. How much water?"

What I wanted to ask was *where* the throttle had been found. But such a question is a breach of protocol in every branch of saltwater discipline: fishing, diving, and salvage recovery. So I tried to narrow it some by adding, "The planes ditched in the Atlantic, from everything I've heard. Even Palm Beach, where the Gulf Stream sweeps in close, it still had to be within a few miles offshore."

Futch was smiling—he knew I was getting into it. "The Atlantic is another 'fact' that's never been proven. Keep reading. I've got a box of Pine Island grapefruit promised to the ladies aboard *Tiger Lilly*. And a bag of stuff your sister wanted from the Bahamas. I'll be back in fifteen and tell you what's on my mind."

I don't have a sister. The man was referring to my cousin, Ransom Gatrell, who introduces me as her brother because I'm her closest blood relative. The woman is quirky, wonderful, and sometimes tricky. Rather than correcting him, I'd offered good advice. "Don't let Ransom talk you into anything stupid. What'd she make you sneak through customs this time?"

Futch dismissed the question by motioning to the stack of research. "I tried to separate confirmed facts from the bullshit and then summarize—all numbers in civilianspeak so it would be easier to share. Read through it and see what you think. Oh, there's one more thing"—he paused in the doorway—"there was no moon that night. You'll understand what I mean. And military logs confirm the planes all left Lauderdale with a full load of fuel."

My curiosity spiked.

So I read, skimming through bios of the fourteen dead airmen, then a weather report out of Miami dated 12-5-47 that suggested flying conditions were *not* ideal as commonly believed. On that

31

long-gone day, there were scattered squalls along the coast, some generating winds in excess of fifty knots, with clouds that limited ground visibility to less than a thousand feet. Worse, after sunset— which was at 5:36 p.m.—a massive cold front was expected from the northeast. Instead of ideal conditions, the fourteen aviators had, presumably, been aloft when a meteorological collision had occurred: a high-pressure mass met a low-pressure phalanx of thunderstorms.

I leafed through two pages of diagrams, several maps, then began to read more carefully.

The first indication the squadron was in trouble came ninety minutes after takeoff, 3:40 p.m. A senior flight instructor in an unassociated aircraft intercepted a radio exchange that suggested Flight 19's pilots were confused about their location and their heading. The senior instructor reported hearing the following from one or more of the squadron's pilots: "I don't know where we are . . . We must have gotten lost after that last turn . . . Anyone have suggestions . . . ? What's your compass heading?"

After several attempts, the senior officer made brief contact with the squadron's flight instructor, Lt. Charles Taylor. Reception was poor, often garbled, but the senior instructor reported Taylor as saying, "Both of my compasses are out. I'm sure I'm over the Florida Keys, but I don't know how far down. And I don't know how to get to Lauderdale."

According to logbooks, the instructor told Taylor, "Put the sun on your port wing and fly north until you see Miami"—good advice IF the squadron was over the Keys.

Later, investigators would conclude that Taylor had badly misjudged his location. How could five planes have gone so far south when their mission consisted of a route that took them due east, then northwest, then southwest? Investigators were quick to dismiss the possibility, even though Taylor had served as flight instructor in Miami and Key West during the previous nine months and had logged nearly two hundred hours flying over Florida Bay and the Keys.

The search efforts that December night would only compound the tragedy when a long-range Martin Mariner, a "flying boat," was launched and exploded in midair, killing its crew of thirteen volunteers.

Half an hour later, when Futch returned to the lab, I looked up from my second pass through his summary to say, "You believe Taylor's version, don't you? You think he was right about being over Florida Bay, not the Bahamas. That's what this is all about."

Straddling a lab stool, Dan gave it some thought before replying. "I'm not convinced of anything. But I find it damn interesting that a seasoned flight instructor who'd spent nine months flying the Keys would say, 'I'm sure I'm over the Florida Keys,' unless he was *sure*. But that's just one piece of a mixed-up puzzle. There's been so much misinformation printed about what happened that day and night—including the military's official six-hundred-page report. And dozens of bullshit magazine stories and 'documentaries' that include outright lies. Hell, one of those so-called writers even claimed to have piloted a sixth Avenger on Taylor's flight but survived. Which is total fantasy, but it's still repeated today."

"All because your nephew found this." I touched the throttle assembly. "Or were you already interested?"

"It lit a fire under me, but that's not the reason. I'm a pilot. I don't know how many hundreds of times I've flown that Lauderdale–Bahamas route. And there wasn't a single trip I didn't think about those fourteen guys—plus the thirteen others who died trying to save them. They all volunteered for what they knew was hazardous duty. Men like that deserve to be found—don't you think?"

I couldn't disagree. So I listened to Futch explain that for the last ten years he'd been trying to piece the real story together. Not working on it full-time, of course. He was too busy fishing Boca Grande Pass during tarpon season and flying charter clients all over the Caribbean the rest of the year.

"It's more of an occasional hobby. Doc, you'd be surprised how many men who served at Lauderdale Naval Air Station during the second war ended up retiring to Florida. Some who flew Avengers on that exact same training route never had the first problem. Even a few who were actually there the day Flight 19 disappeared.

"I'm lucky. I fly clients all over the state. When I get the chance, I visit these old pilots in person—a couple times, it was only a few months before they died. I'd look at their scrapbooks and listen to their stories." Futch grinned. "My god, it's fun listening to an eighty-year-old guy who used to be a hotshit Avenger jock get all fired up over some of the crap that's been written about Flight 19. Most of 'em believe government investigators were more interested in placing blame than in nailing down what actually happened that night. So they're eager to help once they know I'm a pilot.

"One thing they're all convinced of, Doc, is those fourteen sailors and Marines were competent men. They weren't a bunch of screwup rookies, like some accounts say. Several were combat veterans from the Pacific war. Some highly decorated heroes, the flight instructor included—despite some of the bullshit that's been written about Charles Taylor. They didn't fly into a time warp, and they weren't the victims of some shady government conspiracy. The men I've talked to are convinced their squadron mates got so damn lost, so turned around in a storm, they didn't have a clue where they were. Didn't even know if they were over land or water. You saw the time line I made of radio transmissions?"

I had. Once the pilots were lost, they began a series of course changes, desperately searching for mainland Florida. Even after sunset, they continued to zigzag their way into oblivion—thus the title of Gian Quasar's book.

Futch said, "It was a black night. A storm ceiling of less than a thousand feet, in planes that had primitive electronics compared to today. No landing lights, no gyro compasses—that's a key detail—and very limited radio range. At a time when Florida was one of the most sparsely populated states in the union."

"No gated communities," I offered. "No bright lights from shopping malls and football stadiums."

"Between Palm Beach and Jacksonville, not many ground ranges to fix on," Dan agreed. "And if they turned inland? Even Orlando was just

36

citrus and cattle. Hardly any lights at all, coast to coast. I mentioned no gyro compasses? I've flown those old warplanes at air shows. Make a sharp bank and the compass spins like a damn top. Even after you level off, they're squirrelly as hell. Which is just one reason our air bases lost *fifteen thousand guys* to training missions. You believe that?"

I said, "That can't be true."

It was. "In only five years," Futch continued, "there were more than seven thousand plane crashes on U.S. soil! I had no idea 'till I did the research—most of those guys never even got a chance to face the damn enemy! Hell, the Gulf and Atlantic are littered with wreckage from old Avengers, B-52s, Mustangs—the whole list. People today don't realize that, to be a fighter jock back then, you'd better have balls of brass and nerves of steel."

Futch named some of the steely men he'd interviewed—several were important players in the Fort Lauderdale Avenger squadron. Then he'd methodically listed a couple of facts that, although historically accurate, only made the story more inexplicable.

At 5:30 p.m. on that December day, land-based radar stations, unable to pinpoint the squadron's location, triangulated a probable location as a hundred fifty miles north of Lauderdale and forty miles out to sea. This information was not passed on to the lost pilots because of poor radio reception, or human oversight.

At 6:20 p.m.—nearly an hour after sunset—Air Station Lauderdale logged its last transmission from Flight 19. Lt. Taylor was heard radioing his squadron, "Close in tight, we'll have to ditch unless landfall. When the first plane drops below ten gallons, we'll all go down together."

Automatically, my brain did the math. The Avengers had taken off at 2:10 p.m. They'd gotten lost. At 6:20 p.m., when the flight instructor's last transmission was intercepted, the planes should have had almost two hours of fuel left. At 160 mph, even one hour in the air was a substantial amount of time. Where the hell had those fourteen fliers ended up?

There was another fact that Futch found perplexing.

"Three weeks after the Avengers went missing, the brother of one of the crewmen received this. *You* figure it out."

Futch had placed a photo of a yellowed Western Union telegram in front on me. The typeface was faded but legible:

Jacksonville Flo Dec 26 10:15 am
Cpl Joseph Paonessa
Marine Barracks 6th and Eye St. Southeast
    YOU HAVE BEEN MISINFORMED ABOUT
ME. AM VERY MUCH ALIVE. GEORGIE

Before I could ask, Futch explained. "George Paonessa was a radioman aboard one of the lost Avengers. His brother, Joe, was stationed at Jacksonville Marine Base the day that telegram arrived. That's a verified fact, by the way, not fantasy. Something else: only the family called George 'Georgie.' And Paonessa's father and mother both said that no one knew that nickname outside the family. Some say until the day she died Mrs. Paonessa was convinced that George sent that telegram."

If Futch expected me to be mystified, he was bound for disappointment. I'd told him, "When a disappearance makes headlines, the kooks and cranks come out of the woodwork. The telegram's a hoax or a cruel joke. Georgie is the common, familiar form of the name, so someone made an obvious guess." Looking through the north window, I paused. Puttering toward my stilthouse was Tomlinson in an inflatable dinghy, his sailboat, *No Más*, floating pale gray at anchor just beyond. He was shirtless, a bottle of beer in his free hand, and wearing a monkish-looking hat he'd woven from palm fronds.

"A very sick joke," Futch agreed. "It hits home, though, because I've been checking the source code. You're going to like it." His tone became confidential as he tapped the paper in front of me. "There's a chance this telegram was sent from *here*. Not Sanibel, but just across the bridge. The old telegraph office is still there, even after they built the condos. You know the place—that little yellow shed off to the left when you leave the island? It was one of the few Western Union stations between Key West and Tampa. No wireless in those days. Everything had to be hard-wired."

He was talking about tiny Punta Rassa, just across the bay. Today the spot is adjoined to the Sanibel Causeway, plus a cluster of high-rises and a resort hotel. For two centuries, the village had been the primary cattle port between Cuba and Florida. When the battleship *Maine* was sunk in Havana Harbor, the first distress message was sent to Punta Rassa, not Key West or Miami. Now Punta Rassa isn't even shown on most maps.

I told Futch, "There's someone coming who'll appreciate this telegram a lot more than me."

A few minutes later, Tomlinson was drinking my last beer while he listened to Futch retell his story. It was no surprise that he—a devotee of the paranormal—loved the connection between a local one-room telegraph station and Flight 19. So the three of us had spent the afternoon discussing details, probabilities and possibilities. Before leaving, Futch loaned us his dog-eared copy of *They Flew Into Oblivion*, assuring us it was the most carefully researched book on the subject.

"You've got the salvage gear and the experience. I know planes," Futch told us. "If you're interested, it's something we can work on independently. You know, get together when there's a reason. Start by talking to fishing buddies, the ones willing to trust us with their private GPS numbers. Chart the unidentified pieces of structure out there and match the locations with Army Air Corps logs. In the meantime, when the water clears up, we'll dive the place where my nephew found this." Futch tapped the briefcase where he'd stowed the throttle mechanism.

Finally, I asked the obvious question, but in the most general of ways. "I assume he found it in the Gulf, not the Atlantic. But was it north of here or south?"

My shotgun tactfulness amused Futch. "If I didn't trust you, I wouldn't be here. My nephew found the throttle in a mangrove creek south of Marco Island. Hawksbill Creek, it's called on the charts. There're a couple of Indian mounds way back in. And something else I'm going to trust you with—is that okay?"

Tomlinson nodded while I waited.

"Near the mounds there's a marl flat there I call the Bone Field. Human bones. They're scattered all over the place, stuck in the roots of trees, sticking right out of the mud. My daddy and I found it too many years ago to remember. We always figured it was an Indian burial ground, so we didn't report it. Now I'm not so sure."

I've known Tomlinson a long, long time, but I'd never seen his eyes glow a brighter shade of turquoise than when he heard the words *Bone Field*.

Futch added, "Tell you what. We'll keep a close watch on weather around Lauderdale. Next time it's similar to the night those Avengers went missing, we'll hop in my plane and fly the area. I've got a theory about what happened to those pilots. I can't tell you how many times I've flown a thirty-knot tailwind east to Lauderdale. Then, on the return trip, I climbed a couple thousand feet to catch a northeast tailwind home. Best way to convince you is show you."

"You did this on the same day?" I'd asked.

"Same afternoon. Couple years ago, in the worst kind of weather, I gained sixty knots of airspeed riding one of those northeast storms home. Wind on the ground was southwest, but, man, I was like a rocket ship going the opposite direction. If it wasn't for my GPS, I'd have been fifty miles out in the Gulf when I dropped down through the clouds instead of over Boca Grande." The pilot's smile asked *See how easily it could happen?*

Which is why the night before something went *BANG!* in the tail section of his plane Dan Futch had bunked on the porch outside my lab. The skies over Sanibel Island were flawless, but NOAA Weather Service was predicting a near repeat of December 5, 1945: next-day squalls along the Atlantic Coast; southwest winds expected to turn by afternoon and blow heavy from the northeast.

"I didn't expect this kind of luck until hurricane season. Maybe even as late as November," Futch remarked that morning as we buckled ourselves into his little Maule floatplane.

The man was right, in a way. Dying in an Everglades plane crash was unexpected luck, indeed.

3

THE PLANE WAS DOING A HUNDRED-plus when I felt the first jolt of our pontoons snagging sawgrass, yet Futch didn't reduce speed. It caused me to wonder if he had frozen at the throttle—damn disappointing to lose my life at the same instant I lost confidence in a legendary pilot. Then a second jolt, much harder, caused a frictional roar and slammed me forward, my belt harness the only thing that saved me from the windshield and the blur of propeller.

Finally, finally, Dan levered the throttle back, concentration fixed on controlling the plane, his feet very busy at the steering pedals. Our pontoons skipped like flat rocks on water, causing us to fishtail wildly between the pond and a wall of cypress trees. Then we began a slow-motion skid that lasted an improbable span of seconds and threatened to dip the portside wing, which would have flipped us upside down.

It didn't happen. Instead, the plane stabilized and began to slow, which stilled the world around us and allowed my hearing to return. By the time sawgrass had clawed us to a halt, I had the door open and was ready to bail. But Futch stopped me, yelling, "We're okay, stay put!" meaning there was no fire, no threat of an explosion, so I pulled my legs in while he killed the engine. Then the pilot leaned back in his seat and took a huge breath, releasing it as a whistle. In the abrupt silence, the plane made creaking, cooling noises. Frogs resumed their steel drum thrumming. Birds chirped. Sun was shining, life was being lived, and the Earth still turned on a solid axis, indifferent to what had just happened.

Through headphones came Tomlinson's voice: "I just made a promise so damn ridiculous, God must have plans for me in Hell. *Hey* . . . my left shoe is soaked! Please tell me we're sinking . . ." Then he began to laugh, a sound that teetered between hysteria and relief.

I looked at my feet, then my hands—they were shaking—and snapped my safety harness free. "Everyone okay?" I said and looked around.

"You okay, Tomlinson? Dan—you hurt?" It seemed important to show concern for others if they were to believe I had remained cool throughout it all. But I had an eerie floating sensation in my head, as if dreaming, when I asked, "What in the hell just happened?"

Futch said, "I need a big shot of vodka. I'd drink one, too, if I wasn't flying." He pulled off his headphones and looked at me. "It makes no sense! Losing pitch control—doesn't make a goddamn bit of sense! A week ago, we did the hundred-hour inspection. Went through the entire tail cluster. And triple-checked the elevator bell crank!"

I replied, "Bell crank," as if I remembered the mechanical significance, although I didn't.

"Exactly! I'm crazy anal when it comes to bell cranks. Maybe a cable broke, but . . . but it *couldn't* have broken. Not in that piddly little bit of turbulence!"

Tomlinson was still laughing, telling himself, "Never get off the damn boat. Goddamn right! Why can't I remember one simple little rule?" while Futch continued, "Always wondered if I could land with just the throttle and a trim wheel. Now we know. But, my god, I don't want to ever have to prove it again." He tilted his head back and took another long breath. "Geezzzus, that was close!"

I said, "Incredible job," and meant it. My door

45

was still open. I poked my head out and looked down. The plane's floats were aground in six inches of water, sawgrass almost as high as our wings as far as the eye could see.

Futch was still talking, dealing with the adrenaline crunch in his own way. "I'll get out and take a look. But I need to sit here a minute, okay?" Then he repeated what he'd said about the recent hundred-hour inspection, adding that he had landed on wet grass lots of times because the FAA required his plane be hoisted off the ground to check the pontoons.

"There's an industrial crane in Arcadia, but it's miles from the water. So I always leave Boca Grande before sunrise and get there while the dew's still heavy. See what I'm getting at?"

No, but I guessed it had something to do with me trying to direct him toward the sinkhole.

It did.

"When we went into that dive, boys, I thought we'd bought the f-ing farm. First thing pops into my mind was, *Keep adding throttle 'till we stabilize, and stay the hell away from water.* If I'd tried to land us in water at a hundred knots, the suction would've grabbed the floats and sent us ass-over-end. Which is why I didn't make for that little pond. Right now, we'd either be upside down and sinking or we'd've skipped into the trees at the other side. Probably on fire, too . . . the tank's still almost full."

My sense of reality was slowly rebooting, details were assuming form as, behind me, Tomlinson also began to recover. "From this moment on," he said, "every second of every day is icing. Seriously. It's like gambling with free money. Balls to the wall . . . savor every beautiful moment. My new motto is *Live like there's a lighted fuse in your butt.* Because you never know when the big boom's gonna come." Then he tapped the back of my seat, demanding, "Let me out, let me out, I need some breathing room!" so I did. But I didn't take my eyes off Dan Futch.

There was a reason. He had been palming the VHF microphone since the plane had stopped but had yet to make a call. Now he appeared undecided. Or . . . maybe there was something else on his mind. So I tried to help him along, saying, "You think traffic control will hear us from ground level? We'll need some help getting out of here."

While we were in the air, Futch had been too busy at the controls to shout a Mayday, but now he seemed to be postponing the inevitable call to air traffic control, and probably to the FAA. I don't stay current on flight protocol, but we'd damn near died. The feds would want to know every detail.

Yes, buying time . . . that's exactly what the man was doing. No doubt about it when he abruptly secured the microphone, then unclipped his harness. "Let's find out what happened first," he said. "You can sit here while I take a look . . . or get out and stretch your legs if you want. If there's no serious damage, it won't take long." Then, nodding at a gauze bandage on my left forearm—a recent injury—he added, "You definitely don't want to get swamp water on a cut."

"I'll risk it if you don't mind," I replied, then attempted a mild joke. "Plane crashes make me restless. Plus, I've got to bilge ship." Which was island talk for urinating.

Futch pulled on a blue ball cap and fixed me with a look that communicated a lot more than what he said next. "Fact is, Doc, we didn't crash. And there's no law against landing hot—long as you can take off again."

He was already out of the plane, so I swung out, too. "That wasn't criticism, old buddy. Anybody else at the stick, I'd be dead. I owe you."

We were facing each other, Dan standing on the port pontoon, me on the starboard pontoon, looking through the empty cockpit. Behind me, I heard Tomlinson drop down into the sawgrass, his big feet kicking water as he hurried away. Dan was studying my reaction when he replied, "Owe me? I may have to take you up on that, Doc. Don't say it unless you mean it."

I shrugged and said, "Sure," but was thinking, *What the hell does that mean?*

• • •

"**I'VE GOT TWO TRIPS** to Key West this weekend. Plus, clients booked through the rest of the month—including a three-dayer to Walker's Key. Then a big polo tournament in Palm Beach with old money clients. Tips alone will pay for my fuel and expenses."

Dan was explaining his cryptic request while he worked at the tail section, unscrewing the inspection plate. He had already done a walk-around and pronounced the plane undamaged, but for a dent in the starboard float.

When the inspection plate was free, he handed it to me, plus screws, and looked me in the eye. "Tarpon season starts in six weeks. August through April, I make my living in the air . . . or I don't make it at all. Kathy wants to remodel the kitchen this fall. And we're going to surprise our daughter with a big wedding reception—Useppa Island isn't cheap, you know. That's what I meant about calling in a favor."

I felt dense because I hadn't figured it out sooner. "If you file an incident report with the FAA, how much air time would you lose? Not to mention all the paperwork, I know. But they wouldn't ground you . . . would they?"

"Grounded? Hell, they'd confiscate my plane. Probably wouldn't see it again until late winter. That's a big chunk of money I'd lose." Futch patted the fuselage. "Which would make sense if

49

I didn't think my aircraft was safe. But I'm a safety freak, you know that. And the feds can't tell me anything I can't find out for myself. Fact is, we didn't crash-land. We just landed hot—which doesn't constitute an incident report, far as I'm concerned."

He motioned to the tool kit that was open on the elevator flap. "Hand me that ratchet, would you? I need a three-eighths, and the seven-sixteenths." Locking one of the ratchet heads into place, he continued, "You mind walking a big circle around the area? There's a roll of mechanic's towels under the seat. Use 'em to mark any tree stumps or rocks. Anything that would knock off one of our floats." Then referring to the bandage on my arm, he warned again, "But don't get that damn cut wet, you could be sick for weeks."

I was less concerned with germs than with what Futch was considering. He was going to attempt a takeoff in dense sawgrass? I wasn't going to question his judgment, but the man knew what I was thinking.

"Don't worry, I've done it before. Never with two passengers—weight could be a problem. Did you check your cell phone? Mine's got no reception."

I took a look and said, "Maybe if we were closer to the road."

The pilot shrugged. "Once you scout the area,

I'll know more. Check our landing track first. We made it in. Get this fixed, we should be able to fly her out. And Doc?"

I had pivoted to leave, but stopped.

"Probably no need to remind you, but tell Quirko to watch his step."

Quirko was Futch's nickname for Tomlinson. I smiled and said, "Don't worry. If you say there's no need to tell the FAA, that's good enough."

"That's not what I meant. A month ago, I flew a couple of state biologists into a spot near here. Herpetologists doing a census on exotic snakes. They showed me a video they had, them opening up a twenty-two-foot-long boa constrictor. The thing had choked to death eating a deer. Caught it just a few miles from here."

"I saw a photo in the paper," I said. "Tomlinson probably did, too, but I'll pass it along."

Futch wasn't done. "I'm serious, I wouldn't want to do much walking out here. In an afternoon, those guys counted eighteen boas and six or seven pythons. And I've spotted two snakes so big I circled around and watched them from the air. Those bastards breed like rabbits—same as the iguanas on Boca Grande. So be careful if you reach to pick up a limb . . . or have to squat for some reason."

"Got it," I said. "No latrine stops, and keep track of my fingers. Holler if you need me." I could hear Tomlinson's feet splashing aft of the

51

plane, so I grabbed two rolls of towels from the cockpit, then slogged off in his direction.

Truth was, some time in the Everglades was just what I needed to decompress. I had followed news accounts that claimed the population of exotic snakes—escapees from zoos and pet store mistakes—wasn't just growing, it was exploding. The media, however, have a long history of sensationalizing stories about Florida, usually exaggerating the bad, seldom the good. From hurricane damage to oil spills to red tides, I could not think of one exception. Now the possibility of seeing a boa or python gave me a reason to stop obsessing about almost dying and think about something else.

I wasn't the only one fixated on our near demise. Tomlinson heard me bulldozing through the sawgrass toward him and hurried to wipe his eyes before turning. He'd had a breakdown, I realized, but I pretended not to notice. "Depending on how much weight the plane can handle, Dan thinks we can fly out of here."

"Fly!" he replied, as if the prospect horrified him.

"Yeah . . . if he can fix whatever happened to the tail section. What? You'd rather hike three or four miles to the road through this stuff?" Sawgrass isn't a grass, it's an abrasive sedge, each three-sided blade defended by serrated edges. It cuts clothing, shoe leather, and skin.

Tomlinson didn't want to be convinced. "Walking's good for you, man. I love to walk. It's, like, one of the healthiest things on Earth. Drink lots of water and walk every day. In the marina office, there's a *Reader's Digest* story if you don't believe me."

I was nodding. "I know, I know, your body's such a temple. But I forget sometimes. Maybe it's all that dope you smoke, plus the nightly pint of rum. And how many beers? Think of it this way—"

"Plus, the wildlife," Tomlinson interrupted. "Hear all those birds and frogs? The Glades . . . it's alive, man. I see this as an opportunity . . . get back to nature. You know: simplify, simplify. And, suddenly, I'm not exactly in love with airplanes—"

"Think of it this way," I said again. "If we hike out, it'll take all day. Then we've got to hitch a ride—and that northeast front is due late afternoon. Hitchhike in the rain? On the Tamiami Trail, where nobody in their right minds would pick us up even on a nice day? Fly, though, thirty minutes from now we'll be back in Dinkin's Bay, sipping a beer. An hour at the most."

I took a step closer and gave his shoulder a friendly shake. "You fall off a horse, ol' buddy— you know the rest. If Dan says it's safe to fly, I think you should fly."

Expression glum, Tomlinson looked at the

ground. "I don't know, man, I've . . . I don't think I've got the balls to climb back in that thing," which was as out of character as the clothes he wore: a khaki safari shirt with epaulets and creased slacks he'd bought at the Sanibel Goodwill store on Palm Ridge. The shirt was baggy, and the pants so short I could see his beanpole ankles sticking out of red Converse high-tops, size 13. Sockless, of course, and he'd used a girl's barrette to clip his hippie hair atop his head—a warrior samurai meets Barbra Streisand.

I tossed him a roll of towels, saying, "Think about it," then motioned toward the plane's landing track. It was a curving swath of sawgrass, bent like harvested wheat that terminated at the seaplane's tail, where Futch was still working. "Use a couple of towels to mark any snags or rocks that would knock the floats off. You walk this side, I'll take the other. Then he wants us to spread out and do the same thing in a circle." I thought about mentioning exotic snakes but decided Tomlinson's nerves were already on overload. So I finished, "The guy's a magic mechanic. It won't take him long to figure things out. Okay?"

"Marion . . . ?" Tomlinson only uses my first name when he's serious about something, so I made a show of paying attention. "Thing is," he said, "getting back in that plane . . . I'm scared to death of dying, man. I've known it for a while and it's time I stopped pretending. I'm a fraud, dude. My whole act about being an enlightened spirit . . . an ordained Zen Buddhist—which is true, officially speaking—but it's total bullshit."

It was a struggle not to smile at his line *I'm scared to death of dying,* but I managed by concentrating as I listened.

He continued, "I'm guessing the Buddha wouldn't be impressed by a guy whose weasel springs a leak whenever the grim reaper takes a swing. I'm supposed to be one of his divine incarnates, for christ's sake! Or pisses his pants when a plane the size of a go-cart falls out of the goddamn sky! I couldn't take it again, Doc. This is the second time in ten days this has happened and I just can't handle anymore."

I was confused. "Second time what has happened? In another plane, you mean?"

"No. But I still had to change shorts." He lowered his voice. "I feel like I have a bull's-eye tattooed on my ass. Hell, you and Danny almost bought the farm just through association. Second time in a week I almost died."

I said, "What in the world are you talking about?"

The last three nights, Tomlinson had stopped at the lab, for one reason or another, and this was the first he'd mentioned a close call. "On your boat? Where?"

From the seaplane, Dan Futch's voice hollered across the sawgrass, "Guys! *Guys.* Get over here. I want to show you something!" His tone had the sound of discovery.

Tomlinson looked toward the plane, then at me. "It was in your lab—under it, actually."

Now I was totally confused. "What the hell are you saying?"

Futch called, "You gotta see this bullshit!"

Suddenly uneasy, Tomlinson turned and began walking toward the plane. "He sounds pissed off. I'll tell you about it later."

I said, *"Tomlinson . . . ?"*

"Doc, it wasn't a huge deal. The night you got called to Tampa, I was messing around near your fuse box and almost got electrocuted. That's why I'm not flying out of here, man. Flipping fate the bird is something I've learned not to do. Trust me, the details can wait."

I was staring at the man's back. I said, *"Electrocuted* . . . Geezus," while my brain tried to make some sense out of what he'd said. The previous week, I'd told my marina neighbors I had to go to MacDill for a couple of days. Because I didn't know how long I'd be gone, I'd arranged for a friend to check on my aquaria and feed whatever needed feeding. Janet Nicholes, who lives in an apartment above the marina, was my regular helper. But she, her husband, Jeth, and toddler son had gone to Key West for a week. So

I had imposed on my new workout partner to help, a tall, athletic, and oddly attractive woman named . . .

Hannah Smith.

When Hannah's name flashed into my head, I suddenly understood why my old buddy was reluctant to share details. I started after him, calling, "Wait until later, my ass!" The man flinched when I grabbed his shoulder, then demanded, "What were you doing in my lab? You knew damn well I was away for a few nights. Just like you knew Hannah would be there—didn't you!"

Sex addiction is a pseudo malady, in my opinion, a term coined to excuse infidelity, but Tomlinson's behavior does border on pathology. It wouldn't be the first time he had broken the first tenet of male comradeship.

"Now, Doc," Tomlinson said, holding his hands up, "you two aren't dating. That's what you said at the pool bar, remember? Then a few days later, in the lab, you told me, 'I'll never lose another good workout partner to the bedroom.' Or something close to that. And Hannah told me the same thing—more or less, anyway."

"*Hannah* told you," I said, glaring. "So it's true! You tried to ambush another one of my women . . . and in my own damn house."

In any confrontation, there is a sly device Tomlinson employs to gain the advantage. He pretends to be patient, empathetic, and eager to understand—which is maddening. He used the finesse now. "I won't bust you by mentioning ownership to Hannah . . . it was just a slip of the tongue, I'm sure. As good as forgotten, so, you know—like, float on, man!"

Float on, his new favorite phrase to wish people well or to avoid responsibility, often both. So I warned him, "You're going to be floating faceup if I hear that again before this is settled."

"Whoa," he said, "you got to get off the violence train, ol' buddy." But then saw the look on my face, so conceded, "On the other hand, you do make a decent point about the shittyness of using another man's bed—"

"Decent?"

Tomlinson put his hands up, palms out, and began to back away. "Hermano—have you forgotten what a putz I am? I can't even keep track of my own schedule, let alone yours. Or Hannah's! Besides, I'm too shaken up to think right now . . . Plus, that night's all a little too foggy—"

"Don't give me that 'I was drunk' crap," I snapped. "I've warned you for the last time, pal. You ever try to seduce another woman I'm dating, a plane crash will be a blessing compared to—"

Which is when Dan Futch silenced us both by saying, "Knock it off, you two! I've got some news, if you're interested: Someone's trying to kill us."

4

TOMLINSON ASKED DAN, "WHO'D WANT to kill a sweet guy like you, Danny boy?"

Futch was glaring at my hipster pal. "That's exactly what I'm wondering. I've known Doc a long time, but all I know about you are stories. Lots and lots of stories, and most of them not exactly PG-rated. So maybe you already know the answer."

I brushed past Tomlinson and was soon peering into the seaplane's aft inspection port, seeing springs, a simple pulley system—the elevator bell crank—and several cables that branched toward the tail fin, trim tabs, and the elevator. The cables were secured to the main pulley, all except one. That cable lay curled on the deck, its crimped eye loop intact, but the line had pulled free for some reason.

"See how they did it?" Dan asked.

I wasn't sure. "Why would someone sabotage your plane?"

"Murder," Dan said. "A first-degree scalp hunter." He reached across the tail and took the stub of free cable in his hand. "See this? This should be bolted to the bell crank—just like the others. And it *was*. How am I so sure? Because I bolted the goddamn thing myself. Sprayed it with LPS 3, then snubbed her tight. Some asshole backed the nut free, removed the bolt, then replaced it with *this*."

Now in his wide fingers he held a twisted two-inch loop of wire fishing leader. The loop had snapped in the middle. "Whoever did this knew planes. The asshole knew the wire would hold long enough to get us into the air. Under any serious pressure, though, the first little bit of turbulence, and *BANG!* This breaks."

Furious, Dan started to toss the wire away, but then reconsidered. Instead, he looked at it for a moment, then placed it in his billfold. "That's what we heard just before we went into a dive. I thought at first a bullet hit the fuselage."

"Jesus," Tomlinson muttered. "Crazies have taken over the planet. It's been coming for a while."

Dan ignored him by addressing me. "I'm surprised the wire held as long as it did, truthfully. I can't find the missing nut and bolt, either, so whoever did this was worried I might do a quick inspection. Military A-N cadmium steel hardware—thank god, I carry extras. So I can have this fixed in five, ten minutes, but I want to ask you something first."

Futch motioned toward the tail and looked at us. "This was intentional. It could've happened night before last while my plane was docked at

Boca. I had smooth air yesterday when I flew to Sanibel, and it's only a quick hop. Or it was last night, someone snuck into Dinkin's Bay and . . . hell, it would only take ten minutes." The pilot paused, his attention inward, before he asked, "Either one of you have any serious personal problems? Somebody you owe money? Or a husband so mad he'd kill us all just to take you out?"

Giving Tomlinson a sharp look, I said, "That is a *possibility,* I suppose. What about it . . . Quirko?"

Instead of being offended, Tomlinson became thoughtful. "I've been seeing a married lady, sure. From New Jersey. Her husband graduated from an engineering school. She's a quality person; not the screw-around type normally, just lonely, plus some personal issues. And ten years older than the guy she married. That information doesn't leave here, by the way. Understand?"

Tomlinson has some maddening flaws, but compromising a lover's secrets isn't among them.

Dan's eyes swung to me. I told him, "A mechanical engineer wouldn't have trouble figuring out how to sabotage a plane even if he wasn't a pilot. Depends on how hard he took the news that his wife was screwing around."

Tomlinson said, "No, she says he doesn't suspect. His family has money—they're big-time developers—and he's made a pile more by

61

investing in Florida real estate. So she spends a week down here every month on business—it's just part of her normal routine. And he's not the physical type. There are a couple more married women on the islands I have a history with—but we're still good friends. Same with their husbands."

"How'd you manage that?" Dan asked. He was sorting through a box of cadmium nuts and bolts, already back at work but paying attention.

"Shameless lies of omission," Tomlinson replied, "and good eye contact. Not that I'm proud of it, but life happens. If everyone knew the truth about their spouses, the world would either be crazy serene or there would be crazy fighting in the streets. Honesty is risky business when it comes to love." Tomlinson glanced at me before adding, "That's why Doc has all sorts of rules when it comes to women and honesty . . . especially married women. So no worries about a homicidal husband in *his* closet."

Dan missed the double meaning and the insinuation. The insinuation was that I don't take *anyone* into my confidence.

The pilot shook his head. "No husbands for me, but some crazy fisherman, that's a different story. I've guided tarpon for thirty years and there are more pissed-off boat captains every season—especially in Boca Grande Pass. Doc knows what I'm talking about. When your study on tarpon snagging comes out—in two weeks, right?—there'll be a lot of people pissed off at you, too. But at least Tallahassee will finally understand the bullshit they've let go on too long."

I nodded, even though the study was already being circulated on the Internet—there'd been a leak when the document was sent out for peer review comments. That wasn't unusual, although I didn't like the fact that an uncorrected copy was out there. I take my work seriously, had invested a lot of effort in getting the project *right*. The data had been collected over six weeks in that unusual deepwater pass during tarpon season; thirty-two consecutive days working with research assistants on a hook placement census—*where* a tarpon is hooked says a lot about *how* it was hooked. Our findings were at odds with a badly flawed study done by the Florida Fish and Wildlife Commission, so it would be controversial despite the convincing data we had collected. Tomlinson already knew something about the project, so I gave him a look that said *I'll explain later* because Dan wasn't done.

"Some of these tournaments I fish, the prize money is big. When the purse gets to be five hundred grand, there're guys out there who'd cut their mamma's throat to win. Outsiders especially. The so-called jig fishermen and us Boca Grande tarpon guides have been in a sort of war since the eighties—that's what's going round and round in my head all of a sudden. What do you think, Doc?"

I nodded because animosity between the two groups had spiked the previous season. I said, "You're a high-profile guy. You're president of the Boca Guides Association, and I see you quoted all the time in fishing magazines."

"This jig-fishing thing," he said to Tomlinson, "it's actually snag-fishing, which we've known all along, but Doc's study actually proves that—"

"The data we collected is strongly suggestive," I interrupted.

"Same thing," Dan said, then continued. "See, what's at stake is some big-money people started a tournament series, an organization calls itself Silver King Pro Circuit. We hate what they do and they're on my ass all the time for trying to make lawmakers understand. Because they know Doc's hook placement study might convince Tallahassee, they'll be all over his ass, too. You just wait. When there's big money involved, some people don't give a damn about the truth."

His talk about tarpon fishing caused me to fixate on *how* the plane had been sabotaged. "The fishing wire used on the bell crank, it looked like the good stuff," I said. "Is it Malin's?" Malin was a well-known tackle manufacturer.

Futch touched fingers to his billfold pocket and nodded, aware of my meaning.

"How many tournaments have you won the last few years?"

"That's something else I'm thinking," he replied. "Somebody wants me out of the picture. My boat took the two biggest pots last season, and we almost always place pretty high. One tournament, my anglers split a quarter million dollars between the four of them. And I went home with fifty thousand cash just from the calcutta. Get rid of me, some idiot might picture himself moving up a few rungs."

The calcutta was an auction-style event in which fishermen bid on the different tournament teams. At the end, the winning bidder got a payout from the pot.

Futch couldn't come to terms with the idea, though, and began shaking his head. "I don't know . . . it's just too damn hard to believe. We get our share of hard cases and assholes fishing that pass, but I don't know anyone who'd do something as crazy as this. Hell, if there'd been rough air when we crossed over Naples, we could have killed a houseful of people. Or that field where we saw all those kids playing soccer? Imagine what would've happened!"

Tomlinson had an alternative ready, one I would have never considered. "Maybe it has to do with Flight 19. Think about that. How many people know we're looking?"

"Nahhh," Dan replied. "There's no money in

finding those Avengers. The government owns them. Because men died, the sites will be protected—nothing to sell. There'd be some fame, maybe, but who cares about that?"

"Almost everyone not *already* famous, that's who," Tomlinson answered. "Maybe some military kooks afraid we'll beat them to the spot. Or just some right-wing freak with an obsession."

Futch mulled the idea over while he checked the other cables, ratcheting the nuts tighter. "Well . . . I sure haven't tried to keep it a secret. At the marina last night, how many people were listening when we talked about flying today? There were a bunch when Quirko told the telegram story. And the fishing guides at Boca Grande, they've known for years I'm hot to find those planes. So, I guess—"

"In an Internet world, fame is power," Tomlinson cut in. "Power can be converted into wealth."

"Nahhh," Dan said again, his tone more final. "If we were close to finding them, maybe. But we're not."

"Could be we're closer than we think but don't realize it," Tomlinson countered. "Either way, whoever did this has a snake loose in his noggin."

I checked my watch—almost noon—then looked to the east where a horizon of gray hung motionless in the jet stream. "That weather's coming," I said, which caused Tomlinson to give me a look, aware I wanted to switch the subject. I didn't want to lie to Dan Futch, but I also didn't want to discuss any killers who might be willing to murder two innocent men just to get at me. As I knew for certain, there were several out there who wanted me dead. A couple of foreign agencies, too. Tomlinson had to at least suspect that.

Ours has been an unusual friendship—one linked by polar differences and secrets. Once upon a time, my peace-loving New Age pal had been the underground revolutionary type. We had both lived covert lives, but at opposite ends of the spectrum, so, unknowingly, we'd been overt, unswerving enemies. I don't perceive any glimmer of good in improvised explosive devices or similar backdoor terrorist carnage—never have, never will. The fact that Tomlinson and I are now friends is irony at its symmetrical best and gives me hope for the other warring coverts in this world.

My boat bum neighbor has gone "straight" by his own twisted definition—although he has still his share of closeted skeletons . . . and possibly secret enemies. I, however, continue to bounce between my public life as a marine biologist and a shadow life that can, with a phone call, send me and my passport packing. It doesn't happen more than a few times a year, but the calls still come, so I continue to create and keep secrets, old and new. The newest was a trip I'd returned from less than a week ago, another name added to my own list of enemies. Yet another reason to dodge the pilot's question.

When I mentioned the storm clouds, Futch stepped away from the plane, wiped his hands on a towel, and looked for himself. "How about you two go back to marking snags while I finish here? Once I know what I have to work with, we can decide what to do."

"I don't mind walking," Tomlinson said. "Doc mentioned the weight problem."

Thinking I must also have mentioned the boa constrictors, Dan showed surprise. "Well, Quirko, you've got a bigger set of balls than me," he said and went back to work.

WELL, I COULDN'T LET him hike out alone, could I?

An hour later, two miles from where we'd watched the seaplane lift off, carrying only our pilot, Tomlinson stopped to rest, saying, "Maybe this wasn't such a good idea. How much farther, you think?"

I replied, "You can't be tired already."

"I keep stepping in holes. Can't see a goddamn thing, the water's so black. How about a drink?"

I was carrying a canvas knapsack over my shoulder. Long ago I learned to never set foot on a boat or a small plane without packing the essentials: flashlight, gloves, knife, first-aid basics, mosquito spray, a clip-on strobe, and a handheld VHF radio. From the seaplane, I had added two bottles of water, a liter each, which wasn't enough for a long hike in the Glades, but it was all we had.

I tossed a bottle to Tomlinson, said, "Hang on to it," then stepped up onto a slab of limestone. The sudden elevation was like surfacing through a flaxen sea. Horizon to horizon, sawgrass reflected sunlight and heat, flagging wind currents that furrowed the surface like tumbleweed, then springing back in flashes of copper and wheat. To the north was an island of cypress trees . . . an orb of shadows, mossy blue, that felt cool to the eye. Behind us was more sawgrass, our trail a temporary scar that was being reclaimed faster, it seemed, than we could walk. To the west, I noticed, a small plane was coming our way. No pontoons, so it wasn't Dan.

"Beautiful out here," I said. "Smells good, too."

Tomlinson took another gulp of water as he untied his basketball shoes, something wrong with his feet. "You're awful damn cheery. I thought you were pissed at me for refusing to fly."

"That's not the reason," I said. "But I am."

"Then let's talk about it. . . Awww, shit. Look at *this*."

"I've seen your feet. No thanks."

"I think I broke my toe, man. Wish we had

69

some ice . . . Crap, I think I'm gonna lose this nail for sure."

"Great!" I said. I took the second bottle of water, found a dry spot for the knapsack, then stood and rolled my shoulders. "Five-minute break. Then we go."

For an hour we'd been plowing north toward a two-lane road that crosses the Everglades—the Tamiami Trail—and this was the first we had spoken other than to kibitz about directions or to call a warning about the terrain. I'd done most of the warning because it was easier for me, wearing leather gloves, to bull a path through the sedge. Water depth varied abruptly, and so did the bottom. After long bouts of muck, we would exit onto a ridge that was a honeycomb of limestone, its unseen holes masked by sedge and water. The limestone was sharp, honed by a current centuries old, and spiked the crevices that consumed our legs to the thigh.

We were on one of those ridges now.

The little plane was still angling toward us, but the landscape was far more compelling. My eyes allowed it to flood in. "It would be nice to spend a few nights out here," I said. "All you'd need is a tarp and one of those handheld filtration pumps for water. I'll bet there're guava trees at the rim of that cypress head. Seminoles did agriculture sometimes, when they camped. And plenty of fish, if it came to that. Deer, feral hogs. I've read there are varietals of orchids and apple snails out here that still haven't been described. Scientifically, of course."

"Fascinating," Tomlinson replied, inspecting his other foot. "You've been crabby as hell lately, know that? But one plane crash later, you're all sunshine and lollipops. I'll never understand the rational mind."

I didn't reply, although there was some truth to what he'd said. We'd left behind the twenty-first-century world, with its cobweb of electronic ties, and it felt good to be dropped into the middle of nowhere. The Everglades was a separate reality from the comfortable existence on Sanibel Island. The region was a self-sustaining biota, an indifferent force. Life was more precariously balanced here. The landscape had an *edge*. I had yet to see a boa, large or small, nor had I mentioned the possibility, but that was part of the edge. So was our near-miss plane crash. And, as I had to admit to myself, so was the possibility that someone was trying to kill me, Tomlinson, Dan, or all three of us.

Churchill said it: *There is nothing so invigorating as being shot at without result.*

We all dodge a few bullets in our lifetimes, and I've ducked my share. After each narrow escape, I'd felt energized, never more lucid and alert. Now, standing on the low ridge surveying wild country, I was enjoying that cleaved sense of awareness when Tomlinson broke into my thoughts, saying, "The hunter is being hunted. That's why you're in such a jolly mood. Your drug of choice, man. Yet they demonize my gentle friend marijuana." He shook his head. "And if losing my toenail puts a smile on your face, this should make you positively goddamn giddy. See here? A chunk of my ankle bone's missing, too. I stepped in one of those holes back there. Your little fish buddies are probably feasting, having a grand time. Filet of primate. Yum-yum."

I hadn't been smiling, but I did now. "The Zen guru wanted oneness with nature?" I said. "Keep feeding the locals, it'll happen." Then I bent to open my backpack.

In a ziplock bag, I'd packed antibacterial cream, Band-Aids, gauze, surgical tape, two military QuikClot compresses for serious trauma, plus a few other basics. I lobbed him the bag, then returned my attention to the airplane, which had banked a few degrees northeast and would soon make a low-level pass overhead. Either the pilot had spotted us or his sudden course change was coincidental. Or . . . something else nearby had caught the pilot's attention.

Into my head came Dan Futch's voice. *I spotted two snakes so big, I could see them from the air.*

5

I LIFTED MY HEAD, SNIFFED THE AIR,
then stood on the balls of my feet and did a slow
three-sixty. Yes . . . Tomlinson and I were not
alone. To leeward, fifty yards away, a slow sawgrass trail was being tunneled, blades collapsing
under the weight of something sizeable. A
southwesterly breeze blew noise and odors away
from me, but, even in a gale, I would have heard
telltale sounds if it had been hikers or an ATV.

No . . . the thing approaching us was alive . . .
and big enough, possibly, to be spotted from low
altitude.

"Get your shoes on," I told Tomlinson.

"Huh?"

"You heard me."

My tone trumped the man's injuries and his
natural aversion to authority. Immediately, he
pulled on one red Converse, saying, "Geezus,
what's wrong? Are those cops?"

He meant the plane, which was now descending.
A Cessna 182, it looked like, a model I'd flown
while logging most of my air hours. The propeller
whine was closing the distance, and I could see
two people in the cockpit, details shielded by the
silver sheen of Plexiglas.

"Maybe Danny radioed someone to keep an eye on us," Tomlinson suggested.

"Hurry up," I told him and turned to concentrate on the approaching animal. Sawgrass was still funneling toward us in a slow riverine swath that created switchbacks. The zigzag path was suggestive. Meat eaters follow their noses, casting back and forth as they close in on their quarry. So do big snakes. I picked up a limb I'd been using as a walking stick, stepped off the ledge into the water, and began to circle away, hoping to intercept the animal.

Behind me, over the whine of the approaching Cessna, Tomlinson raised his voice to say, "Hey . . . where you going? Why you think there's no door on that plane?"

I didn't reply. I was choosing my footing, trying to move fast while the plane masked my noise. I wasn't worried about what I would find, despite Dan's warning—I was intrigued. The list of potential attackers was not particularly long nor formidable: a Florida panther, a gator, a black bear, coyotes, feral hogs, or a hellishly big snake. Those were the most likely candidates, and I wanted to get a look at the thing before it got a look at us.

Tomlinson called, "What's that guy doing? Is that a camera? Jesus Christ, Doc . . . I think he's trying to . . ." My friend's words were lost in the roar of the plane passing overhead. I looked up

74

just long enough to note that he was correct about the missing door. Inside, a male passenger was turning away from us, something in his hands. Yes . . . some kind of optical gizmo, a telephoto lens possibly. A pro photographer or videographer at work, maybe. Why else remove a perfectly good door from a perfectly good airplane?

My eyes didn't linger. I was angling to the left, using my gloves to part sawgrass as if it were a wall of beaded curtains. If I gauged the distance correctly, maybe I could slip in behind the animal before it spooked. That didn't strike me as risky. Black bears and coyotes have yet to place man in the food chain, and I could outdistance an alligator, or even a twenty-foot boa constrictor, if I surprised the thing from behind.

A Florida panther, though, was a different story, as I was aware. Surprising a big cat in the wild was risky. Probably riskier now than ever before. After being hunted to near extinction, they had learned to avoid contact with man. But, for reasons unknown, that is changing in the western varietal. Panthers—mountain lions, they are called—have attacked lone runners, hikers, and bikers. And I knew firsthand of an attempted attack on a pair of Florida hunters.

Even so, I wasn't worried. I'm a biologist and I wanted a closer look. It was a sunny, windy day, so the odds of me surprising a panther were minuscule, and the odds of it attacking me even less.

"Doc! Where the hell are you? That damn plane's circling back!"

No telling why Tomlinson was so concerned. Through a veil of sawgrass, I saw the plane bank to turn.

I kept moving as the plane pivoted toward us, but I was having no luck. Where the hell was the animal's trail? I couldn't find it. Sawgrass, I realized, was as indifferent as seawater when it came to preserving the tracks of an interloper. There was no trail to find. Ahead, a big snake could be lying in ambush. Or a big gator. Not good.

I stopped, did another slow three-sixty, holding my walking stick in both hands. The smart thing to do, I decided, was follow what little remained of my own trail back to the ridge. So I retreated, moving slowly at first, then faster. When the plane roared overhead a second time, I was slogging at top speed so took only a quick look. From my angle, I couldn't see if the photographer was snapping pictures or not. Was it two crazy hikers that had interested them? Or the animal I had failed to find?

When I stepped into a clearing, only yards from the ridge, one of my questions was answered. The creature I had been tracking was there awaiting my exit. I had been outsmarted, which isn't unusual, so I don't know why I was surprised. But I was.

The animal stood on four sturdy legs studying me, yellow-eyed, ears alert, something recently captured in its mouth. I felt a microsecond of concern, then gradual relief. I moved several steps closer . . . stopped . . . then took a few more steps. Then I held out my hand.

"**TELL ME** I'm not hallucinating!" Tomlinson hollered as I sloshed up the ridge, the animal trotting at heel beside me. "You found a . . . *dog?*"

Yes, I had. "I think he's a Lab. Or maybe a mixed breed—see the curly hair? He's been out here lost for a while. Feel him, he's all ribs and muscle. See all the crud in his coat? No collar, no tags. And something skinned a piece of fur off his tail, plus there's a chunk missing from his leg. This guy's had a tough time."

"A dog's a good sign, man. My morale was drooping. But finding a dog in the middle of fumbuck . . . *Whoa* . . . What's he got in his mouth?" As Tomlinson asked the question, his eyes swerved to the Cessna, which was disappearing toward the west.

I felt a cold nose nudge my hand, so I scratched the dog's ears. "A snake. But he won't let me have it. The thing's been dead a couple of days, from the smell, and part of it's still wrapped around his neck. He either bit the thing in half or he ate it. So he had a hell of a battle with a boa or a python, maybe a small anaconda. I won't know until he lets me take a closer look."

Tomlinson grimaced like he'd just eaten something foul. "A serpent is never a good omen, man. It's the worst sort of juju—Christ, a boa *constrictor*, you mean?"

I shrugged and said, "Dan might have mentioned seeing a few in the area."

"A snake cancels out the good dog mojo. Which makes sense after what just happened. The guy in that plane, he shot at me, man! You didn't hear me yelling?"

I looked up. "Baloney."

"No, he had a what's-you-call-it on a small gun. A scope. You know . . . like with crosshairs? Fired once on his first pass, then he shot maybe twice on the second. I remained motionless, that's the only reason he missed. You know, like a chameleon blending into the grass."

"Your powers of psychic cloaking saved you," I suggested.

"Sarcasm—the shield of the unenlightened," Tomlinson replied and tugged at his safari shirt. "It's because of my desert khaki. Same color as the sawgrass."

Even sober, my friend had a vivid imagination. "If someone had been shooting at you," I said, "I would've heard the shots. A gunshot is a hell of a lot louder than a Cessna passing at two hundred feet. It was someone taking pictures. Now, toss me that first-aid kit. But keep the stuff you need for your feet."

He was still tracking the plane, which was no bigger than a vulture against the Gulf blue sky. Finally, though, he lobbed the kit to me, saying, "I'm surprised they gave up so easy. Someone's out to get me, man. I told you." He nodded at the retriever, which had yet to leave my side. "Like I said, snake's bad juju."

My pal was making no sense whatsoever, so I knelt and inspected the dog's ears and neck, ignoring the carrion stench of the snake in his mouth. He was a fully grown retriever, medium height, a hedge of curly charcoal hair along his back, still a young dog, from his looks, but now oddly stoic after the excitement of being found. I removed several ticks, probed an infected wound above the left leg . . . then discovered why the dog refused to release the snake.

"You're not going to believe this," I told Tomlinson.

The man was concentrating on his shoelaces. "Hah! I'm the fool who believes *everything,* remember?"

Constrictors aren't poisonous, but their jaws are lined with recurved teeth that angle inward toward the throat. The teeth provide a secure loading system for muscles that convey food to the stomach. Once a boa, python, or an anaconda

79

latches onto its prey, the only escape is to forfeit a chunk of flesh or to kill the snake. The retriever had killed this snake, but the head and fangs were still anchored deep in the baggy fur around his neck, the snake's upper and lower jaws spread wide. Dragging six feet of boa would have been painful, so the dog was carrying the thing in its mouth. Smart.

"Get over here. You need to keep him calm while I do this. Once you see, you'll understand." I had the first-aid bag open, laying out gauze, disinfectant, tweezers, and salve.

"One more shoe. If the bastards come back, I want to be ready."

I stood to grab a bite of clean air. "You sold drugs too many years, that's your problem. Guilt isn't as easy to quit, is it?" Several seconds went by. I looked at him and said, "You did stop selling marijuana . . . right? That's what you told me six months ago."

"And it was true—six months ago," Tomlinson said, getting to his feet, then he looked toward the horizon. "Life is a fluid, not a solid. I probably should have told you and Danny, but it's something I can't admit to the cops. That's why I didn't say anything."

"Admit what?"

Tomlinson cleared his throat. "Well . . . two weeks ago, I found out I've seriously pissed off a Caribbean importer."

"I knew it, here we go," I muttered.

"I wasn't looking for trouble! How was I to know I was undercutting his prices? We're only talking a dozen *veinte* baggies to a few trusted clients. But this particular dealer is very territorial. Turns out we have a customer or two in common."

"A Colombian," I said.

"Haitian," he replied. "A voodoo sacerdotal with zero tolerance when it comes to competitors. Even boutique operators like me, connoisseurs with big hearts and low prices. When a Haitian turns capitalist, trust me, the gloves come off."

I wasn't going to ask what *sacerdotal* meant. It would only encourage more esoteric gibberish.

Tomlinson provided it anyway, adding, "His name's Kondo Ogbay, which is Swahili—you don't even want to know what it means. The night you left for Tampa, one of Kondo's people put an assault fetish on my dinghy. Blue stone and turpentine on a bundle of dried grass, which is obvious enough—the man's a damn witch doctor. That's sort of why I almost got electrocuted in your—"

"I don't want to hear it," I said. "No more talk until we get the dog fixed up."

I waited while Tomlinson, making soothing sounds, got down on his knees on the opposite side of the retriever. His confession hadn't convinced me, and I wanted time to think it through. The gunshots from the Cessna were imaginary. Had to be—how would anyone have known we were out here in the first place? And my friend had missed the significance of the wire used to sabotage Futch's plane. Tarpon guides in Boca Grande have used Malin's leader for a century. As do other discerning anglers, including the so-called jig fishermen—but only when *not* fishing for tarpon.

There was something else Tomlinson didn't know. I hadn't gone to Tampa, as I'd told my marina neighbors. I had spent three days in a Central American city where I had added a new enemy to my list. Not just one man. It was an emerging terrorist cell founded by a Muslim cleric.

The cleric had recently disappeared. The bandage on my forearm covered the last evidence of the man's final moments—a bite wound that was less severe because of the cleric's missing teeth.

"Good god, the snake bit him and wouldn't let go!" Tomlinson whispered, when he finally figured out what he was seeing. "Damn head's the size of my fist." Then cooed, "Brave doggie . . . yes you are," before saying to me, "This guy's a hardass, huh? The snake, too. Neither one would quit—you've got to love that."

"He's a survivor," I said, then looked at

Tomlinson. "We both have enemies, and we both have reasons not to involve the police. So let's keep all this to ourselves when we get back. Okay?"

"About Kondo, you mean. Sure."

"All of it," I told him, and should have added *especially about the plane* but didn't, which would turn out to be a mistake.

We'd be home before sunset, hopefully. Dan Futch was to call Dinkin's Bay Marina from the air, so, once we made it to the road, our ride would be nearby, only a text away—if we could get a signal.

Tomlinson nodded in agreement, then dismissed it all, looking into the retriever's eyes. "You're gonna love living at Doc's place . . . aren't you, big fella? Sharks to swim with, pissing in the mangroves . . . and maybe help us find our missing cat—"

"I'm not keeping him," I interrupted. "I travel too much. And so do you." I wiped the tweezers with an alcohol pad, then slowly, slowly slid my glove toward the snake's head. The skull was coffin-shaped and solid on the retriever's pliant skin, fangs buried at an angle. The pain caused the dog to drop the snake long enough to slap my cheek with his tongue, but he remained steady.

Tomlinson watched, a familiar knowing expression on his face that I find particularly irritating. "Don't worry, we'll find a home for him," I added after backing the skull free. "Maybe use some of your illegal drug money to pay the vet bills first. How's that sound?"

When a wet tongue whapped me a second time, Tomlinson gave me a *What a crazy day!* sort of look, then confided to the dog, "He can be an asshole . . . yes he can! Prudish as a damn arrow . . . and jealous. But that's not going to stop us from picking out a good name!"

6

DAN HAD BEEN TRUE TO HIS WORD AND our ride was waiting for us when we got to the Tamiami—thankfully, just before the rain hit.

The next two days, I had plenty to do in the lab, so I really didn't spend much time thinking about the near plane crash or the many theories about who might be trying to kill us.

Until I met one of the theories in person at Dinkin's Bay.

IT HAD BEEN A STRANGE NIGHT to begin with. I'd been standing by a fire near the marina docks with my friend JoAnn Smallwood, a chunky, busty woman with big bones and a handsome face, who'd just had a fight with her boat partner, business partner, and on-again off-again bedmate, Rhonda Lister, and so was feeling weepy and fragile.

Then she looked at A-Dock, where the deepwater boats are moored.

"That's something else that's making me crabby," she said, staring.

"What?"

"That."

I followed the lady's gaze to a neat and incremental line of oceangoing sailboats, sails rolled, portholes dark, trawlers, cruisers, and blue-water sports fishermen, most cabins buttoned tight. But a few of the regulars were alive with light: Mike Westhoff's Sea Ray *Playmaker*, Dieter Rasmussen's Grand Banks, Geno Lamont's *Birdsong*, a classic Hinckley, and JoAnn's boat, *Tiger Lilly*.

Because it was two weeks before Easter, a lull in high season, there were a few open slips, but not many. Two spaces down from *Tiger Lilly* was a new arrival, a sleek powerboat, thirty-plus feet of Kevlar Stiletto that looked more like a futuristic spaceship. Dark hull, low black flybridge that tapered aft toward a transom compartment which hid two or three mega-horsepower engines. The engine space was decked with plush cushions, roomy enough for a dozen starlets in bikinis. Oval ports showed lights inside. A string of LEDs mounted under the hull transformed the water beneath to lime Jell-O. No name on the stern, either. Unusual.

I said, "In showrooms, boats like that are missing only two options: an ego big enough to buy it and a lackey to start the engines."

"It showed up last week. Came in at night, the engines so loud it shook the windows. I should've got up and taken a look, but I didn't. You were away on one of your mysterious trips."

"Tampa," I replied automatically.

"Whatever," JoAnn said, giving it a mall-girl inflection. "Sure, you expect some bigmouthed real estate tycoon or a trust fund brat. But we're two slips down, and Rhonda and I haven't met the owner or even seen him. Woke up next morning and there it was."

I was thinking, *Mysterious. Just like Tomlinson's mistress,* as my neighbor continued talking.

"At a marina this small, you expect people to be friendly . . . or at least sociable. I'm telling you, Doc, Dinkin's Bay is changing. This place used to be more of a crazy little family, but now the rich ones come and go, and Mack doesn't give a damn as long as they bring cash or euros. That, plus Rhonda's crazy mood swings, I'm starting to feel too old and tired to put up with this bullshit much longer."

Just then, I saw headlights of a luxury car illuminate the parking lot, then a man get out and open the gate. It was Tomlinson, with his married mistress, returning from South Trail Animal Clinic, where he'd taken the dog.

JoAnn nudged me and said, "Looks like your dog's home."

In the two days since we'd returned from the Everglades I'd repeated "I'm not keeping the dog" too many times to count, so I didn't bother. Instead, I switched the subject to the married mistress by nodding toward the car. "Has anyone seen her? I know she's been in the lab. There was blond hair in the shower drain, and someone refolded my kitchen towels. Then she neatened up the drawers."

JoAnn replied, "Except for the towels, it could've been Tomlinson."

"Not a chance. There was still a quart of beer left in the fridge."

That was enough to convince her. "So he admitted using your bedroom?"

"Why ask?" I replied. "After I've been away, I change the sheets and soak my toothbrush in alcohol no matter what. Laboratory grade."

JoAnn said, "I saw her once . . . at Bailey's grocery. Just a quick glance, though—I recognized her Mercedes SUV. She's everything I'll never be: tall, Nordic, rich, wears tailored clothes— even to grocery-shop—and too damn skinny for tits the size of hers. Plus, she's *married*. Not happily, which is obvious, thank god. Otherwise, I don't think I could bear it. It's women like her who make me want to curl up in a ball and cry myself into a puddle."

As if on cue, she appeared with Tomlinson, he laughing at some punch line, full of life and the awareness of a burning fuse in his backside. She was a tall, vertical presence softened by estrogen contours and a halo of golden hair. The two walked up to his dinghy. The dog, at heel, walked with mechanical care—maybe because of the leash clipped to a new collar—but didn't hesitate to follow the two into the little boat.

That was the first time I saw Cressa Arturo. It would be far from the last.

JANET NICHOLES, the wife of one of our guides, Jeth Nicholes, had come racing onto the dock saying she'd spotted Crunch & Des in a nearby wilderness preserve being chased up a tree by a panther. We'd gone tearassing out of there, and the whole thing had been a farce—no Crunch & Des, and I'd ended up with cuts, scrapes, and bruises for my trouble.

Late that night, the moon was still high in the winter sky as I limped toward the boardwalk and my stilthouse. Then I stopped dead because an odd shape blocked my way. A solid shape . . . an immobile darkness in the shadows . . . weighty enough to be threatening, but not tall.

I stopped, squinted, took another step, then stopped again, reaching for my little flashlight. I switched it on, then immediately off again and whispered, "What the hell . . . ?"

A thousand times I had walked this trail, sober, drunk, preoccupied, dazed, and occasionally eager as hell to disrobe whatever lady I had in tow. But this was a new one.

The dog blocked my path. When I had gone running off, he'd tried to follow and I'd ordered him to stay. "Understand? Stay here!"

And here he was. Sitting exactly where I'd left him. The *precise spot,* as I knew better than anyone could know. The retriever's posture straightened when I approached, he thumped the ground with his tail a couple of times, but otherwise remained a statue. Even when I switched the light on again, he didn't budge, although his eyes revealed a mild enthusiasm that suggested he was *willing* to move if so ordered.

"Amazing," I said.

The dog's ears stiffened, possibly while its brain sorted through a vocabulary list. Then his ears relaxed, the word now rejected as unrecognizable.

In my mind, I replayed the scene prior to getting into the truck to look for that damn missing cat. I remembered telling the dog he couldn't go. But had I also told him to stay? Yes . . . yes, I had. No doubt in my mind.

I looked at my watch—Tomlinson's watch, actually—a Bathys Benthic with bright green numerals that told me it was ten 'till ten. More than an hour ago, I had told this dog to stay and, by god, here he was. To him, *stay* wasn't just a command. It was a mandate.

Despite my throbbing knee and the scratches on my face, I smiled and said, "Who are you?" which brought the retriever to attention. The search for Crunch & Des had been more painful than productive, but the night was suddenly improving.

"Truly amazing," I said again. Then, as a test, I walked past the dog to the boardwalk without looking back. When I did look, the retriever's head was turned a full one-eighty, but he hadn't moved.

Enough testing for one night. I tried the most common release command—*Okay!*—and watched the dog bounce to his feet. He trotted toward me, circled away, then got derailed by a buttonwood, which he sniffed with expertise. When the ideal spot was located, he hiked a leg and marked the place with an uninterrupted stream that would have put my best and beeriest night to shame.

Comfortable again, the dog's brain returned to another subject, so he backtracked to where he had dropped—a fish? Yes, a three-pound mullet still kicking, freshly caught. Where the hell had he gotten that? By the time I'd opened the security gate, the dog was heeling to my left but slightly behind because of the narrow walkway, the mullet sideways in his mouth like a bone. The excitement of locating a spot to piss had been replaced by his dominant temperament, which seemed to vary between boredom and dutiful awareness.

I find animal behavior interesting, seldom amusing, but I was having fun with this. Well-trained dogs are a rarity, in my experience. A well-trained retriever—if he had been trained to hunt—was also a valuable commodity. How had this dog ended up in the middle of the Everglades, hunting for food and battling snakes to survive? I would know more after I spoke to Tomlinson. A valuable dog would have had an ID microchip inserted somewhere under his skin and the vet would have found it. Until then, there were a lot of unusual scenarios to imagine.

The mystery was so entertaining, my bruised knee was forgotten. Nor did I notice that I had a visitor waiting on the porch outside my lab. When I hit the dock lights, though, she was there in the shadows of the upper deck: lean and blond, an elegant silhouette sitting in one of my cane-backed rockers. Looked right at home as if she'd enjoyed the view from that spot many times.

Maybe she had.

It was Tomlinson's mistress. The married woman who'd claimed her wealthy husband didn't have a clue.

Not a lie, exactly. But neither was it true.

7

SHE'S NOT AS NERVOUS AS SHE PRE-tends to be . . .

That was my initial impression when the married mistress greeted me with a request, calling softly, "Mind turning off those lights?" Then, when I was close enough, offered an apology. "This is very rude, I know. But your buddy is headed for trouble, I think. And you're the only one who . . . well, who knows about us. Is it okay?"

Could she stay and talk in confidence, she was asking—as if I had a choice now that she was standing, watching me climb the steps to the upper deck.

"I'm Cressa," she said, extending a hand. "Or maybe he already told you. Cressa Arturo. So I'm sure you understand why I'd rather not attract attention."

I asked, "Where's Tomlinson?" Beyond the porch railing, *No Más* was pointed into the tide, its yellow cabin lights afloat on a breezy moon-roiled bay. No dinghy tethered off the stern, so my friend was somewhere ashore.

The lady allowed her hand to linger in mine, then made a dismissive gesture, her white blouse hinting at angles and contours in the moonlight. "He took off on his bike looking for you and the dog. That was more than an hour ago, so I have no idea." She looked past my shoulder. "Where is the dog? I thought I saw him."

I was more concerned with strangers who behave as if they own the stilthouse I call home. "You've been here the whole time?" I asked.

"My house is on the beach, not far, so I drove home, got restless, and walked back because I know the gate's always locked." She hesitated. "Tomlinson doesn't know I'm here, if that's what you mean. Is that a problem?"

The question seemed innocent enough, but could have been interpreted as suggestive. I told myself I was being cynical and judgmental—no way to live for a man who'd been given yet another chance at life by an expert pilot. So I reassured her, "Probably not. Depends on what kind of trouble you think he's in."

Details were softened by the dusky light, but I sensed a smile. "He says such nice things about you. Sometimes he calls you Indiana Jones. Or Captain America, but not in a mean way. I guess it's true."

Before I could reply, her attention swerved to the dog who had stopped to lap from a bucket of water on the lower deck, then do some exploring. "My god, there you are! We looked all over the place!" She knelt and reached, but then immediately stood. "Ohhhh god, what stinks! He must have rolled in . . . no, a *dead fish*. Silly dog . . . and you smelled so nice after your shampoo!"

In response, the dog's tail whipped the back of my leg once, then he ignored us by walking to the farthest, darkest corner of the deck to enjoy his mullet in peace.

I stepped toward the breezeway that separates the lab from my living quarters. "You can wash your hands while I find something to drink. What did the vet have to say?"

"I stayed in the car, but Tomlinson has a sack of stuff, pills and salve. Nothing serious, I guess. Oh—they did an X-ray and found a computer thingee under his skin, but it doesn't work."

So the dog *had* been microchipped—another indicator he was valuable. "I'll get details later," I said. "Come on in, there *might* be something to drink, but don't bet on it."

The lady's laughter seemed genuine, just the right touch of self-deprecation when she replied, "I'm already a little stoned or I wouldn't have had the nerve. A year ago, even two months ago, if someone had said I'd be high on weed, or standing here telling secrets to a stranger, I would have called them crazy. Just the way I say it— 'smoking weed'—it sounds ridiculous for someone like me, doesn't it?"

Yes, it did, and yes she was a little stoned. But still articulate and in full control, which she proved as she followed me into the house, saying, "Hope you don't mind, but I already closed the shades. Just in case you didn't shoot me for trespassing, then we could talk privately without having to sit in the dark."

I flicked the light switch. "My house is your house," I said, giving it an edge.

"I deserve that, I guess. Tomlinson said that about you, too. That you can be intimidating. He's even hinted you might be a little dangerous, depending on the situation . . ." She emphasized the last with a pause, her tone oddly hopeful. Then said, "But he trusts you. So I've decided to trust you. Is that so bad?"

That was my cue to turn and look at the woman now that the shades were drawn and a light on. Time to smile and stop the sparring. If she was as attractive as JoAnn had said, Cressa would expect it. She would be poised and ready to take advantage of my bedazzled reaction—or was I being the cynical misogynist once again? I might have played along if I hadn't noticed that the coffee mug I'd left in the sink was now washed, and a stack of research notes had been straightened and squared on the desk beside my shortwave radio.

"Obsessive-compulsive behavior isn't a bad thing," I said, opening a cupboard. "We'd still be living in caves if the gene pool didn't pick a few of us. And there wouldn't be meds to treat the symptoms when they get out of hand." I turned for the first time, adding, "Has your doctor tried prescribing something? Or would you miss the mood swing highs?"

The lady was almost as advertised—attractive in a moneyed way that relies on style and cosmetic augmentation, but she also emanated a fleshy sensuality that I associate with ripeness or willingness—both, possibly, in her case. The woman had chosen the Grace Kelly look, Nordic face and hair, long legs in designer jeans, but the indignation I expected from my crack about obsession wasn't there. Instead she appeared stricken as she stepped toward me. "My god, were you in a fight?" She reached to touch my cheek. "You're scratched all to hell . . . and your shirt's ripped. No wonder you're in such a vile mood. What happened?" Her fingers were warm and confident, right at home, as she inspected my face.

That fast, I went from distrusting the married mistress to liking her—in a guarded way.

USING A CORKSCREW on a bottle of Concha y Toro merlot, I explained the scratches on my face and forearms. "I fell out of a tree trying to rescue a cat. Our marina's cat, but it turned out to be a different one—they're both black, so no way to tell from a distance."

"So that's where you disappeared to." Cressa

was inspecting my wounds, standing close enough that I got a whiff of body lotion. Girl scent and leather, a hint of soap. *Nice.* "A cat scratch can be serious," she told me, then hurried toward the bathroom where, presumably, she had already gone through my medicine cabinet and knew what to look for.

I continued to talk while I poured wine into a pair of Bell jars. "Well . . . actually, I didn't fall. There was a big bobcat above me and the limb broke when I looked up. I overreacted, entirely my fault. It was a stupid thing to do."

Her voice, silky feminine, didn't carry far, but I heard her well enough. "*Bobcat.* I had no idea."

"They're common on the islands. Anyway, this big male had flattened itself in the branches, all it wanted to do was blend in, which is why we didn't see it. Plus, we were all focused on that damn stray cat. So I sort of lurched—you know, surprised when I figured out what it was?—at the same time that idiot cat tried to shoot past me. It was a gumbo-limbo tree, very brittle limbs. But only about ten feet off the ground. Somehow, the cat and I got all tangled up. Or maybe it was the bobcat, I'm really not sure. But it could've been worse."

Cressa Arturo reappeared, salves and bandages in hand, an endearing smile on her face. "Tomlinson told me about your plane crash-landing. Which I suppose explains why—"

"I think you misheard," I interrupted. "We didn't crash-land."

She responded with a shrug. "What I'm saying is, I understand. After almost dying in the Everglades, nothing seems like a big deal. You're both looking on the bright side of life—pain, love, everything. I get it. How could anything be worse?"

No point in explaining I had landed on top of Jeth, the fishing guide. Or possibly Jeth, a big, strong guy, had tried to catch me, I didn't know. Afterward, he was dazed and stuttering so badly I had yet to get the story straight. But I didn't want to go into it.

"You mentioned something about our mutual friend being in trouble," I said, placing her wine within reach, then sitting at the little galley table. She obviously knew about the plane, so I asked, "You were with him last week when he touched a wire and got shocked?" I had already seen where someone had left the hose on near the breaker switch downstairs. Because my power was off when Tomlinson had arrived, he'd been standing barefoot in water when he'd tried to fix the problem.

Cressa nodded. "Scary, but it was an accident— or so I thought at the time."

"So that's it. You're worried someone's trying to kill him, right? He told me the same thing. Look"—I put my glass down and tried to make my point—"you two are romantically involved. You care about him, maybe think you're in love with him. Fine. But you haven't known the guy long and he goes through these periods of—I don't want to call it paranoia, exactly, but—"

"I'm not in love," the woman cut in. "Neither of us are in love." She was arranging first-aid items on the table as if preparing for heart surgery, but stopped long enough to joke. "Besides, I find the smart dangerous types more interesting. They're damn rare these days." Then laughed as if she wasn't testing me.

I countered, "Maybe Tomlinson's not as safe as he appears—we all have a darker side."

Her expression read *You've got to be kidding!* "That dear, sweet man? I've only known him a few weeks, but that's impossible. He's too . . . free, too open to be dangerous. And so insightful. I didn't believe him at first when he told me he's an ordained Zen Buddhist teacher, but it's true, isn't it?"

"You really don't need to do this," I said, meaning clean my scratch wounds with the Betadine she was dripping onto a gauze pad, probably counting each drop.

Cressa made a shushing sound and continued. "He says people call him *the guru* sometimes."

Among other things, I thought, but said, "Yeah. It seems to fit him."

"*Guru,*" the woman said again, musing. "Must

be true because he's opened my mind to a lot of things. I was ready for a change, don't get me wrong. But if I hadn't've met him, well . . . let's just say I'm way ahead of schedule when it comes to getting to where I want to go. He reads to me—he's a beautiful writer. We meditate, we laugh, and he nails me on some of the totally bullshit lies I try to tell myself. Tomlinson's more of a teacher . . . but fun, with absolutely zero inhibitions—I can't tell you how refreshing that is for someone like me. And I don't want to see him get hurt. Or you either."

She attempted eye contact, adding, "It makes you uncomfortable, doesn't it? Talking about yourself."

No, she was wrong. Even so, I allowed myself to be distracted by the rumble of a boat idling into the marina basin—Captain Alex returning from a dinner trip to Useppa Island or 'Tween Waters. Just in time, though, I noticed Cressa reaching for the bandage on my arm and slapped a hand over it before she saw the teeth marks beneath.

"Good god!" she said, giving me a look. Surprise, a hint of fear, then approval—an odd mix.

"I just changed it," I explained. "Barnacle scrapes take awhile. It'll be fine in another week."

The woman took an uneasy step back and trashed the gauze pad as if I'd soiled it, then selected another. I watched her fold the pad into a perfect square, then dab Betadine on it, a precise circle of red. "I think my husband knows," she said, finally getting to it. "I think he has someone watching me."

I waited, letting her explain in her own way.

"His name is Robert—Robby. I was fond of him once, but ten years of marriage has turned our age difference into light-years. The younger man!" She laughed, an older woman amused by her own naivety. "I keep expecting him to grow up, but it's not going to happen. He refuses to divorce. Now it's getting ugly—only I didn't know it was ugly until I started putting things together."

"Tomlinson said something about him being the nonviolent type," I replied.

"I still believe that. But I'm starting to wonder. Robby and his family are in the development business—beachfront condos and shopping malls. Mostly in the Vineyard and Buzzard's Bay, but a few projects in Florida, too. See, we signed a prenuptial—"

"Where in Florida?" I asked.

Cressa didn't like being interrupted. "I'm trying to explain my situation. Can you save the interrogation for later?"

"I'm trying to understand," I replied. "Background would be helpful. Their projects in Florida, what kind?"

101

"Rob doesn't exactly include me in the company's business. I don't know . . . they do gated communities . . . some low-cost housing if Tallahassee offers the right perks, and they speculate on real estate, which has gone to hell in the last few years. That's what I was telling you—we signed a prenuptial agreement. I didn't want to, but Rob—well, his father, Robert Senior, actually—he insisted. Which didn't turn out the way they expected, because the prenup figures we agreed on don't fluctuate with the housing market. That's why his family's so against a divorce."

I nodded the way people do when they're impatient with the obvious, saying, "*Money*, of course." Then winced when she pressed the gauze to my face and scrubbed harder than was necessary.

"Cat scratches are dangerous," she reminded me. "If I don't get deep enough, you could end up in the hospital. They're carriers, you know. A type of fever."

I wondered if there was a message hidden between the lines but resigned myself to her nursing. The woman was thorough. While she worked on me, she addressed the dangers of cat scratch fever, but soon returned to the thread.

"Rob never calls between ten and eleven—*ever.* That's when he meets with his online fantasy-league guys, and he's a sports junkie. A tornado

102

could land, a burglar could break into our house at ten-fifteen, it wouldn't matter. But last night, around nine, I don't know why, I turned off the GPS thingee on my cell just to see what would happen. And an hour later, my phone rings. Rob. It was ten-thirty."

I acknowledged the significance with pursed lips.

"Tomlinson and I were on his boat playing Beach Boys cassettes. Maybe I shouldn't have answered my cell, but I was thinking, you know, an emergency, like someone in his family had died. But it was nothing like that. Rob told me he called because he'd had a 'premonition.' He was worried I was hurt or in trouble. That's what he said, anyway. Trust me, men like my husband don't have premonitions. Especially not on the nights they're drafting their fantasy baseball teams."

"That was it, no details? How long did you talk?"

"He was checking up on me, that's what I think. It still gives me goose bumps, the feeling I got"—Cressa held out an arm to prove it—"like he was watching me. Could see me right through the phone. His tone was weird, too. Suspicious . . . passive-aggressive. My husband *knew* I was with another man, I'm sure of it."

I glanced out the window toward A-Dock, where the no-name Kevlar Stiletto was moored.

103

Then said, "The guy's ten years younger than you, but has no problem with his wife spending part of every month in Florida?"

"Nine years," she corrected. The woman was adding salve to my scratch marks, but gentler now. "I'm not getting into our personal life. He's not gay, but sometimes men get injuries playing sports . . . or there's a chemical imbalance. I've stopped wondering or blaming myself. So let's just say he prefers fantasy sports to *fucking*."

It wasn't just the profanity, it was the angry emphasis that caused me to look up. But the woman was still focused on her work and carried on. "Robby might be laid-back, but Robert Senior isn't. Robby has a younger brother, too, who's crazy—I mean that literally—and seems to be getting crazier. The Arturo family is very powerful in some circles"—she let it float there a moment—"if you know what I mean."

I understood. She was insinuating a popular fiction about Italians and an underworld organization that had been dismantled by the Justice Department decades ago.

"No kidding?" I said. "So the crazy brother or his dad might have Tomlinson killed because you're having an affair? A debt of honor? Swimming with the fishes?"

"Make jokes, if you want, but I'm scared. Something's going on. I've never given Rob or his father reason to be suspicious—until the last month or so." In response to my expression, she snapped, "That's the truth!"

"If you say so," I replied, then looked at my watch. "It's getting late. Full day tomorrow." I was thinking, *I need some ice on this knee.*

Still standing, the woman picked up her wine and took a first sip, her mind working at something. After several seconds, she said, "You can be an ass. Tomlinson said that, too."

I wasn't going to deny it, plus I like assertive women. Somehow she'd sensed this and was still trying to win me over. *Why?*

"What time do you leave?"

I replied, "For where?"

"*Tomorrow.* You're flying to the Everglades in that damn seaplane again. Tomlinson told me all about it—those five Bermuda Triangle planes from World War Two. Then, next week, it's some cleanup project in Boca Grande. More flying, more diving. It worries me. Couldn't you two just play it safe for a while?"

I got to my feet and went to the fridge. "Why not relax for a few minutes, enjoy your wine. Then I'll drive you home."

"Especially diving that goddamn pass!" she said.

The cleanup project, she meant. Every winter, scuba volunteers sweep the bottom of Boca Grande Pass, a saltwater canyon that separates two barrier islands, Gasparilla and Cayo Costa.

Annually, groups collect more than a ton of lead fishing weights, hooks, and miles of mono-filament line, much of it residue from fishing tournaments. What I saw would be a useful follow-up to the project I'd done there.

I wrapped ice in a towel, asking, "You scuba dive?"

The woman shook her head, still preoccupied. "No . . . Robby's brother and his father are into fishing. I went out with them twice in Boca Grande Pass, but never again. It's a circus with all those boats flying around at full speed. Even on the charter boat they hired."

Once again, the lady had earned my attention. I wondered if I should press it and ask if the Arturo males fished the big-money tournaments. Before I could decide, she returned to what was actually on her mind, insisting, "It is *true,* you know."

She'd lost me again. "What?"

"I've never been unfaithful! Ten years living like a nun and not one single slip. That's what's so maddening about you, Ford. I'm the private type. I come here—which wasn't easy to begin with—and I tell you something honestly. Your reaction? Like it's no big deal! And that I'm lying to somehow hide my lustful ways. Please don't expect me to feel guilty for finally having the nerve to—"

"I don't," I said. Then added, "That was unfair," even though I wasn't persuaded.

Cressa Arturo touched my shoulder with tentative fingers—a request for permission, it seemed—then softened her tone to share another secret. "You're forgiven," she said. "The truth is, I am worried . . . but mostly glad. If I'd only *known* what freedom feels like . . . so now I'm making up for lost time."

Her meaning was obvious enough for all but the naive and slow-witted, which is why I had to bumble along, saying, "With Tomlinson, you mean."

My answer was delivered via green eyes, an acetylene look that left no room for doubt. "Tomlinson and I are friends and nothing's going to change that. The chemistry, though . . . let's just say the pheromone wallop wasn't the same as the one I just experienced on your porch when we shook hands."

My second impression of the married mistress was now tied to my own internal struggle:

Take advantage of this woman, just to even the score with Tomlinson, and you are scum, Ford. Scum.

8

CRESSA'S VISIT WAS UNSETTLING, BUT I thought I could move it to the back of my mind at least while Dan, Tomlinson, and I resumed our search for the missing Avengers the next day. As it turned out, though, she wasn't my only visitor that weekend—and this one set off alarm bells.

We weren't leaving until later in the day, so Sunday morning I was attempting to capture on video something I'd never witnessed—a southern stingray giving birth—when a man called from the boardwalk gate, "Dr. Ford? You have a moment?"

No, I did not and said so. It didn't deter him. He opened the gate and came toward the lab. "I heard through the grapevine that you and your partners have an interest in Flight 19. Maybe even found wreckage? I think we might be able to help each other."

Another fast look: a genial smile on a big man in his twenties, the successful outdoorsy type, in slacks, waxed boating shoes, and a silver Rolex, but still hip enough to wear shaggy hair tied in a ponytail. Just a hint of accent, enough of a scar showing on his forehead to suggest hockey or boxing, and weight room muscles but without the bulk—a weekend athlete who stayed in shape.

"Not now," I told him. With my digital camera, I gestured to the shallow water below. The stingray was a meter wide, a diamond-shaped slab of brown muscle, with a reptilian tail and undulating wings for lateral fins. It was behaving erratically, spouting water from spiracle vents aside its big shark eyes, gliding in short bursts from one end of the netting to the other as if pacing.

"Is it sick?" My visitor sounded concerned.

"I'm busy," I replied. His accent was Boston, I decided, but unusual in that it seemed forced. Grew up there but moved, I guessed . . . or wealthy enough to have attended private school in the area for a few years.

"I've seen thousands of those things," he told me. "At night, their eyes glow if you hit them with a light."

A phenomenon caused by *tapetum lucidum* in an animal's eyes, but all I said was, "Feeding time is when they come in shallow. They're common here."

"So . . . how's this stingray different?" A moment later, though, the man was saying "Good boy, it's okay," then asked, "What kind of dog's that?"

I looked up. The retriever was at the top of the steps, staring, eyes like two yellow lasers focused on this stranger. If a message was being communicated, the content was neutral, but my visitor read it as a threat.

"Does he bite?"

"I don't know."

"You don't *know?*"

"He's a stray," I said and signaled the dog with a hand, palm out, that commanded *Stop there!*

A stray that obeys hand signals? If that's what the man was wondering, the answer was *Yes.*

It was another fun discovery I'd made about the mysterious retriever. Instead of anchoring him with a sit or stay command when he followed me, there was a more tolerant way. Hold up a hand like a traffic cop and a boundary line was created. Since I'd noticed the stingray's erratic behavior, the upper deck was now the dog's to roam, but the steps were off-limits. Because of this new arrival, though, the dog was tempted, so I signaled him again, then returned to what I was doing.

"A runaway, huh? That's why he's so skinny. I've seen lots of chocolate labs, but their coats are different. So he's probably a mixed breed, you think?"

I was concentrating on the ray: something was happening. So I dropped onto my belly, eye to the camera, and said, "I think it's starting. Don't talk while I'm filming."

The man said, *"Oh . . ."* but caught himself. Then we both watched the stingray float free of the bottom, an envelope of flesh now protruding from its uterine vent.

"I'll be damned," my visitor whispered.

I shushed him and continued to film.

A week earlier, in my trawl boat, this ray had tumbled from the net along with a flopping heap of pinfish, grunts, grasses, hydroids, puffer fish, plus several sea horses that I needed for a recent order. Stingrays are common on the Gulf Coast and considered a dangerous nuisance by some. At the base of the tail is a venom gland and a modified denticle—a long, serrated barb that's sharp as an Amazon spear and sheathed with a slime of nerve toxin. Seldom fatal, unless the barb pierces the heart, but the sting is excruciating.

Little is known about stingrays because they live in the scientific shadow of their close relative, the shark. So I was interested. The absence of claspers told me this ray was a female. Her size told me she was sexually mature (males are dwarfs by comparison). Her belly appeared engorged, so I'd taken a chance and brought the ray back to the lab, handling her as carefully as the delicate sea horses. Here, beside the dock, where stingrays came to feed nightly, I'd created a temporary pen that was roomy enough to forage and shallow enough for observation.

Now, one day before the full moon, my interest was being rewarded.

The man knelt beside me. "In the car, I've got a waterproof Sony. Slip it inside the netting on a desk tripod and use the remote. You'll get the underwater angle."

"Quiet," I told him. "You'll spook her."

Not true. The stingray was lost in the birth process, but I didn't want his voice cluttering the video I was shooting. Inside the ray's uterine brood chamber, eggs were now hatching, and the first pup had appeared. I braced the camera against a railing, lifted my head and watched.

Soon, from the uterine vent, something that resembled a roll of pie dough jettisoned free . . . floated downward . . . then, before touching bottom, blossomed into a pair of elegant wings. The wings were a parachute. Beneath them, saltwater was weightless, buoyant. Chemistry sparked some ancient knowledge, and the wings stroked in unison. Then stroked again. Several strokes later, a miniature stingray, no wider than my hand, swam free.

"When I was a kid," the man told me, "I stepped on one of those and my whole left side went numb. One of the most painful damn things I've ever experienced. What about you?"

I have a low tolerance for the pushy types. In a different mood, I might have told him to get the hell off my property, but I was elated by the video of the live birth, so I replied, "When I was wade-fishing once. The woman with me asked why I was crying. I wasn't, but damn close. Hot water is the only thing that helps—meat tenderizer is useless, even though the poison's protein-based. Longest stingray barb I ever collected was eight inches."

"Really," he said, interested. "They sell them in shell shops, places like that, but nothing that big."

"Quiet," I replied. "Here comes another one."

The visitor stood, olive brown eyes hopeful as he threw back his golden ponytail. "Like I said, my camera gear's in the car—I'm a filmmaker. Do we have time?"

"I don't have time," I snapped.

The man was unfazed, which was irritating or to be admired, I hadn't yet decided. When it was over, five stingray pups were winging the water near an indifferent mother. After confirming I'd gotten footage, I got to my feet, saying, "If you have a business card, maybe tomorrow. I'm busy all day. Sorry."

It was true. In half an hour, Tomlinson and I were meeting Dan Futch at Punta Rassa on the other side of the causeway. There's a shallow flat there near the boat ramp, a good spot for a seaplane. Tomlinson's idea. I had a guess about motives, but he hadn't explained.

The card my visitor presented said he was *Luke Smith, President* of something called *Adventure World Productions, Tampa, Santa Monica, New York.*

"We do reality adventure," Smith explained, following me across the deck. "Our Atlantis piece, maybe you saw it? Or the thing we did on hyenas in South Africa? I just spent three weeks in Key West filming the offshore boat races. It'll be a series on Guys' Network. Flight 19, though—"

The man tapped my shoulder to ensure my attention, so I stopped and turned.

"—Flight 19 is a project I've wanted to do for years. I'm no bullshit amateur looking for a free ride, Dr. Ford. My company's willing to front expense money. Start with ten grand, say?"

I retrieved his card from my pocket for review, straightened my glasses, then looked north beyond the bay where a miniature plane topped the mangrove rim. A Cessna, so it wasn't Dan Futch.

"Interesting," I said, "but I'm already late, Mr. Smith—"

"*Luke.* And your friends call you Doc." The genial smile reappeared as he offered a hand. "I do my research, Dr. Ford." The man was fit, confident, and didn't attempt to crush my fingers when we shook—an asinine gambit that signals a garden variety of male assholishness.

"I'd shoot all the early stuff personally and oversee the whole project once my partner gets involved. But *only* if you're really onto something. Convince me, and we'd have a hell of

114

a good time, I think. Make a fair chunk of money, too, doing what we love—isn't that what life's all about?"

I returned the business card to my billfold, asking, "Who said we found wreckage?"

The genial smile broadened. "Like Jimmy Buffett says, 'The Coconut Telegraph.'"

"It's not true."

"Oh? Well, you can't blame me for trying. You're not the first group I've approached that's on the trail of those Avengers. I'm at a local bar in Florida, talking to fishermen? I always bring up the subject." Smith shrugged in a way that added *So here I am.* "Mostly they're screwballs— UFO hunters who've been probed by aliens, psychics, weirdos. You know the type."

That caused me to look at *No Más* in time to see Tomlinson appear on deck, soon followed by a man in a Rastafarian hair net with the body of a miniature sumo wrestler.

"Yes, I do," I said with feeling.

Smith took that as encouragement. "That's exactly why I've got a good vibe about this project—trust me, I've been on both ends of a camera. I don't care what you're shooting, you have to start with quality talent to end up with quality product in the can."

Movie jargon, I guessed. Now in the rubber dinghy, Tomlinson and his friend were laughing, but possibly sober, while sumo-man bounced as if testing a trampoline—the Haitian drug dealer, perhaps. Kondo-something, I couldn't remember—a "witch doctor." I kept an eye on the two as I continued to listen.

"You're respected in your field—I've even read some of your papers. And your friend Tomlinson's book. And there's not a marina in Florida that doesn't know the name Dan Futch."

I expected Smith to stress the point one more time and he did, adding, "But it all depends if you've actually found those missing planes."

"We haven't," I replied, which only convinced the man we had. He raised his eyebrows and gave a knowing grin.

"Trust me, I understand you've got to be careful. But why not let me tag along in the early stages of the hunt? Start getting it in the can while we hammer out details." He motioned toward the parking lot. "I never go anywhere without my gear." When I failed to respond, the man added, "I'm willing to risk my time and money. What do you have to lose?"

I had been cheery, relaxed, and preoccupied, which is probably why I hadn't noticed the alarm bells until they suddenly hit max volume. Luke Smith—if that was his name—knew our plans for the day. Had somehow found out that we were flying to the Everglades and possibly also knew we were to dive a remote creek where the Avenger throttle assembly had been found.

There is a creaky old maxim often repeated but seldom applicable, even more rarely workable: *Keep friends close, enemies closer.*

The maxim applied now.

"Are you staying on the island?" I asked.

"I can."

I shook my head. "No need. This afternoon we're just reconfirming landmarks. I'll talk to my partners and see what they think. Can I call tonight?"

"Landmarks," Smith echoed, fascinated. "Sure. My cell number's on the card."

"Just to be safe," I smiled, "why not dial me now? That way, if your card gets soaked, I'll have it in my contacts."

Soaked. I watched the word register. My visitor translated the implication, then covered his tracks, saying, "Sure. Can't tell you how many times my billfold's gone through the washing machine." But then hesitated, hand on a pocket that contained his mobile phone. I could see the outline.

"How 'bout I call from the car," he suggested. "What's your number?"

It was a long shot, but I'd guessed right—Smith had two phones. He didn't want me to know his personal number. Enough Third World countries have cell towers that, in recent years, I had employed the same cloaking strategy while traveling on assignment.

My stilthouse has a tin roof. I gestured and used the roof as leverage. "Reception sucks in there." Then pointed at his pocket to block any more excuses. "So why not call now?"

WHEN HE HAD GONE, I finally did what I should have done two days ago.

Alone in my lab, I went to a steel cabinet, dialed the padlock combination, and opened the door. Inside were the few Schedule III drugs used in my work, a couple of notebooks, and also a military SATCOM phone. It was a much smaller version of the iridium transceiver it had replaced.

I entered a security code, touched my thumb to the screen to verify user access, then told the thing, "Call Donald Cheng." My vocal signature matched the voiceprint, so the connection was made.

Cheng works for an intelligence agency that operates worldwide, but is based in our nation's largest unnamed city. I greeted my old friend. "It's in the low eighties here. You still got snow in Maryland?"

Our conversation lasted all of two minutes while I provided the details necessary to preface the question I posed to Cheng: Was somebody gunning for me? Had a foreign agency or a terrorist cell issued orders to kill me?

As I signed off, the dog appeared at the screen

door, his wolfish eyes mildly interested. Let him in, fine, or he could watch fish from the deck, no big deal. A dozen times already the dog had leaped over the railing in pursuit of a passing dolphin or a school of mullet. He was dry for the first time in an hour, so I let him in, and he tagged along while I packed a few things and made a second call:

"Dial Bernie Yeager," I told the transceiver.

Bernie, among other things, is an expert on Internet systems and computer warfare and a legend among the elite few who do similar work. As a young man, he became a secret star by unscrambling the Soviet nuclear sub code progression. It was Yeager who discovered that the Mossad had the cipher key to transmissions between the U.S. and Panama, compliments of a Mossad agent named Michael Herrera. Incredibly, Herrera was put in charge of the Panamanian air force by dictator Manuel Noriega. Find a photograph of the former dictator in uniform. Note the inverted paratrooper wings of the Israeli army—an honor bestowed on Noriega by a grateful nation.

All true.

We are old friends, Bernie and I, and the man was eager to help even though he is semiretired and living in Scottsdale. As always, though, he was also eager to talk.

"Another time, Bernie," I told him. "I've got a

plane to catch," then repeated the same question I had posed to Cheng.

"Such a pal, always too busy!" Yeager chided. "So what president's wife are you sleeping with now? Just name the country, and I'll put two and two together. Sovereign nations don't terminate fishmongers without a reason. That is my personal experience."

"Bernie," I said patiently, "there's some other information I could use. Nothing to do with the intelligence community, so it's a little out of your line. There's a guy who calls himself Luke Smith, says he's a filmmaker. If you can find something on him, great."

"*If* I can find it, he says! In my heart, such a stabbing pain I felt just now, you wouldn't believe." I heard a sound that might have been Yeager tapping his phone against a desk before he returned, saying, "Hello . . . hello? Operator, I think we have a bad connection. I was talking with a friend who only calls to ask favors, then insults me!"

I laughed, but was also aware that Bernie sounded more frail than the last time we had spoken. The man was right. It had been too long since I had called simply to trade stories and catch up. There are certain people in our lives who are so powerfully linked by events, or chemistry, that we are lulled into believing contact is unimportant. These rare few, it seems, are always there, close at hand, their presence unaffected by distance or the passage of time.

By the age of forty, most of us have learned that this is not true.

So I told Bernie Yeager to block out an hour, if he was willing, and I would call about ten-ish, Arizona time. "I've got at least one joke guaranteed you've never heard. And a story about an ambassador in a certain South American country you won't believe, but you'll love it. Oh, and there's something else"—I was seated, the retriever beside me—"I've got another mystery going. But this one's fun."

Bernie was delighted. And also touched, I could tell. But he couldn't let me off the phone without offering his usual advice. "Move here, get out of that terrible business now! Are you listening to me? Make friends with the cactus and the old women with their shopping carts. Pushy old broads, but at least they've stopped getting their periods! And sidewalks so hot, my god, why bother? But Marion, I tell you this—Scottsdale is better than a bullet in the head from some putz in a turban."

Through the south windows, beyond the mangroves, I could see Tomlinson and his sumo-shaped friend talking with Mack. I had questions for Mack, too, questions about the Stiletto—go-fast boats, they are often called—but they would have to wait.

"I'll give it some thought and discuss it tonight," I told Bernie before signing off.

JoAnn had promised to stop, check on the dog's food and water supply, and give him his pills. Later in the day my fishing guide friend and workout partner, Hannah Smith, would redo the dressings if needed. So I grabbed a bag, closed the gate, pausing only to hold up an emphatic hand.

The dog understood and didn't much care. He sniffed the new boundary line, yawned, and turned, all muscle and bone beneath an oily coat, moving away at a lazy pace. A strange animal. I had expected a hint, at least, of disappointment or willfulness . . . something. So I waited.

Finally, the retriever stopped and looked back at me. His tail swung a single stroke of recognition. That was it. Then he lumbered up the steps toward the lab.

A small thing, but I felt my worth had been acknowledged. Possibly even elevated. Irrational, of course, and I realized it. But who would ever know?

9

OUR FIRST STOP BEFORE FLYING TO
the Glades was just across the bay. Dwarfed by a
ridge of condominiums, I followed Tomlinson
into a one-room cabin at the water's edge,
Tomlinson slipping into a receptive state of mind,
his bare feet absorbing vibes from the cabin's
pine floor where the imprint of a potbellied stove
was centered, brick chimney above, three
windows conveying dusty morning light.

"Wood absorbs energy," my friend replied.
"Control your breathing . . . open your receptors.
You'll feel it, Doc. A lot of life flowed through
this tiny space."

Tiny was right. The shell of what had once been
a telegraph office was the size of a gardening
shed, an incongruous element among towers of
concrete, gated grounds trimmed with palms, the
Sanibel Causeway within shouting distance, if
not for all the traffic.

It was from there that "George" had supposedly
sent his telegram.

I tried to ask Tomlinson about his Haitian
visitor, but he hadn't said much, only that he and
his competitor had decided to be friends. Kondo
Ogbay—finally, I could pronounce the drug

dealer's name—was supposedly a reasonable man, and also very spiritual, which apparently was required of witch doctors.

Tomlinson had dismissed my warning *Keep your friends close, your enemies closer* with a laugh that informed me I was guiding my life via clichés. Now Kondo's trusting pal was immersed in vibrations so deafening, he could neither hear nor respond.

"When the battleship *Maine* exploded in Havana Harbor?" Tomlinson tapped his foot, mimicking Morse code. "This is where the news first touched land. Almost three hundred men dead. Eighteen ninety-eight. It was in January, so this room was still decorated for Christmas."

He sniffed the air, perhaps in search of a holly wreath, then held up a finger to request silence. "The clicking of a telegraph key. Copper hitting copper. Smell it?"

No . . . but the room had a pleasant odor, typical of old Florida structures. Pine sap, wood, and dust, a hint of warming tar on tin.

Behind us, Dan had set a temporary line to secure his seaplane and now appeared in the cabin's open door. Unaware we were communing with history, he asked, "How the hell did you get the key to this place?"

I told the truth. "He stole it. The lady he wanted us to meet wasn't feeling well."

"*Borrowed* it," Tomlinson corrected, peeved at

the interruption. "She's getting up there in years or she wouldn't have canceled. I wanted you to hear the story for yourselves. Like that's a federal crime?"

"The lady who told you about the telegram," Dan nodded. "And she knows for sure it was sent from here?"

Tomlinson opened his eyes, surrendering the mood. "I should have gotten her on tape. The man who used to run the ferry to Sanibel, before the bridge was built, he's the one told her. Leon was his name."

I wasn't surprised. In my teens, I'd known the old ferryboat captain. He was an accomplished waterman, and fun to be around because he told riveting stories—some not easy to believe. Tomlinson was on stage, though, and Dan was interested. The facts could wait.

"The telegram was sent three weeks *after* those planes disappeared," Dan reminded him. "Which supposedly means one of the crewmen lived. This lady believes that?"

Tomlinson nodded, an emphatic *Yes.* "Leon told her about a wounded airman limping down the street, then into this room. Try to picture it—no condos, no bridge, but the same narrow street along the bay, just like now. It was Christmas Eve. That's why he was so sure."

Dan and I exchanged looks. Punta Rassa had once been an isolated village. In such a place, an

125

event witnessed on the day before Christmas would be anchored in memory. Didn't mean it was one of *the* missing airmen, of course, but the story became more credible.

"Five missing warplanes was big news," Tomlinson continued, "but details about the telegram didn't come out for a while. When he found out, Leon put it all together. It's been two weeks since the lady first told me, but I've spent time alone in here since." He tugged at his hippie hair while his senses absorbed vibes from the little room. "Flight 19 . . . they didn't all die."

The pilot gave it some thought. "You never know," he said in the way that open-minded people do, then herded us out the door. "We want to be in the water by noon, the sun directly overhead. Visibility's bad enough down there without us being dumb, blind, late, and lazy. *Okay?*"

WALKING TOWARD THE WATER, Tomlinson confided to me, "I took three Xanax. You're sure he inspected that damn plane. Right?"

"Drank them down with a shot of rum, I suppose," I replied.

"Coors Light. I'm nervous, not suicidal."

"You and Kondo, two drug dealers having fun. Let's hope your new buddy didn't slip a half dozen roofies into your beer as a send-off."

"Nothing wrong with fun," Tomlinson responded,

126

changing his tone and the subject. "As long as you don't break the karmic rules."

My god . . . was he referring to last night, me and Cressa Arturo? I couldn't help laughing. I've heard the man say some outrageous things over the years, but this was a new low in hypocrisy. "You're something, you know that?" I told him. "A real piece of work."

"Don't worry, it's cool, Doc, it's cool. Crescent said she had a *fab* time at your place. Very bubbly on the phone this morning—but sounded, you know, like she overdid it a little."

It took me a moment. Cressa was short for *Crescent*, but I didn't stumble.

"Oh?" I said. "Good."

He hadn't mentioned the scratches on my face but did now by pretending to notice for the first time. "Looks like you might have overdid it yourself."

"Nope," I told him. "Did some work, then hit the bed."

"*Hit* the bed," he said. "I just bet you did."

I derailed him by telling him about my adventures with the dog. "He's valuable. He belongs to someone, I bet—they're running ads in magazines. Hell, they might have even hired a search plane—which would explain why we got buzzed. That's why you and JoAnn and the others can't let yourselves get too attached."

For some reason, that helped Tomlinson rally.

127

"Attached emotionally to your dog, you mean?"
"The dog we found," I said. "He already has an owner."

"*Sure,*" Tomlinson said, smiling. Then added, "*Now* who's a real piece of work?"

SOUTH OF MARCO ISLAND and Everglades City, we dropped to six hundred feet and followed the wilderness shoreline, the seaplane's shadow linking white sand beaches with blue water and swamp. All around us was a region called Ten Thousand Islands—a mosaic of green that, from altitude, resembled an algae bloom of islands adrift on a shallow sea. No villages, roads, trails, or houses . . . Even boats became a rarity as we flew south.

"Lostman's River," Dan said through the intercom, pointing. Then tapped the GPS, his finger on some unnamed bay. "We'll land here. Then it's a hell of a hike to Hawksbill Creek." He glanced over his shoulder. "Everybody okay? How you doing, Quirko?"

"Dreamy," Tomlinson replied with a Xanax sigh, his nose pressed to the window. "Know what I've noticed? The busy multitude doesn't hold a damn candle to nature in the flesh. Photosynthesis and saltwater . . . *my god,* the power of it all. I wouldn't mind taking a piss, though. How much longer?"

"We're gonna follow Lostman's almost to the

sawgrass," the pilot said. "We'll drop to tree level . . . a few sharp banks, but don't let it scare you. This plane's solid now."

He turned to me. "I'm glad I didn't tell the cops. Hell, I didn't even tell Kathy." He shrugged. "Probably some guy with a hair up his ass and Johnnie Walker courage. A last-minute deal when he saw my plane unattended—then spent the next day scared shitless, hoping it was all a crazy dream."

I didn't agree, but would know more when I heard from Cheng and Bernie—something I couldn't discuss. Ahead, a black crevice appeared in a canopy of green: Lostman's River snaking its way inland from open sea.

"You ever fish the oyster bars at the mouth?" I asked.

Futch grinned. "Granddaddy told a story about setting trotlines there. Not really a trotline 'cause they'd tie the lines to trees. You know, camp, roast some oysters, then do a check. One morning they came back, the damn tree was missing. He swore it was true!"

"Big snook there," I agreed.

"Or tarpon. The bull sharks get in that river sometimes and just tear it up. Or a big gator. I've seen lots of gators, they don't mind brackish water."

The prospect of a big bull alligator had been on my mind since packing my dive fins and mask

129

that morning. And was still in my mind when Futch said, "You boys hold on," and banked the plane sideways, Tomlinson's voice moaning, "Whooooooa, Mamma!" through my headphones. Then: "Float on, Sky King!"

At tree level, water glittered beneath us as we carved a switchback trail, following the river at a hundred knots. Geysers of wading birds, egrets and herons, erupted off our wingtips and sprayed white arcs into the sky. Manatees, four or five adults, plus infants, gathered like hippos in the drop-off pools, and cormorants slapped the water ahead of us, desperate for flight.

"Up here's what I want to show you," Dan said. "We'll circle it so you see what I mean."

It was the only explanation he offered for suddenly climbing to fifteen hundred feet and flying east until mangroves gave way to sawgrass, which marked the freshwater boundary of the Everglades.

"Now we circle back," Dan said. And we did. Lostman's River was to the north, mangroves below, when he pointed again and said, "See the scars! Right there!"

No . . . not at first. But then I did: slight furrows in the mangroves. Two . . . maybe three separate lines not easily noticed because the tree canopy was so dense. The curvature of each indentation reminded me of old propeller scars on a grass flat.

We began to circle while Futch oriented us. "Years ago, something cut a path through those trees. Cut their tops off. I didn't notice until after Justin found the throttle plate."

Justin was his nephew.

"One night I was on Google Earth, that's when I spotted it. They're more visible from five miles up. This is the first chance to actually look for myself. See there!" The seaplane's portside wing provided an axis for a tight circle that froze the spot beneath us. "Two definite scars . . . but I'm seeing three now."

"Could've been tornados," I offered. "But I know what you're getting at." Planes, out of fuel, could have also plowed those furrows.

"Okay," he said, "here's the best part." He turned the wheel until the plane leveled, then dipped our starboard wing. "One of the scars ends here. See it? That's Hawksbill Creek."

Below was a vein of glittering water, not much wider than a sidewalk, that disappeared into a mangrove island. Several hundred yards into the interior, though, was an abrupt crown of gumbo-limbo trees. High ground.

"There's the Indian mound," I said.

"Calusa pyramid," Tomlinson corrected. He used the name in a generic way meaning Florida's first people.

The pilot shook his head. "The highest mound's pure sand. A burial mound, we figured, so always left it alone. There're a couple shell mounds, too."

"The Bone Field," Tomlinson said softly.

"Nope. The Bone Field's off in that marl flat. You can't see because of the trees. If we had a canoe, I'd put us down here and we could paddle. Instead, we'll land on the other side and hike in."

We didn't respond, so Futch agreed with us, saying, "Thick as hell, I warned you. I've never cut my way in before—the times I've been here, we trailered a boat to Everglades City. So, who knows, maybe we'll find something new."

It's the sort of thing people say even though they don't expect to be surprised.

Not this time.

10

IN THE FABRIC OF UPROOTED TREES were bones. Human bones.

It took awhile to train the eyes. A cranial plate blended with clamshells. A jawbone was lichen-splotched, edged with brown—just rotting wood until the teeth jumped out at you. Human incisors, a partial skull grinning. Half a grin here, an upside-down smile over there.

There was a technique. Kneel and focus on one small spot . . . allow details to blur, then refocus.

Once my eyes had learned the trick, the next step was to reconstruct.

An unbroken piece of femur . . . so the ribs should be . . . where?

More than once, I marveled at my blindness. When parts of human scaffolding finally assumed form, I would scold, *How in the world could you have missed that!*

Once unmasked, though, it was the bones themselves that refused to liberate my eyes. Soon, I was surrounded. Pieces of the dead lay everywhere: sprouting from gray marl where nothing grew, scattered beneath a mangrove cavern that did not permit sunlight. People who had lived and laughed and dreamed, Tomlinson reminded us when we'd made our first discovery, and who had ended their journey here.

So we looked but did not touch. Moved from spot to spot, calling out our finds, but in low voices. Then knelt to inspect.

Tomlinson, to my right, was kneeling now over some new revelation, then abruptly stood. "That's me all over," he said, meaning an area of scattered bones. And then smiled.

Futch was the first to realize it was a joke and he laughed. I laughed, too, which changed the dark mood of this place, but not much.

"You've been here how many times?" I asked.

The pilot was on his knees by an uprooted tree. "Uhhh . . . third trip since I was a kid. About a twenty-year gap between then and a month ago when I brought my nephew. I don't think anybody else knows about this place." He looked around. "I don't see any sign, do you?" Garbage, he meant, the tin and plastic spore of our species.

Tomlinson said, "That's wise. Keep it in the family."

"That's what we decided. We'd been exploring the creek, Daddy and me. Used a saw to cut our way in—this was back in my teens. He spotted those gumbo-limbos and knew there must be an Indian mound. I don't know why he wandered this far back in the mangroves."

"State archaeologists have to know about it," I said. "From satellite photos, if nothing else."

"Sure. But I've never seen another human footprint on this marl flat. That tells you something."

Futch turned in the direction of the mound, a hundred yards to the west, the ridge shielded by swamp. Then looked up at the tree canopy, his mind still on the missing planes. "Thing about this place is, back in the forties it was off the normal flight grid. Key West, they'd fly up the coast to Buckingham or Fort Myers. Orlando, the flight line runs north of here. The air base at Miami or Lauderdale, it's way to the southeast."

"A plane crash wouldn't have been spotted," I offered. As I said it, we were suddenly aware of the sound of an approaching airplane. Single engine, a private plane, maybe a Cessna, flying low.

In unison, we looked up, but foliage blocked the sky. The engine noise suggested the aircraft was passing to the west where Dan had landed his Maule, then secured it with anchors and spring lines hitched to mangroves. So we waited.

"They noticed your seaplane," Tomlinson said after several seconds. The aircraft had circled, but was now heading away. North or northwest, from the sound.

Dan shrugged, then returned to the subject of finding wreckage. "Even if search planes were scrambled—a spot this thick?—they might have flown right over. A lot of wrecks were never found. Just a few years back, I probably already told you, an Avenger was found in the Glades. Took a grass fire to uncover it. Ten years ago maybe? First time the wreckage was ever seen."

His eyes returned to the uprooted tree while he laughed, "Besides, I just proved this place isn't easy to find. Even when you know it's here."

We'd gotten lost. Despite a handheld GPS, for more than an hour we'd wandered in zigzags through swamp and ridges of shell. Finally, we'd hacked our way straight to the creek, then waded against the tide looking for familiar landmarks. Even then Futch wasn't sure this was the place— one marl swamp looks like another—until he remembered the trick from childhood, how to focus and refocus until the bones made themselves known.

"I don't think these are our pilots," I said, getting to my feet. "The incisor teeth, you notice? They're all filed flat on top . . . the ones over here, anyway. But it's not intentional. I think these people ate food that was loaded with sand."

"An ancient place," Tomlinson agreed, referring to contemporaries of the Maya. The Calusa had been sea people, living mostly off fish and clams, anything they could kill and cook over a beach fire.

Dan said, "Then why aren't they in the burial mound? That's what doesn't make any sense. Bones just laying out here on open ground. Or . . . it's possible that we're looking at remains from two completely different time periods."

The remains of World War II pilots mixed with those of an indigenous people, he was thinking.

I turned to Tomlinson and suggested, "Burial platforms, maybe? I didn't find any charred bones, so pyres are out." Then said to Futch, "It's just an idea, but think about getting archaeologists involved with this place. Discuss it with Kathy and the rest of your family, this could be an important discovery. How many know?"

Tomlinson was walking away from the creek toward a wall of vines, then stopped. "Not wind burials," he said, shaking his head. Then stood in silence for several seconds, hands at his sides, before saying it again. "Definitely not wind burials. No platforms . . . no ceremonies. The people who died here"—my friend appeared to wince and then straighten—"they weren't buried. These people were . . ."

I gave it some time before asking, "Were what?"

Futch had picked up his backpack and was walking toward the same wall of vines, a satellite photo from Google Earth in his hands. "If there was a crash," he said, "it either came from this direction or hit the trees from behind us coming from the northeast. Which would make sense."

The pilot was swinging a machete as I asked Tomlinson for a second time, "These people died how?"

When he still didn't answer, I shouldered my pack and walked toward him, saying, "What's going on? Whatever you're thinking, it's purely your imagination. Don't believe me if you want, but it's true."

Maddening, but it was classic Tomlinson: making jokes one moment, the next he's mired in some dismal trance—the paranoid residue, possibly, of one hallucinogenic voyage too many.

I put a hand on the man's shoulder and turned him. "You okay?"

Tomlinson didn't look okay. His face was pale, beaded with sweat. Eyes dazed, but they also communicated suffering. "You're dehydrated," I told him. "How many times do I have to say it? If you wait until you're thirsty, it's too late. Here . . . drink this."

"I need some sunlight, Doc," he replied, then brushed past me, ignoring the canteen in my hand. "I'll be at the creek when you're ready. I'm done exploring for today."

Tomlinson, the sensitive psychic, was wrong once again.

Futch had vanished in the foliage, already some distance between us, but close enough there was no reason for him to yell, "My god! Oh . . . my . . . god!"

I spun, feeling a familiar burn down the back of my neck.

"Doc! You won't believe this!"

Inexplicably, as I headed off at a jog, Tomlinson called after me, "I *knew* it was there."

Unlikely. Not when I saw what the pilot had found.

No one but an expert could have identified a wedge of metal, six feet high, that had buried itself in muck like a hatchet. Then had remained there, stationary, while seven decades of vines and tree roots had winched it deeper into the earth.

The Grumman TBF-1 had several distinctive features, as only someone like Futch would know. He had found an aluminum component. Just the tip—the rest of it, like an iceberg, was implied.

"It'll be obvious when I cut more vines," he told me, sounding numb. "But you see it, right? See the shape?"

Yes, I did.

It was the tail rudder off a World War II torpedo bomber. I could only guess, but Futch seemed sure.

An Avenger.

AFTER HOURS OF BATTLING mangroves and mud, I settled back and relaxed while the seaplane transported us from the silences of history and wilderness, toward Sanibel Island, where the bridge would be busy with twenty-first-century traffic and where Dinkin's Bay awaited, a time warp in its own way.

The giddiness of discovery had worn off. We were tired, bruised, and I'd had to break out the first-aid kit more than once. Now, while insulated from the world below, was the time to discuss how to proceed.

"We need to do this right," Dan said through the intercom. "We're equal partners. So let's hear some suggestions."

"We don't tell anyone," Tomlinson said immediately. He was still subdued, but at least had returned to the current decade. "Not about the wreckage or the Bone Field. I have some close archaeologist friends, but that spot is sacred. It's too late for us. We've already breached the capsule. So I say we ask their permission to find what there is to find. One way or another, we'll get our answer—and god help us."

"From the archaeologists, you mean?" Futch was confused, but already didn't like the idea.

"From the people who died there," I translated. Then said to Tomlinson, "He's asking for ideas. We want to uncover enough wreckage to ID the plane but without messing it up contextually, or getting arrested. In other words, what's our next move?"

"Exactly," the pilot said. "We're going back there, that's a given. I am, at least. But we need to agree, come up with a plan that's organized. Something low profile that makes the best use of our time. And we still have to dive that damn creek!"

He had known from the start that there were realities and obligations that, if not handled properly, could bite us in the butt. Possibly even put us in jail or nail us with a heavy fine. Early on, he had stepped away from the tail section and made that clear, saying, "Let's think this through before we do something really stupid. We're on government-owned land, okay? The government still owns this plane—what's left of it, anyway. So let's take a minute and talk."

This was before we'd searched the area for more wreckage, but after we had cleaned away enough foliage for Dan to be certain he'd found a

140

tail rudder off an Avenger. On his iPhone were photos of Avengers in flight, and he'd waited while Tomlinson and I compared them with the buried monolith.

Yes . . . we were looking at the aft section of a tail fin, minus the wings, elevators, and the tail. The fin's top edge was flat—distinctive. Same with the contour of the aft edge. According to photos, Avengers carried ID numbers on the tail and rudder, numerals painted in white, two yards high. There was too much moss and mud to see if paint had survived.

The shape of the tail matched, though. Tomlinson was convinced. I was willing to be convinced. There were certainly similarities.

Dan had explained, "I've read books on aviation archaeology. I don't claim to be an expert, okay, but I know that amateurs can screw up everything by changing the context of a crash site. We're not going to do that. Just like back there"—he had tilted his head toward the Bone Field—"we look, we take all the photographs we can. But we don't touch. At least, we don't move anything. Not yet, anyway."

The temptation to see more of the tail rudder, though, was overpowering, and the pilot wanted to remove the detritus that cloaked it. Were we okay with that?

"If there's a number," I'd asked, "it might confirm the plane's from Flight 19?"

"Helpful, but no," was his answer. Confirmation required something called a data plate.

"It's sort of like a ship's bell when a diver finds a wreck. Positive proof. On a plane, the data plate's under the fuselage, port side, on the stabilizer. But a tail number would narrow it down. So I say we clean off what we can—not all of it. Then search for the fuselage. After that, the photograph-only rule applies."

So we did it. Wearing gloves and using dollops of freshwater, we took turns peeling the decades away. Soon, a faded numeral was revealed: 3. Only the top half, though—the tail rudder had hit the earth like a spear, so the rest was buried.

When Futch had seen enough to be convinced, he stepped away and began to pace, ignoring Tomlinson's rapid-fire questions about the significance.

He's hiding something. That was my impression. Or Dan, too, realized that a section of paint might have been sheared away by the crash. In the military, letters and numerals are segmented because paint is applied over a stencil. Instead of a 3, it could have been an 8.

All Futch would say is, "It's not *bad* news, I can tell you that much. In my flight bag, I've got the squadron list, numbers for all five planes. Judge for yourselves when we get back. Right now, we spread out and search. Doc, do you have a notebook? I wish to hell I'd brought a measuring tape!"

Each small discovery had been photographed, then dutifully paced off, all bearings anchored to the Avenger's tail rudder. Then the spots were given a tagline and added as waypoints in the handheld GPS.

We didn't find the fuselage. We didn't find much, in fact: fragments of metal, the remains of a gigantic tire, a cache of .50 caliber cartridges, unfired, in a rusty linkage belt. And a piece of fabric that might have been an airman's inflatable vest, a Mae West. A couple of other objects that had less to do with an airplane than the men aboard: what might have been a survival kit, the metal husk too fragile to touch. A collage of straps, buckles, and a sheath of leather that had been lifted off the ground by a tree and was now embedded in the bark. Several more bits and pieces that while undoubtedly man-made had disintegrated beyond identifying. Not recognizable in the field, anyway, but photos might yield something if we did the research.

Combined, the things we found confirmed that an Avenger had crashed in the area or—as I was already thinking—had exploded or collided with another plane overhead.

The tail rudder was the most compelling evidence of all. As we'd strapped ourselves into the seaplane, Dan had opened his flight bag and produced a sheet listing the ID numbers of the missing Avengers. All numbers were prefaced by the letters *FT*—Fort Lauderdale; Torpedo—but only numbers, he said, appeared on an Avenger's tail.

No wonder the man had paced when a 3 was revealed. On the Flight 19 list were Torpedo Bombers FT-36 and FT-3.

If a chunk of paint had been sheared away, there were also planes FT-28 and FT-81.

The pilot was excited for good reason. So was I. Tomlinson galvanized his own interest by matching tail numbers with the names of pilots and crew. What he discovered was a surprise to all but him: the telegram sent three weeks after Flight 19 had vanished still meshed with the wild story he'd told at Punta Rassa. "Georgie" had been the radioman aboard FT-36.

Now, flying toward Sanibel at two thousand feet, Futch was trying to rein in his partners, and also come up with a plan. "Here's what we need to keep in mind, okay? I mentioned the Avenger found in the Glades a few years back. From the moment word got out, the place was a circus. Everyone from UFO nuts to local historians wanted to be the first to prove it was one of the famous missing planes."

Through my headphones came Tomlinson's voice. "The wrong types would flood the place. Yeah."

"We've got to protect the place," Dan agreed. "Believe me, I flew over the Glades the day after it hit the papers. Must have been thirty cars, plus TV crews, parked along the Tamiami Trail. None of them knew the exact location, of course. Even with the sawgrass burned away, the wreckage wasn't easy to find—you know, parts scattered everywhere. But souvenir hunters hauled off a bunch before the experts got a chance. Not the data plate, though. The data plate proved it wasn't a Flight 19 Avenger. But you see my point."

Tomlinson said, "We need a beard. The right beard, no one will ask questions."

I understood, but Futch was confused again. "Try English, Quirko. Except for Miami, they speak it almost everywhere."

I said, "He means invent a reason why we're interested in the Lostman's River area. He's right, people will want to know. When that plane flew over awhile ago? Someone's probably already curious. So we need a story. Something believable, but also so damn boring no one will bother asking. Or *follow* us. Flying around in a seaplane isn't cheap—we owe you money, by the way. It's best if people at the marina see us writing out checks." I looked over my shoulder at Tomlinson.

"Doc's a beard expert," he said. A private joke, which he covered by asking, "How often do we come back? That's important. I'd be fine with a few times a week—you know, as long as we show proper respect—but people would get suspicious."

The pilot was mulling it over. "A story that's believable but boring . . ." Then said, "I'm booked through Thursday. So Friday morning? Maybe camp, which would give us more time. I can't go anywhere once tarpon season starts . . ."

As they talked, I was thinking about the guy from Adventure World Productions, Luke Smith. I hadn't mentioned him and wouldn't until I found out if he was legitimate or not. Either way, Smith would have to be dealt with. Throw him off the trail with a convincing story . . . or invite him along?

Some enemies require more attention than others. So it depended on what my friends Bernie and Donald Cheng had to say.

11

MACK, WHO OWNS THE MARINA, intercepted me near the gate, warning, "You've got to do something about your dog! Anybody else, I would have called Animal Control. Or the Marine Patrol. Where've you been?"

I was shouldering my backpack, a quart of cold beer still unopened in my free hand. "Marine cops?" I joked. "What'd he do, Mack, steal a boat?"

My smile vanished when the man replied, "No—three of them! Two kayaks and Stu Johnson's Whaler. He was chewing the lines on a Donzi when we caught the bugger or it would've been four."

I was confused. "From the water? The boats drifted off—"

"No! He chewed through the lines and swam them back to your lab! We can't have it, Doc. My clients pay good money for slippage. Just because he's your dog doesn't mean he can nick any boat he fancies. Mooring line's expensive."

I was surprised. The behavior didn't mesh with the well-trained retriever I'd left on the porch. I placed my bag on the ground and held up the quart of beer, asking, "Want a glass? Come inside and calm down while you tell me about it."

Mack shook his head, and said, "Jesus, what a day!"

Mack is Graeme MacKinley, a New Zealander who sailed to the States years ago, and took the big step. He bought controlling interest in a marina. Like many immigrants who've prospered, he's wildly patriotic but also a raging libertarian who despises government interference. But he's not the type to rage at me, or any other local, unless there is good reason.

"He's not my dog," I heard myself say, trying to

147

picture what had happened. "You say he swam the boats back to my place? With his *teeth?*"

"The kayaks, he pulled them up next to your gate. But the Whaler was too heavy, I guess. God knows where he'd've ended up with a thirty-foot Donzi. The bugger did it all from under the docks. That's why we didn't see him."

Mack isn't one to exaggerate, so it must have been true. "We'll find the dog's owner," I told him. "My guess is, there's a reward. A big one possibly. The money's yours, would that make you feel better? Until then, I'll pay for the damage."

The man sighed and patted his pockets, looking for a fresh cigar. He's a wide-bodied, bighearted man, but he loves money and is not ashamed to admit it. My offer softened him. "The kayaks, no worries about those. They're rentals. But the Whaler and the Donzi, I should replace all the lines so they match. Doesn't hurt to be classy. You know, have the moorings in Bristol shape before I have to explain to the owners."

I said, "Tell me how much, I'll write a check." Then, because I know Mack well, suggested, "Or would cash be better?"

That softened the man even more. "Oh hell, Doc, it's not that big a deal. I shouldn't dump on you, but the crazies were out today. A woman bought a pound of squid for the pelicans—never mind the damn *Don't Feed the Birds* signs—then went screaming off the dock, about thirty pelicans chasing her. Probably end up with a lawsuit because of all the barnacle cuts on her legs. And I had to send Jeth to pull another rental boat off the beach—it was swamped, of course—then . . . then the lady I've been seeing calls and cancels dinner. Which I'd been looking forward to all bloody day." Mack sighed and lit his cigar, suddenly uncomfortable.

Sunday is always the busiest day of the week at the marina, a crush of vacationers in a rush to have fun. That wasn't the real problem, though. So I took a guess about one of the ladies aboard *Tiger Lilly* and asked, "How *is* Rhonda doing?"

Mack's no actor, but he did a decent job of appearing confused. Midway through an intricate lie, though, he paused, disgusted with himself, and said, "Awww, hell with it. Are you the only one who knows?"

I shrugged, "Probably. JoAnn doesn't, if that's what you're asking."

"She suspect?"

"No. She would have told me."

"I'm a fool," Mack said, "a bloody fool. But I've always had a soft spot for Rhonda. And she's been having a tough go of it lately. Hormone issues—happens to a lot of them, she says."

I offered the unopened beer again, saying, "Why not come inside and talk."

The man thought about it a moment, pushed the straw hat back on his head, then redacted his confession and our exchange. "When we finally got your dog out of the water, a woman offered to help, so I let her take him. A Mrs. Arturo—lives on the beach, third house down from the Island Inn? That's what I really came to tell you."

I looked at Mack and nodded, "If that's the way you want it," meaning his relationship with Rhonda was not to be discussed.

"She said she's a friend of yours. Damn striking woman, you ask me." Then Mack sealed our bargain, and turned the tables. "You know, local gossip has it that someone's trying to kill you or Tomlinson, or both. Maybe a jealous husband. I know it's not true, of course, or cops would be all over the place asking questions. Boat people love to talk."

"Yes, they do," I replied.

"But a rumor like that makes the locals nervous. No one wants to get caught in the crosshairs of another man's trouble. Not that we wouldn't stand up for you if it's true."

I said, "Tomlinson gets in these moods and he thinks everyone's out to get him. He's probably the one started it."

The man nodded and pretended to be convinced. "That's what I figured. Plus, you would have gone straight to the police." After a beat he added, "Right?"

"Someone's trying to kill you, it would be stupid not to," I replied.

No . . . he wasn't buying it. I've lived next to the marina too long, and this wasn't the first unsettling rumor that had made the rounds about me. Even so, he said, "Good. I was almost convinced that's why you asked Jeth about that Stiletto. You know—worried about some jealous husband spying."

"Just curious," I said. "JoAnn said she's never seen the owner."

"Nothing mysterious about that. A hired captain brought her in one night, and the owner made all the arrangements online. Some corporate secretary, anyway. Paid by wire transfer. That's not the only boat new to A-Dock. That big Lamberti? Probably a million-dollar yacht, but no one's said a word about it. The owner's Brazilian and he paid the first week cash. In euros. The guy's a jogger, you haven't seen him? Runs every morning."

I made a mental note to have a look at the Lamberti but stuck with the subject of the Stiletto. "It's probably all that carbon fiber that makes people suspicious. Tinted windows, a black hull. What's the name of the corporation?"

Mack blew a cloud of smoke toward the sunset sky, pleased he had finally confirmed the rumor was true. "I'll find out what I can and let you know. Can't have the marina's most respected citizens bullied by some jealous tycoon, now can we?" He turned to go but then stopped. "By the way, where *did* you and Tomlinson disappear to today?"

Less than a minute into my cover explanation, the marina owner checked his watch to keep from yawning. "Doing a fish count in Lostman's River," he said. "Love to hear about it—but later, Doc. Okay?"

I WAS IN THE WATER, opening the gate of the stingray pen, when my cell phone beeped. When I looked I saw that I'd missed two calls, not one. Mrs. Crescent Arturo and my new workout partner, Hannah Smith, had dialed simultaneously—a coincidence I wouldn't risk sharing with Tomlinson.

Hannah, I wanted to speak with. No doubt she had stopped to tend to the dog, as I'd requested, but had found the dog missing. This after driving her fast little flats boat from across the bay to help, so I owed the woman an explanation.

It wasn't just about courtesy, though. Hannah is one of the rare independent ones, tall and confident in the way she moves, but also guarded at times—a private woman who protects personal boundaries or, less likely, who is aware of some inner frailty that she keeps hidden from outsiders. She is complex, like all interesting people, and I was just getting to know her. For now, we interacted on the most basic of levels. Hannah was a superb fly fisherman with a good laugh and among the few willing to swim a quarter mile along the beach after a three-mile run with me.

Cressa Arturo, I *had* to speak with. I'd enjoyed parts of our evening together, but now I was obligated. She'd rescued the dog from Mack's wrath, and my mental image of her elegant beach house didn't include paw prints and room for a rangy, sodden, oily-coated retriever.

Even so, both would have to wait. After opening one side of the pen, I sloshed my way to the back of the netting, then stomped around until the female stingray spooked in a jet stream of silt. Her wake left the five immature rays rocking like drunken birds, so I stepped into the pen and shooed them carefully, very carefully, toward the opening. My lone stingray wound had come from a ray no bigger than a plate. If body size was in any way proportionate to the amount of poison and pain inflicted, god help the poor bastard who stepped on a big one. The pain is so intense that the Maya used fresh stingray barbs to induce trances and also to prolong the agony of human sacrifices. It's because the barb is a saw-blade of spines composed of vasodentin, a substance harder than bone, and each spine is grooved to transport venom-secreting cells when the barb is plunged into a victim. As long as the spine remains in the flesh, the venom continues to flow. Among Mayan ruins in Guatemala, I'd seen stone carvings of stingray barbs protruding from the hearts and necks of tormented priests and contorting victims. Damn right, I was being careful!

Sissified—if someone was watching, that's how they might have described my careful use of feet and hands. I didn't care. Soon the family of six had disbanded, each stingray flying its separate way, all singular links in an ancient chain, indifferent to everything but survival.

Then I headed upstairs to clean up before returning calls and tending to lab specimens. Later, I would decide on dinner.

MY HOUSE IS ACTUALLY two small houses on a platform, both perched above the water on stilts. It's an old place built to store ice and fish in the days before refrigeration, so it has an outdoor shower fed by a cistern that collects rain from the roof. I was just finishing beneath the shower, the bottle of cold beer finally open, when my phone beeped again.

Hannah Smith.

So I wrapped a towel around my waist and answered, "I owe you dinner. Name the place, and I'll explain why the dog wasn't here."

Southern women who are natural contraltos have an edge when their tone turns icy. "Why, bless your little heart," I heard in reply. "Aren't you the sweetest man ever? No wonder you're so popular with the ladies."

I cleared my throat and said, "Uhhh . . . did I do something wrong?"

"Not the first little thing. I'm just calling to make sure that bad memory of yours didn't put you on a plane to Alaska. Or wandered off in some supermarket and locked yourself in a freezer. A man gets a certain age and—well, I don't much care for the term *feebleminded*. And *senile* is such an ugly word—"

I interrupted, "I would have called and saved you the trip, but I didn't know the dog was gone. It has nothing to do with my memory—"

"Well, the important thing is, you're okay," Hannah breezed along. "At a certain point, a middle-aged man, he starts doing things that are sorta clumsy. Like walking into walls or, you know, that cause him to look just plain dumb and thoughtless. A Christian girl has a duty to check on a person like that or I wouldn't've risked interrupting your nap."

"Hannah," I said, "you've made your point. Only thing missing now is the part where you tell me what you're talking about."

The woman's tone returned to normal, but more businesslike than friendly. "So I finish up my six-hour charter. I drop my clients at Boca Grande, then run like crazy 'cross the backcountry to tend to your dog, just like I promised. And what do I find?"

My brain had raced ahead in search of a scenario that could cause upset, which is why, just in time, the image of Cressa Arturo surprising Hannah popped into my mind. Two women meet unexpectedly in a small house. *My* house.

"I can explain that," I said.

"There's no need, Marion. We're friends. It's okay." Hannah's sudden sincerity only caused me to feel worse when she added, "We're fishing pals and swim buddies. I understand that. What I don't understand is why a woman I've never met—a girlfriend you've never even mentioned—would talk that way right to my face."

I dreaded the answer but had to ask, "What did she say?"

"I don't use rude language as a habit. You know that."

"We're both adults," I replied. "And she's not my girlfriend."

"It's not the sort of thing I'd repeat. What kind of parents would name a girl Crescent, anyway? Flower children, is that what you used to call them? Probably where she learned it was okay to use raw talk."

I said, *"Hannah?"*

"Okay! 'Doc only picks workout partners he wouldn't screw.' That's what the woman said! But didn't say 'screw,' if that's plain enough. So it made sense to her—after looking me over—that you partnered up with a woman not nearly as pretty as her. Is it true you talked that way about me?"

"No," I replied. "Not to her, not to anyone."

To mask the hurt, the woman added, "My lord, as if I'd even think about hopping into bed with a man who dates married women! Just because she's rich and owns a beach house? It's not my place to judge, but there's some who consider stealing another man's wife to be shabby behavior."

Hannah's gambit of using pride as a mask was even more upsetting. I was thinking, *Tomlinson did this!* He had dredged up some throwaway line I'd used months ago, probably after a few beers: *I'm not going to lose another workout partner to the bedroom.* Then he had blabbed it to Cressa Arturo, oblivious to the possibility of her storing it away to use later if needed.

I said, "The woman had no right to be in my house, Hannah, let alone confront you. I have no idea why she'd say something so mean."

"You don't remember asking her to check on your dog?"

"Absolutely not. I barely know the woman! And she knows even less about me."

In a very different tone, Hannah said, "Please don't lie to me, Marion, or I *will* get mad."

Once again my brain raced ahead, and I pictured the married mistress moving around my

157

house like she owned the place, already familiar with every drawer and cupboard. So that's how she had played it. Hannah was the unwelcomed outsider, Cressa a member of the Ford and Tomlinson inner circle. No one in their right mind would believe that Cressa Arturo and I weren't close after finding her alone in my house.

What to do?

Beyond the porch, fragments of a winter sunset told me it would be dark soon, but the moon, almost full, would be up in an hour. Perfect night, cool and calm, to travel by boat. I'd had a long day, but it was only six-thirty. Plenty of time to retrieve the retriever, say a sharp word to the married mistress, then win back Hannah's respect over dinner. But at what risk?

The truth was, Hannah Smith scared me— scared the bachelor in me, anyway. She is not the type to share her favors, or even confidences, without first establishing a relationship based on trust. With the few Hannahs that exist in this world, a date was not just a date, secrets were not just secrets, and bed was a hell of a lot more than a recreational trampoline.

No . . . I was walking a fine line. I had already lied to her more than once—most recently about my trip to "Tampa" and the bite wound on my arm. My god, deception wasn't just a tool in my life, deception was my *profession,* and I had no right to lead someone like Hannah on. Yet, now this good woman with the solid laugh, and her gift for honesty, was warning me not to lie again and she meant it. Had in fact, I sensed, come very close to hanging up on me.

So I said, "I only met her last night for the first time and she's Tomlinson's friend, not mine. And I *did* tell Tomlinson once that I didn't like losing workout partners to the bedroom, but it wasn't about you. He must have mentioned it to her, anyway, and she decided to use it. I don't know why, Hannah. I'm sorry."

There was a long silence. Finally, the woman said, "Thanks."

"I really am," I told her.

"I can tell . . . or we wouldn't be talking."

Yes, she had come damn close to hanging up. For Hannah, there would've been no going back. The relief I felt was unexpected. Way out of proportion to saving what, until now, I had considered to be an interesting, peripheral friendship. So I prattled, "I just got out of the shower. I'm out here walking around in a towel, so I skipped the truth to hurry the conversation along. Stupid. I feel like an ass."

"We've all got one. Sooner or later, we show it," was the reply.

I laughed. Probably overdid it, because Hannah quickly amended, "That didn't come out right. I wasn't hinting around about . . . Not that I'm a prude, because I'm not!"

"If you are, who cares?" I said. "How about a run and a short swim tomorrow. Around sunset?"

For some reason, that prompted another thoughtful pause before I heard, "You don't care, huh? I guess that's a good thing."

"Sure it is. Your personal life is none of my business."

"But I'm not a prude. Just careful when it comes to men—unless I was actually *interested* in someone."

"If you say so. Point is, it doesn't matter. Not to me, it doesn't."

"I see," she replied, then thought about it some more before telling me, "I don't make friends easily, Marion. Wish I could. That's one of the things I admire about you. If you don't mind, though, let's take a week or two off. I understand the way things are now. By then maybe I'll feel like running."

End of conversation.

I stood there mystified, phone in my pocket, wondering what new blunder I had committed. I walked a few feet, then stared at the dog's empty food bowl. Then a few feet more and my eyes found the empty bench that was the cat's favorite spot to doze in the sun. A black cat gathers heat like an oven on winter mornings, so Crunch & Des had been as warm to the touch as freshly baked bread.

I berated myself: *You live alone by choice,*

160

Ford—THEIR choice, every woman you've ever met.

Then Mack's voice came into my head: *I'm a fool, a bloody fool.*

No shit, Sherlock! Six words that summarized the regrets and dumb behavior of every male who has survived the slippery trip through the womb and then stumbled through life.

I went into the house where I changed, then continued to wallow in self-pity as I did the grunt work required of an aquarist. Three times the phone rang and I ignored it—Cressa Arturo was pissed, apparently, because I had yet to appear. *Good.*

But not a word from Hannah Smith.

Can you blame her?

When the phone beeped a fourth time, I looked and read a text. Bernie Yeager wanted to make contact via military SATCOM. That, at least, presented an opportunity to think about something else. So I dried my hands, hung my lab apron on a hook, and called.

FIFTEEN MINUTES WE TALKED, Bernie doing most of it while I made cryptic notes. He didn't have all the information I'd requested, but enough to snap me out of my piteous mood. My wise old friend also grounded me with an axiom I had jotted in a notebook and shared with him long ago:

The fact that unexplained elements are noted within a similar time frame while in the field does not guarantee those elements are linked or are even significant.

He was referring to the jumble of unknowns I'd dumped on him: a strange boat, missing planes, a married mistress, and a filmmaker who seemed to have ulterior motives.

"Focus," Bernie told me after he'd shared what he'd uncovered. "You don't have to be a botanist to cut down a tree."

The homespun aphorism wasn't an exact fit, but close enough to get his point across. And by the time we signed off, I *was* focused, fully in the moment, even though there were plenty of blanks unfilled.

The hunter is being hunted, Tomlinson had told me. *That's your drug of choice.*

Apparently so, because the buzz of elevated awareness returned. I switched off lights in the lab, slipped a tiny semiauto pistol into my pocket—a .32 caliber Seecamp stainless—then headed for the door. I lived alone—so what? Their choice, my choice—either way, traveling life single was the least cluttered of vehicles. More maneuverable, life was cut closer to the bone.

As I closed the walkway gate, I was trying to convince myself. *The less baggage, the less chance of leaving something behind.*

12

JUDGING FROM THE WAY CRESSA
Arturo was dressed, she was, indeed, eager to
make up for a decade of celibacy. She greeted me
at the door in a bathrobe that was belted loosely,
the bikini top or bra she had selected right there
for me to see, two black hammocks of lace fully
laden, the breasts separated by the palest of milk
cleavage.

If she had seduction on her mind, though, it had
been earlier, before the dog had dampened her
mood on this night of dry wind and moon.

"My god, where have you been?" Cressa
demanded, motioning me inside. "I can't control
that animal. Take a look at what he's done to my
house . . . and my pool!"

Swimming pool, too? I managed to conceal my
delight as I took a last glance behind me, then
stepped inside.

I had arrived by pickup truck, a blue '72 GMC
now parked conspicuously in a drive that weaved
through palms and landscaping to three tiers of
stucco that was visible through the trees. The
house was built on the beach close enough that I
heard waves sluicing sand when I got out and
pretended to yawn. While yawning, I scoped the

163

area. If someone was watching the place, where had they concealed themselves?

Thanks to Bernie, I now knew things about Cressa, her husband, and her husband's family that suggested the woman was dangerous company, possibly very dangerous. And that she was being watched.

I had narrowed it down to three likely spots before touching the doorbell, then covering a smile that now broadened as I followed Cressa into the living room.

"I think the rug's ruined," she said. "And my couch . . . I can't make him get off the damn thing. It's a Lilly Pulitzer, white sea worsted wool." She pulled my elbow against her breast and pleaded, "Doc, please do something!"

The dog, asleep on his side, lifted his head for the first time and blinked at me while my eyes took in the room. White throw rugs on a black marble floor. Chrome-and-white furniture. It was an expensive couch. I had no idea how much something like that would cost, but the brand Lilly Pulitzer sounded pricy. Which only made sense in a beach property worth six, maybe eight million. No doubt about it, Rob Arturo and his family, father and crazy brother included, had done very well investing in Florida. "Are the rugs real sheepskin?"

"What could it possibly matter!"

"Dogs are drawn to animal smells."

"The only animal in here that smells is him!" she snapped, then headed for the kitchen.

I called after her, "He usually minds pretty well. You tried the basic commands?"

"Yes!"

"Single words only?"

"For christ's sake," Cressa replied, "I tried everything but shooting him in the eyes with mace."

"They can't pick commands out of a sentence. You know, say it once in a normal voice. *Sit-stay-come.* Like that."

Even though I strung the words together, the dog came to attention. So I signaled him with an open palm: *Stay.* Which caused the retriever's head to teeter sideways, his fur darker for the white wool, and he was asleep when his jowls hit the cushion.

I asked, "Did he mind Tomlinson?"

"*No!* Well . . . not for long, anyway."

The seaward side of the house was glass, sliding doors ten feet tall, one linked to another on tracks so the wall could be opened wide at sunset or on balmy nights like this. But the married mistress was an air-conditioned girl, so the room was warm as an orchid house in a structure sealed like a capsule.

The woman was obviously a compulsive neat freak—but she had kept the retriever inside, so there had to be a good reason. Did she know she was being watched, but didn't want the dog to sniff out her observer? Was she manipulating the person who was paying to have her watched? If so, playing to the camera benefited the woman in some way. If true, I was now part of the act. So was Tomlinson.

I snapped my fingers and instantly had the attention of two alert yellow eyes. I motioned *Come,* then I said, "Heel," which caused the retriever to circle behind me and sit beneath my left hand. Didn't say another word as I marched the dog across two white throw rugs, detoured to hit a third island of white in the dining room, then backtracked across the rugs, out the door and down the steps to the caged pool.

Maybe he's bipolar, I reasoned, surveying the wreckage. Like most swimming pools, this one had a robotic cleaner that chattered along the bottom, linked by accordion hose to a pump. A retriever's job, of course, is to retrieve objects from the water. Possibly because there were no boats moored in the Arturo's pool, this retriever had gone to work on the cleaning system. Chunks of hose and robotic parts everywhere. The detritus of what might have once been a sun mattress lay on the bottom of the lighted pool.

"Or possibly just neurotic," I said aloud.

The dog, indifferent to the mess he'd created, nudged my hand as if inviting a reward. Which he'd earned, by god, so I scratched his ears on behalf of Hannah Smith, a friend who had been intentionally insulted. Offered to scratch his belly, too, but the retriever balked at this wild display of emotion. Preferred to take two galloping strides, then went airborne, crashing into the glittering pool of turquoise to continue an assault that had been interrupted by his nap on a couch of white virgin wool.

I was thinking, *Maybe I remind him of his owner.*

There had to be a reason why he was an obedience champ when I was around, but the Creature from the Black Lagoon when I was away. I don't believe in pull-a-thorn-from-the-paw fables. Lions don't befriend mice, and fairy tales don't explain loyalty, let alone obedience. I had freed the retriever from a snake's teeth, but Tomlinson had helped, yet the dog didn't obey him, according to the married mistress, and obviously preferred to be with me.

Interesting, but I had more pressing matters to deal with.

"Please, *please* get him out of that pool. I was thinking we might go for a swim." Cressa, at the top of the stairs, was standing with a drink in her hand, bathrobe open now. Her string bikini cupped a triangle of shadows on a torso of Nordic white.

"Sorry. I'll have to take a rain check. Better get this dog back home."

And I left her there, with her drink and her bikini, and her mouth wide open.

THAT DIDN'T MEAN I didn't come back, though.

When I was sure she was asleep, I returned to the beach house on foot, a canvas bag over my shoulder. In the bag were tools that I use overseas, seldom on Sanibel Island: night vision optics and a military Golight with an infrared cap over the lens. Cap off, the spotlight threw a mile-long beam. Cap on, the beam was invisible unless using night optics. I used the night vision to search the Arturo property. I found what I was looking for, all right, and much more. I didn't know why Cressa was being watched, but it was the sophistication of the surveillance that concerned me most. The married mistress was being watched by pros.

13

NOON THE NEXT DAY, TOMLINSON puttered up in his dinghy and called my name through the open windows of the lab. I wanted to talk to him about Cressa, but I couldn't just then. I'd almost forgotten about a rush order I had to fill and now I was seriously behind.

On the counter were four Styrofoam containers used to ship live specimens. Two were already loaded, two dozen hermit crabs in each, plus heat packs to keep the animals warm on their flight. It was part of a drop-shipment order I'd received from Carolina Biological Supply: send the crabs to Eden Prairie High School in Minnesota; box and ship sixty marine invertebrates, at least eight genera, to the science department, East Stroudsburg University in Pennsylvania.

Which was why I was busy selecting a mix of small whelks, sea urchins, brittle stars, and sandworms when my self-absorbed pal hollered from outside. And why I didn't answer. When I felt his dinghy bump my dock, though, it was time to act. I threw my rubber gloves into the sink, removed my apron, and went to the screen door, which I didn't bother to open.

"I'm right in the middle of something," I told him. "I can't stop now."

I could see Tomlinson's head bobbing above the dock. "I know what those straps are," he hollered back. "What looked like leather we found in the tree . . . where bark had grown over the straps? Flight 19. I can tell you now, but it would be better if I showed you."

I replied, "If you'd ever had an actual job, maybe you'd understand—I'm *working*."

"Doc, we found a parachute harness! Plus, something I should have shown you and Danny but didn't. Here . . . it's in here. It all makes sense now!"

I had turned away from the door but looked back to see a boney hand holding a small bag. He was waving the object like a surrender flag. Tomlinson, I realized, had *taken* something from the crash site.

When irritable, I'm prone to snappishness. When angry, however, I retreat into a sphere of calm. Emotion clouds clarity, which is why I opened the door and in a tone that crackled with clarity said, "When the feds bring charges against you, I'll be the first witness. So, you bet! I'd love to see what you stole and then lied to us about."

Tomlinson's hand and head disappeared beneath the dock, and his became an invisible voice. "If I caught you at a bad time, just say so, man! No need to fly off the handle. How 'bout I come back, oh . . . say, around six?"

I was peeved but also curious. He'd found something interesting, that was obvious. I was eager to have a look, but I wasn't going to fold that easily. Tomlinson's uninhibited zeal can also be read as shameless manipulation.

"Give me an hour," I countered, "I'll be done by one-thirty," then had to add, "as if being punctual means anything to you."

The phone rang. At first, I didn't recognize the area code but remembered calling the offices of

Gun Dog Magazine, *Retriever Magazine*, and a couple of others. So I answered. It was one of the editors. I put the lab phone on speaker so I could work while we talked.

"This would make a terrific article," the editor said after I had given her the condensed version. "What kind of snake attacked the dog? Poisonous?"

My eyes shifted to a jar where the reptile's skull, recurved fangs bared, was curing in preservative. "A Burmese python," I said. "Or possibly an African boa. I sent photos to a herpetologist friend, but she hasn't gotten back yet. An anaconda is a longer shot."

"*Incredible.* A dog who survived a snake that size, my god," the editor said. "And you say he's well trained. Field trial quality, do you think?"

I had yet to work with the dog on retrieving, which I told her, then added, "I'm a novice on the subject, so I'd be a poor judge. But he's definitely been through the upper levels of obedience training."

"A Lab or a golden? You didn't say."

"A Chesapeake, maybe, or one of the rarer breeds," I said. "I'm guessing."

"A *Chesapeake,*" the editor said as if it was significant. Apparently it was, because a minute later she was explaining. "A common mistake people make is thinking that retriever breeds are all similar. You know, sweet, good-natured—but they're not. In terms of breeding, Chessies have nothing in common with Labs and goldens. Totally different animals. All great in their way, but Chessies are . . . well, they have a much harder edge to them. They're not a breed I'd recommend to the average owner."

"He's so skinny and scarred-up," I told the woman, "it's hard to be sure what breed he is. Not from photos on the Internet, anyway. But someone put a lot of time and money into this dog. No way of telling how long he was lost in the Everglades, but yesterday I picked him up and stepped on the scale. He weighs fifty-two pounds. An adult male retriever, average size, should weigh seventy or eighty, right?"

"Poor thing!" the editor sighed, then became overly polite to excuse what was on her mind. "A fascinating story. But before we go any further, well . . . thing is, we have to be careful when it comes to animals that disappear, then show up in the hands of a second party. I believe *you,* of course, but there are other types out there. I'm sure you know what I mean."

No, but I took a guess. "I don't want publicity or a reward unless they want to pick up the vet bills. In fact, I won't allow my name to be used if you do write something. I called about a lost dog, not to suggest an article."

"The way I put that was clumsy," she said. "Dognapping. I should have come right out and said it. We just ran a piece. The FBI goes after kidnappers, everyone knows that. But a blue-chip stud, or a field trial champion worth forty, eighty thousand dollars? Sure, dog theft is against the law, but low priority. The highest ransom on record is twenty-five thousand—a toy Pekingese owned by an actress—but most owners don't report it. Why would they? Police can't do much, and all they want is their dog back alive."

She added, "So if a blue-chip retriever was stolen, chances are we wouldn't hear a word—not if ransom was demanded. Dognappers, the real professionals—and there are probably a hundred theft rings around the country—have it down to a science. They demand an amount just low enough to stay under the radar but high enough that it adds up to a multimillion-dollar industry.

"Another technique these people use is they pretend to find the dog. Usually under terrible circumstances—save it from being run over by a truck or find it starving in some garbage dump. See what I'm getting at? They contact the owner anonymously, then hint around about a big reward for their trouble. To a family, of course, a dog's real value has nothing to do with a price. It's purely an emotional decision. There's a rumor an oil sheik in the Hollywood Hills paid half a million for his daughter's missing Afghan."

Interesting.

We talked for another ten minutes. The editor provided me with a few names to call, and I promised to e-mail a couple of photos.

Then back to work. While I packed the Styrofoam containers, I took occasional breaks to check on the retriever. Early that morning, to stop him from vandalizing boats, I'd loaded a crate of crab buoys onto my stand-up paddle board, then paddled toward the marina basin. The dog had followed, swimming as if at heel until I granted him freedom with a wave of my hand.

While he freestyled after birds and chased dolphins, I used the weighted buoys, dropping one every ten yards, until they formed a perimeter that made the marina off-limits. To each buoy I also tied surveyor's tape, Day-Glo orange, to make them more obvious.

When finished, I had summoned the dog. It took half an hour for the retriever to learn he *could not* breach that sacred perimeter. Once I felt confident, I had returned for a quick morning workout: forty minutes on a ballbuster of a machine called a VersaClimber, made tougher by wearing a forty-pound vest. Then ten minutes of stretching followed by abs, then squat thrusts, but no pull-ups, although the bar beneath the lab summoned me. A partially torn rotator cuff is a bitch of an injury that heals—if ever—at its own lazy pace.

Sunset was for running, swimming, and

surfing—on those rare occasions when Sanibel Island has waves. Hours nine to five, seven days a week, were for work.

Working now, packing the order for Carolina Biological Supply, I went to the north window and searched for the dog. It took awhile. Finally, I spotted him. He was a quarter mile offshore, laboring toward the lab with something large and dark in tow.

Geezus. The marina was now off-limits, but I had allowed the animal the option of open sea.

I used Soviet binoculars, forty-some pounds of glass on a tripod, the superb optics once used to snipe East Germans crossing the wall to freedom. Palm fronds, that's what he'd found. A large section of a tree canopy blown down by a squall. *Good.* The dog was neatening up Dinkin's Bay. No one, not even Mack, could complain about that. The man's story about purloined boats and kayaks had seemed far-fetched until now. Never had I seen an animal move so powerfully through the water.

A Chesapeake Bay retriever? Maybe. Or . . . *otterhound.* The name popped into my mind because the animal was oily-coated and swam like a damn otter. I'd seen the name somewhere, but did such a breed exist? There was probably a long list of esoteric retrievers. Later, it would be a fun topic to research.

I returned to my work, aware I had to have

the Styrofoam coolers at Pak-n-Ship by one. Time and the UPS truck wait for neither man nor invertebrate.

TOMLINSON TOLD ME, "One of the crew injected himself with morphine. Or someone else who survived the crash. See where the needle's broken off?"

Glasses on my forehead, I was looking through a microscope at an object two inches long, half an inch wide, trying to get the focus just right. "How in hell did you find this? Something so small . . . Pretty weird."

"The tube's made of an alloy—lead and tin, I think. I felt it through my feet. Like an electrical charge, I don't know how else to describe it. So I dug down a few inches. It didn't look like much, that's why I didn't mention it. Just a glob of mud, so I put it in my pocket for later."

I was thinking, *He can't sense camera surveillance, but his radar picks up a speck of buried metal?* Even so, I grunted to communicate disapproval, then asked, "How far from the parachute harness?"

"Ten yards, I stepped it off. The tube's rolled flat, see? Like an empty tube of toothpaste, which proves it. I found photos on the Internet. Mind if I use your printer? Space is one of the drawbacks of living aboard."

"Nice of you to bother asking," I replied, then

told him, "The tube's made of a lead alloy, you're right. Or rust would've . . ." I paused and changed power by rotating the lens head. "The label isn't paper. It was die-stamped, red on white. Squibb, that was the drug company. Morphine Tartrate, but I can't make out the dosage. The needle . . . yeah, it's a very simple injection system."

Because I'd been angry with him, Tomlinson was eager to make amends. "I'll never take anything from the crash site again, promise. A syrette, that's what they called it. A first-aid kit was attached to every parachute issued to aviators. A half grain of morphine, which is a decent hit if it's recreational—but not nearly enough if you're in serious pain. Someone survived the crash, I knew it first time I stepped into that telegraph office."

I rotated the lens head again and said, "The muck probably saved it. No oxygen, no oxidation, so we need to get photos, then figure out the best way to preserve it." I stepped away so Tomlinson could take a look, adding, "Because the tube's smashed doesn't prove a wounded man used it. You're guessing. More likely, it was damaged in the crash. See how delicate the needle is?"

"Ten yards from where we found the parachute harness?" Tomlinson argued. He gestured toward his little Mac laptop, where he'd opened several photos. "You knew what it was, didn't you?"

I cleaned my glasses, then sat in front of the

laptop, seeing photos of parachute harnesses issued in the 1940s and another of a small yellow box labeled *Solution of Morphine WARNING: May Be Habit Forming!* Beneath the box was a syrette tube of malleable metal, the needle protected by a glass tube and a safety key. The die stamp matched what I'd seen through the microscope.

I leaned back and said, "The D rings and clips told me it was some kind of harness, but the canvas fooled me. I could have sworn it was leather." After scrolling through several more photos, comparing what we'd found melded into a tree with vintage harnesses, I added, "These are so simple compared to what they issue at Fort Bragg. Integrated parachute systems, sort of like BC vests for diving. But, yeah, I suspected."

Tomlinson stooped beside me, the scent of patchouli not as strong as usual. He'd done his homework and pointed out similarities that seemed to prove we'd found what the old Army Air Corp called a Quick Attachable Chest harness. A remnant of red material at the shoulder, he claimed, proved the harness had been produced after 1943. Then he turned toward the door, asking, "You want a beer?" and left me alone to try to picture the unlikely scenario he was suggesting.

Just before his Avenger crashes, a pilot or crewman throws open the heavy canopy and jumps into the darkness. His chute opens, but he's so badly injured when he lands he needs morphine. Or he finds an injured crewmate and injects him with the morphine. All possible but for one glaring detail: on a stormy night, how in the hell had a parachute drifted down within fifty yards of where the Avenger had crashed? Where pieces of the airplane had landed, anyway. Even if the man had jumped at a crazy low altitude, the parachute would have put on the brakes while the plane rocketed onward. Unless . . . unless there was a strong tailwind and the chute had followed the same trajectory and landed *after* the plane had crashed or—as I still suspected—broke up before hitting the ground.

I was interrupted by the sound of the screen door banging open and I looked around to see Tomlinson, fresh beer in hand, a wild smile of discovery on his face. "We're idiots!" he said. "All three of us, it was right there and we missed it!"

I edged my chair back to create more space. "Are you okay?"

"Move . . . move—I'll show you!"

Tomlinson couldn't wait to get at the computer, so I stood and got out of his way. It took him awhile, but he finally brought up a photo of an Avenger taken in the 1940s. Then he opened a photo he'd taken of the tail rudder we'd found, a portion of a 3, or possibly an 8, faintly visible. He touched his finger to one, then the other. "Now do you understand?"

No . . . but I was working on it. In the old photo, the bomber appeared pristine, painted black or navy blue, the number 79 stenciled in white, huge, on the tail. The shot was taken from the plane's starboard side. In Tomlinson's photo, the rudder section Dan had found was also shot from that side. The top edge of the rudder was crowned with a hinge but otherwise flat, angled slightly aft. Distinctive. No chance the number we'd revealed was upside down.

My eyes moved back and forth. Finally, it hit me . . . a detail so damn obvious that I could only agree with Tomlinson.

"Absolute idiots," I said. In the old photo of Avenger 79, the number 7 covered the rudder. The 9 covered the solid section of the tail. On the port side of the tail, though, the numbers would have been reversed. To prove it, I ripped a sheet from a notepad and just for the hell of it wrote 36 on both sides of the paper—the ID number of one of the missing Avengers.

"The second number will be on the port side of the rudder," I said, flipping the paper to illustrate. "If there is a second number. And if there isn't, it proves we found Torpedo Bomber FT-3—one of the five missing planes. How many crew was she carrying?"

I moved to my own computer and opened a

folder I'd created for research on Flight 19. Tomlinson was up and pacing, tugging at a strand of hair, when my cell rang. Dan Futch.

Ideas are in the air, Thomas Edison once wrote. Maybe so, because I heard Dan tell me, "We've got to get back there, Doc! I just realized something about that tail section—"

A minute later, I said to Tomlinson, "Dan's booked the next four days, so we fly down Saturday morning. Or you and I take my new boat and go without him. He doesn't have a problem with that." Then I said into the phone, "Are you sure?"

"Tomorrow!" Tomlinson replied, "Or . . . Thursday—I'm teaching Beginner's Mind Wednesday night."

I covered the phone with my hand because I didn't want Futch to hear. "First, we need to have a serious talk about your married girlfriend," I said. "*Then* we decide."

14

AND I HAD SOMETHING ELSE TO DO AS well. Mack had given me some interesting info this morning. Bernie had given me even more.

At sunset, my shorts dripping seawater and sweat, I finished a long swim and gimpy run at

A-Dock, my Clydesdale weight causing the planks to vibrate, which announced my presence to all deepwater vessels and passengers aboard.

Exactly what I wanted to do.

Sitting aft on the recently arrived Lamberti yacht, reading a magazine, was a lean, aloof man who could have played Zorro in the movies. Errol Flynn mustache, white cardigan sweater on this cool evening, a long Macanudo freshly lit—the vessel's Brazilian owner, presumably, who jogged every morning when he wasn't smoking cigars. His name was Alberto Sabino, according to Mack, and had paid cash in advance. Euros.

At my approach, the Brazilian looked up, then pointedly ignored me by finishing the last of his white wine and checking his watch. After a glance at the pumpkin moon blossoming from the mangroves, he stood, then disappeared into the cabin with a dancer's easy grace that I've always envied but will never possess.

What does come naturally is imitating the cliché American boob. Big smile, loose-limbed, I clomped up to the boarding gate and rapped on the yacht's hull. Twice I had to knock before the Brazilian finally poked his head out.

"You wish something?"

"You're new to Dinkin's Bay," I smiled. "I always like to stop and say hello to the new ones."

"*Es* fascinating," the man replied with sarcasm,

"I am, though, busy at this particular time." His English was flavored with Portuguese and a whiff of German; articulate, but in a way that caused me to picture him as a boy practicing the tough words: *fass-cin-A-ting*, *par-r-r-tic-U-lar*. Working at it hard to impress important people down the road.

I said, "My name's Ford, but everyone calls me Doc."

The man stared at me as if he'd discovered a new type of bug. So I bumbled along, saying, "I'm not a real doctor, but you know how folks are. I'm a biologist. I hear you're a runner—I'm always looking for running partners."

Silence, the man staring at me through wire-rimmed glasses, not blinking. So I pointed down the shoreline to my stilthouse. "I've got a lab there. You're welcome to stop by anytime—your wife, too. You have a wife? There're some really nice places to shop on the island."

The man was entertained, possibly also reassured by my vapidity, which accounted for his expression of contempt. "This area is private, no?" he said, then looked toward the dock juncture where a sign read *Owners Only!*

"That's to keep outsiders away," I explained, then hurried to add, "Great fishing here. Tarpon are already showing up. Maybe you've met some of our fishing guides—they're the experts."

For an instant, just an instant, I saw a glimmer

of interest, but it didn't last. "Already I have arranged this matter," the Brazilian said, "now please you go," then he closed the door with a sound that only oiled teak and brass can make.

For several seconds I stood there, then clomped down the dock to the sleek Kevlar Stiletto and banged on that hull. Lights showed through porthole curtains, but no telltale shift in trim to suggest the boat was inhabited. And still no response after I'd knocked again, so I backtracked to *Tiger Lilly*, where I would have stopped but just in time heard the fragments of an argument that froze my fingers inches from the visitor's bell.

JoAnn accusing, ". . . might as well just admit you're seeing someone!"

Rhonda firing back, "As if you'd notice . . . and so damn self-righteous—"

"I've never done that to you! Who is it? Tell me!"

"So now you *own* me, too, is that it—"

"An appointment with a doctor, that's all I'm asking! Honey, your hormones are all screwed up!"

Turning a blind eye to the small, inevitable indignities that befall us all is one of the duties of friendship, so I hurried away doing my version of a tiptoe jog. By sparing the ladies aboard *Tiger Lilly*, I was of course also sparing myself the role of mediator, but I chose to believe I was being courteous, not cowardly.

Mack and Jeth were still in the office, so I waved good-bye, but Jeth had already unlocked the door. "Tom . . . tah-tah-Tomlinson was looking for you," he stammered, " 'bout fifteen minutes ago. Said you two were doing somethin' tonight—I forget the word he used. But he was gonna be late, so I should tell you."

Surveillance? If that was the word, it was true. We planned to visit the Arturo property before joining Cressa for dinner, although no telling why Tomlinson would share the information. Jeth seldom stutters these days, but still avoids problematic syllables so I didn't press the issue.

"He'll be late," I said. "What a shock." Jeth was still smiling as I stepped inside and spoke to Mack. "Did you find anything else on that Stiletto and the Lamberti?"

"Already have it out for you," he replied, then looked at Jeth. "This is just between us. Understood?"

I spent a few minutes going through documents while Jeth and Mack went back and forth, having fun rehashing details of our encounter with the bobcat, then the limb breaking.

"Bloody drongos!" Mack roared. "Had to be like trying to catch a damn refrigerator—surprised either one of you can still walk."

Jeth agreed by rolling his sore shoulder, and they were both still laughing when I left to jog home, where instead of showering I filled the dog's water bucket, then lugged the heavy Soviet binoculars outside to the porch.

To the east, the moon was huge, a blaze of smoky orange, and sunset clouds were still streaked with tangerine. A wooden courtesy screen shields my outdoor shower from the marina, so I moved the screen to the railing to create a hidden viewing station. When I had the tripod positioned the way I wanted it, I swung the binoculars toward A-Dock and took a look.

The Lamberti Custom, sixty yards away, was partially blocked by other boats, but I could see enough. It was a beautiful yacht, white-hulled, with a white upper deck that was trimmed with mahogany, teak, and stainless steel, Palm Beach registration below the name *SEDUCI* in luminous gold script. Translation: "seduction," or the masculine spelling for "seductress"—several possible meanings, in Portuguese, I guessed. The Brazilian had taken his bottle of white wine and cigar to the flybridge, where, I realized, he had a clear view of my stilthouse. But his attention wasn't on me. He was sipping wine and talking on a cell phone, his expression blank, movements relaxed and fluid.

According to Mack and the paperwork I'd seen, now and earlier, Alberto Sabino was CEO of an import-export company that had offices in Rio, Luxembourg, and Dubai. His real name, though, was Vargas Diemer, originally from São Pedro,

Brazil—information provided by my aging pal Bernie Yeager.

Bernie had some other interesting tidbits. The area around São Pedro was settled by Germans in the 1940s and known for the freakish number of twins born there—the result of experiments done by Dr. Josef Mengele, some geneticists believe. The Nazi physician had posed as a veterinarian during the years he'd lived in São Pedro. It wasn't until long after 1979, when Mengele was drowned by a SEAL-trained Mossad agent, that researchers made the connection between the reclusive veterinarian and a small village where for three generations more than half of the infants born are fraternal or identical twins.

"They are very, very German," Bernie had told me, then informed me of something unexpected and disturbing. Vargas Diemer was the son of a locksmith and now a pilot for Swissair. It was ideal cover for an elite thief and sometime assassin—which he was, according to Yeager, although his avocation was known only to a few in the international community. Diemer was an articulate man, picky about assignments, who specialized in recovering compromising letters, photographs, and videos for blackmail victims. Contract assassination was the natural and more lucrative next step. Vargas Diemer, according to Bernie, had amassed a fortune working for a jet-set clientele—the politically powerful and ultrawealthy whom the Brazilian had met on the social circuit.

I'd been looking for someone who might want to kill me. Well, here was somebody in my own backyard. Automatically, I connected Diemer's Sanibel visit with the Muslim cleric who had vanished after burying his teeth in my forearm. This wouldn't be the first time a fatwa had been issued declaring that, as adjudged by Islamic Law, I deserved to be executed. But then, as I thought about it, I wasn't so sure. Hire a Germanic Brazilian pro to mete out Muslim revenge? Money wouldn't have been a problem, but that was not the way the religious crazies usually work.

Bernie had agreed with me. "There's not much on this man, Diemer. Never is in his particular line of work—the true craftsmen, I'm saying. As if I'm telling you! For one thing, he's not Muslim. He's Lutheran—still attends church when he's not building toy planes or tying those whadda-ya-call-its . . . the feathers at the end of a fishing pole. If Arizona had an ocean, maybe I should know the word, but it's slipped my mind."

"He ties flies?" I'd asked. Yes, it turned out, Vargas Diemer was also a fly fisherman, which is why I had paid attention to the Brazilian's reaction when I'd mentioned fishing.

"Fish that eat flies," Bernie had grimaced. "So

remind me next time not to order the fish. But, yes, this is what I am telling you. Professional thieves and assassins with money sometimes take vacations. You know, get away from the hustle-bustle of killing and stealing for profit when he's not flying around in jet planes. Fishermen love Florida, that is the rumor, so maybe it's a coincidence, but maybe not. Either way, stay out of this man's way, Marion . . . or stay *very* close and watch him.

"Personally, what I think you should do is take a vacation yourself. Four bedrooms in this house of mine, so much room we wouldn't have to see each other's faces 'till cocktail time. Since Helen died, I wander around and get lost, the place is so big, don't ask me why I keep it. Like I keep telling you, Scottsdale isn't perfect, but it's better than a bullet in the head."

Now as I watched Diemer savor his wine and cigar, it seemed even more unlikely he had accepted a contract to kill me. He was a fishing *enthusiast,* that was evident even from his mild response. And why would an elite pro risk something so obvious as using my own marina as a base? If the man was being paid to watch me or even steal something from my files, it was possible. Otherwise, Diemer's presence was at odds with the four basics of a successful hit: *anonymity, surprise, disposal,* and *escape.*

Murder is easy. Eliminating a target, then

disappearing unnoticed, is not. It would be doubly difficult if the killer owned a fifty-foot custom-built yacht that was moored a hundred yards from his victim's home.

Sanibel Island is a favorite destination of the affluent who keep a low profile: the famous, the wealthy, international politicos. Could one of them be his target? But I couldn't think of anybody staying there now who would fit. Or . . . had Diemer been assigned a person within striking distance of the islands? I thought of Tomlinson. I thought of Futch.

Either way, Bernie had been right. Diemer— Alberto Sabino—required watching.

Less troubling, after speaking to Yeager, was the Stiletto ocean racer. Dark rumors about the boat were already being exaggerated by locals, but they were baseless, apparently. As Donald Cheng had confirmed, the vessel was owned by a Miami company that sponsored boats in the Offshore Grand Prix, an annual May series, and the Key West International races in November. In Florida, there's a megalist of tournaments and events that appeal to the big-business types who mix recreation with profit. Still, it was odd that the boat's occupant had yet to appear, but should that oddity concern me? I recalled the maxim Bernie had shared:

The fact that unexplained elements are noted within a similar time frame while in the field does not guarantee those elements are linked, or are even significant.

It was an important point, yet didn't alter the fact that someone *had* sabotaged our seaplane and almost killed us. But who?

My thoughts went again to the supposed filmmaker, Luke Smith. The only thing I knew about him was that his business card was as fake as his name. Even the Bernie Yeagers of the world can't conjure up information on a faceless person named Smith who disappears after the briefest of encounters. I had tried Smith's cell phone and the business number on the card—both no longer in service. I had searched for his film company on the Internet but found nothing. Frustrating. The man knew a lot about me, but all I knew for certain about him was that someone familiar with the marina or people living in Dinkin's Bay had provided him with information about me and possibly still were. He had a working knowledge of cameras, which was suggestive, but didn't prove he was a filmmaker. Smith's interest in Flight 19, real or not, might also be a gambit designed to get me and/or Tomlinson and Dan Futch alone in the Everglades.

While I stood at the binoculars, the dog appeared and made a grunting noise. Thus far, the sound was as close as he'd come to whining—his signal he needed to visit the mangroves. Because I'd yet to hear him bark, either, it crossed my mind that maybe the snake had damaged his vocal cord. I pointed toward shore and said, "Okay," thinking, *Is this the perfect dog?* But abandoned the notion when, instead of trotting toward the walkway, the retriever took a shortcut by vaulting over the railing. He hit the water with a cannonball crash that displaced a shower of golden spray, compliments of the last rays of a winter sunset.

It was six-thirty. Tomlinson would arrive in less than an hour, so I showered and tried to finish some work in the lab. My mind kept wandering, though. I wasn't obsessing about the supposed filmmaker or the articulate perfectionist who might have been sent to kill me. No . . . my fixation was more mundane. Dinner with the married mistress was at eight, and I dreaded the inevitable awkwardness. Just the three of us, alone, making small talk?

Dinner was Tomlinson's idea, of course.

ONE BY ONE, I retraced my steps from the night before and led my hipster pal to three video cameras hidden in foliage outside Cressa Arturo's beach house, each time touching a finger to my lips to remind him to keep his eyes open but his mouth shut.

Using night vision, the units were easily found. Infrared lights were mounted atop two of the cameras, and the camera positioned at the gate fired a laser across the driveway—a trip wire that recorded all comings and goings associated with the married mistress. Which is why we'd parked my truck at the Island Inn, just down the beach, and had cut in through the side yard.

Last night, after discovering the cameras, I'd been tempted to steal one of the data cards in hopes that the shooter would accidentally appear at the start or end of a video. But a missing memory card was too damn obvious. So tonight I'd brought an exact replacement, a thirty-two-gig SanDisk with contact ports intentionally fouled—a way of explaining why the card was empty. Believable, but not if more than one camera had failed. So I told Tomlinson, "Wait here," then worked my way toward the swimming pool and made the switch after confirming the camera there wasn't already filming.

Risky, and I knew it. The cameras were all keyed by auto triggers of some type—a heat sensor, in the case of the camera near the front door—but it was possible the shooter was also stationed nearby. Dozing in his car maybe. Or had a room at the Island Inn where he was watching the house live on a computer screen. Jostle a camera, a motion sensor might flash an alert. But what was the worst that could happen? If the shooter surprised us, we would take off running like a couple of kids after TP'ing a house. This wasn't the jungle after all, this was affluent Sanibel. No one would appear with guns blazing.

Changing the memory card didn't set off lights and alarms. No *obvious* problems, anyway. Soon we were walking West Gulf Drive toward my truck, casting giant moonlit shadows while we talked.

"She signed a prenuptial," I explained. "So the question is, does it contain an infidelity clause? If so, maybe that's what the cameras are about. Maybe even the sabotage of our plane, too, to get to you. Depends on how crazy the husband and the in-laws are. Or how crazy *she* is."

"Prenuptial agreements," Tomlinson mused. "Never even crossed my mind before I married the Dragon Lady. There's your answer to the one thing that me, the Beatles, John Lennon, and the battleship *Arizona* all have in common. A genuine ball breaker sent from the East. Female variety of the Asian flu."

He was referring to a tiny little Ph.D. he had once lovingly called Moontree, although her name was Musashi. Their daughter—whom Tomlinson has had to retain a lawyer to even visit—is Nicky. The wife's Anglomaniac choice, not his. He had lobbied for the names Coquina or Junonia, but had been overruled. At the time, Tomlinson had been heavily into animism and also inhaling some kind of surgical gas, halothane I think, which he had balanced (I'm guessing) with amphetamines. "My synthetic period," as he calls it.

I said to him, "Don't get fixated on your ex-wife. You need to pay attention, buster. I just told you something important and it went right over your head."

"If some little yellow succubus had stuck your Zamboni in a light socket, you'd understand," he replied.

"Let's stick with your new girlfriend. If the prenup has a fidelity clause, Cressa loses money and you might end up in court when she fights it. If it doesn't, then she *wants* her husband to know she's screwing around. Cressa is throwing it right in his face to force a divorce and you're her costar. So if the husband or one of her in-laws is nuts, guess what? You're the one they're trying to kill, not me or Dan, so think about your buddies if nothing else."

Unruffled, Tomlinson replied, "From what I remember, you were here last night, too, Doc. You could end up on the big screen. You know, best supporting actor? I think it's safe to say we are officially Eskimo brothers."

"Eskimo?" I asked, then waved it away. "Forget it, I don't even want to know. Tonight, just pay attention, okay? We could level with Cressa about why the seaplane almost crashed— put it out there and see how she reacts—but, personally, I don't trust her. Or try to finesse the

truth out of her about the prenup. I'll follow your lead, you're the gabby one—unless you drop the ball."

"Baseball metaphors," Tomlinson smiled, getting into my truck. "You really don't know what it means?"

Eskimo brothers again.

"Get your seat belt on," I told him, then drove to the beach house and parked in the drive, indifferent to the invisible laser that recorded our arrival.

15

CRESSA ARTURO LOOKED FROM ME TO Tomlinson, then back to me and smiled, "Why is it I feel like a kid in an ice-cream store?" which was her way of proving she could relax and have fun with the subject, a soon-to-be divorcée whose new life was already on a roll.

Tonight, her outfit matched the meticulously casual décor: a white linen dress that caught the patio breeze, with straps more like two scarves that lifted her breasts in suspension and framed cleavage. Beige sandals, silver bracelet, and a white ceramic watch, but it was the beach dress that added a bounce to her step as she exited the kitchen carrying drinks.

I could sense Tomlinson about to reference ice cream—*Eskimo Bars,* possibly—and was silencing him with a look when Cressa stiffened. "Was that a car? I think someone just pulled into the drive." She put the tray down and tilted her head to listen.

"Cress, sweetie, your whole breathing rhythm changes when you're nervous. Realize that?" Tomlinson, eager to help, was already relighting the joint he and the woman had started. I scooted my chair back to avoid the smoke.

The married mistress was still attuned to sounds outside: tree frogs, the wash of waves . . . then the *BANG!* of a heavy car door.

I thought, *Uh-oh,* wondered if I'd been unwise to trip the laser-beam camera sensor.

"Can't imagine who it could be," the woman muttered, then hurried inside the house to have a look, her sandals clicking on tile. After a few seconds, she called to us from across the house, "My god, it's him! It's Rob! What the hell is *he* doing here?"

Tomlinson was looking at me, smiling through a cannabis haze as if he'd been surprised by jealous husbands a thousand times, and was now pleased to share the experience with me, his ol' buddy. "This should be interesting," he confided, leaning back in his chair. "Just stay cool, man. If we tried to escape over the railing, he'd know for sure we're lovers. This way, we're just two neighbors who stopped by for a drink. A welcome-to-our-island sort of visit."

I turned to face him. *"Cameras,"* I said. "Or did you forget?"

Yes, judging from the man's reaction. "Oh, yeah . . . that," he nodded and sat up straighter. "Well, I've jumped off higher balconies, but I wouldn't panic just yet. Always let the woman handle these situations. No matter what they say, they've rehearsed their story over and over in their heads. A guy gets involved, though, the husband dude really will get pissed off."

I replied, "Some vet should have neutered you years ago," then got to my feet and had a last sip of beer. I wanted to be ready just in case the husband dude came crashing into the room with a bat in his hand or even a gun. It was possible. Who could blame him?

When Robert Arturo Jr. appeared in the foyer, he was fuming but not enraged and polite enough to wipe his feet before sliding past his wife. Instead of the couch potato she'd described, I was looking at a man, late twenties, who might have played college basketball or was a competitive swimmer and still competed weekends. Tall, good-looking, slacks pleated, shirt fresh from the laundry, his hair combed just so. Tortoise-rimmed glasses added a professorial touch and gave his nervous hands something to do when he turned to Cressa and accused, "Screwing my brother wasn't enough? What do you think Dad will say when he sees *this?*"

I was thinking, *She's sleeping with the crazy brother-in-law, too?* while Arturo drew his arm back and hurled something across the room that bounced off the soiled couch, then spun to a stop on the floor.

A DVD, I realized. Video of the married mistress with another man fresh from the surveillance cameras?

Tomlinson, still sitting, informed me, "It's always a bad sign when they throw stuff," which caused Rob to notice that two strangers were listening in. My truck was in the drive, I don't know why he was surprised but he was. The man stabbed at his glasses, unsure about how to handle the situation, then glared at his wife. "You are un-goddamn-believable. Know that, Cressy? Doing threesomes now, are we?"

"How can you be so filthy-minded in front of my guests?" the woman countered. "That's just sick. My god—your *brother?* Take that back and apologize right now!"

"It's true and you know it!"

I decided it was time to get the hell out of there and I tried, saying, "We were just leaving," then indicated the patio door, the steps to the pool just beyond. "Thanks for the drinks."

"The hell you are!" Arturo shouted and came toward us with long strides, but slowed when he got to the couch. He was momentarily distracted by the mud stains, then got madder when his eyes settled on Tomlinson as he knelt to retrieve the DVD. "It's *you,*" he said finally. "It *is* you. Of all the goddamn gall!"

He turned to his wife. "You can't do better than this? Some pathetic hippie loser? As crazy as Deano is, he was right about your whoring. Here"—he shoved the DVD at her—"*you* tell my father to watch this sick . . . garbage for himself. I dare you."

Cressa said, "Robert, are you insane? I have no idea what you're talking about! Is it Dean? Call the goddamn facility if he's making threats again."

Now I was thinking, *The crazy brother's in an asylum?* a question that was answered when Rob Arturo told his wife, "This was playing on the screen when I started the Lexus," meaning the DVD clenched in his hand. "The car at our condo twenty *miles* from here?"

"That can't be!" The expression on the woman's face suggested shock and also asked *How?*

"I didn't catch a five a.m. flight for the fun of it," Robert snapped. "Dean escaped!" He turned to me. "My brain-damaged brother ran straight for Florida when he took off. More than a week ago, and she's been here the whole time. What's that tell you?"

The wheels in my head were turning. I said to him, "Let me ask you something. Did you plant the cameras outside? Because if *you're* not paying for the surveillance . . ."

"*Surveillance?*" The husband looked at the wife, both of them confused, or at least pretended to be.

"What cameras?" Cressa demanded.

I nodded toward the patio door. "I can show you—but I'd be surprised if at least one of you didn't know."

Husband and wife, two icy spheres, followed me down the steps, through the pool area, outside, where I didn't expect to need night vision to find what I was looking for.

But I was wrong. The cameras were gone. Just like that, someone had slipped in and collected them all, two tripods included.

When Tomlinson suggested, "I left a joint upstairs. How about we take ten, then come back with flashlights?" the search ended abruptly.

"I'll call the cops if you're not off my property in ten *seconds,*" Rob Arturo told us. He meant it.

IT WAS ALMOST MIDNIGHT when I heard the soft clang of the bell at the walkway gate.

I stood, hesitated—this couldn't be good news, and I was right. It was the married mistress bundled in a trench coat and stocking cap. Even

201

at a distance, I could see that she was dabbing a handkerchief at her eyes.

The evening had turned chilly, a northeast breeze sufficiently brisk. I had lighted a fire in the woodstove that heats my quarters when I'm in the mood. My mongrel heart was certainly in the mood, but logic demanded that I look at the ceiling and wonder aloud, *"Why me?"*

Curled near the fire, the dog looked up, thumped the floor with his tail, then went back to sleep. If that was a warning, the animal definitely didn't possess extrasensory powers as Tomlinson claimed.

Clang-clang. The bell again. Crescent Arturo was getting impatient.

I was wearing sweatpants and a tank top that could have stood a washing. Should I hurry up and change?

Who you trying to kid, Ford? A rational man would tell her to go away . . . At most, offer to drive her home.

That's exactly what I decided to do while I pulled off the tank top and chose an old Egyptian cotton shirt. I had the shirt on by the time I got to the door and called to the woman, "Come on in."

While she crossed the boardwalk, I suffered a moment of clarity and used the cell to call Tomlinson. I was staring through a window at the cabin lights of *No Más* when he answered.

"Get your ass over here now," I whispered.

"Trouble?" he asked. He sounded hopeful, which suggested he'd done more drinking than smoking.

"I think your girlfriend needs a place to sleep." He replied, "Huh . . .? Oh—*her!* Be there soon as I get this damn caulking off my hands," then a clattering sound that told me he'd dropped the phone.

From the porch, I heard, "Are you alone?"

"Depends on your definition," I said, stepping over the dog, then opening the screen door. An attractive woman who's been crying projects a childlike quality that dampens sensuality, yet it softens the heart. "Everything'll be okay," I assured, steered her inside. "What happened?"

When Cressa had a glass of wine in hand and was seated in the chair next to my telescope and books, she answered the question, explaining, "We had a terrible fight after you left—no surprise, I'm sure. Robby went storming out. His family has a condo near the airport. I thought about calling Tomlinson, but I hate that little rubber dinghy boat of his. It's so wet, and the wind's freezing."

"The condo where your husband keeps a Lexus," I said.

"His family's car. I was glad he left, at first, because usually I love being alone in the beach house. But . . . then I got scared." She looked at me, her jadeite eyes glistening. "It's because of Deano. He's around here somewhere. I believed you about the cameras. How else this?"

She was still wearing the trench coat cinched tight by a belt. From a pocket, she pulled the DVD Rob had found and placed it on the desk. On the disc was a little label, the stick-on type, one word printed in caps: *WHORE!!!*

"Looks like someone doesn't approve of your new freedom," I said. "Your brother-in-law for sure?"

"Who else?"

"There has to be a reason. Why would Rob's brother give a damn?" I pointed at the DVD. "In the video, who's the guy with you?"

"How would I know!" she snapped. "I watched just enough to see where it was taken. That's all. Just the thought of someone spying gives me the creeps."

"I assume you were with Tomlinson," I said. But also knew the married mistress could have added another man to the list in her eagerness to make up for lost time.

Cressa began to fidget. "Of course it's him, but that's not the point. What really hurts is that a member of Rob's family is behind this. Dean—it's got to be him. How could he do such a thing!"

I said, "Dean as in Deano?"

"If it's serious, *Dean,*" the woman said, then focused her attention on her handkerchief while I touched a hand to her shoulder but also tried to keep her talking.

"You should be telling this to the police," I told her. "The brother, Deano, just how crazy is he?"

"That's what's so upsetting," she replied, "I don't even know anymore. A year ago, a judge signed papers and put him into a private facility. Very expensive, but it seemed to help. Everyone thought Dean was getting better." Cressa sniffed again and added, "The judge was a friend of the family—of course."

"A full year?" I said. "Then he must have some kind of history. You can't just sign a paper and put someone away for a year."

"No, he's been in and out, getting treatment. You can only make them stay seventy-two hours. It's not his fault, that's the sad thing. Used to be, Dean was a terrific guy."

A hint of family loyalty or had Rob been right about Cressa sleeping with his brother? The latter, I began to suspect.

"He's a speed freak," she explained. "Not the pill type—not at first, anyway. He raced moto-cross, boats, you name it. He was just getting into planes, probably skipping steps, I don't know, but Dean managed to crash one into a hangar. The doctors said he was fine, just a concussion. But that's when he started to change—two years ago in December. 'Prescription drugs,' people say it like they're safe, but they're even worse than the other type I think. Dean never told me, of course, but I think a year on painkillers got him into other stuff. Drugs he had to buy on the street."

"Vicodin, Oxycontin, it's a big problem," I said, hoping empathy would open her up. "A man in pain, addiction is the least of his worries."

Cressa seemed to appreciate that. "That's what I keep telling Rob and his father! Sometimes, he'd be like a zombie—sit around and stare. Next day, he'd be banging off the walls, full of ideas and new projects—and he is always broke, even though Robert Senior still gives him an allowance. That's a sign, according to what I've read. Of drug abuse? The abuser is always desperate for money."

"A head injury and chronic pain," I said, "the guy needs some help." Then tried to get her back on topic, asking, "Behaviorally, though, he hasn't done anything to suggest he's dangerous?"

From the woman's reaction, the way her eyes moved to the ceiling, I suspected that what came next would be an evasion or a lie. She told me, "No . . . not in the way you mean. Oh, he *likes* all the macho stuff—same as most guys. But he's usually very sweet. Deano and I always got along—friends, you know? At least, we *were* friends."

"What kind of stuff?" I asked. "Guns, knives, bowling? I'm trying to get a sense of what he's capable of doing. The police will ask if you report the cameras, so you might as well think this through."

"He would never hurt *me,* I'm sure of that."

"He already has if he's the one shooting video. I'm not a physician, but brain trauma can cause all sorts of unexpected changes. And if the guy does have a history of violence—is he a gun buff?"

"No!" she said.

"I'm not accusing him," I said, continuing to empathize. "Does he hunt?"

"Yes, but he doesn't use a gun. Didn't think it was fair. I don't think Deano even owns a gun."

"He was a bow hunter?"

The woman was getting frustrated. "Probably—I don't know! He didn't believe in killing animals with guns. Doesn't that tell you something?"

"Cressa," I said, "I'm trying to help," then sat back and waited while she thought it over.

Finally, she looked up from the table and said, "I'm being overly protective. Sorry. Cameras, that's what he hunted with—at first. Deano used to say a clean shot is a clean shot. He had Nikons, then he got into shooting videos. He's always loved movies—he studied it in college."

For the first time, it crossed my mind that Deano Arturo might also use the name Luke Smith. "Was he in the business?"

"He *wanted* to be in the business. Still does—and maybe it'll happen if he gets well and finally gets a break. Five or six years ago, he did a camera safari, and he put together this incredible film about a tribe in East Africa, the men still hunt with spears. That's when he started getting serious about documentaries. I don't know if he did the bow-and-arrow thing, but he thought using a spear was the fairest way to hunt. No, 'the noblest'—the corniest line in the film, I thought. But that's not the reason the cable companies wouldn't buy his film. Said it was racist, even though Deano loved the natives he worked with. Took him two years to get that film right. Damn near broke his heart."

"Spear hunting," I said. "That's what you meant when you said 'at first he just used cameras.' "

"What I'm telling you," Cressa replied, her tone severe, "is that Deano was a fairly normal guy before the accident. Always pushing the limits—just the opposite of Rob. But, you know, in a healthy way. Like an athlete."

"Sure," I said, playing along. "Your brother-in-law was perfectly normal before the head injury. How about some more wine?"

I used it as an excuse to check the window and see what was keeping Tomlinson. For some reason, the man was rowing his dinghy, not using the engine. That was okay. He'd be here in time to guarantee I didn't do anything stupid. And, so far, the odds against it were improving by the second—with every word that came out of the woman's mouth.

"**WHERE WAS THIS SHOT?**" I had refilled Cressa's wineglass and picked up the DVD. The woman had used the bathroom, returning fresh-faced and under control.

"I don't want to talk about it tonight," she replied. "You mind? I'd rather not start bawling again."

The word *WHORE!!!* on the disc label had been typed, not printed, I noticed for the first time. "You might have a serious problem. You should go to the police like I suggested."

Cressa tugged the belt of the trench coat tighter and folded her arms as she replied, "Rob's father wouldn't like seeing the family name in a newspaper. I wouldn't like it, either."

"Even if he's dangerous?"

"Deano's not dangerous, I just explained that."

"You don't know for sure it's your brother-in-law," I said, then tried a more direct approach. "In your prenuptial agreement, is there an infidelity clause? I'm trying to think of every motive possible. Whether it's Deano or someone else, there has to be a reason for putting so much effort into the surveillance. Your husband says he didn't know about the cameras. And if you've got nothing to do with it—"

"If I'd thought a clause about screwing around was necessary, I wouldn't have gotten married," Cressa cut in, then surprised me by taking the disc from my hand. I watched her grimace, struggling to bend the thing until it broke— *CRACK!*—then she sealed the subject, saying, "There. Like it never happened," and handed me the pieces. "Can we please change the subject? I've had a terrible night."

I was thinking, *Any second, Tomlinson will be here,* as the woman stood and told me, "All I want to do is pretend like it's a month from now. That I'm here to relax and behave like a normal woman. Like I haven't wasted ten years of my life in a platonic marriage—or should I feel guilty about that, too?"

I shrugged, meaning *Whatever you say,* which gave her permission, apparently, to unbuckle the trench coat and remove it one slow arm at a time. "It's warm in here, but I love fires." Cressa held the coat out for me to take. "Where should I hang this?"

Eye contact: rainforest eyes still glistening, but nothing broken behind those two sharp lenses, and curious about how I would react. It was because of what she wore beneath the coat: a pale lemon chemise that hung to her thighs, spaghetti straps that allowed her body to move cleanly beneath the satin sheen.

"I went running out of the house," she explained while I turned toward the hat rack. "I was lying there in bed listening to all the sounds, then suddenly just panicked. Threw a few things in a bag and ran. You know how that happens sometimes?"

"It's important to feel safe," I agreed as I hung the coat, then immediately headed to the galley to check the window again.

"Don't get the wrong idea about the night-gown."

"Why would I?" I replied.

"I'm an emotional wreck, so it's not the way it might look to your neighbors—but no one saw me."

"It happens," I said.

She used the handkerchief to wipe something invisible off a chair, then sat at the table. "I knew you'd understand. I hate Tomlinson's damn little wet boat . . . Plus, I feel safer with you." Cressa hesitated, then decided to risk asking, "You're supposed to be the dangerous one, right?" In her tone was fascination.

Outside, I heard the clank of a plastic paddle, then a wet little rubber boat went *THUMP!* against the house.

"Who could that be?" I said, breaking the beam of the dog's eyes. When I got to the door, I added, "Geezus . . . you're not going to believe this."

The woman stood. "Oh, no . . . you've got to be kidding! *Doc?*" The married mistress's voice could also command, so I turned. "Let me ask you something. *Honestly.* Are you afraid to be alone with me?"

I focused on her almost Grace Kelly face and answered, "Yes . . . yes, I am." Which was true—but not in the same way that Hannah Smith scared me.

"You shouldn't be!"

"It's a rule I have about breaking up marriages. I try not to rationalize what I personally wouldn't tolerate."

The woman was miffed. "But you're wrong. Rob and I, our marriage is so *over*—Tomlinson understands that, and we're still friends."

Opening the door, I replied, "Tomlinson is a more spiritually advanced person than me. He'll be up here in a second—just ask him."

16

THE NEXT MORNING, I AWOKE BEFORE sunrise in a hammock I'd brought back from Nicaragua and strung between two hooks outside on my porch. It's a double-wide, woven from fine heavy cotton in a mountain village where hammocks are made for sleeping, not decoration. Plenty of room and lift for two, but I awoke alone.

I threw off a blanket and sat up. Dew was heavy, dripping off the tin roof, the morning gray and still in the silver predawn light. But not too early for a boat to be idling down the channel toward my house. One of the fishing guides, I guessed, who'd spent the night aground. Or had fallen into the Budweiser trap at 'Tween Waters or Temptation Bar on Boca Grande. The boat was returning, not leaving, that was obvious, so I untangled myself from the hammock, found my glasses, and went to the railing to have a look.

It wasn't Jeth, or Neville, or any of the other guides. The boat was a twenty-one-foot flats skiff, a custom-built Maverick with an oversized outboard. Even through fogged glasses, I had no trouble recognizing the lines because the skiff had been mine up until a few months ago when I'd sold it. Standing at the wheel, wearing a dark foul-weather jacket, black hair spilling from beneath a visor, was the new owner—a fishing guide . . . *Hannah Smith*.

Yep, it was Hannah . . . no mistaking those long legs, the lazy country-girl way she moved, or the angularity of her face. Coming to pay me a visit, apparently.

I was wearing running shorts, nothing else, so I walked back to the hammock to get my clothes, wondering, *Why the hell didn't she call?* You don't just drop in at a friend's house before sunrise on a Tuesday morning. I hadn't heard a word from Hannah since our phone conversation, so the thought that something was wrong crossed my mind. Privately, though, I was pleased that her hardheaded ego had been softened by a sudden need to see me.

My shirt was dew-sopped, so I was wearing only jeans when I returned to the railing and motioned Hannah toward my dock. She replied with a vague salute, then focused on the marina, which, I soon realized, was her way of communicating her actual destination. Not just the marina basin, either. I stood there feeling dumb, then confused as I watched her swing the Maverick expertly toward A-Dock and throttle into reverse when she was abeam the swim platform of the largest vessel. It was the Lamberti, *SEDUCI* in gold letters on the stern.

What the hell was she doing?

It was a question soon answered when a smiling Vargas Diemer, the Brazilian thief and hit man, appeared in the cabin doorway. He waved and called, "*Es* precisely timed, captain! I have tied several new flies for today!" Sound carries over water, the man's words and accent—*Pre-zicely timed cap-a-tan!*—were clear.

Un-damn-believable. Diemer, the jet-set assassin, had booked Hannah as his fishing guide! No other way to explain it. And nothing I could do but stand there feeling even dumber as I watched him duck into the cabin, then exit carrying a fly rod case and an equipment bag, which he handed down to Hannah, who was waiting on eager tiptoes.

The man—Alberto Sabino, I had to remind myself—looked ready for a day of gentleman's sport: loose pleated khaki slacks and a long-sleeved shirt that would have looked baggy on any guy who didn't move with the same prissy, catlike grace. I watched as Diemer and Hannah shook hands, standing eye to eye. Then the man stepped aboard, saying what sounded like, "I have *un* nice *char-DON-ay* on ice . . . and *sand-weeches* for our lunch."

I couldn't hear Hannah's reply over the noise of the engine as my former skiff pirouetted smartly, then started for the channel, the bow of the skiff—and Hannah Smith's eyes—pointed directly at my stilthouse.

That's when, from behind, the voice of another woman intruded, asking, "My god, what are you doing up so early? Your whole house shakes when you walk. I thought we were having an earthquake."

I said, "Huh?" too dazed to grasp a situation that was deteriorating fast. Crescent Arturo had slipped up beside me, a beach towel around her shoulders for warmth but wearing nothing else but sandals and her pale lemon chemise.

Cressa said, "Like in a dream, you know? A bad dream about earthquakes." Then she yawned, "You didn't happen to start coffee, did you?"

"Go back inside," I said, but kept my voice down. "And put some clothes on."

"Well, excuse me all to hell," the woman shot back in a way that guaranteed she wasn't budging.

I remained focused on Hannah, watching as her expression showed surprise, then tightened and became grim. Shaking my head, smiling and holding my hands up to declare innocence didn't help. Hannah only turned away and said to the jet-set assassin, "Pay no attention to those two on the stilthouse, Mr. Sabino. Most folks on the islands wear clothes and they're sober by sunrise—but that's for God to judge, not me."

Diemer, who had his nose buried in his equipment bag, was confused for a moment but figured it out when he looked up. Even with a towel around her shoulders, Cressa Arturo's physical assets were obvious, and the Brazilian's eyes latched onto her body, a feral expression on his face. "Ahhh . . . yes, I see. Perhaps you can introduce me to that lady sometime. *Es possible?*"

Hannah, the fishing guide, knew damn well sound carries over water, but it didn't stop her from replying in a sturdy voice, "*Her?* I wouldn't advise it. That woman's married and she's already rich—not that it seems to matter much."

Cressa stepped to the railing and asked, "Hey . . . is that bitch talking about me?"

Hannah put her hand on the throttle and warned, "Hang on, Mr. Sabino, those fish aren't going to hook themselves." Hannah gunned the engine, and my custom-built skiff launched itself onto a bay that was a gray mirror, mangroves to the west now golden with the light of a new day.

The towel dropped from Cressa's shoulders while she gripped the railing and watched the boat. "That oversized Amazon *was* talking about me. What a catty bitch she is!" But then saw the look I was giving her and amended, "Although I suppose she could have gotten the wrong idea. Are you sure you two aren't more than jogging buddies?"

I took a breath and let it out slowly, my eyes still on the skiff, watching a silver rooster tail appear behind the engine as Hannah jumped the sandbar off Green Point, no need to run the channel because she knew the water so well.

From inside the house, I heard Tomlinson call, "Who wants coffee? We've only got two beers left!"

The screen door opened, banged shut, and I heard the claw clatter of a dog trotting toward us. When the retriever came around the corner, he sat and made the grunting sound, his request to go ashore.

"That horrible dog," Cressa said. "I'm going to have to wash all my clothes when I get back."

I turned and signaled the dog—*Heel*—as I replied, "When Tomlinson comes out, tell him we're not leaving for the Everglades today. I'll be in the mangroves if he wants an explanation."

I TRIED HANNAH'S CELL and left a message: "When you cool down, give me a call. It's important."

When I hung up, I thought, *Bonehead. Too dramatic—how are you going to explain yourself?* But then thought, *A Brazilian killer shows up at Dinkin's Bay and hires my running partner? Not likely.*

I was standing at the edge of the mangroves, waiting for the dog to finish, when Tomlinson appeared on the walkway. He wore a towel knotted around his boney hips, yawning while he rubbed a fist at his eye like some six-year-old who's miffed about his missing Cheerios. When he was close enough, he cupped his hands and hissed, "What the hell did you say to make her so mad?" then motioned toward the porch.

"If you want to talk, get your feet wet," I replied, which motivated him to drop down off the boardwalk and wade the sand perimeter. When he was closer, I told him, "We'll go to the Bone Field tomorrow or Thursday. Something came up."

"Tell me about it!" Tomlinson replied, which apparently meant something from the way he glared at the house before facing the bushes, then parted the towel. "A long piss on a cool morning has put a smile on more than one man's face—but this one won't be easy. Not after the night I had."

Down the shoreline, my eyes found a pod of nervous water to inspect; behind me, the dog was breaking mangrove branches with his weight, or maybe his teeth, while Tomlinson added, "Medusa has nothing on Crescent Arturo, by god."

A blue-hued fin breached the water's surface—a fish rooting for crabs in the shallows. I watched a second tail fin appear, then a third, before I suggested, "Pretend you're in an airplane. Maybe it'll help."

"*Hey* . . . that's cruel, man."

"Just an idea."

"I'm trying to relax. Priapism is no laughing matter—check the medical journals."

I said, "There's a school of redfish over here."

Tomlinson lifted his head. "Cool."

"Feeding in a foot of water. Nice-sized, too. I'm tempted to get a fly rod."

"Fish for breakfast, that would brighten up my day. Fried in a slick of peanut oil. Or poached in coconut water and lime. I've got fresh grapefruits on the boat—" After a long pause, Tomlinson made a victorious *Awww* sound, then continued. "And some nice mild jalapeños with a cold beer. I doubt if she'll stay and eat, but we should at least ask."

"Nope," I said.

"You seem undecided."

"I'm not."

Now there were a dozen blue-hued tails teeter-tottering in the shallows, each dotted with one or more eyespots that, over eons, had evolved to flummox predators by mimicking a two-headed fish. I watched for what seemed like minutes before I heard Tomlinson sigh, *"That's* better," then return to the subject of the married mistress as he joined me at the edge of the mangroves.

"I think it's okay to push our no-talk rule about women by saying it's not easy to sleep in the same bed with the Crescent Arturos of the world—not if she won't even let you spoon in a friendly sort of way."

I said, "I'm surprised."

"That was *after* I promised to keep my hands out of the goodie basket. True . . . I did try to sneak across the foul lines a few times, but it was strictly reflexive behavior. Like a guitar—Jimi Hendrix picks up a guitar, his fingers automatically go for the strings, right?"

I said, "You wouldn't believe that, why should she?"

"No, but I'd be willing to pretend just to keep the peace. Or, you know, help a treasured friend deal with an obvious problem—it's a matter of hydraulics, for christ's sake, not morality. You're the scientist."

"I think that woman's big trouble," I told him.

"You're being too hard on her. Crescent is

confused—and she's at one of life's shitty little crossroads. Plus, she also has a bad case of Marion Ford—that's the most recent affliction. It's one of those alpha male phenomenon things. People think the beautiful ones have it easy, but nothing's easy if you're a woman."

Eyes fixed on the water, I said, "A couple of those fish are right in the slot, eighteen to twenty-six or -seven inches." Then added, "You usually have better judgment when it comes to sniffing out the bad ones."

"When people are down, at their personal worst, those are exactly the ones who need me most. True, the fact that she's a five on the Budweiser scale helped move her to the head of the line. But I would have found her anyway."

Budweiser scale—I knew the crude punch line so didn't ask. "You're a regular bridge over troubled water," I replied. "Which makes it easier for me to ask a favor. It'll take half an hour at most. Today; hopefully this morning."

Stand lookout while I snuck aboard Vargas Diemer's yacht is what I wanted him to do. Mack didn't mind helping out marina neighbors, but he would draw the line at breaking and entering if it put a fat weekly rental fee at risk. I couldn't let him or anyone else at Dinkin's Bay see me break into that boat.

Tomlinson didn't process it, though, because he was still talking about Cressa. "Women with a body like hers, and that face, she meets very few men who won't jump through hoops, then roll over and show their bellies. That's gotta get old after a while—which is why she's got smoke eyes for you. Crescent's never had an alpha male in her life."

"I wouldn't bet on that," I told him.

Tomlinson was two more sentences into his theory before he stopped and refocused on me. "You can't be talking about her husband. Rob almost had a hissy fit when he saw what the dog did to his couch."

I checked the porch—Cressa was still inside—then looked to make sure the retriever was within whistling distance before I said, "Here's what I think. Rob's brother, Dean, is as alpha as they come—according to what Cressa says, anyway. I think she was sleeping with Deano up until he started having mental problems a couple years ago—head trauma after an accident. Afterward, maybe they kept the affair going, but then the guy started getting too weird. Even scary, but who could she go to? Tell her husband, 'I've been screwing your brother, now please make him go away'? I don't think so. Meeting you was the safety net she needed to cut herself free from the whole family."

Tomlinson said softly, "Hmmm . . . the crazy brother who tried to kill us," as if presenting the idea to his brain for consideration.

"He was learning to fly planes until he hit a hangar," I continued. "He's been seeing shrinks, in and out of twenty-four-hour-care facilities, ever since. Plus, abusing pharmaceuticals, maybe some other drugs, too. When the crash happened, Deano was trying to get into the film business. Documentaries."

A light went on behind Tomlinson's eyes. I'd told him about my visit from Luke Smith and he now made the connection. "Jesus Frog. Did she show you a photo or something? The crazy brother's got some balls if he showed up at your doorstep."

"See if you can talk her into showing you a picture of Deano. You'll have to borrow it or set it up so I can get a quick look."

Tomlinson's face took on a wilted expression as if he'd been slighted. "Cressa never told me any of this. And I didn't pick up on it, man! Makes me wonder if my precognitive powers are on the fritz."

"You figure out how to work it. But don't tell her too much. Last night, she tried to cover for the brother-in-law. I think she's been feeding Deano details about Flight 19. I think the guy stays in touch—possibly even stays with her some nights."

Tomlinson was having a tough time coming to terms with what I was suggesting. "I can't picture her doing harm to anyone—not intentionally—

but you sound like you've made up your mind."

"Nope, not even close. Like I said, it's a possible explanation. This one, at least, we can take to the cops. The brother-in-law tried to kill us, but we don't have to involve Dan and his plane. I can call Moonley or Lieutenant Brett and mention we know a lady who's being stalked. Blindside the brother with a lesser charge but still get him out of our hair."

"I don't know, man, I think you're headed down the wrong road. Crescent is covering for a guy who tried to kill us? That's a pretty heavy accusation."

Tomlinson didn't want to believe it, so I humored him by saying, "There *is* another possibility. Which brings us to a second favor I need—if you're willing."

My pal's expression replied *Aren't I always?*

It was safer to wait until dark to search the Brazilian's boat, but Diemer and Hannah would be back before sunset if it was a standard fishing charter. Plus, I was too antsy to wait. In my mind, a question kept repeating itself: *Why did an elite assassin hire Hannah?*

"See that big Lamberti on A-Dock? The owner just left on a charter, and I want to go aboard alone and have a look around."

"Why?"

"It's better if I don't share the details. I don't want to be seen, so I need someone to keep Mack busy and stand watch. *You*—that's the favor I'm asking."

"The guy Hannah just left with," Tomlinson said, looking at me. "Good-looking foreign dude, he owns that monster."

"Twenty minutes tops," I said, then repeated, "It's a business matter, so, I'm serious, the less you know, the better."

A slow smile signaled that Tomlinson had sorted through the data but had misread my motives. He said, "Torpedo the rich bastard— how else you gonna compete with a dude like that? Sure, I'll do it. Just tell me one little thing: are you going to steal his shit or plant some dope? Either way, I know the drill, so float on, man."

17

I WAS IN THE AFT SECTION OF THE Brazilian's yacht using a flashlight to search his stateroom when my cell buzzed: Hannah was finally returning my call. I told myself it was idiotic to attempt a conversation while trespassing on a million-dollar yacht, but I answered anyway. Lucky me for trusting bad judgment.

Sounding formal, I heard Hannah's voice say, "My client forgot something, so I've got about five minutes to talk if it's that important."

I stiffened and asked, "You're at the marina . . . *now?*" As I said it, I heard Tomlinson's warning whistle—my pal's criminal skills obviously rusty. I rushed to a starboard porthole and brightened the room by pushing the curtains aside.

On the phone, Hannah replied, "I don't know why I'm not surprised you didn't notice my skiff come back—you're such a busy man."

I was too rattled by what I saw through the window to respond to the barb. Vargas Diemer was already on the yacht's boarding ramp, his knees visible only for a second before I heard the sound of his shoes on the upper deck. Two . . . three . . . four graceful paces, and I knew the Germanic Brazilian had stopped to deactivate his security system—no need to bother, but, hopefully, the man wouldn't realize it.

Tomlinson whistled again. Three sharp blasts, fingers to his lips.

Whispering into the phone, I demanded, "What's he looking for?" The door to the master stateroom was open, I realized. It had been closed when I arrived, so I had to make a decision fast.

"Who?" Hannah said. "You mean Tomlinson? I guess he's whistling for your dog." Then asked, "Where *are* you? Don't tell me you're whispering because of that woman."

I replied, "No, what's your *client* looking for?" while my brain wrestled with two options: I could either run for it or sneak the door closed and hope the Brazilian had returned for something he'd forgotten in the main cabin.

Hannah asked, "Are you drunk or just nosy?"

I came very close to replying, *Neither, I'm on your client's boat,* which would have required the woman to take action—possibly attempt to help me even though the right thing to do was call 911 on behalf of her paying customer. I couldn't put her in that position, so said, "Call you back," and jammed the phone in my pocket, the Brazilian's footsteps above me now, crossing the cabin toward the stairs.

Click-click. The bedroom door made a pistol hammer sound when I closed it, the brass latch sliding home, then I turned and used the flashlight, looking for a place to hide. The room consumed most of the stern area and seemed roomier for the mirrors above a bed that was framed in mahogany and joined to the wall. A dresser, two vanity mirrors, the closets and the entrance to the master bath were done in teak and brass, the curtains gold, the bedspread blue on green—the colors of Brazil's national soccer team, I remembered. Lots of closet space, but none big enough to hold a man my size. On the bed, I also noted, was a tiny hip pack, SAGE RODS embroidered on khaki canvas. It was a fly case—probably the reason Diemer had come back.

Damn it.

No doubt about it, he'd come back for his newly tied flies. I heard the gangway door open, then Diemer's feet on the stairs, so I crossed the room into the master bath. It smelled of after-shave and diesel. There was sink space, an antique tub bolted to the deck, a cylindrical shower beside it, the floor still wet. The shower was ringed with a privacy curtain, but it wasn't drawn. I thought, *Like I've got another option,* and stepped into the shower, then swiped the curtain closed. Blue with green stripes again—the assassin loved his soccer.

I switched off the flashlight and waited.

Diemer wasn't a man to whistle and hum. He came down the steps on rubber-soled shoes at a gallop that is typical of sailors. I heard the door of the master stateroom open, and didn't hear anything else until the shower curtain rustled against my nose. The Brazilian had pushed a volume of air as he came into the room toward me but then stopped abruptly at the bathroom door.

He's an articulate, precise man, Bernie Yeager had warned. If true, Diemer might have stopped because he noticed something different about the shower curtain. I shifted the flashlight from my left hand to my right and held it like a dagger.

"Humph." Diemer said it with the descending inflection of a person who is puzzled. It

suggested, yes, he had noticed the curtain. Now he was probably backtracking his steps that morning, visualizing his movements after exiting the shower. I would have done the same.

Slowly, so as not to disturb the curtain, I raised the flashlight to waist level, palm up—it would add the torque and lift needed if I used it to drive the Brazilian's nose into his skull. And I *would* if he found me. What happened afterward, I didn't want to explore, but couldn't block the obvious: I might have to kill a man to cover the minor crime of trespassing. Sobering . . . No, I was sickened by the thought, never mind that Diemer might also kill me. One was as bad as the other, I realized in that instant. Either way, life in Dinkin's Bay as I knew it would be over. Grab the false passports, pack a few things, then flee to Central America, where at least I'd be closer to my son. Or Cuba—a government in chaos that might welcome someone like me.

Dumbass!

The prospect of ending my years on Sanibel this way, because of my own stupid misjudgment, was as distressing as falling from the sky in an airplane. There was nothing I could do now, though, but let it play out.

Focus, I told myself. *He's coming.*

Like a psycho in some movie, I waited behind the curtain, flashlight gripped, as Diemer voiced puzzlement again—*"Humph"*—then muttered a

Latin profanity that had the ring of surprise. When his feet moved on the varnished wood, I got ready, certain he knew my location, when I heard the man say, *"Hello?"* Said it in a testing way as if he expected an answer.

I didn't respond, of course—why make it easy for him? Still crouched, I coiled my body to the right so hips and thighs could generate power when the curtain was thrown open.

Then I heard, "Where are you?"

Why the hell was an elite killer asking me an absurd question instead of taking action? It made no sense until I heard Diemer say, "I didn't expect you to call," which is when I realized the profanity he'd muttered was in response to a cell phone vibrating in his pocket.

I released a slow, hushed breath and listened to a one-sided conversation. It was in English, which suggested the call was from somewhere in the U.S. No . . . the call was local because I heard Diemer say, "I see . . . Yes, I see . . . But why so important? Okay . . . yes, *yes*—I will be there in one minute!"

More Portuguese profanity, but not heated. The Germanic Brazilian wasn't a man who lost control of his temper. Two staccato zipping sounds also proved his attention to detail—Diemer was confirming the fishing lures were in their case before he closed the door to the stateroom, then galloped up the stairs.

Seconds later, I could hear his footsteps above me, but I wasn't in the clear yet. Was the jet-set assassin so compulsive that he would actually test the security system before reactivating it? If he did, the mysterious shower curtain would explain why the alarm had been silenced. I had used a portable jamming unit no bigger than a book, set on a frequency that didn't interrupt cell service—a lucky coincidence that I didn't fully appreciate until more seconds had passed and I watched the Brazilian exit the boarding ramp, then stride gracefully away from A-Dock.

I needed air, felt a dizzying oxygen debt that couldn't be replenished until I was off the Brazilian's damn boat and back in the lab. The logician that steers my behavior argued against abandoning a search I hadn't yet started. Called me a *fool,* and explained quite logically that Diemer had probably left to deal with some irritating detail. Afterward, he would hurry straight to Hannah's boat, eager to enjoy a fishing trip that was already behind schedule. Statistically speaking, the logician told me, now was actually a broader, safer window in which to paw through the man's personal possessions.

Screw the odds, I told the logician.

Coward, the logician concluded accurately.

I didn't care. Never again did I want to experience what I'd felt while waiting for the Brazilian to throw open that shower curtain. I'd made a basic error in judgment and wasn't going to compound it. In the Homo sapiens' guidebook, the reasons should be bulleted under the heading *Don't piss in your own pond or crap in your own nest*. I had done exactly that, but for the last time.

Taking calculated risks in South America, Asia, Africa—fine. All part of the job. But how I live, and where I live, composes the fabric of who I am. Death? It's inevitable. Living among friends in a good place, though, is a temporal pleasure, an inviolate choice not to be risked because of something I had always suspected, but now believed: a life well lived trumps every damn drab, existential alternative, so don't screw it up!

I was getting off that damn boat fast, but *safely*.

Like a teenage burglar, I hurried from porthole to porthole monitoring Diemer's movements. He didn't rush, a man with dignity who enjoyed attention. Which gave me time to notice the room's only personal appointment, aside from soccer team colors, was a photo on the cabin wall: a teenage girl; blond, gawky, with braces, but cute in an agrarian way. A family resemblance in her aristocratic nose, the Germanic cheeks— Diemer's daughter, I guessed, or a niece. The photo seemed out of place in a space so impersonal and utilitarian, and also because it was the bedroom of a bachelor. The man had at least one sentimental bond, apparently.

I moved topside and peeked through cabin curtains. Finally, when the Brazilian was aboard Hannah's skiff flying across Dinkin's Bay, I exited the yacht as if I owned the thing and went to find Tomlinson. He was under the poinciana tree next to the gift shop.

"I didn't notice Hannah come back because I was busy herding Jeth away from the docks," he explained, his nervous fingers twisting a lock of hair. "Damn, that was close, Doc!"

I said, "You turned that guy around just in time—thanks. How'd you get his cell number?"

Tomlinson gave me a blank stare in response: *Huh?*

My friend tugged at his hair and shook his head. "I didn't call the man. I *wanted* to call, but you're right, his number isn't in the office. So I was on my way back to A-Dock to maybe kick the side of his boat or scream 'Fire!' I don't know . . . do something that would distract him, but then the dude reappears. Looked like he was in a hurry . . . and I didn't see any blood on his hands, so"—Tomlinson shrugged—"I figured everything was copasetic. What the hell happened in there?"

I was flipping through various explanations. Barring coincidence—which was possible but unlikely—there was only one possibility.

My eyes searched for my former flats skiff, scanning from west to east across the bay, while I explained, "He got a phone call seconds before the shit really hit the fan. The caller said they needed him right away. He took off."

My skiff was *there,* just off Woodring Point, a mile away, a dark husk supporting a lean vertical silhouette that was Hannah Smith.

"Saved your ass," Tomlinson agreed, "whoever made that call."

"Yeah," I told him. "She really did."

THAT NIGHT, because the moon was too bright for sleeping, I rode my bike to the beach and jogged a mile of ocean, turned, then picked up the pace all the way back to Tarpon Bay Road. Because I was without a running partner, I took the dog, who trotted at heel when he wasn't trying to retrieve waves.

Vargas Diemer was in the lab waiting when I returned, a day's growth of beard sculpted onto his Zorro face—the Hollywood look. *Surprise!*

I'd left the lights on, the doors unlocked as always. Even so, it was unusual to find an elite killer sitting at my desk, reading from a folder I'd left on the autoclave. Worse, there was a black semiauto pistol near his right hand. A sound suppressor lengthened the weapon. It added a look of surgical intent.

When I pushed the screen door open, the man didn't bother to look up as he said with only a trace of accent, "I decided to return the favor, Dr.

Ford." To his left was a photo, and he spun it in front of me. An unseen lens had caught me studying his yacht's security monitor while in search of unseen lenses. Stupid, that's how he expected me to feel. I did.

"A filament camera," Diemer explained, "self-contained in a memory stick. Remember moving it? *Chiflado*, you break into my vessel, that is a very sloppy thing to do. Now you're surprised I'm here? Come on, man!"

His stilted English, no longer stilted, had a touch of the barrio now that he had me alone, a pistol within reach. No point in denying I'd been aboard, so I let the door close behind me, saying, "Breaking and entering usually isn't a shooting offense. But maybe the laws are different in Brazil."

The pistol—did he intend to use it? That's what I had to know before I took another step. Behind me, the retriever made his grunting sound, and I thought, *Now? Why not a mile ago!*

Diemer, still reading, said, "I know something about these missing planes—is a hobby of mine, the European war. So I sit down expecting to read the same old stories, but no, man, instead I find some information that's new to me. *Interesting, some of this shit.*"

He had picked up the folder on Flight 19, I realized. It contained Dan's summary as well as photos of the tail section and other items we'd uncovered. Now I was wondering, *Is that why he came to Dinkin's Bay?*

Or . . . maybe wrong yet again because the man looked at me for the first time, adjusted his wire glasses, and left the barrio behind. "Until tonight," he said, "when my computer showed a security breach, I'd never heard of you. Thought you were just another American hick because of that dumb act you used yesterday. Christ, and I bought it! So I"—the man became more animated—"you know, made some calls to my people, asked around. After what I hear I'm, like, Wow! How could I be so wrong 'bout a guy might be a badass!"

Diemer was showing off, changing accents with the ease of an actor—a useful tool for a jet-set assassin but irritating. Nothing I could do but stare at the pistol and gauge my options as he dropped the act. "We have things in common, Dr. Ford. But no one mentioned your interest in aviation archaeology. Could be, though, *your* sources are better. The National Security Agency has a ton of money"—he motioned vaguely to indicate the lab's construction—"but obviously doesn't pay worth a damn. You ever get tired of being a poor working slob? Consulting work is something you might consider. The finest of everything, and a better class of people."

The Brazilian had dark eyes, more Latin than German, but his superior demeanor added attentive sparks. The man who'd forgotten his fly case seldom missed a detail, and I got the impression he wanted me to know he was good at what he did. I looked from him to the pistol, then back, and said, "I need some Gatorade and a towel. You want anything? Or did you already check the fridge?"

A smile, definitely a smile—the guarded variety used by neurosurgeons and others who've been taught that emotion signals deficiency. "A census switch on my cabin door told me you stayed for only nine minutes. Nothing missing, so I figure you got nervous. Surprising behavior"—he paused for effect—"for an operator who's supposedly a legend in the field."

The Brazilian's middle finger was tapping the pistol grip as I replied, "Your boat's too close to home, so I pulled the plug. Maybe it'll happen to you one day."

"Is that an explanation—or an excuse?"

"Committing a felony isn't as much fun in your own backyard," I said. "You're a long way from São Pedro, but I'm counting on you having better judgment."

"And that means . . . ? Oh! You're worried about this," Diemer said, then swept his hand over the pistol and had the muzzle pointed at my face before I could react. Held it there for a second, savoring the power, then pointed it away. "I thought this might help convey a message.

237

Bad form to board a private vessel without permission, old boy. Particularly my vessel." He glared at me. "Don't *ever* do it again, homey—*o es fodido*! Understand?"

Portuñol slang. *Or you're screwed,* it probably meant, but I was more concerned with the damn pistol. If the Brazilian was crazy enough to shoot me in my own home, submissive behavior wouldn't stop him. So I asked, "A Beretta?" Said it coolly to negate the way I'd almost thrown up my hands in surrender.

"Sig Sauer," he answered, lowering the weapon. "Called a Mosquito—a stupid name for a piece that chambers twenty-two hollow-points as smooth as this little number. Care to try?" Diemer popped the magazine, cleared the weapon, then held it by the barrel for me to take. That quick, the real Vargas Diemer—the articulate killer— was replaced by Diemer the charming foreigner who had worked hard to learn English. His standby persona, I guessed, when dealing with those who might be of some use.

My fists relaxed, but I wasn't going to let the man see me take a deep breath. "I need something to drink and a dry T-shirt," I said, turning. "So go ahead . . . make yourself right at home."

Diemer didn't miss the sarcasm. "Americans are such a friendly people!" he said, then coughed. No . . . it was the way he imitated laughter.

18

I WAS STILL WONDERING, *WHAT DID Hannah say to get the Brazilian off his yacht so fast?* as the Brazilian said to me, "Call me Alberto . . . but not Al. The name makes me think of canned beer and condom dispensers. Doesn't really fit with Sabino, either—lyrically, I'm saying. Not that I'm a snob, but one has the right to choose one's own alias. Don't you agree, doctor?"

The polished syntax again, which suggested a boarding school, or Jesuit, education and old Brazilian money. According to Bernie, though, Diemer was the son of a locksmith, born in a rural village. So it was another act. But maybe a man who'd finessed his way up the social ladder while amassing a fortune had earned the right to play a ruling-class Castilian. The role suited him: a member of the arrogant glitterati who was willing to bond with an inferior—me, in this case—if the inferior was deemed worthy.

Diemer and I had changed places, me sitting at my office desk, him in a metal chair, but the folder was still in his lap and the book *They Flew Into Oblivion* within reach. I hadn't showered, but I had changed into sweatpants and a pullover before returning with a Corona for each of us and an extra Gatorade for me. "Most people call me Ford," I said in reply to "Alberto." "Or Doc."

Beer in hand, the Brazilian nodded *Salute*, then placed the bottle near the pistol, which lay unloaded, still separated from its magazine. It was a quarter 'till eleven, the moon dazzling outside, where the retriever dozed after returning from the bushes.

The Brazilian wasn't chatty, but he was comfortable saying whatever he pleased, which struck me as unusual for a criminal operative. Acting or not, he had an elevated sense of entitlement, the imperious Castilian who doesn't socialize with the uncultured. The reason, I guessed, was that Diemer perceived us both to be isolates in the same lonely profession, which was accurate in some ways—not that I was going to admit it—and it explained why he was so forthcoming.

I reminded myself, *He also wants something.* The man hadn't mentioned seeing me with Cressa Arturo earlier that morning, which was puzzling. The feral expression on his face had been intense, unmistakable. He couldn't have forgotten the blonde in the lemon chemise.

So I played it loose by playing along, but paid attention. I hadn't confirmed his suspicions by using Diemer's real name, nor had we returned to the subject of me checking his background through intelligence sources. But the man *knew* it was true. In his mind, at least, it allowed us to explore safer topics, such as Flight 19, as well as other missing ships and planes that interested him—a B-25, flown by Captain Gene Nattress; a German sub loaded with gold bullion that had disappeared en route to South America. I was now convinced that World War II and its missing relics actually was one of Diemer's passions. He had already told me about a DC-3 he'd helped salvage in the Bahamas and had mentioned details from a "drawer full of files" he'd collected on the gold-laden submarine.

"Is all of this information accurate?" he asked, taking several papers from the folder. "For instance, says here that parents of the missing men were convinced some of their sons survived and—most surprising—that they lived 'like animals' in the Everglades, according to this. In this newspaper . . . no, *this* one—have you read it? The story made headlines in many of your papers."

I replied, "I skimmed through them," and let him talk.

"Then you've missed important details," Diemer scolded. He held up a clipping from the *St. Louis Post-Dispatch* that ran January 1946, then adjusted his glasses so he could quote directly: " 'Hunters from the Seminole Indian Tribe of Florida have reported finding an isolated camp and bootprints deep in the swamp. Along with the remains of a campfire, and many bones from animals that have been eaten, this tells us our boys might still be alive.'" His eyes continued to scan as he said, "I wonder if this is possible."

I said, "A grieving mother would believe anything if it meant her son was still alive."

"You're convinced there were no survivors. *Es* fascinating. Newspaper reporters from that time obviously disagree."

"It could have happened, but there's not enough information to go on," I answered, aware that his attention had shifted to a photo of the parachute harness.

The Brazilian leafed through more papers, then said, "The telegram to the missing aviator's brother is a new one on me. Bizarre, huh? The newspapers published three, four articles about it, but not until"—the man squinted at the small type—"it was several weeks later that these stories appeared. To them, at least, the telegram appeared to be genuine."

I said, "The information put together by my pilot friend, yes, it's accurate. The book by Quasar is the best on the subject. The other stuff, though—the newspaper stories especially—I don't think it's credible." I looked at my watch to communicate impatience, then offered the man another chance. "How'd fly fishing go today? I saw the rod cases when you left this morning."

Diemer had yet to ask about the photos of Avenger wreckage stacked on the desk, so he ducked my question by saying, "Quite good—but back to these planes. Almost seventy years later, they still haven't been found." He made a *tsk-tsk* sound. "Mysteries, the few left that are real and important, they deserve to be solved—incredible they haven't. I become obsessive about such things." Finally, he reached for the stack of Avenger photos, adding, "It's something else we have in common, Dr. Ford," and held up a photo of the buried tail section.

I finished my Gatorade and replied, "Two peas in a pod . . . Alberto."

The slang amused him but didn't budge him. "You probably know that, by profession, I'm a jet jockey—an airline pilot. I've visited Germany too many times to count—finest military libraries in the world, trust me. But even the Germans can't locate several submarines that went missing during the war. And your government with all its money! How can they not account for five torpedo bombers? Or a ship the size of a B-25? I dislike sloppiness"— Diemer's eyes moved around the lab, which I keep tidy but was now robotic in appearance thanks to Cressa—"particularly sloppy work. Once again, we are similar. So, to me, it's no surprise that someone like you has found the missing planes." He slipped the photo into the stack and held up another, the parachute harness, and mused, "No survivors—how strange that you are so certain."

I told him, "I'm working with two friends and we have an agreement. A few pieces of wreckage, that's all we've found so far. Unlikely it's from Flight 19, but we're not sure. That's about all I can tell you."

The man nodded in a way that said he understood, but I knew he wasn't done, so I pressed, "It's getting late. You can take the book, but I need to keep the folder." I slid *They Flew Into Oblivion* toward him and began to collect papers and photos. Then tried again to switch subjects, asking, "You caught fish today?"

"I had a very good guide," the Brazilian said, getting to his feet, then gathering his pistol. "You know her?"

No searching look, no trickiness in his tone, so I answered, "Hannah Smith. A nice girl. Did she put you on redfish? Not twenty yards from here, I saw a big school this morning. Only in a couple feet of water."

"I read about Captain Smith in *Florida Sportsman*," Diemer explained. "From her photograph, I didn't expect her to be so attractive." He smiled. "I think you agree."

I said, "She's a fishing guide. It's her business and . . . I don't mix business and pleasure."

Diemer nodded. "Few would understand your

meaning, but I do. Maintain personal discipline when traveling—tourists and amateurs have no concept of the importance. For example, I seldom socialize unless work requires it, and never drink more than two glasses of wine in an evening. Women, though"—shaking his head, Diemer leaned to confide—"they are *mi defeito*, my weakness. Even when I was married, I couldn't help myself. It's perhaps unwise to admit weakness, but there you have it."

My chance to use a scolding tone. "All it takes is one slipup," I warned. Then opened the door and followed the man onto the porch. "You'll be leaving Dinkin's Bay soon anyway, so why risk it? Probably never see her again."

Somehow the Brazilian had lost the thread. "Who?"

"Your fishing guide," I said.

In the porch light, the Brazilian's expression asked *Are you kidding?* "I didn't say that! I've hired her boat for the next three days. Perhaps more, it depends on how things go."

"How the fishing goes?" I offered.

The man shrugged, and blinked at the brightness of the moon. "She took me to a group of tarpon. Which I didn't believe because it's the wrong time of year—for tarpon. Yet she saw a fish jump—more than a mile away, she saw it. Then off we were."

I was jolted. Was that the reason Hannah called

the man's cell? If so, it meant she didn't know I'd broken into her client's yacht. Definitely good news . . . So why did I feel disappointed?

Diemer was now locked into the subject of fishing. "I've read about tarpon in the journals, but, my god, so powerful, I never imagined! All morning we followed those fish, no other boats to bother us. Incredible sport. And she's quite a good fly caster herself. Not as technically skilled as me, of course, but a trained eye for tarpon."

It was beneath me to attempt a juvenile blocking finesse, but that's what I did as I trailed him toward the mangroves. "You're a man with money," I said, "you must be a target for the blue-collar working types—the treasure hunters."

"Blue-collar?" he asked over his shoulder, then figured it out. "My god, so right! American women, the nine-to-five class—even more devious than the lower classes of Eastern Europe." Then used barrio talk to caricaturize his point. "Bro, you been to Prague? The *chicas*, they wanna see money *before* Mr. Penga. But their big *fondos*, man, those sweet-ah *bucetas* are worth it!" His accent wasn't bad for English, and his enthusiasm added *I love that city*.

I replied, "Not Prague, but I've heard. Nordic genetics—similar to the blonde you saw this morning. On my deck. You seemed to notice."

The Brazilian stopped and turned in the moonlight, taller than me but not as broad. When he replied, "The blonde? Yes, I did. I assumed you were sleeping with her."

"No," I replied, "she was a houseguest."

The man laughed, but in the probing way that expresses doubt to confirm the truth.

"She needed a place to sleep," I explained, "that's all. Going through a bad divorce, the first and last time she stays here as far as I'm concerned."

"Because she has money and you don't," he translated. "That's the way it works. One night of sport, but don't expect anything more. Ah— women!" he said, then commiserated with a shrug and tried to work his own deal. "I don't suppose she happened to notice *Seduci*?"

"She asked about it," I said. "Cressa asked about you, too."

We were near the docks where his yacht was moored. One of the last pay phones on the island is bolted to a wall outside the marina office. Seldom used, but its neon flicker provided the opening the Brazilian had been waiting for. "I just realized—it's only a little after eleven. Was your blond friend expecting you to call?"

"Her name's Crescent," I replied. "No, but I have her number if you want it."

"Well . . . if the poor woman's restless, upset about her divorce. And we're both alone on this damn little island . . ." He allowed himself all of two seconds to decide before asking, "You don't mind sharing?"

"Just her phone number," I reminded him.

"Of course! I'd be willing to call myself."

I didn't mind, and he did.

AT SUNRISE, fly rod in hand, I was sliding through turtle grass, looking for redfish on a feed, but also keeping an eye on Hannah Smith as she idled down the channel. How would she react when she saw me?

Civilized. It was the kindest way to describe the glance she allowed me, and the acknowledging wave. Then done with it, her eyes focused on Diemer's yacht until she was abeam the swim platform, where she tied off and waited.

Hopefully, the self-important bastard had overslept after a night of "sport" with the married mistress.

Maybe it had happened, but I doubted it. Around one a.m., still unable to sleep, I had carried a bottle of beer outside and saw that *Seduci*'s flybridge lights were off. A timer switch possibly, but it was more likely that Cressa had sent the man packing early. I didn't believe that Tomlinson was her only extra-marital conquest, but there was something calculating about the married mistress that told me she wasn't an indiscriminate screw-around. True, Diemer resembled a Germanic Zorro. True, he was rich, connected, and met the requirements of a *genuinely* dangerous man. So . . . so what the hell was I thinking? Of course Cressa Arturo found him attractive! Hannah probably did, too. *Wrong again, Ford.*

I flexed my jaw and continued wading the shallows, pretending not to notice that instead of oversleeping the Brazilian was already getting into my former skiff aided by the attentions of my former jogging partner, who was laughing about something. Some ingratiating remark, no doubt, about the Western-looking shirt Hannah wore or the length of her buckskin brown legs. And why should I care?

Stick to business, I reminded myself. *Where the hell did those fish go?*

Thirty yards away near the ruins of a long-gone fish house, that's where. Concentrating on a bloom of nervous water, I moved to within striking distance after I'd checked my leader and lure—a Chico's Deceiver: mylar and synthetic hair wrapped on a one-ought hook. I pretended to be unaware that Hannah and Diemer were to my left, idling away from the marina in pursuit of more sport. One or both would be watching me because fly fishermen are shameless voyeurs when it comes to evaluating the competition. So now would be a good time to show off my casting skills—*if* I were an ego-driven adolescent.

I'm not, yet I did it anyway. Couldn't stop myself from unfurling forty feet of line with a roll cast . . . stripped off another fifty feet to float near my knees . . . lifted the rod to reduce drag while I single-hauled and popped the line free . . . edged a step closer to tighten my back-cast loop and waited, waited as the line deployed behind, loading the rod . . . then hauled again on the forward cast, which vaulted the line like a slingshot toward the fish, a hundred feet away, where the Chico's Deceiver slapped flat on the surface, then sank, undulating like wounded bait.

Not a flawless cast, but so craftsmanlike I was tempted to steal a glance at two admiring gazes—how could my observers help it? I didn't, though, even when Diemer's laughter carried across the water and he commented to Hannah, "Tailing loop—typical of novices," which was total bullshit. Well . . . my line hadn't tailed as badly as *usual,* so his criticism was rooted in envy—had to be.

A Holocaust butcher, Bernie had said, was responsible for the genetics in the village where Diemer had been born—no surprise there. I was thinking that when I heard Hannah tell him, "Hold tight," then throttled away at speed—she wasn't interested, apparently, in whether I was on fish or just blind-casting.

I thought, *Nazi prick!* but then had to smile at my own childishness. Truth is, I found Vargas Diemer interesting. Intimidating, too—not physically, but because he assumed his various roles so naturally, each tailored to camouflage the dispassionate, manipulative brain that directed his moves from within.

The man was the superior actor, no denying that. A private contractor in an unusual craft who had gotten rich—no, richer—and who had the balls to brag about it to me. Whether he was in Dinkin's Bay on vacation or on an assignment, I still didn't know. The high profile he maintained suggested recreation . . . but the Sig Sauer with a sound suppressor was indicative of a hit man on a mission. The same was true, perhaps, of the way he had used me as a conduit to access Cressa Arturo. For all I knew, Cressa's wealthy husband, or her father-in-law, or even Tomlinson or someone else I knew, might be the man's actual target—if there was a target. Hannah Smith, though . . . *that* connection grated at me. I didn't like the fact that she would spend the next three days alone in a small space with a professional manipulator whose hobby while on the road was seducing the local women.

I stripped my line home and told myself, *Forget it—she's an adult*—then waded closer to the schooling fish, sliding my feet to spook stingrays, and made another cast. On the second strip, the hook jolted as if it had snagged a limb, so I locked my index finger over the line and lifted. At the same instant, the angle formed by rod and fly line transected a gelatinous swirl forty feet away—a redfish had eaten my lure.

I smiled—a man whose world had been simplified—as the fish turned with intent, generating enough torque with its tail that my seven-weight fly rod bowed as if to snap. I held tight and watched a dozen other reds spook away in comet streaks of silver. The fish I'd hooked boiled again and attempted to join them by peeling off line at a speed more suitable to a motorcycle. The run would have blistered my index finger, so the finger became an attentive guide. It would have bloodied my knuckles, so I cleared the reel by yanking my left hand high not unlike a bronc rider who has been overpowered and seeks balance.

On its first run, a redfish often mimics an arrow's trajectory, straight for the mangroves. Some atavistic memory, perhaps, associates shadows and tree roots with safety, unaware that barnacles colonize there, sharp enough to cut the stoutest fishing line. Oysters, too. This fish bulled its way *under* the roots where, by all rights, it should have broken free, but I speared my rod tip into the water, almost to the bottom, and kept the line horizontal. For several seconds, I was linked to a whirlpool of detritus by a thread that vibrated like a violin string, but the thread held. Then, walking backward, I tractored the fish away from the bushes, a blue-hued fin showing on the surface when it was finally in open water again.

A minute later, I held a six-pound redfish by

the lip, a sculpture of mahogany and bronze so perfectly utilitarian that its belly-toothed croaking struck me as anomalous. Because the school had regrouped, I was tempted to land another just for fun but decided against it. I had a lot to do today, it was true. There was work in the lab. Plus, I'd received two e-mail replies to my lost-and-found ads about the retriever. Both parties had to be answered in a way that tested without offending.

More time-consuming would be getting ready for our trip the next morning. Tomlinson and I were returning to the Bone Field and the wreckage of the Avenger. It was possible we'd camp a night or two, depending on how our search went and if Dan Futch would be able to join us on Saturday as he hoped. Before leaving, though, there was an important detail to clear up. I wanted to find out if Luke Smith was actually the troubled brother-in-law, Dean Arturo.

Confirm it too late, we might have unwanted company.

19

TOMLINSON CAME TO THE HOUSE JUST before sunset and said through the screen door, "Something smells good! Mind if I use your computer?"

Kidney beans had been simmering all day in a Crock-Pot. Plus, I had six sweet potatoes in the oven. Two were for dinner along with the redfish filets and plantains now in stages of preparation. The other potatoes would be packed along with a half gallon of beans, salt, grapefruits, fresh chili peppers, coffee, and a slab of bacon for the trip. On the fifty-mile boat ride, I hoped to supplement the larder with more fish: tripletail, hopefully, but king mackerel steaks or cobia would be fine, too.

"What did she say?" I asked my pal. I'd sent him to Cressa's house to gather information and was surprised he was back so soon. Two hours wasn't a lot of time in the world of the married mistress.

Tomlinson sounded harried when he answered, "I'll tell you about it in a sec. She's supposed to e-mail me photos of the brother-in-law, so I want to check Yahoo first. But I think you're right. I think he's the guy who came here calling himself Luke-something. He actually is in the documentary business—or tried, at least—and there's another connection, something neither of us knew."

"She admits they had an affair?"

"Uhhh . . . can't talk, gotta hit the head ASAP," he replied, which explained his antsyness. "It's something I ate, I think, or I would've used the bushes. Give me a couple of minutes, okay?"

I put Danny Morgan's *Captiva Moon* in the CD

player and spent the time getting dinner ready. The redfish had been filleted, washed, and stored on ice but kept dry. I dried the filets again, then poked holes in a Persian lime and drizzled the juice over the fish. In a plastic sack, I made a rub of salt, ground pepper, a pinch of cumin, and freshly powdered jalapeño, then turned my attention to the skillet. Peanut oil doesn't burn at high temps, and is also acceptable to vegetarians like Tomlinson. I poured a quarter inch into a skillet, then turned the flames high. When the oil was spitting, I dumped the pan, then added only an eighth of an inch. While it heated, I applied the rub, and also tended to a skillet of plantains that was sputtering on the second burner of the little ship's stone. I wanted to try fish gravy—a recipe I'd gotten in Panama—so I was adding spices to flour when Tomlinson reappeared. He carried two photos recently printed, his face and hands still wet from the bathroom sink.

"Is it him?" he asked.

I turned off both burners, saying, "Let me take a look," and carried the photos to my reading chair.

"I hate lying to friends, and I couldn't think of anything believable anyway, so I told Cressa it was better if we knew what her brother-in-law looked like—just in case he is snooping around. Which is sort of the truth."

"Dean Arturo," I said, turning on the lamp.

"Then it *is* him."

No, but I didn't say it. I was looking at photos of a rusty-haired man who had the height and moneyed bearing of Rob Arturo Jr. but none of the most commonly inherited features—earlobes, nose, chin, width between the eyes. Hair and height were similar, that's all. But what I saw fit Cressa's description of an adrenaline junkie who stayed fit by pushing the physical envelope.

In the first photo, the man had just completed what might have been a triathlon. He was at leaning rest, hands on knees, corded biceps and thighs extending into spandex shorts while he smiled at the camera: teeth of orthodontic quality and square chin, but a nose that had been broken, and oddly large eyes that were set close together. It gave the man a Bambi look. In the second photo, though, Bambi and an African tribesman were posed beside a recent kill: a small warthog hanging by its back legs from a limb. Both men wore a swath of cloth around their waists, and they'd used mud, or camo grease, to camouflage their skin. Only Bambi held a spear: a tri-edged steel point on a thin wooden shaft.

"Scary-looking dude, huh?" Tomlinson said. "Especially if he's, well . . . if he is psychologically prone to being goddamn crazy."

"It's not the guy I met," I told him.

Tomlinson stood straighter and wiped a hand across his forehead. *"Really* . . . you're sure?"

I was reexamining the first photo. "Not even close. I'm not convinced it's Rob Arturo's brother, either. When you asked for a photo, did Cressa give you a hard time?"

"No, man. She was very *tranquilo* . . . which, you know, happens after smoking a doobie. Just a couple of tokes. Cressa's wifely duties more or less orphaned her from the Toker's Union, so I'm easing her back into the dealie."

It crossed my mind that Vargas Diemer might benefit from Tomlinson's efforts later in the evening. I asked, "She didn't hesitate? She must've—why else use e-mail."

Tomlinson exonerated the woman with a gesture and took the photos. "If you say it's not the film guy, I don't doubt it. But why do you think it's not her brother-in-law?"

"Picture Rob and compare the faces. Do you see any family similarities?"

Tomlinson carried the photos to the window, saying, "This guy's obviously not the investment type, which means he's not a totally tight-assed dweeb. Couldn't get sunlight up Robby's khakis with a harpoon—that alone might throw you. Both of 'em, though, they're tall . . . got that country club swagger . . . I don't know, man, they look like they could be brothers to me." Then, turning to me wide-eyed, added, "Jesus Christ, he kills animals with a *spear?*"

"It's the latest thing with the survivalist types,"

I replied. "I looked it up. They hold tournaments. The world finals are in South Africa. In the U.S., a leading manufacturer is Primal Steel. They sell six different types of spears, and they give the spear tips tribal names. Of course, purists prefer to make their own out of flint or bone—bone is a favorite."

"You're scaring me," Tomlinson said. "Why do I get the feeling you enjoyed reading about this shit?"

"Good clean fun," I replied. "Most productive strategy is spend hours in a tree over a game path. Or in a watering hole, breathing through a tube. Most productive technique isn't *throwing* the spear—that's not up close and personal enough. Either thrust up from the watering hole or lock your hands and legs around the spear and fall on your quarry from above. You know, become part of the weapon. Lots of blood and squealing—but none of the articles explained what to do if your quarry has long sharp horns."

"Savages," Tomlinson said. "The best argument against evolution looks back at those bastards from the bathroom mirror every morning."

The man was sweating, I noticed, face paler than when he'd arrived, and his hands were shaking. I asked, "Are you okay?"

He rolled his eyes in a way that told me he was struggling with something.

"I thought you had a meditation class tonight?"

"It went great, and we were done before cocktail hour. Seven eager spirits psyched about receiving their mantras, man." Then said, "I brought this, too," and reached into a purselike bag he's taken to carrying over his shoulder. It was a DVD. Unlike the disc Cressa had destroyed, this one was colored Macintosh white and was professionally labeled:

"GUY'S TRIBE" PILOT (1-of-3)
1. TARPON SLAYERS (RAW FT)
PRODUCER: C.K. BONO

"*Guy's Tribe*," I said. "Cressa told me Deano wanted to make documentaries but this sounds like he was shooting for his own series. Or a network. '*Tarpon Slayers*'—yeah, a series. She gave you this?"

"I need some water," my pal said, then explained as he went to the fridge, "I found it next to the TV. Know what I did? I leveled with her—in a way. Told her I was hurt *emotionally* because she'd never confided in me. That she'd lied, in fact, about her family situation, but didn't have a problem opening up to you. That really got to her, the honesty of it."

"I wouldn't say she opened up," I replied. "It was more like she was trying a different lure."

"I'm just not that cynical about people. Point is, Crescent got very soft and misty. Plus, after just a couple of hits, she was like *stoned,* as mentioned. Some of the stuff I found out about Rob's dad and the brother—very interesting. Just when she was getting into it, though, she got a phone call and went outside to speak privately—a man she didn't know well from what I overheard. So I decided it was okay to borrow the DVD after she had more or less handed me the keys to the family secrets."

The Brazilian calling? I wondered about that as Tomlinson poured beer, not water, over ice and continued, "The father-in-law, Robert, he's the king asshole in the family. Deano, the youngest son, has been a professional screwup most his life, so Daddy gave him one more chance by financing a production company. The kid borrowed against his inheritance for years, so his chunk of the fortune was gone long ago. Rob, the boy dweeb, has also lost patience. He wants to have Deano put away permanently. Cressa said she's starting to agree."

I asked, "Was Deano disinherited before Cressa married the older brother or after?"

Tomlinson gulped half his beer, then paused to consider what I was implying. "That's a stretch," he said finally.

"Depends on when the father cut him out. Did she say? If it happened before the marriage, it's unlikely Cressa would mention it—too embarrassing and *incriminating*. Hate to tell you, old buddy, but I think your extrasensory powers were blurred by testosterone when you met that woman."

Tomlinson said, *"Whew,"* as if enduring a

cramp, then wiped his face with a towel while he tried to process it. "Okay, okay . . . so let me try and picture what you're saying: the beautiful older woman loves the wild brother, Deano, but marries the straight brother, Rob, because he's going to inherit the family fortune. Which means"—my pal didn't want to believe it from the way he was struggling—"which means you think Deano knew from the beginning why Cressa married Robby. Went along with it to keep Cressa in the family. Like a secret pact, you mean."

Placing the DVD on the counter, I replied, "I put scenarios together based on what we know, then project how people behave. What elements catalyze what actions. That's where it usually blurs. It's all subjective, of course, but if there's enough motivation to sabotage a plane and kill three people, I file it away. If it doesn't, I trash it. So far, this is one of three scenarios that works."

I picked up the DVD again. "You said Deano *was* in the film business. Does that mean his production company went bust? If he was trying to sell a series on tarpon tournaments in Boca Grande Pass, that's big. My hook placement study could help put an end to the snag-fishing tournaments. Dan's a high-profile opponent. If the Fish and Wildlife Commission does its job, the TV tournaments should be out of business in a season or two—in Boca Grande, anyway. No snag-fishing means less action. That translates into fewer viewers and sponsors. Plus, you were sleeping with the Arturo brothers' secret treasure, so there's plenty of motivation to kill all three of us."

Instead of listening, Tomlinson was squinting at the palm of his hand for some reason, moving it incrementally closer, then farther away, as if testing his eyesight.

"What did you have to eat at Cressa's place?" I asked. *Maybe she or Deano poisoned the guy* is what I was thinking.

"Not a thing," he answered after I'd asked the question twice. "It's what we were smoking, I just realized. Kondo gave me some samples of what is turning out to be amazing shit. Diarrhea should have tipped me off—small price to pay for a chance to actually see the bones in my hand."

I pushed the DVD toward Tomlinson and told him, "If you can manage, put this on the computer so I can see the footage—no, wait. Call Cressa first. If you're having a tough time, think about what she must be going through. Who else did Kondo target?" The question keyed a link I hadn't made before, which is why I demanded, "Was Cressa one of his customers before you two met? Tell me the truth, damn it. Her brother-in-law's addicted to something—painkillers, crack, for all I know. Deano would need a steady supplier."

Because my pal didn't respond immediately, I reached for my cell, adding, "I want to have a talk with your Haitian buddy. That's another scenario that works, by the way—one drug dealer wiping out another. You have Kondo's number, right . . . *right?*"

Tomlinson peered into the depths of his beer glass and replied, "Marion . . . I am so damn glad we didn't die in that plane crash, I could cry, man. I really could."

A LITTLE AFTER NINE, Vargas Diemer came into the lab, put his plate on the sink station, and popped a bottle of Perrier water before telling me, "I've never heard of fish gravy. Such a strange idea but excellent—nicely spiced, pepper and limes, yet . . . subtle. I also have an interest in native recipes of the Caribbean. Willing to share once again . . . Doc?"

We were on a first name basis now that the man had eaten the dinner I'd made. My "friend" Cressa Arturo, who'd had a far stronger reaction to the drug, was in my bedroom recovering. I was sitting at the desk computer, ten minutes into the raw footage Dean Arturo had shot of a Boca Grande tarpon tournament a few months earlier. I touched the space bar to freeze-frame, then reached for a pencil, asking, "How's she doing?"

"Calmer, but not asleep," he replied, clearly unconcerned. "Tell me, do you use juice from the fresh lime?" The man swiped a finger across his plate and tasted it. "How does one keep it from curdling when you create the roux?"

One adds the lime afterward, but I'd let the jet-set assassin figure that out for himself. "Maybe you should ask Cressa if she wants something to eat. She has to be drained after the night she's had."

No doubt. The woman had been in a drug-fueled hysteria when I'd telephoned her cell. Diemer was at the beach house with her and moments away from dialing 911—or so he claimed. More likely, though, he'd been weighing the risk of exposure against his opportunity to be alone with a vulnerable woman he had yet to bed. When the Brazilian realized it was me on the phone, he'd had no choice but to join Cressa's rescuer by pretending to lead the way. Now he was the reluctant nursemaid, but only after Tomlinson had agreed she was stable enough to be left alone with the man.

"I heard Tomlinson go out the door," I said to him as I wrote *½ cup sifted flour, a pinch of sea salt* on a legal pad. "Where'd he go?" I craned to have a look through a south window. "Or is he still on the porch?"

"It was because of your dog," Diemer replied. "Whenever I moved, he showed his teeth, so your hippie friend led him ashore. Why people tolerate untrained animals, it is something I will never understand."

"An impressive dog," I agreed. "Unless you're talking about Tomlinson."

The Brazilian hesitated, then decided it was a

joke. "Yes . . . very funny. Actually, the hippie appears to be fine. Not totally coherent, but no serious side effects from the drug. Mysterious, no?"

I shook my head—*No*—while I worked on the recipe. "I think the drug dealer underestimated my friend's experience with hallucinogenics. Cressa only had a couple of puffs and look what happened to her."

"Why would a person do this intentionally?" Diemer said, maybe interested, maybe not. It was the second time I'd baited him on the subject but still wasn't convinced he had no knowledge of the Haitian drug-dealing witch doctor. The matter became no clearer when he added, "Smoking marijuana puts women in a more receptive mood, this I understand. A useful tool. But, personally, I think it's silly—pay money to behave stupidly and laugh at nothing funny?" The man shrugged as he crouched to look over my shoulder and then switched the subject to what he saw on the computer screen. "Ah! Tarpon fishing! Why such ugly little boats?"

In a frozen frame of the video Deano had shot, a dozen high-speed outboards were clustered like bumper cars over a pod of tarpon that had just sounded, the tails of two fish throwing a beaded veil of spray. The hulls of the boats were vacuum-wrapped in neon plastic—yellow, tangerine, pink—then tattooed with advertising logos—Yamaha, Spiderwire, Shimano, Miller Lite—

which fit the NASCAR attire of the anglers.

"A tournament," I told him. "You ever hear of the Silver King Professional Circuit?" I was four ingredients into the fish gravy recipe but looked up to gauge the man's reaction when I added, "A Florida investment group owns the television rights. Tomlinson found that out this afternoon. This footage was shot by someone who wanted to copy the format, but he also wanted to start a whole new series of tournaments. There's a lot of money involved. People will do all sorts of crazy things for money—or to eliminate someone who gets in their way."

Diemer nodded. We were on his home ground now. In fact, it gave me an idea. "Would you mind giving me your opinion on this footage?"

He was an observant man. I was interested in what he had to say about the tarpon footage, but I was more interested in what he knew about the dysfunctional Arturo family who vacationed in Europe and had plenty of money.

20

I HIT THE SPACE BAR WHILE THE Brazilian pulled up a chair, both of us cleaning our glasses in prelude to commenting on the action. The footage was raw, without a sound track or voice-over. As we watched, I explained to Diemer that it was shot in Boca Grande Pass during the last hour of the last tournament of the season and three of the boats in the bumper car jumble were tied for first place.

"Grand prize was a quarter million dollars," I told him, "so tournaments like this have the built-in drama a television series needs—*if* they land fish. That's the key: catching lots of fish."

"How do you know this?" he said.

"I was there finishing a project," I replied, aware that a more obvious question would have been to ask if I'd shot the footage. Had the articulate professional slipped?

If he did, the man recovered seamlessly, saying, "Good. The framing is passable . . . but amateurish. This person's equipment lacks a stabilizer . . . and his lens is filthy. I should have known it wasn't you behind the camera."

The Brazilian might struggle with the subtleties of Yankee humor, but his powers of observation were first-rate. Something else: he knew photography.

"Watch how the boats move," I said. "You're a fisherman, so speak up if you see something . . . well, unusual. If you want it played back or stopped, just say."

"You have never seen this before?"

Shaking my head, I tapped the screen to focus the man's attention. "Watch . . . the school of tarpon is moving. *See?* Notice that all seven boats take off full speed after them. Now watch what happens when they're over the school again."

Diemer was getting into it. "Bizarre," he said. "An entirely different technique than Captain Hannah uses. Far more aggressive. Why don't the fish run away?"

I told him the fish we were watching *had* run. Boca Grande is the deepest inlet on the coast, so the fish had fled by sounding. "Picture a limestone basin with crevices," I added. "The tarpon have dropped down into one of those crevices."

We watched the boats roar to a stop above the fish . . . watched anglers drop weighted hooks, a plastic worm on each, deep into the invisible crevice. When their lead weights hit bottom, a few anglers cranked reels furiously to retrieve the hooks at high speed. Others held their rods motionless.

"The fishing lures are like none I've seen," Diemer commented. "Heavy sinkers attached directly to the hook. Humm."

"Four ounces of lead or more," I replied and hit the space bar, turning to him. "You just nailed an important point. Big weights on hooks that are tied to leaders—but *light* leaders, almost invisible . . . See?" I tapped the magnify key. "Look at the rig near the bottom of the screen"— then zoomed closer—"and not much thicker than the fishing line they're using."

"Yes," Diemer said. *"Unusual."*

I hit *Play* and explained that the technique we were watching worked only in Boca Grande Pass and a few other similar areas worldwide.

For several minutes, the Brazilian stayed close to the screen, studying every move, but then sat straighter and said, "I understand now. In the crevices, the tarpon are trapped. Then, like small bombs, the hooks are dropped into a group of fish. Often the hooks are rapidly retrieved, which makes it more effective. Yes . . . I see what these men are doing."

"Not trapped," I corrected him, "the fish are packed tight into a hole that has walls. Limestone walls, mostly, and chunks of archaic coral."

"Trapped," Diemer insisted, "unable to react when a fishing line brushes against their gills or the hinge of the mouth. I *know* this technique. The Indios use a similar method in streams in the Amazon . . . in Europe, too—Ireland most especially. I've seen it used to catch salmon with very light lines, but only in fast water when the salmon are spawning in groups. There is a term for it—you do not know this term?"

"Floss-fishing," I replied. "Or snatch-fishing—but there the weight is usually molded onto a treble hook. It's the same principle, though."

Nodding, the Brazilian did a quick pantomime of flossing his teeth. "The line slips into a narrow hinge of the mouth or gills. Yes? Then the hook

269

buries itself when the fish attempts to flee." His eyes returned to the computer screen. "This is called professional fishing in Florida? Forgive me if you disagree, but it's hardly *fishing*."

I replied, "It's for a television series, remember? They call it jig-fishing to make it sound legitimate, but it guarantees they'll land tarpon even when fish aren't feeding. Can you imagine investing a quarter million or more in a TV tournament but getting no action footage? That's why an agency hired me to do a hook placement study."

"Outrageous," Diemer said.

The irony caused me to smile. A man who robbed and sometimes killed for a fee was offended by a breach of sporting ethics. It confirmed, though, that he had connected the disparate elements and had quickly figured out what, over decades, Florida's legislators had failed to understand. A moment later, the Brazilian snapped his fingers to get my attention. "Two boats—they have hooked tarpon!"

I had been in Boca Grande on that summer afternoon and had no interest in watching what happened next. I knew that one fish had been hooked in the eye socket, the other beneath a boney plate outside the mouth. Just before it was landed, the eye-hooked tarpon was then hit so hard by a hammerhead shark it exploded in a cloud of blood and silver scales, scales that glittered like confetti as they spiraled into the depths.

I got up and walked to the file cabinet. "Keep watching. Then you might want to read the conclusion of the report I did."

My back to the screen, I took my time locating copies of the study. Not until I heard Diemer exclaim, "My god! You must see what just happened!" did I return, a copy in hand. "A shark," he said, "a shark just ate a tarpon . . . I *think,* but the camera work is so poor . . ." The man added something in Portuguese to vent his frustration, then asked, "Who is responsible for this camera work?"

When I did a quick replay, I saw that the Germanic Brazilian was being too harsh on the shooter—presumably, Dean Arturo. Arturo's camera had been blocked from the shark attack by the tournament's own camera boat, which was no surprise. As I watched, though, I was startled when the lens panned the flotilla and then suddenly stopped when it found me and two assistants aboard my new boat: a twenty-six-foot Zodiac with a T-top, radar, a weather console, twin Mercs, and *Sanibel Biological Supply* stenciled on the side. The shot was out of focus, at first, but then zoomed until the frame was tight, just me holding a clipboard. For the first time, I heard the cameraman speak. But he spoke to himself, not for an audience, or possibly to a

271

friend, because he muttered, "That's him . . . the asshole biologist, it's gotta be." The shot zoomed out of focus, then sharpened again. "Yeah . . . the one who wants to screw our chances before I even get started."

The shot tightened on my face, which made what came next more personal. "Marion Ford . . . you fuck. Stick a spear through your neck and wait for the sharks. Put *that* in your research paper."

No fake Boston accent, but I recognized the voice. I'd heard it the morning I'd witnessed the stingray giving birth—Dean Arturo had posed as Luke Smith. I didn't know why Cressa's photo hadn't matched, but I didn't care. I had proof. Proof enough even if I never again met the man face-to-face.

THE SHARK FOOTAGE ENDED, and the next shot was of the winning boat dragging a tarpon toward the weigh station. The sling that awaited the fish resembled a body bag, which added implicitly to the tarpon's humiliation.

Diemer was confused by what he'd just heard Dean Arturo say but interested. "This person, the cameraman, is he not your associate?" Then added a smile to his voice and confided, "Sounds rather dangerous to me. Why . . . that man just threatened your life!"

Seldom does the solution to a problem flash

into my head without the plodding logic most solutions require. It did now. The catalyst was the way the Brazilian had said "rather dangerous." It was a warning, but he was also having fun with it. Diemer relished the potential those words offered—a hunter who got an adrenaline kick from projecting how *he* would deal with such a matter.

Two peas in a pod, I had joked.

Maybe Diemer would have his chance. Which is why I decided to tell him the truth and explained, "A few days ago, he did try to kill me. So it's not surprising."

"How?"

I shook my head. "It doesn't matter."

"But you do *know* him?"

"If it's the same voice—and I think it is—I only met the guy once. Three days ago, Sunday morning. He offered me ten thousand dollars to come along on our search for Flight 19 and film it. Obviously, he has some personal issues, but that's not why I said no. And the tarpon footage was shot months *before* he made his offer."

The man's posture changed subtly, no longer interested in sportfishing or anything else. "Then you *have* found the planes."

I touched the space bar to stop the video . . . thought about it for a few seconds . . . then decided to take a bigger risk. "You mind telling me something . . . Vargas? Are you really here on vacation? If it's business, I know better than to ask details."

The man remained unruffled, but neither was he amused. "Why did you deny checking my identity?"

I said, "Just being careful."

"Humble," he replied, staring at me. "And you have the resources to check on a stranger from Brazil." He smiled. "A Swissair pilot. Why would you care?"

"I have an idea," I said, "if you're willing to listen—but let me make sure what we say stays private."

I went out the door, across the breezeway to my living quarters. A singsong garble of voices told me that Tomlinson and Cressa Arturo were in the bedroom talking. The dog, sleeping in the middle of the floor, told me the chaos was over—for now. I returned to the lab with two cold beers, turned a chair backward, and said to Diemer, "Your business is your business, but I think maybe we can help each other. We have things in common, like you said. For instance, I have a lot of contacts in Central and South America—Cuba as well. I suspect you know that's true."

Yes, Diemer knew. He gestured in a way that said *I'm listening* while he removed his wire glasses and cleaned them.

"I'm a biologist, you fly for Swissair. Fine. Doesn't really matter what we do for a living, but traveling is easier—and a hell of a lot safer—if a person has trusted assets scattered around. That's what I have to trade—information when and if I can help you out. A month from now, five years from now, all you have to do is call."

Diemer misinterpreted the offer—intentionally, I guessed. "Intelligence," he said carefully. "Information provided by contacts from the National Security Agency? I'm confused about what you are asking in return."

"No," I said. "Just me. If you're in a jam, I'll give you a name or a contact number that might be helpful. I have nothing whatsoever to do with government agencies. Let's make that clear."

"Of course," the Brazilian replied, said it the way it is always said by people in the black ops business. "And what do you want from me?"

I told him, "The man we're talking about—the guy who offered me ten thousand dollars, then just threatened to kill me?—he's Cressa's brother-in-law. I don't doubt he's actually interested in Flight 19. Even a novice producer like him, a piece on those missing planes might sell to a cable network. Maybe even get him a deal for a guy's adventure series. He owes his father a lot of money, apparently, but he's also mentally unstable—a head injury puts him in and out of institutions. Two days before he made his offer is when my two friends and I were almost killed."

Say something like that to most people, they will ooh and ahhh, then press for the gruesome details. Not Diemer. He tilted his head as if to declare neutrality, then responded, "An experienced man would handle the matter himself."

"Do what, invite him outside to fight?" I said. *"Don't piss in your own pond*—it's a saying we have. If I did something about this, I'd have to leave the country. That's why I need an outsider with the right skills to help."

The Brazilian gave me an indignant look. "If you're asking me to . . . *eliminate* your threat, the idea is stupid." He spread his hands to indicate my lab, the stilthouse, everything I owned, and explained, "You couldn't afford the minimum price that"—he caught himself—"that people say such work requires. From an expert technician, not some 'Yo, dude' *viciado,* a drug addict from a ghetto."

The man, getting impatient, sat back in his chair. "This is a dangerous subject. Even to discuss such a thing is . . . well, here, you like old sayings? *Pull the trigger, and you can never stop the bullet.* Understand my meaning? Go to the police, Dr. Ford, that's my advice. I can't help you."

When I replied, "That's exactly what I plan to do," I watched his impatience transition into curiosity. "Tonight," I added. "I want to scare the brother-in-law off this island before someone really gets hurt. To make it happen, I need evidence the guy is making illegal videos of Cressa while she's with male visitors. She's been protecting the guy, so it's better if she doesn't know what's up. This is a wealthy little town, and the local cops don't tolerate the blackmailer types. Approach them in the right way, with the right evidence, there's a chance they'll run the guy off without arresting him. Everything nice and quiet and my problem's solved."

"He actually is filming her?" Now Diemer was interested, probably because there was a chance his visit had been documented by a camera.

"His name's Dean Arturo," I said, "but he also uses 'Luke Smith.' He sets up cameras outside her house and the pool area. Three cameras that I've seen, all activated by laser trip wires or sensors. With that many sensors, it's likely that he appears in some of the footage—a shot that proves it's him, *that's* what I need."

"Then he *is* blackmailing the woman."

"In a way. I think the brother-in-law trades the videos to Cressa in exchange for protecting him, probably gives him money, too. When she doesn't play by his rules—and it's happened only once that I know of—the guy punishes her by delivering a DVD anonymously to her husband."

"If she was filmed in bed with another man," Diemer countered, "*in flagrante* or just having fun—it depends on the husband, of course—then the damage has been done. Why would the brother-in-law continue such a pointless threat?" The Brazilian, an expert on blackmailers, asked the question in a dismissive way, meaning Dean Arturo's hold on the woman had already been neutralized.

I said, "I don't know why. But his reasons won't matter as far as the island cops are concerned. That's the important thing. Personally, though, I'd like to find out. Cressa and her husband signed a prenuptial agreement. If we had a copy, it might explain his behavior. Hers, too."

I had taken only a few sips from my beer, but now picked up the bottle and took a drink. The move gave Diemer time to sit in silence until he finally attempted to cloak his curiosity by saying, "I find Mrs. Arturo to be . . . *sensual.* For this reason, I'm interested."

"An attractive woman," I agreed. I took another drink and waited.

The man tapped the desk with an impatient finger, then pressed, "I don't suppose you know where she keeps her valuables? If it is a local bank"—his expression read *Impossible*—"but her home's another matter. People tend to entrust their cash, their jewels, et cetera, to the same hiding place. The videos and her personal papers might be there as well. But not actual videos, if I am right. She's an intelligent woman. She would insist on having the original memory cards from the cameras. Not copies. My point is, if I . . . if a *person* found them, he would have no way of knowing in advance if the photographer himself is in a shot—and that's the proof you need. Understand the problem?"

Diemer loved women and the adrenaline rush he got from stealing, so fretting about details didn't disguise his willingness. *Good.* I placed my beer on the desk and tried to set the hook. The night I had gone to her house after she was asleep and found the cameras? I'd also done a little stealthy snooping in the house itself. Hadn't found much, but I had found one thing. "At her beach house, there's a hidden wall safe in the study. She doesn't know I found it. A good one, modern, larger than most I've seen, and it's wired into the security system. Even if it wasn't too close to home, I don't have the skills to breach something like that." I gave it a beat before adding, "The son of a locksmith might be able to do it, though."

For an instant, what might have been a knowing smile appeared on the man's face but vanished when he said, "How would the locksmith's son profit?"

"I've already told you."

"Nonsense," Diemer said. "I already have more contacts in South America than I can use. There is another way, though. Let's assume there are other items in this safe, valuable items. Her husband is wealthy, you say. How wealthy?"

I looked in the direction of my living quarters, then got up and closed the heavy plank door I seldom use. When I was seated again, I kept my voice low. "She can't know she's been robbed. That should be obvious to someone like you."

"Done properly, she won't—not for a period of time. It depends, of course, on what's in the safe. Gold coins and bars are an investment, not something to be fondled. I know women who seldom touch the actual diamonds they've had replicated for a ring. A matching necklace and bracelet, it's common. Months go by, they never look."

Was he serious? "Not only do you want to get the woman in bed," I argued, "now you want to steal her jewels, too? That's coldhearted even for a . . . Swissair pilot. No, you can't touch her valuables. I'm after leverage, not profit."

"The risk taker *takes*—it is always part of the deal," Diemer shot back, then added in a tone that sealed the subject, "If your ethics don't allow it, the solution's simple: find someone else."

I shook my head, frustrated, and tried to regroup by repeating, "She can't know. You have to understand that or there's no point in going any further."

"And here is what you must understand," Diemer countered. "I've been in the woman's house only twice and I haven't seen the safe. If I do this and anything looks wrong, or feels wrong, I will leave. *My* rules, not yours. You mentioned your local police—that's another concern. I think it's idiotic to involve some uneducated *campesino* with a gun. I won't be a part of it."

Peasants was the translation.

"This isn't Brazil," I reminded him, "it's Sanibel Island, which means the guys I know are probably overtrained, so you can stop worrying."

Diemer immediately shrugged his acquiescence, which told me I'd just been hand-fed the only concession he was willing to make. I was thinking, *He won't stop there,* which the man proved by saying, "There's something else I want—and it's not negotiable."

Flight 19. That was his price. The jet-set assassin wanted to be included in the search. He wanted to be along every step of the way and receive an equal share if there was profit.

"I have partners," I reminded him.

"Telephone them now," he said, getting to his feet, "but no mention of why I'm to join you. Then call your policeman friend, if you must—but speak as if you *already* have the evidence. It's smarter to document ownership in advance of stealing it."

I didn't take his advice; waited until after eleven p.m. to telephone Lt. Kerry Brett and tell him I had photos and video of a stalker.

By then, it was true.

21

THE NEXT MORNING, IN THE GRAY AND silken heat of a stormy Thursday, Dean Arturo confirmed a couple of things when he crashed through a glass door he had shattered with a camera tripod, then sprinted across the parking lot of a hotel, my off-duty cop friends in pursuit.

"Crazy as ten loons," Tomlinson muttered, dazed by what had just happened or the hallucinogenics still in his system.

"That's him, the one who came to my lab," I said, meaning that Deano was also Luke Smith. Then added, "Stay where you are. I promised Kerry we wouldn't get involved."

"Involved?" Tomlinson said. "Hah! I want to get the hell out of here before the Earth catches fire!"

"Stay calm," I told him. "Just sit there and let them handle it."

Easy for me to say, but not so easy to heed as I watched Deano, ponytail swinging with every stride, hurdle a bike rack and disappear around the corner of the hotel. Kerry and his partner, Moonley, followed, Moonley pulling a radio from his pocket, not a firearm, before they, too, vanished behind the building.

"He's headed for the beach," I said, unaware I had opened the driver's-side door and was standing outside my truck.

"This is your idea of nonviolent intervention!" Tomlinson hollered from inside. "I told you bad shit happens when I'm around cops. You and our new partner, the Nazi Brazilian—suddenly, it all makes sense!"

My pal was still brittle from a long night spent dealing with chemical demons and comforting the married mistress. For the past twenty minutes I'd been telling him the truth about how I'd discovered where Deano was staying. Shared it despite the Brazilian's instructions to remain silent about the burglary. How else could I explain why we were in my truck, watching from a distance, while Kerry and his partner Moonley paid an unofficial call on the crazy brother-in-law? I had gone into detail—but also left out several key bits of information—about how my pact with the Germanic Brazilian had turned out better than expected.

Much better—until seconds ago when Dean Arturo crashed through the sliding glass doors of his hotel room and fled. And much too smoothly, as I was just now realizing, for the odds not to wipe the smug look off my face and remind me of something I knew better than most: in the field, nothing *ever* goes as planned.

• • •

UNTIL THAT INSTANT, my plan had gone without a hitch. At a little after eleven p.m., Vargas Diemer exited the side lawn of the Arturo property, wearing a jogging suit and surgical gloves. I had been standing watch near the street, which was where he'd slipped a candy box into my hands. Did it without slowing his breezy stride or saying a word, then disappeared toward the beach: a tourist out for a jog in the moonlight.

Impressive. Same with the Brazilian's cat burglar skills demonstrated during the twenty-seven minutes it had taken him to override the security system, crack the safe, and reappear. Along with the candy box, Diemer had exited carrying an unfamiliar shoulder pack—a detail I had not shared with Tomlinson.

The bag wasn't full, but it had looked heavy. Diemer hadn't offered an explanation. I didn't ask.

My truck had been parked at the Island Inn, and I waited until I was on the road to glance inside the box. It contained several video memory cards, a copy of a legal document—Crescent Arturo's prenuptial agreement, I correctly assumed—along with an envelope and a Post-it note, something written on it in pencil.

The parking lot at Lilly's Jewelry, on Tarpon Bay Road, was empty, so I pulled in and took a closer look: eight memory cards, which was promising.

In a week of surveillance, Dean Arturo, hope-fully, would appear in at least a *few* pieces of accidental footage. Finding the shot might take hours of scanning but worth the effort if it got him off the island.

My laptop and a card reader were in a computer bag next to me, but I had decided to wait. Wise choice, it turned out. The envelope, when I opened it, contained photos that spared me all that scanning. The Brazilian cat burglar had found a packet of photos that showed Deano in action. In one, he was peering through the curtains into Cressa's home—the patio railing was wood on chrome and as distinctive as Deano's own facial features: a good-looking guy, but for the scar on his forehead, and blazing pale eyes. There were two shots of him looking up from the lighted pool deck. Several more of Deano in a hoodie, setting up his surveillance cameras: shadowy images that wouldn't hold up in court but good enough for my purposes. The photos were taken by Cressa, presumably, and probably shot as insurance against a denial from Deano that he was spying.

The photos alone, I'd hoped, would be enough to convince my cop pals that Deano was stalking his own sister-in-law—a woman who wanted to protect the family name and was too frightened to file a formal complaint. Lt. Kerry Brett was a rational man and a total pro. Same with his partner Moonley. Show the cops the photos and suggest they give Deano the option of leaving the island or face charges. No rough stuff, no intimidation, just an honest warning that videoing unsuspecting citizens wouldn't be tolerated on our happy little island.

Convincing Kerry Brett had been key—and not just the key to scaring off Deano. At first Dan Futch had refused to honor my agreement with Diemer. No surprise. So I'd spent ten minutes on the phone arguing the wisdom of banishing an enemy quietly but without admitting my plan required breaking and entering and theft. "No headlines, no harm, no FAA," I had assured him. Then even Tomlinson had balked at sharing the Bone Field with an outsider until my nonviolent approach finally won him over.

The success or failure of the plan all came down to a fifteen-minute meeting that took place around midnight in the jewelry store parking lot. Brett and his partner Moonley were on duty and had some time on what they'd said was a "very quiet night"—good news in itself after I'd just helped burgle a house.

The two cops had listened to my story, and they'd studied the photos while their squad car's computer turned up something I didn't know: Dean Arturo had a police record—misdemeanor assault and resisting arrest—that added weight to my claim the man was mentally unstable.

Friends of mine or not, though, cops are rightfully guarded when dealing with civilians who try to tell them how to do their jobs. Sanibel is among the most desirable billets in law enforcement, and I was dealing with top hands, not affable good old boys who were easily manipulated.

The Post-it note Diemer provided had made finding Deano almost too easy for them to refuse. On it, written in a woman's hand, were initials and an address: *DA West Wind, Rm 243-244.*

The obsessive Cressa Arturo had done the last of the drone work for me. *DA* was Dean Arturo, and he was staying at a beachfront hotel, rooms 243–244. To me, booking two rooms suggested Deano's affair with Cressa hadn't ended. I could think of no other reason, so it didn't strike me as odd—although it *should* have. A dangerous man books two adjoining rooms? But I was too preoccupied . . . no, too self-satisfied with what I'd accomplished to bother exploring the implications.

Which is why on this gray and stormy morning in the West Wind parking lot, while watching my nonviolent brain child come unraveled, I stepped away from my truck and whispered, "You bumbling dumbass. You idiot!"

Meaning me, Marion Ford.

WHY DOES A DANGEROUS MAN, operating alone, book an adjoining room?

The bumbling dumbass got his answer less than a minute after Deano sprinted toward the beach: because he wasn't operating alone. A second man had appeared in the shattered doorway, looked both ways, then stepped out into the parking lot. I recognized him: triathlete muscles on a rangy frame, maple-colored hair, and close-set Bambi eyes. It was the man in the photos Cressa had e-mailed. All along she'd been misleading us, protecting her brother-in-law.

Tomlinson spotted him, too. "Christ A'mighty," I heard him say. "It's the spear hunter—freaking pig killer, man!" As he said it, Bambi scanned the parking lot, found my truck, then me, while Tomlinson muttered, "Get thee behind me, Satan!"

The man glared at us for a moment, then turned away.

"Stay here," I told him, then hesitated. "Call Cressa—find out who that guy really is."

" 'A quiet little warning,' " Tomlinson replied, mocking me. " 'The peaceful approach,' he says. Marion, *you* try weathering this bullshit with acid in your brain!"

I went after Bambi who had turned toward the street, not the beach as I'd expected. He was carrying a camera case and an overnight bag—all packed and ready to go—leaving Dean Arturo to his fate.

Loyalty wasn't part of their tribal code, apparently.

One glance over his shoulder, Bambi walked faster. So did I. After another look, he set off at a jog, taking long triathlete strides. Even though I wasn't carrying luggage, I had to push to keep up.

22

DEANO'S PARTNER WAS TRYING TO escape on foot? To *where?* Taxis don't cruise the island, and the hotel's main bike rack was empty.

On a run, I followed the man under the check-in canopy, where he veered right into a second parking lot, only a few vacant spaces showing puddles from a recent rain, and populated by a family of six, twin girls wearing Mickey Mouse ears, pillows in their arms.

When I hollered, "I want to talk to you!" the father looked up, correctly read the faces of the two strangers, and ordered his kids, "Get in the van—*now.*"

Bambi slowed, then sprinted into the cluster of children, shoulder-butting the father while the mother screamed. The move created a temporary shield that forced me to detour around a Winnebago while he beelined through the bushes toward an adjacent hotel, where there was a tennis court and another parking area.

A rental car, that was his destination. A white Jeep wagon, Florida plates, that Deano and Bambi had been smart enough to park a safe distance from their rooms. They'd also daubed mud over the plate. Bambi was in the Jeep, stabbing a key at the ignition, when I reappeared from an unexpected angle. Didn't notice until I had a hand on the passenger door, which he tried to thwart by slamming his hand down on the electric lock button. But too late . . .

"I want to talk," I said again. I was standing in a puddle of crushed shell, the door open, but then swung into the passenger seat when the engine started.

"Get out!" Bambi ordered.

I shook my head. "Your friend has some serious mental issues, you know that."

I didn't expect the rage the comment sparked. "You don't know a goddamn thing about me! Or about Deano. So shut your mouth! I'll call the police if you don't get out right now." Didn't expect a Boston accent, either, but it made sense.

"The two men chasing your buddy *are* cops . . . so, yeah, I think that's a good idea. I'll come along, you can tell them all about it."

Looking straight ahead as if he hadn't heard, Bambi scowled, then put his hand on the gearshift as if to drive away. I was deciding whether to go for an arm bar or just go along for the ride when, instead, he used the hand to turn down the music—tribal rap, it might have been, drums like electronic thunder that kept pace with the chanter's piercing hip-hop.

"You buy that in Africa?" I asked.

Arturo's partner ignored the question for several seconds, then turned to me. "Those assholes had no right to question Deano! Not after all the garbage he's been through. And he's trying, man, he's really trying to get it together! Then the cops pull a stunt like this."

I said, "It's not like they accused him of attempted murder," and watched how he reacted to my double meaning.

He didn't. Bambi stayed on track by continuing to transfer blame. "I heard the way they came into his room—pretending like they wanted to help, then started right away with the questions. Shrinks and cops, we've talked about it, they're always trying to trap you with questions. Well, bullshit, that's not the way you deal with someone like the Deanster. Force an alpha lion into a corner, man, how goddamn dumb you got to be not to know what'll happen?"

Eyes straight ahead again, the man's jaw muscles flexed. "They're lucky he didn't have a weapon, you know," he confided. "We don't need firearms. We do it the *real* way."

A threat. But I let it go, asking, "What's your name? Mine's Ford."

Finally, a reaction. "I know who you are. We saw you almost every day in Boca Grande during tarpon season—the guy who was going to ruin it for everybody. We had a cable deal all lined up until word got out."

I said, "Word got out about what? Deano's brain injury?"

Bambi's brown liquid eyes flared. "No, you prick! That the state might shut it down once your study comes out. Sponsors are going to take a risk like that? Jesus Christ, and we had everything all set to go, then you come along. Must make you feel real important, huh? Fucking up other people's lives? I was surprised when Deano gave you another chance."

Another chance at what? "He might still be willing to work something out," Bambi said, "if you've actually found something. Just one hit on cable, just one goddamn break, that's all we need. We can't pay the ten thousand—never could. But if you had just given us a chance, none of this bullshit would have happened."

What the hell did that mean?

Bambi looked at his watch, his mind working on something, then explained in a tone so suddenly optimistic I felt a chill, "Dean's really good, you know. So am I—not that the networks give a shit about talent. The project we're working on now, though, just wait until those hacks see it. Millions we're going to make . . . because it's timeless!"

I was thinking, *Big ego, built-in excuses,* and baited him, saying, "Then you're better off. We found something—but a few pieces of airplane wouldn't make much of a show. Cressa didn't give you the latest update?"

The man who'd killed a pig with a spear smiled, letting me know he was too savvy to fall for it. But then revealed more than I'd hoped. "Don't ever trust that bitch. She even came on to me one night, and Deano hates her. If his old man ever stops thinking with his cock, she'll be out the—" Bambi caught himself, stopping midsentence, then switched off the ignition for some reason. Or was he baiting me . . . ?

Apparently not, because he popped the trunk and got out, explaining, "I'm going to check on Deano. But I'm taking a camera—cops act almost human with a camera around."

Sirens—a chainsaw warble that found its way inside the Jeep. More than one squad car, sounded like, coming fast from the direction of the Rum Bar on Rabbit Road. I got out and spoke to him across the roof. "I'll be right behind you."

The Bambi-eyed glare again from the back of the Jeep. "I don't give a damn what you do. Unless you want to make a film with a couple of first-rate shooters, stay away from both of us." Then leaning into the vehicle, he appeared to fumble something, and I heard, "Shit . . . right in the water," before he disappeared from view.

A setup of some type, my guess. Rather than wait, I hurried to the back of the Jeep in two fast strides, hoping to catch him unprepared. Bambi had thought it through, though, and was ready. As I came around the rear fender, he stood and swung a bamboo staff that whistled with velocity, but I got a shoulder up in time or it might have killed me. He lunged and swung again. I tried to step inside the staff's power radius, crouching as I threw out my left hand and tracked its path. The bullwhip smack of bamboo on skin wasn't as piercing as the pain, but I caught the tip of the staff and managed to hang on when he tried to pull it free.

"I think you're both insane!" I heard myself shout. The pain was numbing, but I wasn't in shock—I was mad. What I wanted to do was bust the bamboo over my knee, then use it to spank the bastard. Which is why I yanked too hard and why I went backpedaling into the bushes when Bambi suddenly let go and sprinted to the driver's-side door. It was still open—just as he'd planned, I had no doubt.

Mud! He or Deano had used it to camouflage the license plate. Two letters—*RK*—was all I could decipher before the Jeep spun out of the shell parking lot onto West Gulf Drive, then was gone.

I got to my feet, momentarily heartened when a Sanibel squad car braked out front, lights flashing.

Before I could get the officer's attention, though, he accelerated to the West Wind and turned. Seconds later, another blue-and-white followed, then a big diesel EMS vehicle. It confirmed what I had suspected: Kerry Brett or his partner Moonley had called for backup. But why the ambulance?

I PICKED UP the bamboo shaft and rushed back to the West Wind. Beneath a covered walkway, next to a coin laundry, I scooped ice into a bag and held it in my throbbing hand as I jogged past the pool, relieved the area hadn't been emptied by some bloody clash nearby. Then stopped among sea oats on the path to the beach.

No . . . not a bloody scene, but damn ugly. Beyond a gaggle of tourists who'd gathered to watch, I could see Tomlinson standing at a distance as my friends Kerry and Moonley were joined by uniformed cops who came on a run to form a restraining semicircle around Dean Arturo.

They, too, maintained a guarded distance. It was because of Arturo's behavior and the mad dog look on his face. He was handcuffed and shirtless on his knees, the Gulf of Mexico behind him, but continued to fight by lunging and gnashing his teeth . . . then spearing his legs at anyone who got close enough. My first reaction was pity. A strapping big man with a healthy body who'd been felled by an accident and a brain injury—it could happen to anyone. Could alter the behavior of the most stable among us.

But then Deano's threats, which reached the ear as a sustained flow of profanity, began to register, and my pity was replaced by a clinical interest. Soon, that changed to disgust. Brain pathology might exacerbate anger, but it is not the source of hatred. Dean Arturo's contempt for people originated from within, the plane crash had only released his hatred into the world. The man raged, spittle flying, in barbed sentences that were vicious, vile, full of self-pity, but he crafted his insults with *purpose,* methodically targeting the physical flaws of his enemies.

"Hillbilly genetics from a used rubber!" Deano screamed at a woman cop, then ridiculed her teeth, her body, her "white trash" income, then her chances of happiness, before aiming his venom at a new target. The woman bore it stoically, eyes hidden behind sunglasses, but I noticed when she touched a hand to her mouth, took a slow, involuntary step back, then folded her arms as a shield against another attack.

Something else: the scar I'd noticed on Deano's forehead was only the first inch of a injury that dented his skull like a walnut. His long hair, molded in place by a ponytail, had hidden it that morning on my dock. Not now as he thrashed around on his knees, flinging himself at anyone who came too close.

Pity. Once again, that dominated my perception—or clouded it. After watching for another minute, though, I was done wondering about it and went to fetch Tomlinson. "Let's go before he spots us," I said, putting a hand on his shoulder.

An actress friend once described Tomlinson's eyes as "pools of lechery and wisdom," but only his scars were showing when he turned to me and said, "He's possessed by demons. There's a decent man in there somewhere, but handcuffs aren't the way to set him free."

"Yeah?" I responded, "His partner just tried to knock my head off with this." I tapped the bamboo shaft in the sand. "The best way to deal with the homicidal crazies, I suppose, is stay out of their way and hope they kill someone else, huh?"

Tomlinson winced, but it was because Arturo was now screaming, *"You're all fakes, you're clowns!"* which touched a chord in him, apparently. "Doc," he said, "I've been in that guy's *shoes,* man. Handcuffs just press the *Crazy* button. Jail and shock treatments don't help, either."

When he has downed enough rum and is in an autumnal mood, he sometimes talks about the shock treatments prescribed during his college years to jolt him out of a sustained depression that (I suspect) put him at risk of suicide. This was the first time, though, he had alluded to being handcuffed and the center of a similar demeaning insanity. I wanted to spare us both the details, so I steered him toward the parking lot, saying, "Don't worry about it. They'll wait until he calms down, then commit him for seventy-two hours. Couple of days in the psych ward might help him snap out of it. And"—I hesitated, thinking it could wait. But it couldn't, so I continued—"and one of us needs to phone Cressa. She'd probably rather hear it from you."

Deano had spotted us and was now lying on his belly, spitting sand, yelling, "Hey! I'm talking to you, Ford! Fuck up my life, then turn your back on me! Hear me, Forrrrrd?"

Tomlinson slowed for a moment, then decided, *Hell with it,* so Arturo had to address the cops and the crowd, yelling, "Those two—they're both screwing my brother's wife! *That's* what this is all about. The hippie, I've got video! And the big-shot biologist—I know he's doing it, too! They're friends with all the local cops!"

My turn to consider stopping, but Tomlinson kept me moving. "Challenge him and people will think it's true."

"We've got nothing to worry about," I countered. "No video of us—not after last night."

"Who cares if he does? Doc, next time you come up with a peaceful solution, don't bother because—" We were in the parking lot now, shattered glass on the walkway outside Deano's room, so Tomlinson paused to look. A cop stood guard inside the sliding door, framed by a jagged hole, so it was like peering into a cave where sunlight touched a tangle of broken furniture, the detritus of a brawl.

I was ready for what came next, so prodded, "Now you're against nonviolence?"

My pal shook his head to shush me, derailed by something. After a moment, he asked, "Did you hear a cat?"

No, just the diesel rumble of the EMS truck and Deano's distant howling. "From inside the room?" I asked. "I don't know the officer, maybe he'll let us take a look. But, hey, you know it's a waste of time. Crunch & Des would have bolted when the door broke."

Tomlinson's eyes were linking images together: a TV screen that had been ripped off the wall, mattress overturned, minibar bottles scattered . . . the cop's meaty hand resting on his holstered Glock, aware of us but unconcerned. My guru pal appeared to shudder, said, "Forget it," then continued walking and soon remembered that he'd been saying, "Next time you come up with a peaceful solution, Doc, do me a favor: *please don't*. Stick with what you're good at."

"Deano can't kill us from the psych ward," I reminded him, but was thinking, *I will!*

23

THAT AFTERNOON, I WAS ALONE IN MY lab awaiting a telephone update from Lt. Kerry Brett while I also kept an eye on the drug dealer, Kondo Ogbay. With Ogbay were three associates, all voodoo devotees judging from their head nets of red and black, who had loaded themselves into a rental boat—a twenty-foot tri-hull with a sun awning and red plastic upholstery from a marina on the other side of the causeway. When they were seated, the little sumo-shaped man freed the lines, then idled out the channel. Tomlinson's dinghy was ashore, but his absence didn't stop the drug dealer from waving at *No Más* and calling a cheery greeting that sounded like: "How you doin', mon? We gone check'n you maggy drops! Be fun, you joyin' us!"

Which was nonsensical until I played with the phonetics, replaced a few words, and finally understood. "We're going to check on your magic crops!" is what the witch doctor had said. It was a reference to mangrove islands with enough high ground to plant seeds and harvest crops. Pot was the money crop, in Tomlinson's case, and there were several secret spots he tended with a shepherd's tender care. Now Kondo

300

and friends were on a raiding trip, apparently, and had challenged Tomlinson to interfere with this cryptic taunt.

Watching through the north window, I spoke softly to Kondo, who was a football field away, saying, "Break a leg," and I wasn't smiling. One option was to get in my boat and follow. Instead, I called my cousin Ransom, who knows about voodoo and obeah because she was raised in the Bahamas and who might even recognize Kondo if she stepped out on her dock—she's popular with the wealthy nightclub set from Naples to Sarasota. The channel from Dinkin's Bay exits at Woodring Point, where Ransom lives—rents among the last of the old Cracker houses—and Kondo's boat would soon be passing by.

"Why you think I be home on a Thursday 'stead of working?" she asked after answering her cell phone.

When I told her why I hoped she was home, Ransom said, "That not his real name, why you have truck wid that bad man? His real name, it Sylvester—like in the *Rocky* movies his unedu-cated mama probably loved, but who knows?" After a thoughtful pause, she then asked, "You say Kondo's in a rental boat? A man wid his money, what the hell he doin' in a damn rental boat? Think he lives in Kingston, but he got a place in Naples, too. A bad boy like Kondo, he'd have him a fast boat."

"You've met him?" I asked.

My stubborn cousin replied, "Tell me how much Tomlinson owe that midget 'fore I tell you another damn thing."

"Ransom," I said patiently, "this might be important."

She sighed, but gave in. "Even a dumb Haitian know an island woman not put up wid his bullshit, so, no, Kondo, he avoid me. But the money people—at parties, at the clubs, I'm sayin'—they treat him like somethin' special. You *know* what does. Sells 'em herb, then a Santeria blessing if they pay four, five hundred cash to buy a damn dirty pigeon that Kondo call a dove. Or cast an assault obeah on some business enemy—these smart people, I'm talking about, good-looking, wid cars and houses. I hear them at parties whisperin', thinkin' they very cool to have they own Haitian voodoo man can invite for drinks when they in Jamaica, Saint Martin—that boy get around. You know what else he do . . . ?"

As I listened to Ransom talk, I slipped outside to the porch and peeked around a corner at the yacht *Seduci*. The Brazilian was there, sitting with coffee on the flybridge. He, too, was following the progress of the rental boat, but was only vaguely interested. If he had wanted details, there were binoculars next to him.

I retreated behind the corner, asking, "Have you told Tomlinson any of this?"

In her mellow, singsong way of speaking, my cousin replied, "Mary, Mary, you quite contrary today—*Marion*. Why waste time speaking reason to a scarecrow who think wid his dick, not his brain?"

I knew better than to reply, *Because you're still in love with him?* so postponed more details, saying, "I'll be away this weekend, but how about dinner next week?"

"Don't you bring that damn Tomlinson. He better off standin' in some cornfield. Not speaking wid that particular person never again."

"Just us," I assured her. "I'll leave him behind, and you promise not to bring one of your brownnosing boyfriends."

For some reason, Ransom thought that was hilarious. "Brownnosing, ho-ho-ho, oh lordy, the words come out your mouth! So quick 'n' clever, I love you, brudder!"

Not clever at all because the joke was accidental, which I didn't figure out until watching the Brazilian again, who still hadn't reached for his binoculars.

Fascinating, Diemer might have commented because I still couldn't fit the man into a schematic that made any sense. True, unexplained elements noted within a similar time frame aren't necessarily related, but I had witnessed, with my own eyes, the Brazilian's talent for black ops and burglary. His skills were too finely tuned to risk inactivity, plus he thrived on the adrenaline rush—why waste time on anything but a working vacation?

He wouldn't. Yet, a Caribbean dope dealer would be of no concern to Diemer or his wealthy clients. Neither I nor Tomlinson were his targets, I was convinced. And it was unlikely a man of his experience would've risked burgling Cressa's home in advance of executing someone who could be linked to the place. So why the hell was the Brazilian in Dinkin's Bay?

I stepped out from behind the corner and picked up the dog's water bucket. Diemer failed to notice, so I emptied the bucket over the railing just to see how he reacted. As I did it, he looked up, focused, and then acknowledged me with a slight bow—a European touch that I returned via a friendly salute.

Maybe he won't be such a bad partner after all, I was thinking.

DIEMER HAD BEEN RIGHT about the burglary— so far. I had no idea what he'd stolen in that shoulder pack, and was still disturbed by his treatment of a woman he wanted to seduce, but I couldn't fault his expertise. Cressa Arturo, according to Tomlinson, had been actress enough to feign surprise when told that Deano had been arrested and his partner had fled, but she showed nothing close to the agitation of a woman who's discovered her house has been robbed.

Months go by, and they never look, Diemer had told me about the wall safe. Theft for personal gain is gutter behavior, but the guilt I should have felt was blurred by the victim's own twisted conduct. Cressa had damn near gotten us killed, she'd lied to us, insulted my running partner, and she had finagled information from Tomlinson about the Avenger wreckage and then passed the details along to Deano, who, I was convinced, had booby-trapped our plane. If my assessment was right, and if Bambi was to be believed, she had also used Tomlinson either to sabotage her marriage or to end an affair with her own father-in-law—maybe Deano, too—and had then tried to seduce me, a "dangerous man," to protect her from the fallout.

The woman was poisonous even from a distance. I was done with the married mistress, which is why I focused on matters at hand as I carried the bucket to the lower deck and filled it with fresh water.

Pull the trigger and you can never stop the bullet, Diemer had told me, which now applied to the deal we'd made. But even if working with him turned out to be a pain in the ass, I could accept that, because some good had already come from it. Along with eliminating Deano and his spear-happy partner from the scene, the Brazilian playboy had canceled his fishing trips with

Hannah. Good news, particularly because it had been Diemer's idea to cancel, not mine. He would be meeting Tomlinson, Dan, and me off Lostman's River on Saturday morning, so had to get his boat ready for the trip. Hannah hadn't returned my calls, but if the subject came up, I looked forward to explaining that aside from telling Diemer he should pay for the canceled trips I was innocent of all involvement.

It was pleasant to linger on how our conversation would go—me saying something like, "All you've got to sell is your time, so of course you should be paid." Then Hannah saying, *You're such a thoughtful man!* Or, *I owe you dinner, Doc. Maybe after swimming the* No Wake *buoys off Blind Pass?* Back on friendly terms again, which would be nice.

Which is why I was in a cheery mood when the retriever appeared, already dry after swimming the afternoon away, and grunted his request to visit the mangroves. I still hadn't heard the dog bark and was picturing how a snakebite, or constriction, might damage canine vocal cords as I filled his bowl with Eukanuba, then flipped the recliner pad where he slept. I'd replied to the pair of inquiries regarding my lost-and-found ads so might soon have to explain the injury to the dog's rightful owner. That's when my landline phone rang, so I hurried inside to answer. Lt. Kerry Brett calling.

First, my cop pal gave me some unsurprising news: Deano had been committed and would be transferred from county jail to a hospital once his family had been notified. Two bottles of generic Vicodin, plus pot, assorted pills, powders, and a cube of hash, found in the man's backpack would add to his legal difficulties. Deano's partner, whose name actually was Luke Smith, had been stopped and questioned in the Hertz lot at Southwest Regional but released because, as I'd already told Kerry, I didn't want to press charges. I just wanted the guy gone from my life.

Then, phone to my ear, Kerry told me something so totally unexpected I replied, "If this is a joke, people here won't find it funny."

"Come see for yourself," he replied, and I went out the door again in search of Tomlinson. At a jog, I crossed the boardwalk, through the mangroves, then picked up speed as I approached the marina, fighting the absurd urge to call out what I'd just heard like some horseless Paul Revere. Mack, who'd stepped out to light a cigar, gave me a lunatic look as I ran past and asked, "Where's Tomlinson?" The man pointed and said something, but I didn't hear.

My hipster friend was by the boat ramp, leaning over a spigot, using some kind of biodegradable goop to wash grease off his hands. Instead of blurting out the news as I clomped to a stop, the adolescent in me decided to play it cool.

"Working on your engine?" I asked, even though I knew that was unlikely. He'd just bought a new kicker for his dinghy and the thing was under warranty.

"Nope," Tomlinson said in an airy, self-satisfied way that was unusual.

The marina's good tool chest, I noticed, was open near his feet—another oddity. "Mack didn't give you permission to use those, did he?" Mack didn't let anyone touch his tools.

"Nope," Tomlinson said again while his eyes drifted toward the mouth of Dinkin's Bay, then studied the area. He, too, had been following the progress of Kondo Ogbay's boat, I realized.

"Ransom had some interesting things to say about your Haitian buddy," I told him. "I just talked to her—he's bad news, pal. Did you hear what the guy yelled as he went past *No Más*?"

Tomlinson found a mechanic's towel, and began to clean a ratchet he had used. "Yep," he replied, "every word."

A spark plug ratchet—that's what he was cleaning. It caused me to hope there was an association. "You were screwing with Kondo's engine, weren't you?" I said. "While they were eating lunch."

Tomlinson stood, offered me a wink, and said, "Yep." Then inquired, "How far would you guess it is between here and the sky bridge at Fort Myers Beach? Tide's ebbing—a full moon tide."

He had loosened one of the spark plugs, that was my guess. "He'll be running on only three cylinders, so the tide will push him into the Gulf and he'll have to idle twice the distance. Like a warning to leave you alone—good for you!"

No, Tomlinson had done worse than that because, instead of answering, he explained, "You're a bad influence, Doc. I decided you're right—maybe there's not a peaceful solution to everything. The dude tried to put me in the loony ward—bad LSD, that's what he used to lace that grass. Crescent's still a wreck. He deserved more than just a warning. Maybe it's the rank acid or because I'm sober, but I don't feel bad about what I did. In fact, man . . . I feel *good*."

Had the peacenik guru really said those words? "Tell me you didn't do anything crazy," I pressed. Rig the gas tank to blow up, reverse the polarity of the bilge pump, and sink the boat—there are all sorts of ways.

Tomlinson held a hand up to reassure. "Just the spark plugs," he said, "all four cylinders. Depending on how hard he pushes the engine, the first plug should blow before he gets to the causeway. Which should really piss him off. A dude like Kondo will take it out on the throttle, so the last three spark plugs will hit the cowling like rockets. Scripture tells us, 'Render judgment into God's hands, not thine enemies,' so that's what I'm doing. By midnight I'm guessing Kondo and his witch doctor posse will be somewhere between Lighthouse Point and the Yucatán— within easy reach of the Lord. No help from the Coast Guard, either, because someone stole that bastard's flares."

You're really coming along, I wanted to tell him, but I had kept the news to myself long enough. "Kerry called," I said. "You and I are going back to the West Wind Inn."

Tomlinson's ears or instincts had been right about hearing a cat.

"They found Crunch & Des in the adjoining room," I told him, "but I don't want to tell Rhonda and JoAnn and the rest until we're sure."

"He's alive? Did those bastards hurt him?" Tomlinson sounded damn-near savage.

"Let's take my truck and find out."

24

THURSDAY, AROUND SUNSET, DAN Futch texted me from somewhere over Lake Okeechobee—*Have news, time to talk?*—then landed in Dinkin's Bay twenty minutes later, gunning the engine before shutting down and drifting into the shallows next to my dock.

"Isn't the party usually Friday nights?" he asked, taking the iced tea I offered, then selecting a chair on the porch. He'd brought the leather briefcase again. Something new inside to show me, I hoped.

I popped my first beer of the day and said, "You remember the six-toed cat? Black with scars on his face, been around here for years. The guy who futzed your plane took him. It's a sort of welcome-home celebration."

"*What* guy?"

"The one who kidnapped the cat—I'm getting to it," I said.

"Geezus, every marina has a cat, who cares?"

"I don't think the cat cared one way or another," I agreed, "but you know how some people get attached. The guy I'm talking about—had a partner—the cops found a ransom note, but one of them was sane enough not to bother delivering it. Or maybe they were saving it as a last resort. The cat was fine. Had a litter box, milk in the minibar. Sounds crazy, I know, because it is crazy."

Futch sat forward and pushed his ball cap back. "You mean someone tried to kill us because of a goddamn cat?"

I shook my head and said, "Down there in the Glades, if Tomlinson hadn't been so gallant about his married girlfriend's name, you might have put it together right away. Does the name Arturo mean anything?"

"The *Arturo* family? You're shitting me."

"Robert Arturo Senior," I said. "He's supposedly got a lot of money."

"Yeah. Big-timer from New Jersey, the family charters Frank Davis's boat sometimes. Live bait, not jigging, okay? So a couple seasons back, I fished them because Frank had engine trouble. I remember because of the name—Deano, like the singer?—plus, one of them's married to a blonde who would stop traffic." A light blinked on behind the pilot's sunglasses. "Geezus . . . you're not telling me Tomlinson's screwing *her?*"

I shrugged. "You'd have to ask him. Point is, our problems are over." Then explained the probable linkage: Dan discussing Flight 19 with clients, Tomlinson leaking info to Cressa Arturo about the Avenger wreckage, Dean Arturo's failed TV series, *Tarpon Slayers*, and his fixation on us—the three men who, in his mind, had destroyed his career but could also save it.

"Deano crashed a plane a few years back," I said. "He hasn't been right in the head since. But he'd know how to wire a tail rudder. Maybe he met his buddy in a psych ward, I don't know, but the other guy's no better." Then held out my left hand, which was banded with a bruise, red and purple, my pinky finger black and bent like a can opener.

"Jesus Christ, Doc. You can't leave for the islands tomorrow with a hand like that."

I asked, "You still plan to meet us Saturday morning, right?"

"Yeah—and I might have something new on our Avenger, that's why I came. But I'm not even going to talk about it unless you agree to get that hand X-rayed first, okay?"

"In naval crash records," I said, "you found the plane, didn't you?"

The pilot wanted to tell me, couldn't wait, but he set his jaw and said, "Uh-uh. First the hand. If I didn't have a trip in the morning, I'd fly you to see a doctor friend in Boca Grande right now."

Futch, a stubborn man. Now that Deano was in jail, I didn't mind postponing a day or two, but I wasn't going to wait for news on the Avenger wreckage. "A splint, which I don't need, and they'll tell me to use ice," I replied. "It just looks bad—and could've been worse. The two of them got interested in spear hunting on a trip to Africa. Cressa didn't say it, but I'm guessing it was some kind of therapy retreat—sweat lodges, the primal roots deal. The guy—his name really is Luke Smith, the film shyster I told you about—he swung a piece of bamboo at me and took off. Bamboo as in spear, but no point on the shaft, luckily."

I flexed my left hand without wincing much. "See? Works just fine." Then pointed at the briefcase and said, "Now, damn it, tell me what you found out about the Avenger."

Futch gave me a confused look, then rolled his eyes to put the details behind us. "Where's Tomlinson? He should hear this, too." The pilot reached for the briefcase, something important inside. Should I murk the subject even more with talk of acid-laced grass and a malicious drug dealer?

No . . . so I told him, "He's either at the party, or he's"—I didn't want to bring Cressa Arturo into it—"he's taking care of a friend. She, this friend, they both have what you'd call really bad hangovers. Or they might have gone to Lighthouse Point to watch the sunset."

It was a possibility. Tomlinson had returned from *No Más*, binoculars around his neck, maybe hoping to catch a glimpse of the witch doctor as he drifted out to sea. Only a guess.

Futch, shaking his head again, was opening the briefcase. "You think that guy will ever grow up? *Quirko* . . . I don't know, Doc."

"Actually," I said, "Quirko has made real strides in the last couple of days. Our new partner, he's here, though, so maybe it's time you two met. Or tell me what you found first and then—" A galloping vibration on the lower deck stopped me. It was the retriever coming up the steps, moving almost as fast as he did in the water. He skidded around the corner, claws clacking, ignored Dan's welcoming hand, then sniffed and sneezed as he sat in front of me.

"Blood?" Dan said, wiping the spray off his arm.

I cupped the retriever's head in my hands and

leaned my nose close to his. "Humm . . . looks like you finally met Crunch & Des, huh?" Then said to Dan, "Just a couple of scratch wounds, so it wasn't much of a fight. But deep. I better tend to this."

As I got to my feet, the pilot asked, "Crunch and *who?* What the hell are you talking about?"

"About an hour ago, I got an e-mail from the dog's owner," I explained. "Well . . . the family he belongs to. The cat I mentioned—that's why he's bleeding. When the family sends someone— this weekend, possibly—I don't want the dog's nose to be infected. He's got scars enough to surprise them."

Then added as I walked toward the lab, "I'll call Vargas, too, and see if he can stop by."

The pilot, getting frustrated, asked, "And who the hell's Vargas?"

I had slipped. "Alberto Sabino," I amended. "The Brazilian who owns that big Lamberti yacht. His name throws me sometimes."

"Hold it a minute, Doc." Futch's no-bullshit tone demanded attention. "What *exactly* did this guy do to help us? Sharing the Avenger wreckage is one thing, but taking him to the *Bone Field,* my god."

"I wouldn't have pushed if I didn't think it was the safest solution," I said. "Put it this way: we'd all still be feeling crosshairs on our backs if it wasn't for what he did."

"Why is it I'm thinking you two pulled some-thing that could put all our asses in a sling?"

"You're better off not knowing, if that's what you're asking. If you want the truth, though, I'll tell you."

"Does Quirko know?"

"Yeah. He wasn't involved, but there's a reason he had to know some of it."

Futch, scratching the dog's chest, thought about that for a moment. Then said, "What the hell, go call the guy. His boat's big enough, we could use it as a mother ship instead of camping with the snakes and mosquitoes."

I smiled and said, "Thanks, skipper."

MY FIRST-AID KIT was below, packed aboard my boat for the trip, so I went into the lab and collected what I needed—gauze, spray to dull the pain, antibacterial salve—then turned and noticed I'd left my computer on, a letter from Dr. Arlis Milton of Atlanta still on the screen. So I stooped to read it for the fifth or sixth time:

Mr. Ford,

My wife and I are still in shock that the photos we sent confirm the lost dog is the same one you advertised in the classifieds of Retriever Magazine. With your per-mission, we will arrange to have him transported home to Georgia within the week. I understand your eagerness for an explanation as to how my late father-in-law's dog ended up lost in the Florida Everglades, and we much appreciate your generous refusal to accept a reward, or payments, for your trouble. However, I spoke with our attorney this morning and she advised me that precautions must be taken to protect our interests and yours and the dog's as well, especially since his microchip is no longer functioning and ownership might be in question.

I trust your motives 100%, but as a search on the Internet will prove, what my attorney calls "the dognapping industry" has made it necessary to follow what for me is an embarrassingly strict legal protocol. Please don't be offended, here is what my attorney suggests:

1. You must accept a reward and sign the attached agreement.

2. You must sign a waiver (attached) that holds our family free of any liability.

3. You must sign a release form (attached) that confirms you have no past or future claims on the dog.

These days, nothing is simple, is it? Once you have returned these documents, I will be happy to answer all questions, and look forward to buying you dinner if you ever visit Atlanta. As a reward, I am also pleased to offer you $500—it's great to know my late father-in-law's dog is alive and well, so I really must insist.

Arlis Milton, M.D.

That dog's valuable, I had told Tomlinson, and the letter proved it. No mention of the father-in-law's name, or the dog's name, his breed, his age, nothing—which indicated the information could be linked together on the Internet. And also suggested the animal was worth a lot more than five hundred.

Why? The photos Dr. Milton had sent weren't taken at Westminster or a field trial—not that he would have made the mistake—and the only thing remarkable about the animal was his oddities. Some kind of rare barkless breed, perhaps, known for its willingness to stay for hours on command before savaging the neighborhood boats and pool cleaners.

The only way to learn the truth was to sign the forms, which I had already done—but had yet to hit the *Send* button. No particular reason why. Even if I'd wanted to keep the retriever—which I didn't—the man I see in the mirror, although flawed, had yet to sink to something as reprehensible as stealing a family's dog.

Thinking that reminded me I was supposed to call Vargas Diemer. I did.

"Is this Alberto?" I asked tentatively.

"Alberto Sabino, Rio World Exports," the Brazilian replied, meaning we would stick with his alias.

"Dan Futch is here," I said. "I was thinking you two ought to meet."

"That explains the seaplane tied to your dock," Diemer replied—an attempt at humor, possibly. Then he offered further instructions, saying, "I hope you've told him I have a commercial license. So we can discuss airplanes sensibly?"

"He'll know it by the time you get here," I said.

Diemer ended that. "Your dog, I don't care to have him show me his teeth again. I'll open a Malbec and have cheese out. Your friend with the long hair, will he be—"

"Tomlinson has other plans," I interrupted.

"I see. Too drunk last night? Or was it drugs?" A judgmental tone that disapproved.

I responded, "You hear the music outside your door . . . Alberto? It's called a party. He's around here somewhere and he's doing just fine."

If I'd told the truth, Diemer's little trap wouldn't have worked, but I had stepped right into it. "*Really.* On the phone this morning, Cressa told me your friend gave her LSD. She sounded frightened, said he was in bad shape, too."

"Dan and I will be there in a little bit," I told him. "Anything else?"

"Ring the bell before coming aboard. And Dr. Ford? After the pilot leaves, I would like ten minutes alone to discuss something."

Back on a formal basis again. Which is why I tried a preemptive strike. "I had to tell Tomlinson about breaking into the house. I never said I wouldn't."

"That's not what I want to discuss," the Brazilian said and hung up.

25

WE WERE SITTING ON THE YACHT, cheese, wine, and a NA beer for Dan within reach—three wealthy dudes as we might have appeared to any stranger who had stumbled upon the party going on ashore. The fishing guides were done for the day, and some clients had stuck around to watch them cast-net mullet, then gut them for the grill, where hot dogs and oyster were already roasting. Several slips down, on *Tiger Lilly*, JoAnn or Rhonda had hit the outdoor speakers, and Buffett was doing "Havana Day Dreaming," recorded live, the volume just right so we could talk.

Dan was talking now.

"There's an old gentleman in Naples I've been after for years. He wouldn't talk to me, though.

But this morning—I'd just cleared customs, coming back from Nassau—and, out of the blue, I get a call. It's from the gentleman's granddaughter. Get this"—Futch, excited, put down his bottle—"he'd heard about the tail section we found. Suddenly, he wants to meet me. See, these old guys, they have their own network—"

Diemer interrupted, "He was a pilot during the war?"

Futch said, "Doc knows all this, but I should back up. The last ten, twelve years, I've been tracking down the Avenger pilots, a lot of them retired to Florida. Good guys, everyone I've met. After the war, they did their forty-year hitch at some job, you know, shoveling snow, raising kids, the regular crap, then came back where they trained as young guys. Palm Beach, Lauderdale, Key West—the military built more than fifty air bases in Florida within two years after Pearl Harbor—which makes it easy for me, 'cause I hit all those places on my charters."

"You have contact information for these men?" Diemer asked. "How many? They must be in their eighties or older."

From his briefcase Futch had taken out what looked like a scrapbook sheathed in plastic— "All family stuff. Don't even bother. Here's what's interesting"—then produced an envelope of old photos, some of them framed, others still Brownie-sized, with scalloped edges, and began sorting through them, his patient expression telling Diemer *I'm getting to it.*

He and the Swissair pilot had already gotten their sparring out of the way, each proving to the other that he knew airplanes and the esoteric language of aviation. Diemer, the ruling-class Castilian, and Dan, an heir to Florida history, hadn't exactly warmed to each other, but at least they weren't throwing punches.

Dan handed a photo to me and another to the Brazilian, saying, "So the guy's granddaughter calls—her name's Candice—and Candice tells me her grandfather is Angel J. Sampedro, then asks if it's true we found the tail off an Avenger. I recognize the name right away, so I know what's happened. See, that's what I was telling you, these old Avenger jocks, they have their own network. Tell one of them something it's, like, 'Screw the shuffleboard, get me a telephone!' and the information goes right down the line."

Futch, getting into it, and pleased with himself, turned to me. "So I called two Avenger pilots I know and told them what we'd found. Not exactly where, of course, but the general area just to see what would happen. Two days later"—he motioned toward the photo I was looking at— "Angel Sampedro suddenly says he wants to talk. A man who'd already turned me down twice, and his granddaughter says never even talks to the family about what he did in the war. Candice lives in Delray Beach, so I made a quick stop, and she loaned me these."

Photo in hand, I asked, "What's in the scrapbook?"

"She made me take it, but keep your grubby paws off. Christmas parties and dried flowers that I want to return in one piece. You're looking at the important stuff."

I asked Dan, "Which one is Sampedro?" then asked Diemer. "You have the same picture?"

No, but similar. Three aviators, skinny as teenagers and dwarfed by a single-engine Avenger, looked snappy in their flight suits and flotation vests, goggles silver in the Florida sun, which added a *Wings of Eagles* touch. *Dad, Feb. 1944*, in a woman's hand at the bottom. Sampedro was a head shorter than the others, although they all had a gaunt Tex-Mex look. He was one of those ropy, flyweight dudes you didn't mess with and you knew it from his cocky, combat-ready smile.

A second lieutenant, Dan told us, Navy, then added, "But all flyers were Army Air Corps back then. Mr. Sampedro finished his training just in time to see action in the South Pacific. Only three months before we dropped the bomb, but he still managed to win a Bronze Star, a Purple Heart, and his first lieutenant bars. That's why Candice is excited about her granddad talking to me. The man's ninety-one years old. He's running out of bypasses and time, and the family would like to know how he got those decorations."

"Fascinating," Diemer murmured, his glasses reflecting the faces of three young men who had learned to fly planes and fought a war that only seventy years later was already light-years in the past. "This," Diemer said, "was the time of *aviators,* not trained monkeys with computers. And autopilots and avoidance sensors and—what is the term?—*redundancy systems!* Hah! To live in the days of the Luftwaffe and Mustangs and those beautiful P-38s, I would"—the man removed his glasses to bring himself back—"well . . . it's why I find the subject of particular interest."

Futch and I exchanged looks. The Germanic Brazilian had actually shown emotion—a lapse he now tried to explain as he cleaned his glasses, then strapped them around his ears. "My grandfather was in . . . he was an elite soldier in the European Theater. I envy him. Even though he was killed in that war, I envy him"—Diemer focused on the photo—"all these men. They must have experienced an unusual . . . *clarity?*" He looked at me and shrugged. "English is a deficient language. *Êxtase y clareza*—that's what I'm describing is . . . it is a state of being that elevates the brain." Then sniffed to suggest *You wouldn't understand.*

But Futch did and pushed his NA beer away,

nothing more important than getting this straight. "Sure—I know exactly what you're saying. Just you, alone, an actual damn aviator with cables for arms and feet—part of the plane. Right? Throw the cowling back, you're *there*—a hundred fifty knots of wind in your face. Or do it in a cloud—you're soaked, but it's *real*. And the other guy, whoever you're fighting, it's real for him, too. A .50 cal machine gun in both ships—so you've got to find the line faster than him, make the right moves, do it all yourself—not like some video game where you can hit *Play Over*. Comes down to who's the better flyer."

Diemer's eyes sparked, but he tried to sound matter-of-fact. "The technical skills, yes. At air shows—fly into a cloud—in fact, I've done this. Silly, but it's something one tries. A Messerschmitt—my god, start the engine, how you say . . . *Seu coração treme*—your heart trembles! The meaning, though, is more masculine in my language."

Dan was smiling, enjoying himself, but didn't want to take this bonding bullshit too far. "Um-huh . . . but back to what I was saying—"

Which gave me a chance to hand him the photo and ask, "Is there one that shows the tail section of Mr. Sampedro's plane? Or maybe you already know if he trained at Lauderdale."

"That's the interesting part, if I can find the right one." Dan resumed going through photos,

325

careful to touch only the borders, a show of respect. "I'll know more after I talk with him tomorrow—that's if my Key Largo charter cuts me loose in time. If not, I'll visit him on Saturday, which means I'll get to Lostman's River whenever I get there, but Sunday for sure."

I asked, "Why not just call the granddaughter, set it up for late Sunday? He's at a place in Naples you said?"

"A full-care facility."

I looked at Diemer. "We spend all day Saturday, part of Sunday documenting wreckage, maybe we'd have something interesting to show the man. I'd like to hear what he has to say."

Dan said, "I'll call Candice to make sure it's okay." Then handed me a print with scalloped borders, asking, "Isn't that great?"

Just Angel J. Sampedro in the photo now, looking tiny because he was framed by two Avengers, only one of them showing big white numerals on the tail, 113, and white letters, FT, behind the starboard wing, which stood for "Lauderdale Torpedo." Maybe it was great, but I was confused. "You're not saying Sampedro crashed a plane when he was in training? I don't get the connection."

"Maybe there isn't one," Dan said. "I don't know which plane in the picture is his and neither does his granddaughter. That's the problem. But he spent time in Miami Naval Hospital a month before they shipped his group overseas. The Bronze Star and Purple Heart, the other Avenger pilots told me he was a combat vet, but Candice knew he was injured during training from her grandmother's old love letters."

The pilot reached into the briefcase again and brought out an oversized book, then paused, finally getting to what he'd wanted to tell me all along. "The Avenger in that picture *crashed*. On a night training mission. I was going through the book, made the connection about an hour before I landed here. Two planes went down that night somewhere between Cape Sable and Bonita Springs. Torpedo Bombers 113 and 54, neither ever found. And the timing's right—here, look for yourself."

Dan stood to give us room. "It took me two months to track down a copy of that book. It didn't arrive until two days ago, and there aren't many copies left, guys, so don't spill anything on it. Geezus."

Twelve hundred pages thick, cheaply bound: *Army Air Corps Statistics Division* *Airplane Accidents, Continental U.S. 1941-1946*

"They don't even list the crew!" Diemer said after a minute. "Not even a mention of the training mission—other crash records, the mission, are cited—I wonder why?" He sounded surprised— odd after what he'd said earlier. "How can an agency, anyone, maintain such sloppy records?"

"February seventh, nineteen forty-four," Dan said. "See? Even if Mr. Sampedro wasn't aboard, one of those planes could still be our Avenger. Which of course means we didn't find Flight 19 wreckage, but . . . what the hell. That's what we'll find out. Okay?"

I looked to see how the Brazilian accepted that. Not devastated, but maybe a wince of disappointment—hard to say, his face didn't show much. Then he dismissed it by opening up discussion, telling us, "Still an interesting project. If it's on federal land, as you say, we couldn't file claims on it anyway . . ."

WE SPENT ANOTHER half an hour going through photos and charts, letting it all hang out now in front of Vargas Diemer, who I was finally getting used to calling Alberto. He paid attention, took copious notes that he entered into a pocket notebook. Charts and satellite photos—I printed copies of both, then he pressed Dan and me for details. Was there a protected anchorage nearby? A place to camp since the nearest deepwater anchorage for his yacht was three miles away? Cell phone reception? Did the feds patrol the area by plane or boat? The Bone Field—like Tomlinson, Diemer was fascinated by the name and the ancientness of the place, but was frustrated by Dan's reluctance to share information.

"I'm not a grave robber. I respect history," he

said. "The age of this shell mound you describe—how old?"

"Long before Spanish contact," I said. "Two, three thousand years ago. The first archaeologist to visit this coast—this was in the late eighteen nineties—even then the mounds had four distinct sides. The archaeologist made drawings—they were actually pyramids, not just mounds." Because I'd answered for Futch, I sought his approval by asking, "Frank Hamilton Cushing, right? Sent by the Smithsonian."

Dan said, "He didn't visit the place we're talking about, though. Far as I know, no one's been there—*that's* what I want you to respect."

Diemer was ahead of him, already agreeing, saying, "I know of a similar place—of course! I've told no one. I say to you the word *Amazon,* you picture primitive people, jungle, yes? Yet, only a few years ago, I myself found the remains of a city. I was flying over the remote Xingu region. A bright day, the light shining just so, and I noticed the jungle was scarred by what looked like grids. A year later, I returned by canoe and hiked in. Alone. Always, I prefer to travel alone. What I found—*roads*. Evidence of roads built in grids. Remains of central plazas, what might be an aqueduct—and pyramids such as you describe. Made of stone, not shell. Built two thousand, three thousand years ago—the same time period as your Bone Field. I've told no one—the research . . . history, it's my passion." Diemer and Futch exchanged looks, one pilot asking another *Trust me now?*

Dan did, apparently, because he answered a dozen questions about the Bone Field and the plane wreckage, using satellite photos on which the Brazilian made tiny, precise notations.

Three times while they talked I texted Tomlinson, wanting him involved in this unfolding story of Florida and aviators during the 1940s but received only one response, which explained his inattention: *CA out of woods but still riding the snake. Pray for squalls.*

CA was Cress. The squalls were for Kondo the drug dealer, who quite possibly was adrift in moonlight miles from shore.

I gave it some thought while Futch and Diemer veered off into more esoteric talk of aviation. Tomlinson could play catch-up, and it would be fun to throw various theories back and forth on the boat trip to Lostman's River. So, yeah, it was okay.

I was getting a vacation feel for the project. Deano was in jail, his Bambi-eyed friend had been warned away, and the married mistress, once she recovered, would soon lose her ties to Dinkin's Bay. The heavy lifting was over. It was time to kick back, relax, and enjoy this new project.

I, too, am a history buff—prefer pre-Columbian to lost bombers, but all history is grafted from the same rootstock. A few days camping at the edge of the Glades would shear the electronic ties, plus the multiple bonuses of Tomlinson finally showing some backbone, finding the dog's owner, *and* recovering Crunch & Des—all in the same day—were reasons to celebrate. True, the problems with my running partner hadn't been resolved, but Hannah would come around. Other than that, how much better could it get?

What is often referred to as "life's flow" can as accurately be described as a stationary awareness of cascading events. Contextual changes that impact our individual reality—a reality that oscillates in operatic patterns, the waves sometimes spaced like teeth on a buzz saw. So we hunker down, weather the troughs, grab a breath through the foam, and hang on, awaiting that next glimpse of sky. This was one of those rare days, though, when the buzz saw had been flattened by a sudden and glassy wave. True, I'd made a bold move. And, yes, Diemer had appeared in my lab at precisely the right moment—but who knows why or what changes the polarity of our own luck, good or bad?

It was happening, that was enough. The wave was starting to curl nicely, so I was going to sit back, pack a book or two, maybe even my Celestron telescope, and enjoy the ride.

"Doc?" Diemer said. "Captain Futch says we're done. Something on your mind?"

Dan was standing, packing his briefcase, I realized, so I got to my feet, saying, "I was thinking about a waterproof bag for my telescope. I'm looking forward to this."

At the boarding ramp, though, the Brazilian stopped me again. "Oh! A question about marina policy. Five more minutes, Doc?"

Five minutes took only two, but what Diemer had to say was more than enough to put my vacation mood on hold—until I'd exited A-Dock into a party that was becoming a holiday in itself.

No way to dodge the voices hailing me or the beers thrust into my face.

But I did manage to text Tomlinson: *Call ASAP.*

26

IT WAS AFTER TEN, LATE FOR A Thursday night in February, when my pocket vibrated an alert. So I rushed to have a look at Tomlinson's response to my urgent text. It read:

Out of beer. Feed dog?

Which caused the woman at my shoulder to inquire, "I guess I should have asked: Are you *married?*" Then apologize, "Peeking at your texts! My god . . . what's in this punch?"

I didn't know. After two beers, I'd switched to iced tea. Giving her shoulder a squeeze, I replied, "The first time you came here, remember the hippie-looking guy I avoided because I figured he was a druggie, nothing but trouble? Well, he was—and he is. Hang on, I need to answer this."

"Tomlinson?" she asked. How many times had I winced at that rock star inflection? But it was a first for this woman.

"In fact," I said, "I should probably go. I need to leave before sunrise and I still have to go over my checklist on the boat."

Her hand slipped comfortably to my wrist, fingers light at first, but then they explored and tightened by rote—checking my pulse. "Not yet, Doc. *Please*—did I offend you?"

A hint of affection, which was nice but unnecessary. "Just the opposite," I told her. "You made my night."

Well, she had made it more fun, at least. But I still had to add, "Sher, I really do have to go."

It had been ten years since I'd seen Dr. Sheri Braun-Richards, but I'd recognized her immediately as I exited A-Dock, a woman who had been ripened, not diminished, by the years. Fuller-bodied, but still willowy in the way she moved, elfin hair, now auburn, to her shoulders, wearing a business skirt and jacket instead of hip-hugger jeans. Not tall, but the way her eyes panned, searching the marina, had isolated her even in a crowd, and I'd locked onto her face at the same instant she spotted me.

"Marion Ford . . . ? My god! You really do remember . . . ?"

Yes, I remembered.

"The first vacation after my internship—I'm *still* embarrassed about how I behaved!"

I remembered that, too.

So the doctor and I had spent an hour catching up. Nice. A decade is a solid chunk of time, so there was no posturing, no need for the plastic smiles or uneasiness typical of former lovers who meet unexpectedly. And because our relationship had been brief as the lady's vacation, there were no old wounds to deal with. On the other hand, I didn't feel an instant abdominal lusting or the drive to hustle the lady home to restage past bedroom scenes. But talking with Sheri was fun, produced a pleasant patina of nostalgia that was . . . well, *nice*.

The attractive gynecologist with the probing smile and sharp blue eyes had moved her practice from Davenport to Atlanta and then shortened her name to Sheri Braun after the divorce. Now she was head of her department, no children, just a cat, living fifty miles up the beach in Venice. She hadn't returned to Sanibel until agreeing to speak this weekend at a conference at "Port Sanibel"— the newest marketing perversion of "Punta Rassa," where the old telegraph office had somehow managed to survive.

"Venice is so pretty, and it isn't far," Sheri reminded me. "Maybe we could have lunch sometime."

Lunch dates are time wasters to be avoided like

the plague but I heard myself reply, "I'd like that a lot," then glanced at the time before explaining, "Look, Tomlinson's dealing with a sick friend— that's why I have to run. It's not just the boat trip."

When Sheri replied, "I *am* a doctor and I *am* licensed in Florida," it also meant *I'll leave my friends and come along.* A good idea, it seemed, but then pictured Cressa Arturo waiting in my lab, drug-addled but still assertive in a space that she behaved as if she owned. So I dodged the offer by tapping my head and saying, "The friend's problems are up here, but maybe this won't take long. You plan on staying awhile?"

When the lady nodded, her hair bounced, framing the good smile that had not changed in a decade and, hopefully, would not be changed by the marauding decades to come.

Our farewell hug was longer, tighter, included a quick brush of the lips, then I was off.

"**SHE'S WAITING IN THE MERCEDES,**" Tomlinson told me when I came into the lab. Cressa, he added, was suffering what he called a delayed lysergic reaction, which I realized, after a moment, referred to LSD in the pot they'd smoked. He was sitting at my desk, watching the wall of lighted aquariums, ribbon streaks of fish within, as if it were a theater screen—*Fantasia*, perhaps. The dog, lying near the desk, used one droopy eye to convey boredom. He had been chewing at a hunk of hawser line, pieces everywhere.

"How are you feeling?" I asked my pal.

"Came down slow, but I'm back on the planet," he said. "Not Cressa. It hits her in waves, the panic, then paranoia. She seemed okay last night, but it came back. That's unusual—flashbacks were invented by screwheads and *Reader's Digest*. Makes me wonder how the Voodoo Prince poisoned our shit. Christ, belladonna, plant alkaloids, who knows? Cells from a pituitary gland ripped from a human throat, I wouldn't put it past him."

I said, "I'm driving you both to the ER. Don't argue." The swelling had gone down in my left hand, I could use it, no problem, but it crossed my mind to maybe get the damn thing X-rayed while we were there.

Tomlinson turned away from the fish tanks, startled. "I'm fine, man, really. And she's getting better. The shit was more like a Nitrox dive. It takes you deeper and longer, but you still have to put in the decompression time. Mostly, she's paranoid about her father-in-law. That's why she locked herself in the car and won't come inside. Nothing to do with you."

I moved toward the door, but he stopped me. "I just checked on her. She's in a calm cycle now, but still scared. Doesn't want to be around people."

"Can't hurt for me to say hello," I replied, then went out the door after signaling the dog not to follow.

The Mercedes SUV was parked inside the gate, engine running, a strand of white LEDs showing beneath each dark headlamp. I let Cressa get a long look at me before I approached yet she lowered the window only a few inches.

"I'm staying here, so don't bother!" Her voice was shaky, but had an aggressive edge that warned me not to push.

"Need some water, a blanket maybe?" I asked. "It's cooling off tonight." To put her at ease, I'd stopped two paces from the door.

"The police arrested Deano today! He told me you watched the whole sick business . . . that *you* set him up! Tomlinson says no, but I think you lied to him, too."

The windows were tinted, but moonlight showed a band of blond hair and two haunted silver eyes that, at once, accused me and feared me. Music played inside, classical and soothing— therapy of Tomlinson's selection, I assumed. Calm, serene, violins playing now.

My voice softened in an attempt to blend. "You're right, you can trust Tomlinson. *I* told police where to find your brother-in-law, you're exactly right. He's dangerous, Cressa. Maybe he'll be okay one day, but he needs downtime. Give him some space. Same with his friend, Luke—"

"Stay away from him, too! You attacked Luke, tried to kill him—that's what he told me, and

Lucas wouldn't lie to me! I know the *real* you. I warned Luke that you were dangerous."

I took a step back. No surprise that she'd spoken to her brother-in-law, and now was not the time to ask about Luke. *Enough,* I decided, so told her, "The important thing, Crescent, is for *you* to be safe. Lock your doors, listen to the music. I'll send Tomlinson out now. Okay?"

The woman sniffled at this unexpected kindness from a "dangerous" man, and I got a glimpse of the familiar handkerchief. "No. Tell him . . . tell him I want a few minutes to ride this out. When I saw you, it came back. Go away. Ten minutes alone . . . I'll be fine."

"Anything else I . . . that *Tomlinson* can do for you?"

Sounding more like Cressa the married mistress, she explained, "I've never experienced anything so awful, Doc. The drugs we smoked, it's like I'm trapped inside my own skull. There's a . . . *burning* sensation, it comes out of nowhere. Then the panic and the crazy colors come next. I just want it to stop. Dear god, how I want it to stop! Ten minutes, tell him . . . I can't talk now."

The window closed.

When I turned toward the lab, Cressa Arturo, in silhouette, had buried her face in cupped hands.

"INSTEAD OF PLAYING GAMES with the Haitian's engine," I told Tomlinson, "you should go to the state's attorney and help put him in prison. The son of a bitch is worse than a killer. Who knows how many people he's screwed up, scarred for life? If you don't, I will. And damn it, take Cressa to a doctor now!"

"Kondo definitely plays by his own rules," Tomlinson agreed but sounded evasive. Then chose to educate me, the unhip biologist, about druggie protocol instead of explaining why he couldn't narc-out a fellow dealer.

"The whole hospital scene—white coats, the stink of alcohol, and elevators—it would only add to her paranoia, Doc. I've been through this too many times. Physical symptoms, sure, you call for help. Twelve hours from now, she's still bad off, you bet. But the acid in her brain is tapering off, man, I can tell—sort of like a clothes dryer at the end of its cycle. Plus, it would be a big mistake to get Crescent's in-laws involved, understand what I'm saying? And that's what the hospital drones would have to do."

"Not even her husband knows?"

Tomlinson's expression replied *No, thank god,* then he continued, "What it all boils down to, man, her head was in the worst possible space to travel chemically. Why? Because she was *already* paranoid. Even a tab of classic Kesey Sunshine can't change what you bring to the party. Don't always blame the drugs! See, Crescent's scared shitless of what might happen if she divorces. That's what the drug is feeding on."

I hadn't mentioned stealing a copy of the prenuptial agreement, but I hinted at it now, saying, "I'm convinced her prenup doesn't include an infidelity clause. She gets written out of the old man's will, so what?"

"No, it's what the old man might do to her. That he might have her killed if Deano squeals about her sleeping with me—*and* sleeping with the guy who whacked you with that spear."

"Smith, *too?*" I said.

"Who's . . . ? *Oh.* Right, the guy who broke your hand. Yeah, she opened up to me last night. Calls him Lucas or Luke. But her thing with him, Luke—*Smith*—was just a one-time deal. Too much wine, a big lonely house—you know how those things go—and very recent. Other than that, Crescent's been a straight arrow, sexually speaking, which would drive anyone into a stranger's bed. Now she doesn't care if Robby finds out or not—force him into a divorce, see? But the father-in-law's a different story. She's afraid of the whole Mafioso deal, that's my read."

Something else I hadn't told Tomlinson was what Smith—Bambi—had said about Cressa's affair with Robert Sr. The married mistress had obviously omitted that little detail, too, but I let it go. "Take her home and get some sleep. Sunrise is around seven, and I want to be on the water by first light."

When Tomlinson replied, "Doc, that's what I stopped to tell you," I knew what was coming. He was worried about Cressa. He wasn't going to leave her alone.

"Can't believe I'm asking this, but maybe I could fly down Saturday with Dan. Or the Brazilian Nazi, is he still taking his boat? A boat that size, he needs an extra hand."

To give myself time I replied, "How about a beer?" before I remembered there was none so switched my offer to Gatorade or tea.

"Rum would hit the spot," he replied. "There's still about four fingers of Eldorado left, but I hid the bottle and can't remember where." He had lost interest in the fish and was attempting tug-of-war with the dog but paused to say, "Doc . . . mind some advice? You've got to start being more careful about who we let in here. Or buy a beer fridge with a lock."

27

I WENT PAST THE BOOKSHELVES INTO the kitchen and opened the little oven where I had rehidden the bottle of Eldorado that Tomlinson had stashed under the sink. As I got ice, I was thinking about my two-minute conversation with Vargas Diemer. The Brazilian had asked—no, *urged*—me to leave Tomlinson behind in the morning. Said he was worried the effects of the LSD would cause some kind of screwup. I'd refused, of course, and was now wondering if he had enlisted Cressa to put additional pressure on Tomlinson to stay.

Why would the Brazilian be so insistent? And *devious?* If Diemer wasn't leaving for the Bone Field until tomorrow night, a Friday, what did it matter if I arrived alone tomorrow morning? My suspicions struck me as nonsensical until I'd sorted through potential motives.

I came up with three possible explanations. In two, Tomlinson wouldn't be able to deal with the fallout in his current state, so the Brazilian was right in a way. He was better off staying here an extra day. In the third, though, Sanibel was the more dangerous place because, in that scenario, Robert Arturo Sr. played the role of Diemer's target. And if Tomlinson happened to be at the beach house, and if he happened to get in the way . . . ?

But as I pictured it, the threads came unraveled. Why would the jet-set assassin court the mistress of a man he'd been hired to kill? Why would he risk robbing Cressa's safe? Why the hell would he moor his yacht less than a mile from her beach house?

As I poured rum over ice, I forged several decrepit explanations, then discarded them. *No . . .*

The father-in-law might be worthy of an enemy's bullet, but he wasn't Diemer's target. The Brazilian was too good at what he did. He was here for a *reason,* I no longer doubted, but he was too skilled a technician to drag his spore over an X spot—a killing zone—more than once.

Convinced of it, I placed Tomlinson's glass on the desk next to him, saying, "I think an extra day on Sanibel's a good idea. Fly down with Dan. But do me a favor—stay off Diemer's boat, okay?"

My pal had given up on tug-of-war and was sitting in front of the computer. *"Whose?"* he asked, not turning.

I'd slipped again. "I mean the Brazilian," I said. "He's got a weird vibe about him."

"The Nazi dude, yeah, no kidding. I don't think he gives a damn about the Bone Field or the wreckage. What's he really up to, you think?"

"He's not a Nazi," I replied, "and he knows almost as much about Flight 19 as Dan. It was a hobby long before he came to Dinkin's Bay, so you're wrong. Thing is, he's got his eye on Cressa. Which means he sees you as competition. That's why I want you to stay away. You two alone on a boat is just asking for trouble."

The letter from the dog's Atlanta owner was on the computer screen, I realized, so Tomlinson only bobbed his head a couple times to agree with me. Then said in an offhand way, "Cressa, she actually is a good person, you know."

He expected a response. Instead, I poured a dab of rum into my iced tea and stirred it with the closest thing handy, a scalpel.

"Women who aren't allowed to follow their own paths," he mused, "either fake it until their spirit shrivels up and dies or they fight for their lives by going underground. Cressa was forced underground. I can't blame her for that."

Before I could tell him he was misguided, Tomlinson shifted the subject to the letter. "This has gotta be a joke, right? You rescue the family dog, now this guy wants you to jump through his legal hoops? Screw him, that's what I say."

"Some of my e-mails are in Spanish," I replied. "If you need help translating, let me know."

Right over his head. "Not a problem, usually, but this one really burns my butt, man."

"Because you're so sensitive," I countered, then gave up by reminding him the woman was waiting in the car, and also offered a warning: "Keep an eye out for the Haitian tomorrow. Sooner or later, someone'll tow his boat in. And he's going to be pissed! Straight for *No Más*, that's what I think. He'll try to catch you alone. So stay at Cressa's place . . . no, that's no good either. Whether she admits it or not, Kondo might have sold Deano drugs through her. So it's better if you both stay here." I waited a moment. "You hear me?"

"Atlanta!" Tomlinson exclaimed, noticing the letterhead. "They're saying the dog ran away and

survived all that insane traffic? Even if he did, this dog's a stud with brains—he would've stopped in Central Florida, not gone clear to the Everglades. All the nice lakes up there, loaded with ducks and trees. Lots of cute little poodles, college girls with golden retrievers—but our guy chooses the land of giant snakes and gators instead? I don't *think* so."

"That's my personal mail you're reading," I reminded him.

"The dog's yours, too, by rights. That's why I'm trying to help."

"Don't help me," I said. "I hate it when you try to help me."

Tomlinson replied, "It's no trouble, really," while his fingers moved like spiders across the keyboard. Now the legal forms were on the screen and he looked up, his expression showing disbelief. "You actually signed this bullshit! Doc, the guy's an asswipe, you can't tell? It was his *father's* dog, not his. And the dog's happy here— aren't you, boy!"

The dog snatched the chunk of rope away as a boney hand sought his ears, Tomlinson adding, "This doctor dude sent you an ultimatum, not a thank-you note. What you should do is refuse to go along with the attorney. Hell, maybe that's what the guy wants. You signed on the dotted line, so what? As long as you haven't sent these stupid forms yet." Tomlinson turned. "You didn't . . . *did you?*"

No, I hadn't sent the documents, but I would, so I nodded as if it was already done, then blocked more second-guessing, telling him, "Cressa needs to go home. And don't forget what I told you about Kondo."

Finally, the name grabbed his attention. *"Kondo?"* Tomlinson spun the chair around. "What about that pigmy bastard?"

Opening the door, I repeated what I'd said, then shooed him outside while the man continued to argue, reminding me that if I changed my mind, I had several lady friends who'd be eager to dog-sit when I was away on trips.

The reference only made me more eager to be alone. Sheri Braun, I remembered, might still be awaiting my return to the party. Then, for some reason, my thoughts transitioned to Hannah Smith. Hannah was still on my mind as I watched Tomlinson vanish into the mangroves.

A THURSDAY NIGHT in February, and for once I had the house and lab to myself. Still plenty of time to . . .

Do what?

I could finish loading the boat: a twenty-six-foot Zodiac I had recently purchased through contacts at the special ops base at MacDill in Tampa—a confiscated drug runner's boat supposedly, but I knew otherwise. Still had my checklist to run through to make sure power and electronics were operational. Talking over old times with Sheri Braun was a tempting option. Or . . . what about Hannah?

My former workout partner, still on my mind as I flexed my left hand, movement and feeling returning.

Hannah lived two miles across the bay where she was fixing up a pretty little Marlow cruiser. Lived alone, I reminded myself, at the fishermen's coop docks. No one else around at that isolated place, just a couple of security lights—a damn lonely spot for a single woman. But was it too late to bother her?

Probably not. Diemer had canceled their fishing trip, so, presumably, she didn't have to be up at sunrise to catch bait. In fact, an hour before midnight was *early* for a woman with a day off, and the party outside was going strong. So why not do the friendly, neighborly thing and call?

I thought about it as I returned to the lab and taped feeding instructions to each aquarium for Janet Nicholes, my friend and occasional assistant. When faced with a difficult decision, I sometimes use paper to list the pros in one column, the cons in another, and then compare. Tonight, though, I did it mentally and was soon disappointed because the cons won: Hannah hadn't responded to messages I'd left yesterday and this morning. Calling now would seem pushy . . . even desperate. Which, of course, I wasn't—an attractive lady doctor was only a short walk away, down the shoreline where music still played and where, as I could see through the window, someone had lit a circle of tiki torches that blazed beneath the moon.

Desperate? Not Marion D. Ford. There were several women available if I wanted company—more, if I put my mind to it. Any of them—well, at least one, maybe two—would be damn happy to get a call.

Nope, I concluded. Calling Hannah Smith at this hour was childish. End of subject.

The decision, however, put me in an inexplicably sour mood that, in turn, caused me to demonstrate my resolve. I sat at the computer, the retriever at my feet, and reviewed the legal documents I had scanned, signed, and that were waiting to be returned to Dr. Arlis Milton.

The forms looked in order. After a second review, I opened the e-mail to which I'd attached the documents and placed the cursor on the *Send* button. Nothing to it. Click the button and the rightful owner could claim the retriever whenever he chose. But then the jet-set assassin's adage came into my mind and caused my finger to hesitate.

Pull the trigger and you can never stop the bullet.

I sat there for several seconds, the concept percolating in my brain. The adage was true. I knew it better than most. The long-term resonance that pulling a trigger, any form of trigger, guaranteed was another truth I had experienced. But there was something else I knew: facts are the least malleable derivative of truth, and a singular fact in this instance was this: the dog wasn't mine.

Pulling triggers is something you're good at, I reminded myself. It was an accusation that fit my perverse mood. So I did it. Used my middle finger to hit the *Send* button with conviction—*WHAP!*—and, a moment later, my decision was irrevocable.

Interested, the retriever looked up.

"It was the right thing to do," I told him. "At least I'll find out who the hell you really are."

The dog's rump arched into a pyramid while he yawned and got his legs under him. He took two steps, then dropped a heavy chin on my knee, his yellow eyes staring into mine.

"Too late for that boloney," I warned him. "Your psychic powers suck."

The dog's ears perked until his brain discarded the words as unrecognizable. Did the same thing when I added, "The cat—Crunch & Des—he'd just make your life miserable anyway."

I was scratching the dog's neck just above the snakebite, the area greasy with salve, which I bent to examine. Big snake, so a big chunk of skin was missing—four inches of flesh fringed by a scimitar of scabs. The boa's recurved teeth had buried themselves there while the two animals had battled it out. Seeing the puncture wounds, the size of the bite, caused me to scratch at the bandage that covered what remained of the teeth marks on my arm and also re-created the reality of what had happened that day. *One hell of a fight,* I'd told Tomlinson. I smiled, picturing it.

Soon, my smile flattened because what I visualized was not amusing. A sixty-pound snake, lying in wait, strikes, locks his teeth into the dog just above the shoulder, then begins to subdue its thrashing prey with the first systematic loop as its body coils. One hell of a fight? No, I was wrong about that. What I visualized was life attempting to snatch fuel from death . . . the indifferent struggle of selection . . . one energized entity determined to ingest the beating heart of another.

The outcome, however, had made a mockery of my Darwinian script. The results defied all odds, all logic, all reason: a reptile perfected over eons, a dog—once a wolf—whose genetics had been artificially selected by hobbyists . . . tinkered with, refined, into a purebred mold that should have banished it from the food chain hierarchy and deposited it *inside* the snake's belly.

In this dog, though, the wolf had resurfaced. He had attacked his attacker and made a meal of him. Imagining how the encounter had actually gone produced in me the briefest flicker of . . .

something. It wasn't emotion—a sense of clarity, the Brazilian might have described it—and my mood changed.

"Screw reason," I told the dog. "You're a survivor."

Impatient with my gibberish, the animal shifted his attention to the chunk of rope as if comparing its entertainment value to my own.

"Screw logic, too," I added, and that did it. The chunk of hawser won out. The dog turned his butt to me and carried the rope to the only clean spot on the floor and began shredding it.

Outside, the moon overhead, I looked north toward the mouth of Dinkin's Bay. Because my cell phone happened to be in my pocket, I called Hannah Smith.

28

AN HOUR BEFORE SUNRISE, I IDLED past the sleeping portholes and listless halyards of A-Dock, where, just beyond solar lights that rimmed *Seduci*, I noticed a gaping hole in the mooring pattern: the Stiletto ocean racer was gone.

How the hell had I missed hearing those big engines fire up?

Well, probably because I'd been on the phone

past midnight talking to Hannah, then pulled a pillow over my head to get a few hours' sleep. Our conversation had begun with a chill, but had ended, an hour later, with admissions that so closely resembled affection I was still rattled. I didn't want to marry the woman, for christ's sake, but the fact she was often on my mind was reason enough to pursue the relationship. Get to know her better—*slowly*. When I saw that the Stiletto was gone, though, all thoughts of that vanished and I veered left just enough to confirm it was true.

Yes . . . during the few hours I'd slept, someone had slipped into the marina, started the boat, and left—the owner, presumably, because the marina gates had been locked earlier when I'd taken the dog for a last visit to the mangroves. Of course, the owner—or thieves—could have come by water. The driver could have also maneuvered the racing boat clear of the basin using steering thrusters—water jets normally used to facilitate docking—then started the engines far from the docks.

What to do? It was 5:45 on a February morning. Over the Gulf, at tree level, the moon mimicked sunset, a pale and heatless hole in the darkness. The east was black with stars that appeared to drift behind immobile clouds. Should I call Jeth? Alert Mack?

Mack lives in a piling house beyond the boat

ramp, to the right of the mechanic's shed. No lights on there. Tomlinson's dinghy was ashore, the cabin of *No Más* dark, so he was staying with Cressa. My attention panned from the apartment above the marina office, to *Tiger Lilly*, to *Playmaker*, then along the row of cruisers and sailboats—everyone still asleep. Aboard the Brazilian's yacht, though, cabin lights were on but dim. A pale blue flickering suggested a television screen or lighted candles. If Diemer was awake, he would have heard or seen *something* because the Stiletto had been in the neighboring slip.

I pushed the twin throttles forward and idled toward *Seduci*. A boat length away, I shifted to neutral and revved my engines a couple of times. Waited several seconds, then did it again. No sign of movement inside, no telltale swipe of curtains, so Diemer was asleep or . . . or he wasn't aboard.

The possibility nagged at me for a moment, then I dismissed it. So what? My pal Donald Cheng had checked on the Stiletto. The vessel was owned by a Miami company that sponsored boats in the Offshore Grand Prix and the Key West International race series. No connection—not with the Brazilian anyway. So I turned the Zodiac toward the channel, running lights out because the moon illuminated Dinkin's Bay with a pumpkin gloss so bright I could see that, aside from *No Más*, the bay was empty.

No Más . . . my eyes settled on the sailboat as I approached the *No Wake* buoys. The cabin dark, Tomlinson's dinghy tied near the boat ramp, as it often was when he was gone for the night—nothing unusual, so why was I still troubled by the missing ocean racer?

Damn it!

I shifted to neutral and called Tomlinson's cell. No answer, and no need to leave a message—the time stamp would tell him the call was important. It did, because my phone flashed a few seconds later, and Tomlinson, sounding groggy, said, "If you're calling about your truck, yes, I stole it."

I asked, "You're with Cressa at her beach house?"

"At the Holiday Inn, unless someone levitated my ass to a different place. Middle Gulf Drive. But don't tell anybody—especially that vicious little voodoo monster, Kondo. Geezus, what time is it?"

"The Haitian came to the marina?"

Whispering now, Tomlinson said, "Could be. I'm in hiding. Geezus, not even six yet, man! Is the dog sick?"

"How do you know Kondo's after you? Someone must have towed him in."

"Hang on, I don't want to wake her up." I heard the click of a door latch before Tomlinson resumed, "Two-bedroom suite, you believe it? Because she wanted me to, I rubbed her neck until she went to sleep, then snuck off to my own room. That was around one, and my willpower is running dead on empty. I thought you'd be on your way to the Bone Field by now."

"Tell me about Kondo!"

"Christ, you don't have to bite my head off. I'm the one he threatened to kill."

"You *did* talk with him."

"No. And I deleted his messages after listening to the first one. But his texts, man, the way they flow—he writes in dialect—they're, like, hypnotic. Can't help myself. It's like reading Matthiessen— *Far Tortuga*—only not as authentic, which is weird if you really think about it."

I said, *"Tomlinson . . ."*

"Okay! A guy out mackerel fishing towed him and his buddies to Punta Rassa. Little bastard had his feet on the ground just about the time the party was ending for Crunch & Des. That was the first message I got. The guy, this mackerel fisherman, turns out he's also a mechanic and he squealed to Kondo that I'd loosened all the spark plugs."

"The mechanic blamed *you?*"

"That *someone* did it, and was lucky the engine didn't blow up. Kondo, he's vicious, but he's not dumb. Plus, he had to pay the mechanic like five hundred bucks, but he's probably lying about that. You know, like I'm supposed to reimburse him before he cuts my nuts off—that was how the first message started. Next one was that he would feed me Epsom salts until I turned into a zombie and parade me around Port-a'-Prince on a leash. You know, let the kiddies have fun with his pet white demon."

"Did anyone follow you to the hotel?"

"Wait, this is how I know he's serious. Next ten texts, he's apologizing, telling me, 'Hey, mon, you doan know a joke when you hear your good frien' Kondo tell a joke?' Wants me to meet him for a drink at the Rum Bar. Then some bar on Fort Myers Beach. See? Guy's *smart*. I call the cops, the only thing I got in writing is apologies and invitations to have fun."

"Did you tell Cressa?"

"Upset her? You kidding?"

"But she knows who he is."

"Turns out, yeah. You were right. Deano bought pharmaceuticals from the guy. She'd lied to me all along, but tonight finally told the truth. Bad as the acid was, it might have opened her up as a person."

"Always a silver lining," I said. "*Cressa* was buying drugs from the Haitian?"

"That part she was vague about. Me giving her a nickel baggie, I think it's what put Kondo on my ass in the first place—that's the way I met her, the two of us shooting the shit on the beach. Nice pretty married lady who wanted to have some fun for a change."

"Cut your nuts off," I muttered.

"Wear them around his neck, yeah, or make a bolo out of them." Tomlinson's voice softened, his way of becoming serious. "Kondo's reputation on the party circuit, he's a sweetheart. A fun little actor, but I knew he was bad. I just didn't know how bad. Cressa's gonna be okay, so what I think I'll do is turn her over to her hubby, hop on *No Más*, and see a new part of the Old World. I haven't transited the Canal in a while, and Panama's got some of the best surfing in the world."

I didn't ask, *What about the Avenger wreckage?* It would only embarrass the man by forcing him to admit he was scared shitless. So I asked him again, "Are you sure no one followed you?"

"How would I know? On Middle Gulf this time of year, everyone drives fifteen goddamn miles an hour. A funeral could have passed us, traffic was so backed up." Then he said, "I've got to piss, so don't worry. It's not your phone."

Engines in neutral, the Zodiac's hull vibrated beneath me and had drifted so I could see the marina a hundred yards away: streamers of silver water linked to security lights that showed A-Dock and the Stiletto's empty slip. I waited until Tomlinson said, *"That's* better," before asking him, "Does Kondo own a boat? Not the rental boat, his own boat."

"Hang on," he replied, and I heard a door click shut. Then, sounding more like himself, "I don't know. Probably. He's got a condo on Naples

Beach—Coquina Sands. There's a steel drum ditty for you: Kondo's Coquina Condo . . . no, Kondo's Cosmic Condo . . ."

"Anybody you could check with?" I interrupted, then told him, "Never mind. It doesn't matter. Did Cressa know you planned to go to Lostman's River this morning?"

"The Bone Field, yeah. But I just told you, I'm not—"

"Does she know you've changed your mind?"

"Well, I'm right here with her, aren't I? At the damn Holiday Inn, with my laundry bag and a shoeshine cloth."

"Stay there," I told him. "Order room service, don't go anywhere—especially not her beach house."

"What about the dog!"

"Between Janet and Hannah, that's all taken care of."

"*Hannah?* It's about time you smartened up!"

"Pay *attention*," I said. "Don't go anywhere until you hear from me. Understand?"

I put the phone in my pocket and throttled toward the mouth of Dinkin's Bay.

29

THREE MONTHS I'D OWNED THE ZODIAC and had come to the conclusion it wasn't the boat for me, but perfect for what I was doing now: running forty-plus in darkness through light chop, lights of the Sanibel Causeway ahead, a few cars already tunneling their way toward the island where windows sparked behind coconut palms.

I'd bought the twenty-six-foot rigid hull inflatable because it was unexpectedly available, it was equipped like nothing on the civilian market, and it would allow me to run offshore in weather that my previous boat, a Maverick flats skiff—as solid as it was—couldn't handle. So I'd made a snap decision, which is the worst possible thing a boat buyer can do, but the result was only mildly disappointing, not disastrous as it is for most.

The Zodiac had all the high-tech touches: a bolstered T-top, radar tower aft, a cavernous console, an electronics suite shielded by Plexiglas, Ullman shock-mitigating seats mounted on a forgiving deck, and a full-length Kevlar shoe beneath a collar of rigid black tubes that looked bulletproof—and maybe were, considering the agency that had ordered the boat as a prototype. For power: twin Mercury 200s, top speed over sixty, a range of three hundred miles with extra gas bladders—to Cuba and back or more than halfway to the Yucatán. Great if you've got to bull through a hurricane and drop SEAL operatives on a beach but too much draft and too much boat for Dinkin's Bay.

A very comfortable choice, though, for a fifty-mile trip to Lostman's River and the Bone Field, so I should have been having fun with my new toy.

I wasn't. The black-hulled Stiletto was on my mind. And a Haitian drug dealer who had an appetite for revenge when he wasn't partying with wealthy clientele. My cousin Ransom's voice reminding me, *The rich ones, they think it very cool to have their own Haitian voodoo man they invite for drinks when they in Jamaica, Saint Martin.* Ransom's voice stressing, *That boy get around!*

Jet-set partiers . . . a Caribbean supplier . . . a jet-set assassin—but there was no tenable connection! One of the country's top intel gatherers, Donald Cheng, had told me himself—the Stiletto was owned by some faceless company involved with offshore racing.

Stop obsessing, Ford. If you cross the line, vigilance becomes pathology. Shallow up! Float on—enjoy the ride.

The Zodiac's storage console was chest high. Big enough for a chemical toilet, a handheld shower, and an electrically cooled Igloo. I told myself to be decadent, break a long-standing rule and have a

360

breakfast beer. Instead, I fished out a Snapple, Diet Peach, the bottle cool in my left hand. Took another look inside the locker and considered my khaki gun bag—an old 9mm Sig Sauer pistol therein, a smaller, lighter 9mm Kahr, too, plus a box of Hornaday Critical Defense ammo and fifty rounds of Remington for plinking if I got the chance.

Put the Sig on the console just in case?

I asked myself the question, then mocked myself by answering, *In case of what? Steer the damn boat and look at the stars!*

After idling beneath the causeway, I muscled the boat back onto plane, bow pointed at the robotic eye of the Sanibel Lighthouse, and left the channel behind, both Merc outboards synced at 4000 rpm. Off the lighthouse, eons of tidal flow have piled sandbars. Cut in close to the point, though, water is deep enough, so that's what I did, aware that the Holiday Inn was only a few miles up the beach. Then steered west toward a blazing moon that was melting into blackness that was the Gulf of Mexico.

Big moon, key lime yellow. Add rings, it could have been Saturn spinning out of orbit and about to collide with the Earth. I pinned the autopilot to the moon as if it were a target, switched the VHF to Weather Band III, then leaned back, checked the gauges, while a digitized voice reported: ". . . Cape Sable to Tarpon Springs, wind southeast ten to fifteen, decreasing by midday . . ."

Good. Finally, a chance to let my mind drift freely . . . free, at least, to browse the universally limited list of male standbys: sex, unfinished projects, my children, sex, how would the Rays do this year? women, sex, surfing—did Tomlinson ever pay me for that damn paddle?—fishing, sex, women . . .

It was a path that soon fixed my attention on last night's conversation with Hannah.

Friday evening, her mother's bingo night a week away, I was taking the lady to dinner. An actual date. Not a typical catch-kill-and-grill at my place, either. We would travel by car, not boat—well, by truck actually—to a fine restaurant, a place with tablecloths, mojitos, and the best Yucatán shrimp on the islands. Later, maybe stop by the lab to have coffee beneath the stars—Hannah's suggestion, not mine. Which still rattled me because, as I reminded myself yet again, to the Hannah Smiths of this world, a date is not just a date, and the bedroom—if *that* ever happened—meant a hell of a lot more than a recreational romp.

Spooky, indeed, yet I'd felt unexpected relief after our talk. Almost as if I'd been waiting to breathe for a short time and could suddenly heave my chest full and enjoy the next big breath to come. No explaining it—I barely knew the woman. Not really. But that good feeling was still with me while my mind returned to browsing: *oil pressure, water temp, all gauges good . . . nudge*

the rpms up to 4500 . . . next lab project . . .
women, sex: Hannah naked, or even topless, my
god!

That was something fun to visualize, and I did
while I turned the boat southeast and typed in a
digital heading of 147 degrees. Hit autopilot, a
sip of tea, reduced radio volume, looked to port,
starboard, spun around for a look aft, then my
brain resumed scanning mode.

Weather radar: *Pod of squalls, red dots off the*
Tortugas . . . how the hell do you reduce range?
Remote toggles? No . . . touch screen . . .
Hannah's a big girl, too, solid . . . so I walk in, no
way of knowing, and there she is in my bed, blouse
unbuttoned, one long leg canted just so—she
pulls a stunt like that, what's she expect me to do?

Open the Plexiglas shield, punch buttons but
without much confidence, engage the radar
system I did not need on this clear black morning,
a rim of orange heat fast expanding in the east.
My mind still streaming:

Too damn many electronics, screws my night
vision . . . the dimmer button, where is it? Or . . .
better yet, find Hannah waiting in panties and
bra, nipples right there under a meshy sort of
material and she knows it! . . . Pale nipples, or
maybe darker, when the straps slide off her
shoulders—unless some drunk knocks on the
door . . . or if the dog . . .

I closed the cabinet and sat, unaware of what

I'd done, as the flow of consciousness continued: *. . . or if the dog, humm, the dog—the owner, bet he's gotten the forms by now. Damn it all, was getting rid of that dog a mistake? No . . . screw it, hair all over my sheets, with a woman lying in bed waiting, her bra on the floor, wearing nothing but . . . Humm?*

Interesting diversion: *By definition, is a woman actually naked if there's a ring on her finger? Argue all I wanted, Hannah would by god expect it!*

The radar system booted, the screen sweeping pixelated circles around the Zodiac: *BLIP . . . BLIP . . . BLIP . . .* Then suddenly faster: *BLIP-BLIP-BLIP . . .*

I studied the screen a moment, thinking: *That can't be right.*

The pulse increased, the sound of an accelerating heartbeat: *BLIP-BLIP-BLIP . . . BLIP-BLIP-BLIP . . .*

Out loud, I said, "What the hell's wrong with the radar?"

BLIP-BLIP-BLIP-BLIP-BLIP! Then a chiming warble—a collision alarm.

"Jesus Christ, there's nothing out here to hit!"

Four minicomputer screens aglow in video game colors: depth, navigation, Doppler weather, and the digital ping of radar. So why the alarm? Why two boat icons, one red, one yellow, on a collision course, not a hundred yards between them according to the grid?

I stood and raised my voice: "What the hell's going on!"

At sea, or in a car, whenever unsure of what lies ahead, you slow down and continue slowing until your brain ferrets out the puzzle. So I did, backing throttles gradually, feeling the Zodiac teeter, stern-heavy, as the engines dropped into a trough of their own making. In a boat, when slowing, you also always, *always* look behind you to make sure some inattentive idiot isn't about to climb your vessel like a ski ramp.

I did.

A lunar halo, a wafer of orange showing—that's the only reason I saw the Stiletto. Thirty feet of boat that punched a black hole in the moon, a silhouette shaped like an axe blade, the sharpest edge rocketing toward me at a speed that exceeded my experience on the water—seventy, eighty knots. The shock of it froze me for an instant: a rodent awareness of a stooping falcon, no point in resisting or attempting to flee—something else I'd never experienced. The Stiletto's Kevlar hull, only fifty yards from impact, cleaved air molecules so cleanly that the warning scream of engines didn't slingshot ahead until too late.

Even so, I lunged and hammered the throttles forward, my swollen left hand spinning the wheel to port. The Zodiac reared itself, bow-high, like a breaching whale, the combined torque throwing me to starboard, which probably saved me from being flung overboard when the Stiletto, engines suddenly in reverse, dug its stern deep to avoid colliding. The abrupt stop ejected a ton of displaced water that hit my aft quarter as a towering wave. For one long, shaky microsecond, I thought my prototype, high-tech, bullet-resistant special ops craft was going to flip like a cheap bathtub toy. To stabilize, I pulled throttles into neutral, as I almost fell but caught myself. One knee on the deck, a hand on the pilot's seat, I looked up.

Sunrise isolated waves with horizontal light, stars still glimmering in the west, the sea gray beyond the Stiletto, which appeared massive because its bow had swung directly above me. Close enough that the bowsprit banged the Zodiac's T-top and caused me to duck. This time, though, when I came up I had the khaki gun bag in my hands, fighting with the damn zipper.

"Morning, Dr. Ford! Imagine running into you out here!"

Vargas Diemer's voice above the rumble of engines while a cloud of scudding exhaust delayed his appearance. He was standing on the flybridge, wearing surgical gloves, I noticed, a familiar pistol in his hand: the .22 Mosquito, sound suppressor attached. Beside him was a sumo-shaped little man in a Nehru shirt of red and green, holding what looked like an Uzi machine pistol.

Kondo Ogbay.

30

JUST TALL ENOUGH TO PEER OVER THE railing, Kondo showed me a party grin and said, "Mon, we just havin' some fun wid you. Stay mellow, no one get hurt!"

Diemer, not smiling, backed him. "It's not what you think. Shut down your engines—and stay away from *that!*"

The pistol case inside the gun bag, he meant, which held my 9mm Kahr. Or did he mean the VHF radio, the mic within arm's reach?

Both. "Move away from the console, Ford. *Now.*" He used the pistol to motion me toward the bow, his voice flat, no accent at all, a man who'd been homogenized by travel.

I might have done it, but the Haitian was on his way down the ladder fireman style, moving fast for a fat guy, yelling, "Come out, come out, scarecrow man! Your good frien' Kondo, I come say good morning to you!" The machine pistol was at his waist, ready to rock 'n' roll when his feet hit the deck.

Diemer told him, "Don't do anything stupid, Sylvester," using the Haitian's real name, which proved a connection, then warned me again, "Step away from the controls—and that goddamn bag!"

I killed my engines and pretended to comply by placing the gun case on the seat, the case unzipped but closed, while Kondo hollered, "Tomlinson! I know you there. Pissing me off again, mon, that dumb!" His weapon now aimed at the Zodiac's storage console, the only place big enough for a man to hide.

I took half a step back from the pistol case, giving myself room to move, and became the indignant citizen. "Who in the hell are you talking to?"

"Who you think, dumbass! Tell yo no-'count surfer dude come out there 'fore I smoke his ass."

"With the Coast Guard coming?" I leaned my head toward the VHF radio.

Diemer replied, "Strange—we had the scanner on, didn't hear a thing." Then attempted to calm Kondo: "Hey, man, *chill*—I'll handle this," sounding Chicano suddenly, because the Haitian, far from home, was getting fired up while he threatened me, "Shoot yo damn boat to pieces, how else that gonna happen without a gun?" but his attention was on the storage console, convinced Tomlinson was inside. Called, "Ain't gonna hurt you, my brother! Not kill you, anyway. You insulted me, though, mon! My respect deserve somethin'! And we here to collect."

The businessman in Kondo then explained to me, "He can pay me in product. Got him some nice sticky buds, that's fine. Or he pay me, oh . . . ten thousand cash. See? I be reasonable. Kill a man, cops be on *all* our asses, understand what I'm sayin'?" Raised his voice, then, to inform Tomlinson, "Not gonna lie to you, though! Embarrass me 'front my 'sociates, you piece of shit! That serious, so you pay—else I cut my 'nitial on yo face, that okay wid me, too. A pretty letter *K*, but small, mon, like a tattoo—let folks know Kondo not to be fucked wid! But, hey, then afterward, you know, we friends again. Smoke herb. Tell stories 'bout this thing between us at parties, make the rich girls laugh!"

The indignant citizen, me, sounding nervous, told the Haitian, "Geezus, okay, look anywhere you want—there's no need for violence!" but I was thinking, *Do it . . . please come aboard and I will try not to break your neck.* Then looked at Diemer and dropped the act, saying to him, "You can't be this goddamn stupid."

The Brazilian held his pistol at shoulder level, pointed at the sky, watching it play out. Clipped to his wire-rimmed glasses were tinted lenses, the flip-down variety I'd seen only in antique shops—the son of a locksmith, fastidious in his equipage. He answered by speaking to the Haitian, but in a guarded way that made me wonder if he was conveying a private message.

"I'll check the storage area, get back up here. You're paying me to do a job."

Kondo looked up at Diemer. "The hell you doin', givin' me orders on my own damn ride, mon? You tell me you see the scarecrow board this rubber piece shit! Now we here, where the hell's my boy?"

Diemer's gaze swept past me—yes, a message attached—while also telling his client, "Didn't it all happen just like I said? Kondo, lighten up. *Listen* to me. The guy, Tomlinson, he's gotta be here, man—if he doesn't come out, I'll open that storage door and show you. But no killing—hey, *campesino*! It's just biz, not worth fifteen to twenty fighting off new boyfriends."

Kondo snapped, "Fuck dat, Pancho!" leveling the automatic at the storage console, then yelled another warning to Tomlinson, one green tennis shoe on the gunnel, ready to leap across to the Zodiac, but then changed his mind, this two-hundred-pound witch doctor, five feet tall, by blaming the Brazilian, "Shit, mon, tol' you keep us close, now we drift back too far. I ain't Batman! Get ta' work up there!"

Diemer, glancing another message to me, said, *"Sorry,"* and flipped his antique shades down, getting ready for something, his eyes bronze-shielded behind wire-rimmed glasses while he placed his weapon near the helm.

The Haitian, impatient with Diemer, hollered commands: "Turn the damn wheel, Pancho! No . . . no! You in neutral, bro!" which gave me time to

370

palm the little 9mm Kahr, my eyes tuned to the Brazilian who was adjusting his surgical gloves—a man who enjoyed sport, preparing to take the wheel of an Italian sports car. That was the impression. But not his intentions, and I thought, *Jesus Christ, what's his next move?*

What Diemer did was click the throttles into slow forward, calling over his shoulder, "Move your ass to the stern, man, stay low. *Kondo*—the dude's dangerous, I mean it! Wait 'till we're alongside, *then* you can board."

Kondo, talking to me like old friends, but walking backward as he'd been ordered, said, "Fuckin' Mexicans, mon, Brazil? Same thing. Spanish-speakin' folks, shit, they doan know nothin' 'bout no oceangoin' vessels." The man shrugged, made a humorous salute with the Uzi, his expression asking me, a fellow waterman, *What you gonna do?* Then shared the insult with the Germanic Brazilian, a wide white smile on his face, until he saw that Diemer had turned his back to the controls and was aiming a pistol at him.

The smile wilted. "Cut the shit, mon! We partners!"

Body squared, Diemer cradled the Sig Sauer Mosquito in two gloved hands, its sound suppressor appearing too long to miss at only twelve feet. His bronze glasses, sparking with sunlight, made a laser connection with the Haitian's chest.

I had the Kahr 9 up now, shielded by the seat's headrest, ready to take them both out, if necessary. Diemer first, because of his elevated position, but then decided, no, *Kondo first,* when Diemer asked the little man, "Where's the money, Sylvester?"

The jet-set assassin was done speaking Chicano, finally playing the role he knew best— precisely why I had already discarded his visual messages as bullshit.

Confused, Kondo took a step back, the Uzi still in his right hand, finger edging toward the trigger, but the barrel pointed up, relaxing on his shoulder at parade position.

"We damn partners!" Kondo said again. "What I say? You find me the scarecrow, five hundred clean, when we back at the dock! Hell, you worried, I pay you now! It in my bag, want me to prove it?"

"The *real* money," Diemer said, "it's on this boat someplace. Force me to search, you won't be around for the split." Then pulled the hammer back, getting down to business, which stopped the slow arc of the automatic weapon, freezing it against the Haitian's shoulder.

"*What* money? Sheeeit, mon!" Indignant, Kondo tried to laugh, but his voice broke, which he covered by saying, "Doan be fuckin' wid a priest of my knowledge! The rich woman, the blonde, her brother, what's-his-name, she not tell you 'bout my powers? Kill me, it doan matter. The shit still gonna come down on yo head, mon. I'm a voodoo sacerdotal, fuckin' highest priest! Guardian is Chango, mon! Brarilia, Rio, ask anybody what that name Chango mean!"

Speaking to me, but not moving his head, Diemer said, "Start your engines—and put that goddamn piece away!" Then got right back to Kondo. "There was a girl on Saint Martin. French, but part Brazilian. Blond, fourteen years old. You remember her name? Two years ago— February. Same month as now."

The way Diemer spoke, trying hard to remain the cold interrogator, brought back the memory of the photos I'd seen on his yacht: pretty girl, gawky, with braces, with a family resemblance. It also stopped my hand on the boat keys and caused me to watch Kondo, anticipating his reaction, anticipating his desperate lie of denial.

Didn't happen. Instead, the man shook his head, honestly mystified, and tried to explain, "My brother, the hell you talkin' 'bout? So many of those tourist girls kind, mon, I can't count! How you expect me to 'member—"

Which is when Vargas Diemer shot the Haitian drug dealer twice near the heart—*SNAP-SNAP,* like a muted cap pistol—punching a clean pattern, inches apart, despite a morning wind that was freshening, the sea gray, the sky a blue pearl edged with night. The rounds slammed Kondo's back onto the deck, not killing him, but it did knock the air out of him, so he writhed and kicked in Charlie Chaplin silence before he spoke, his words a labored hiss because of two sucking chest wounds and the pooling blood: "Call . . . call a doctor, mon! I didn't do nothin'!"

Diemer maintained a clinical disinterest by pushing a warning hand at me, palm out—*Stop!*—because I had my weapon up, sights focused on him. Told me, "We've got to get out of here!" then turned his back . . . hesitated, placed his weapon on the deck, and opened a black tactical bag, first time I'd seen it.

The Zodiac was drifting away, so I had to yell, "You can't just dump him over the side. Not like he is!"

Diemer, taking something from the bag, replied, "Start disconnecting your electronics—the navigation system, anything that gathers a GPS footprint. We have to throw it all overboard—but not here."

"What the hell's going on?"

The man looked over his shoulder, his impatience asking a question I had asked him moments ago: *How goddamn stupid are you?*

"Okay, okay," I said, but was still confused. "Fishing guides, a few of them might head out here after mackerel. We have half an hour at most."

Kondo was groaning, "Chango . . . Chango,

come heal my heart, I bleedin' to death, Chango!" while Diemer zipped himself into a cheap plastic rain suit, then sat and swung a leg over a knee: he'd brought along surgical booties and a face shield, too—a man who knew the risks of forensic evidence. Getting to his feet, neatening the pliant creases, he called to me, "Don't watch this!" but I did. Watched him slide down the ladder with his dancer's grace, pistol in hand, then straddle the Haitian, the Haitian staring up, terrified by this space-age creature garbed in plastic, which is when I decided, yeah, it was better if I looked away.

POP-POP.

When it happened, I was busy disconnecting my navigation electronics, even though I knew my special ops version had a default shredder if disconnected without first typing in a password. No need to explain to Diemer. Once I heard the splash of Kondo's body, we would be going our separate ways. I would reconnect the system later.

No telltale splash. Instead, a full minute passed before I heard the Brazilian call, "I want you to follow me—but run side by side. Better if fishermen mistake two boats for one boat. Understood?" He was topside again, dismantling electronics, hurrying to stack everything in a box, his rain suit blood-splattered, the face shield tilted up like he'd just come from surgery.

I started to say, "Not following you clear to

Lostman's River—" but realized I was being dense again, so amended, "Tell me what you've got in mind. The little son of a bitch was dangerous—I wouldn't have killed him, but that's not the issue. I'm shitting in my own nest here, so tell me the truth."

"No time!" Diemer hollered over the rumbling engines. "Follow for a mile, maybe two—whatever it takes. I'll have the autopilot on. Due west. No radio contact. I'll be down below—but watch for me! When I come up, I'll give you one of these"—he waved an arm side to side—"then I'll dump the electronics and jump. Got it? At twenty knots, planing speed, I go over the transom."

"Jump while the Haitian's boat's on autopilot," I said, confident I'd figured it out, picturing the Stiletto cruising two hundred miles until fuel was sucked dry, a dead man aboard—and hope to hell no innocent vessel got in the way of a drug deal that had, from all appearances, gone bad.

I was wrong about one detail.

"My *client's* boat," Diemer corrected. "It was stolen, the registry, all the papers changed—and Kondo almost got away with it." Then stressed again, "Watch for me! It'll happen fast."

He didn't add *Then you will stop and pick me up.*

But I did.

* * *

I WAITED UNTIL the Brazilian was aboard the Zodiac, hidden from view, sitting beside me on the deck, to ask: "Now what? I'm not taking you back to Dinkin's Bay."

Diemer shook his head. "Of course not!" He had brought only the tactical bag with him—heavier or lighter, no way to know—but it at least contained running shoes, shorts, and swim goggles, which he was changing into. His bloody rain suit, apparently, was already somewhere on the sea bottom with the box of electronics. "The emptiest stretch of beach you see," he added, "a half mile off, that should be safe."

"Sanibel, you mean." I turned the wheel toward a distant hillock of coconut palms and gumbos, south of the Island Inn.

Diemer nodded and asked, "Do you have bottled water?" his accent sharpening as he reacquainted himself with the role of the class-conscious Castilian. When the bottle was empty, he said, "I'll call Captain Futch and ask to fly with him tomorrow."

The man was still interested in the Avenger wreckage—either way, I wouldn't have been surprised—so I nodded. Yeah, it was better if his yacht stayed in plain view right where it was.

"The hippie will be flying?"

I replied, "I knew there had to be a reason you didn't want Tomlinson with me."

"He was smart to hide. Kondo is . . . he *was* a nasty little predator. A lucky break for me, him showing up this morning." Said it in a way that suggested he'd been tracking the Haitian for a while, waiting for an opening.

Again, I nodded. "It happens that way sometimes."

Diemer, too focused to respond, pointed ashore and told me, "Don't slow down. I'll roll off the seaward side, no one will notice. And *do not* look back."

"Swim half a mile to the beach, then run to Dinkin's Bay," I said, impressed. I was thinking, *Whatever happens with Hannah, maybe I've found myself another workout partner.*

Sliding his belly onto the Zodiac's portside tube, getting into position, Diemer reminded me that his alibi had been established, saying, "Every morning, the tourists, your local people, they see me taking my exercise. Always I am friendly. I wave. So friendly, you Americans!"

The jet-set assassin in a joking mood after a good day's work.

I was closing the distance on the *No Wake* buoys, half a mile away, only a few strollers on the beach at this hour, the tide too high for serious shellers to be out. So I glanced back to tell the Brazilian, "A couple more minutes."

Too late—the man was gone.

Still on the deck, though, was his tactical bag.

No accident—swimmers and joggers don't carry luggage, so he'd meant to leave it aboard. But . . . had he left it to somehow damage me, a man he considered to be a competitor in a strange business?

In the space of three days, the Brazilian and I had been partners in a burglary and a murder—crimes that typically divide but can also bond. On a gut level, I trusted the guy, but I wasn't going to risk incriminating myself by muling his luggage to Lostman's River.

I waited until I was four miles offshore, back on a southeasterly heading, before locking the Zodiac's autopilot, then unzipping the bag.

"Holy shit," I whispered when I opened another bag and saw the blocks of oversized euro bills—hundreds and five hundreds. Twenty blocks, give or take—a half million U.S. dollars, by my quick estimate.

In a separate bag was something else: two framed photos, but different shots of the same gawky teenage blonde I'd seen aboard *Seduci*. In one photo, the girl was leering at the camera, hamming it up, fingers inches from her lips as if blowing a kiss. I flipped it over and saw that it was inscribed and dated in Portuguese: *Tu Sr. Vargas mio Tio con amor en todos, Greta.*

"To my Uncle Vargas with total love, Greta."

Diemer's niece. Dated two years ago almost to the day. She had somehow been victimized by the

Haitian drug dealer, that was apparent. Perhaps Diemer's brother had, too—in a village that produced twin siblings, it was unlikely a sister would own an expensive racing boat like the Stiletto.

Or was I wrong about the connection?

There was a girl on Saint Martin, Diemer had said to Kondo just before shooting him, *She was French but part Brazilian.* Diemer had been in perfect English mode. The phraseology *but part Brazilian* had the flavor of secrecy, as if he was revealing something not commonly known. Or was I suspicious because there was so little up front and obvious about Vargas Diemer? Any attempt to assess offered no . . . clarity.

The girl was dead, that was my read. Or had been institutionalized for addiction—or brain damage, perhaps, thanks to a party gift from the smiling Haitian. In the future, depending on how it went, I might be able to ask questions. But not now—probably never.

I returned everything as I'd found it, stored the bag inside the locker, then stood at the helm and punched throttles forward until the twin Mercs were synced at 4700 rpm.

Fifty-three minutes later, I was running the switchbacks of Lostman's River, flushing white birds and a couple of gators, only a few miles from the entrance to Hawksbill Creek and the silence of an ancient, ancient place.

· · ·

THE NEXT MORNING, before noon, the seaplane buzzed me. Tomlinson, Dan Futch, and Diemer— *Alberto,* I had to keep reminding myself—plenty of room for all of them in the Zodiac, plus gear, when I ferried them to the edge of the Bone Field.

We made camp, got out the machetes, a metal detector, string for laying grids, and we went to work. Worked fast, but with the respect and care such a place demanded: four disparate men who shared the curse of obsessive genetics, and all highly motivated because of something Dan had arranged: Candice Sampedro had agreed to let us meet with her grandfather late tomorrow, Sunday, around seven p.m. It would give us a twenty-minute window, she'd told Dan, before the nurse replaced the old Avenger pilot's IV with a bag that contained his bedtime meds.

31

WHEN TOM LINSON AND I TIED UP AT Tin City Marina, downtown Naples, Dan Futch and the Brazilian were waiting with the taxi they'd hired, a Mercedes Sprinter van that, the driver said, usually only shuttled between hotels and Southwest Regional, so it was up to us or his Garmin to find Faith Village Hospice.

"Never heard of the place," he said.

"Only ten minutes from here," Dan assured us, then we sat in the back, talking in low voices, while the driver turned left onto Fifth Avenue and took us north, past all the pretty shops, then turned right onto Goodlette, a faster six-lane, the sky behind us mixing winter gray with sunset rust—6:25 p.m. Just in time to catch Mr. Angel Sampedro, ninety-one years old, before modern medicine funneled him one night closer toward his everlasting sleep.

Or maybe not from the subdued moods of the two pilots among us.

"Candice is worried because of the way Mr. Sampedro reacted," Dan said. "We haven't seen him, of course, but the monitors he's hooked up to, I guess the nurses came running because they thought he was having a heart attack."

"The granddaughter," Tomlinson said, "she showed him the photos?"

"No," Dan said. "But she told him what we found. I didn't want to blindside the old guy. Shit, I don't know . . . just got too much respect for what he did, okay? The old need-to-know-basis guys. Doesn't matter the age, the training's still there, and I can't mislead a man like that."

The photos we'd taken were not yet printed, but they were on Futch's laptop: the tail fin of an Avenger, enough moss and mud cleaned away to show a number the old pilot would have recognized: a big white 11 stenciled portside on the tail, a 3 aft on the starboard side: Fort Lauderdale Torpedo Bomber 113. The same aircraft the man had posed with seventy years earlier.

For us, the discovery had been a disappointment, at first, but we'd rallied. We hadn't found remnants of the iconic Flight 19, true. But what we'd found had played a role in the life of a man we hoped to meet.

Now even that seemed in jeopardy.

"We've got to play it by ear," Dan continued. "It's all up to Candice and the doctors—and Mr. Sampedro, of course. If they do let us in, we have twenty minutes, no more. Oh—something else. We aren't allowed to record what he says, no photos either. Especially no photos. Not even notes. That comes from Mr. Sampedro himself, so nothing tricky, okay?"

For some reason Dan looked at Diemer when he said it. The Brazilian's reaction was typically aloof. "He's dying—a man of ninety years. What could it possibly matter what he tells us? Or even a few photos?"

Tomlinson and Diemer had spent the last two days treating each other with congenial indifference, but my pal now leveled a hard look at the man. "There are people who believe photographs snip away pieces of their spirit."

Diemer countered, "Perhaps you've forgotten

the photos of Lieutenant Sampedro as a young man."

"People change—takes a while to figure out who they really are. It's an individual choice, man. Doesn't matter a man's age. His spirit's still in there, so we've got to respect that."

The Brazilian muttered, "Silly superstition," which Tomlinson talked over, saying, "It might help if I write the old gentleman a note. Let the granddaughter or a nurse take it in first. If he reads it and trusts us, then it's *his* decision." He looked around. "Any objections?"

Last night, by firelight, Tomlinson had played catch-up by going through photos he had yet to see, the old scalloped Kodaks of a young Lieutenant Angel Sampedro and his fellow aviators. Unlike me—Dan, too, probably—he had also plumbed the depths of the Sampedro family scrapbook, Christmas parties, dried flowers and all, often smiling at some fragment of the clan's history. Obviously, he had felt a connection—but didn't he always? I didn't mind him sending a note, nor did Dan, but the Brazilian couldn't resist commenting when Tomlinson folded the paper after only a second or two, pen in hand.

"So few words?" Diemer asked, amused. "Such eloquence!"

"Only two words," Tomlinson replied, flicking a look at me. "We don't want the old guy to kick off before he's finished reading. *Right?*"

NOW WE WERE with the aviator, the four of us, sitting or standing next to a bed that cradled the remnants of what had been a decorated Avenger pilot, a cocky flyweight Latino in the old photos, his combat-ready smile replaced by translucent lips and a tremor.

"Is . . . she . . . gone?"

Tubes in his nose, needles taped to onionskin forearms, gray veins beneath, Mr. Sampedro had ordered his nurse, then his granddaughter, from the room—a surprise to all. There had been no debate because he had issued the orders by refueling his lungs with a breath after each word or two. Decades of Camels—a lethal war wound shared by his generation—had left the man only one other option: a voice synthesizer that vocalized his two-fingered typing. Sampedro, a proud man, had yet to risk humiliating himself.

"We brought pictures, sir. Would you like to see a few? The tail off an Avenger we uncovered yesterday. Torpedo bomber"—Dan hesitated— "well, like your granddaughter said, the ship was out of Lauderdale. The tail section is from a ship you might remember: Avenger number 113."

Yes, the old man had been told, but Dan's offer still caused one skeletal fist to clench while eyelids slammed tight—a reaction of sudden pain. But then Sampedro gathered himself,

tapped the bed, and said, "Put . . . here. Glasses
. . . damn things. Need 'em to see."

I fetched his reading glasses from a table that
held flowers in a vase, a few get well cards, and
Tomlinson's note, still folded. Maybe the message
had done the trick, but I doubted it. Angel
Sampedro, even near death, was determined to
find out what we'd found—the man's last chance
for an update from his old training squadron.
Candice, the granddaughter, was the reluctant
one, but 1st Lieutenant Sampedro, U.S. Navy,
would not be bullied. So here we were, the old
man's hands shaking while Tomlinson helped get
him situated, then Sampedro tugged the laptop
closer, his way of demanding privacy while he
leafed through the images we'd shot. One by one,
the photos were mirrored by his thick bifocals.

Tomlinson, Dan, Diemer, and I also, one by
one, pretended not to notice when the aviator's
eyes flooded and a tear traced a glycerin path to
his jaw. I studied a painting on the wall from the
1930s I recognized—*South Moon Under* by
Eugene Savage. Tomlinson chewed at his hair
while throats were cleared.

Peeved by our transparency or irritated with
himself, the man sniffed and found the breath to
tell us, "Dumb . . . punks. *Allergies.* Stinkin' . . .
flowers," then glared at the vase on the table.

A joke, Dan was the first to realize, and we all
laughed too hard, but a barrier had been broken.

A slow dialogue then began, only the three pilots involved, so Tomlinson and I melted into the background and listened to Dan, a Southern gentleman in the presence of his superior, and Vargas Diemer, the military historian, make the best of what remained of our twenty minutes.

"Is this the tail section from your ship, sir? We saw an old photo, and Candice told us you'd had a training accident."

Bifocals mirroring photos that were bringing it all back, Sampedro shook his head. "One thirteen. My wingman's ship. Unlucky . . . we told him."

"His wingman's plane, that's what we found," Dan translated. He was getting excited but waited for the aviator to finish:

"His name . . . Coach . . . Coachie . . . Oxendine and . . . his gunner. Coachie flew 113. Just him and . . . one crewman."

I wasn't following. Tomlinson stiffened, equally confused but alerted by something, yet the Brazilian understood. "Fighter pilots all went by nicknames," he explained to us, then asked, "Lieutenant Sampedro"—Diemer rolled his *r* but without the aristocratic bullshit—"what caused Avenger 113's crash? We found it listed in Army Air Corps records but absolutely no details. Another ship went down that day, too, neither ever found—"

"Night!" the old man interrupted, the word

387

barked like a cough. "Storm . . . viz-a-bility zero! Hundred feet . . . shit . . shit soup. Out of . . . out of . . ." He tried to sit up but then lay back, his breathing labored. "Out of nowhere, that storm. Lost . . . we were all . . . *lost*."

Concerned, Dan knelt by the bed and said, "Five planes in your group and two went down. Definitely one hell of a storm, sir. But, listen, we don't need to hear all the details now. We'd love to come back. Tomorrow, anytime. Name the day and we'll—"

Sampedro cut him off with a shake of the head. "Two ships . . . *two*—not five. Special . . . training mission. Just me and Dakota—my radioman, gunner. Coachie flying wing with . . . his guy, Harley." Frustrated, out of air, the man's eyes closed, then flickered open. He lay there for several seconds, alone in his head, then sighed and chose Tomlinson to demand, "Hand me that damn thing!"

A plastic keyboard, oversized letters, that worked the voice synthesizer, an unseen speaker close enough to create the illusion that Angel Sampedro was a ventriloquist when he straightened his glasses and began drumming two index fingers on the keys:

Hate this gaddamn thing cant spell or type worth shit awful to get old jest you wait You two boys really pilots what you fly?

A digital voice tweaked to the pitch of a healthy

male robot, so exactingly phonetic that mis-spellings became idiomatic—a clever program designed to make the terminally ill sound damn-near human.

The Brazilian looked at Dan, both men surprised less by the question than this unexpected chance to communicate without sapping the life from the aviator's lungs.

"Fifteen minutes," I reminded Dan, who got right to it, telling Sampedro, "Civilian pilots, sir. This gentleman's big-time—" Diemer, he was talking about. "Swissair. Me, mostly seaplanes. I flew a Mustang once at an air show. My god, you pilots back then, there wasn't room in the cockpit for balls the size of yours."

Sampedro liked that. Squinted at the keyboard and said, "Tell nurse box 'em up. If she finds 'em." Gave Diemer a sharp look, then began an ironic exchange: "From Swit-zer-land?"

"No, Lieutenant."

"Good. Cowardly shits."

"My grandfather was Luftwaffe. Flew Junkers, then Messerschmitts." Which made it okay for Diemer to squat near the old man and point at a photo. "This is from your wingman's ship. You must have been flying the other Avenger. Torpedo Bomber 54? Tell us what happened, perhaps we can find the remains of your ship, too."

Sampedro swallowed, his mind drifting again. There was a reason he had never told his family what had happened that night—guilt, I suspected. Or something so scarring he refused to relive it. Share details now or take the truth to his grave? That was the decision the man was wrestling with—a decision he seemed to postpone by typing. "You have chart? Show where found Coachie's ship. No deal unless show me." Looked up at Diemer and Futch—a fierce look—then his synthesized voice explained, "Mission classified!"

"Uhhh, sure. Understood, sir." Dan began unrolling charts he'd brought along with his briefcase. Selected one of the largest—Captiva to Cape Sable—and enlisted Tomlinson and me to hold it open for the man to see. "You recognize the area, sir? It's changed a lot—"

Sampedro rasped, "Point to spot!" using his own voice, head off the pillow now, excited by the shapes of islands he had once viewed from his own aircraft. Then reached out a pale hand. "Near Estero Bay . . . has to be. Damn it, I . . . told them!"

Dan didn't respond for a moment, then said, "No, sir. We found the wreckage way to the south."

The aviator grimaced, not wanting to believe it, but listened while the younger pilot touched a finger near the top of the chart and worked his way down, saying, "Sanibel . . . Estero Island, Bonita Springs, and we're here, Naples. But we found the tail section and some other wreckage all *here*—about twenty-five miles southeast. A little place called Hawksbill Creek."

The expression of dismay on the old man's face communicated disappointment, pain, loss. His head fell back on the pillow. "Can't be. No! Was . . . so sure."

I was ready to ring for the nurse—the old guy had been through enough. But Tomlinson took charge by sitting on the bed, patting the man's leg. "We can come back another day—*if* you want us. But there's something you should know before we split."

The man lay staring at the ceiling. "So damn sure," he said again. Sniffed, blinked, tired of something, then stole a glance at the note on the table and asked, "How did . . . you know?"

"Your wife's scrapbooks," Tomlinson replied, "and your nicknames, I found a list," which confused everyone in the room, but not Angel Sampedro, who simply nodded while my pal added, "Pawn Man, that's what your crew called you."

"Pawny," the man smiled, thinking back.

Tomlinson gave me a look that meant something. "Yeah—makes even more sense. Trust me on this, Mr. Sampedro, we haven't told anybody anything yet. Use the keyboard, save your air. As far as we're concerned, unless you tell us different, what you say will stay in this room."

Tomlinson had no right to make such a promise, although it contained a kernel of truth: sitting around the breakfast fire that morning, the four of us had agreed to protect the Bone Field and shell pyramid until we had settled on which experts to contact. The tiny amount of wreckage we'd found—so far, anyway—didn't justify revealing the location of a place that resonated with the weight of history, an archaic nucleus that would attract every artifact hunter and Flight 19 kook within Internet range.

The old man had no reason to believe Tomlinson. My impression was that it didn't matter. Sampedro had lived with some secret he had carried for too many years. He was dying. We were his last contact with aviators he had once known, with the man he had once been, and it was time to cut the secret free. He reached for the keyboard and began typing, allowing a computer chip to speak to us from a long-gone night in February 1944.

"MY FAULT, NAVIGATION SNAFU. Killed three buddies, you sure about location?"

Our expressions confirmed the truth, so the digitized voice continued, "Board of inquiry right, then. Sent me South Pacific not as pilot, kept wings but reassigned. Thought Japs would kill me on Saipan, second marines ground unit, wish they had. Never told my son or family, not

Candice. Ashamed." The old aviator shut his eyes, no way to joke about the tears now.

Dan said softly, "You won the Bronze Star, a Purple Heart. You're a hero, sir. My god, a fighter pilot on the ground!"

"Killed my buddies. Lost my ship." His eyes frantic, Sampedro looked at a photo of the tail section, 113, then typed, "Not worst of it. Classified. All cause that damn storm."

A training exercise that had gone wrong, is what he meant, then let the keyboard explain in phrases that had the ring of confession:

Two Avengers, training for a special mission, had left Lauderdale an hour after sunset, each carrying only two men, not three. Sampedro flying FT-54, his radioman and gunner, nicknamed Dakota, sitting aft beneath a glass bubble, no contact between the two but for the intercom. Flying wing to wing with Torpedo Bomber 113, they had crossed the Everglades, bound for a target they had mock-bombed almost nightly, three weeks straight. Details were etched by rote into the old man's mind: 98 nautical miles from Lauderdale, course 263 degrees.

The voice synthesizer explained to us, "Off Key Marco, feds had anchored three, four barges size of a battleship. No lights, shit, you imagine? Coachie Oxendine, me, Dakota, his radioman, Harley—like the motorcycle. All my friends special picked. Private quarters like kings, best

393

chow. Fly nights, sleep days. Damn best at what we did, that's why, and scheduled to fly Pearl late June. Then Guam in July. Special mission, didn't know what. Feds in charge, all hush-hush."

The digital voice paused, which gave Diemer the opportunity to tell us, "Mid-July, Guam. The Americans—*you*—were assembling the bomb."

There are many ways to say that word, but the atomic bomb has earned a unique inflection.

"It was delivered in pieces," the Brazilian continued, "most of it by one ship. A heavy cruiser, not a battleship. She carried your entire supply of enriched uranium. Lieutenant, I have to ask: were you training to escort that ship?"

"Classified!" Sampedro hissed, his real voice less tolerant than the synthesizer. The man looked at Tomlinson, which seemed to relax him, then switched the subject to the storm that had caught the Avengers from the southeast and ended it all. The two planes had lost visual contact. Storm thermals made it impossible for Sampedro to maintain heading or altitude. He had climbed to eight thousand feet, as required by procedure, and attempted to alert Lauderdale and Key West—no response.

Despite the digitized monotone, what came next was chilling.

"Lightning bolt hit our wing. Saint Elmo's fire in the cockpit—blue like Hell, a nightmare.

Didn't know if we were over Everglades or Gulf. Told Dakota, 'I'm taking us down to check.' Second later, my windshield is full of Coachie's ship. Going too slow, that's what I remember, why the fuck he goin' so slow? White strobes blinding me . . . can still see tail fins coming at my head—those damn big numbers!"

Torpedo Bomber 113. The tail section we'd found buried in the earth like a hatchet, the wreckage we had used sponges to clean one slow layer after another, appeared to brighten on the computer screen and caused the old man to cover his eyes.

The planes had collided. Chaos followed . . .

Ten minutes wasn't enough time to finish the story. The nurse knocked and entered, Sampedro's bedtime meds in an IV bag. When he refused, Candice returned with the nurse to plead with her grandfather, the nurse telling us, "Mr. Sampedro needs his sleep! Days here move right along. We keep our guests busy!"

The aviator zapped the woman with a sour look that only Candice noticed, so she kissed her grandfather's cheek, saying, "Don't tire yourself, paw-paw. *For me?*" then left us alone.

In his own raspy voice, Sampedro waited until the nurse was gone to comment, "Bullshit, days don't move when you're dying. Only the nights. That's when I'm alive . . . memories . . . she doesn't understand."

Then he returned to the keyboard, still unsure, seventy years later, what had happened after his Avenger had knocked the tail off his wingman's plane.

Sampedro remembered a night spent alone, adrift in the Gulf of Mexico, his Mae West inflated. He remembered telling his rescuers he had seen a flare to the east—another survivor! The storm had certainly blown their ships northwest, so he shared the logical guess: the collision had occurred north of Marco Island.

For three days, planes and boats had searched, and Sampedro was still bitter—and suspicious— about why it had been called off so soon. Nothing close to the massive efforts he read about one year later when the Flight 19 Avengers vanished. "War was over by then," he reasoned. "Life not as cheap—too late now to worry."

Vargas Diemer, the historian, keyed in on the old man's suspicions when he said, "The heavy cruiser that carried the bomb to Guam—the world's total stock of enriched uranium in one container. You haven't wondered about that, Lieutenant?"

"Yes . . . many times." Sampedro spoke the words, his eyes moving to Tomlinson, who had reached for the note he had written.

"Night torpedo runs," Diemer continued, "that had to strike you as odd. On barges—barges the size of a battleship, you said. Why train to bomb anything bigger than a sub? Unless your government was worried the Japanese might disable or capture the ship carrying the atomic bomb. That they might have to order specially trained pilots to bomb the—"

"No!" Sampedro said. Coughed the word, as he did earlier, angry, but then calmed himself to concede through the synthesizer, "Thought about that, sure. Still do. Order us to sink our own ship—but would never happen. Not us. Not me, Coachie, Dakota, and Harley. Jap subs got her anyway, but later. Still feel guilty maybe could have protected her, Japs would'a been so confused by our talk. Could'a sunk that fuckin' sub! Instead thousand sailors dead on the . . ." The man's finger hesitated—a naval aviator still mindful of his training—then wrote, "Still dream 'bout saving those men on the *Indianapolis*."

Jesus Christ—Dan and I both stunned by what we'd just heard, but not Vargas Diemer, the historian, who was now even more suspicious and started to ask another question, but I cut him off, saying, "Stow it!"

The USS *Indianapolis* . . . my god, a war ship on a mission so secret that sailors who'd survived the sub attack had spent days adrift before radio silence was broken. Sharks had found them the first night among the blood and oil. By the fourth or fifth day, sharks were feeding in mass, killed six or seven hundred screaming men—I couldn't remember the numbers—before the first rescue plane touched down.

Tomlinson stood, slipped the note into his pocket, and took charge of the laptop as he reseated himself at the old man's shoulder, the old man weeping now. Gave the Brazilian a warning look, *Enough!* and put a hand on Sampedro's shoulder. "Mr. Sampedro, you haven't seen where we found the wreckage." Waited several seconds, then said, "We were sent to tell you—help give you some peace about what happened, that's what I think. Please . . . look at these photos."

"Should have . . . died," the man said, but Tomlinson wouldn't let him push the computer away. Instead, one after another, he clicked through photos of the shell pyramid, pottery shards, ancient shell tools. "Look . . . what do you think this is?" until he had the aviator's attention.

Then explained, "There is where we found the wreckage—where your three brothers died. A power spot. *Sacred* ground! Last night, going through your wife's scrapbooks, it all came together in my head and I knew why the spot had called to us. Harley, Cochise, the others, they're still *there,* man."

Coachie had been the wingman's nickname, not Cochise, but Sampedro, sitting upright while Tomlinson stuffed a pillow behind him, was suddenly interested. Looked at a few more shots, then asked, "Bones . . . they died . . . in an . . .

Indian place?" His face, his tone, wanting to believe. There was a sadness in his manner, though, and I knew he was thinking about the flare he'd seen—seven decades spent wondering if one of his men had survived.

Tomlinson picked up on it, too, so closed the computer, sparing the man photos of a parachute harness and a tube of morphine, telling him, "From what we found, the crash happened so fast, none of them suffered. It was the right time for your brothers."

"An Indian place," Sampedro murmured, his mind drifting again.

"Not Pawnee or Dakota," Tomlinson replied to Pawn Man, the aviator. "Ancient, though. See what I'm saying? You didn't kill your friends. Angel—they were leading you home."

As we exited the building, Tomlinson showed me his note, a two-word question: *Code Talkers?*

32

FRIDAY NIGHT, AND MY DATE WITH Hannah seemed a long time coming. The fact that the retriever was gone, claimed by his owner, when I got home late Sunday had nothing to do with it. And it wasn't just because I was nervous about a dinner date—although I was. So

I buried myself in research and started a version of my hook placement study for weekend anglers. I worked out twice daily—running, swimming, wearing a forty-pound vest on the VersaClimber—and I also kept a very close watch on the news.

Sooner or later, someone would find the Stiletto ocean racer, one dead witch doctor aboard, and competent men with badged IDs would appear at Dinkin's Bay, eager to ask questions. Sooner or later, Cressa Arturo would discover she had been robbed—same tight sphincter scenario.

The eventuality didn't seem to bother Vargas Diemer. Probably because the man was too smart, too cool to behave as if he had something to hide. So his million-dollar yacht remained where it was, the jet-set assassin happy to entertain guests, including his beautiful victim, Cressa, the soon-to-be-unmarried mistress. I, too, was a regular visitor during that short span, Monday through Friday, but only when I was bored or restless—which was *constantly*.

It was Wednesday evening, around sunset, sitting topside with Diemer, that I first learned that Dean Arturo had tried to escape from a state psych ward and then, inexplicably, had been released after his father posted bail. The Brazilian and I had been debating the true intent of the old aviator's secret mission while also discussing the role of American Indians in World War II. Many tribes had sent volunteers as "Code Talkers" to befuddle the Japanese and Germans by communicating in their native tongues. Something I didn't realize, though, was that *ninety percent* of Native American males had rushed to enlist after the bombing of Pearl Harbor. Their astonishing loyalty to a government they had every reason to distrust had provided the nation with highly decorated heroes in every service branch— including the Marine Corps' top fighter pilot ace, Gregory "Pappy" Boyington, a Sioux Indian.

It was an interesting irony that called for more research, and my respect for Angel Sampedro, and the airmen who had perished among ancestral bones, had grown exponentially. Same was true of the Brazilian, I think, who that Wednesday evening had turned the conversation to *why* those four men were being trained secretly for a night bombing mission off Guam.

Diemer pressed a three-pronged theory: 1. The U.S. government would have been derelict not to anticipate the *Indianapolis* being disabled. 2. Only bombers flown by American Code Talkers could have breached the ship's security umbrella while also communicating freely among them-selves. 3. The training mission's secret couldn't risk compromise by a prolonged search for three missing men.

Sinister government conspiracy theories are as commonplace as the simpletons who believe them, but this was the jet-set assassin talking so I had to at least listen patiently. Which is what I was doing when Diemer's cell phone rang: Cressa Arturo calling, frightened once again because her crazy brother-in-law was on the loose.

"Why don't you take her on a cruise?" I suggested when he'd hung up, then had to add, "Deano couldn't get to her on your boat—and less chance of her looking inside her wall safe. *Whatever* it was you took."

Diemer dodged the implicit question by asking, "Is he dangerous? I've never met the man."

Later, I would regret my answer, but what I told the Brazilian seemed true at the time. "No, but in the way most snakes aren't dangerous," I said. "The guy will run unless you corner him." I then repeated my suggestion that he take Cressa on a trip—Key West, although she'd probably enjoy Palm Beach more.

The man was already shaking his head. "Even on a vessel the size of *Seduci*, quarters are too close with a woman aboard. Not for more than a day or two. Better, I think, if I simply make nightly visits."

"Just an idea," I said. "A beautiful woman— very *neat,* too, so you have a lot in common—and she's rich."

"Tempting," he said, "but unwise. Risk ugly scenes, emotional involvement? No . . . In certain *professions*"—the man attempted a kindred smile—"romantic relationships are wasted time. Never do they survive more than the first or second new assignment. They ask questions, they suspect infidelity. How does one answer? Impossible!"

That gave me the opening I'd been waiting for to ask about the gawky teenage blonde in the photo—Diemer was smart, he would know I had looked inside his tactical bag—but it would also open up the subject of a half million or more in euros, cash. And did I really want to know the truth in advance of being questioned by police?

No, I did not.

So, instead, I remained silent, which gave the Brazilian an opportunity to add to my restlessness when he said, "You think I'm selfish, don't you?"

"Top-of-the-food-chain selfish," I said.

"You're right. Of course! I have to be—and so do you. But do me the kindness of looking at it from the woman's perspective—Cressa, in this case. I fall in love with her, allow Cressa to fall in love with me, even though I know she will soon hate me—and for good reason. So I keep love in the bedroom, where it belongs. You see? It allows me to be selfish, but also extremely *unselfish*."

The Brazilian, pleased with his rationalization, sniffed, placed his wineglass on the table, vanished for less than a minute, then handed me a sealed envelope as he walked me to the door.

"It has been . . . pleasant working with you, Dr. Ford. I was afraid you would ask all the obvious questions. Instead, you lived up to your reputation."

"At the risk of being obvious," I replied, "what's this?" meaning the envelope, midsized manila, but it had some bulk to it.

"Professionals get paid. Isn't that what the word means?"

When I got back to the lab, I opened the envelope. Twenty thousand in euros—almost five percent of a half mil. Not bad. Generous, actually, by European standards.

I gave some thought to calling the man and thanking him. Plus, I'd forgotten to request updates on Dean Arturo.

I did neither: an oversight a thinking professional wouldn't make.

TWICE THAT NIGHT, I called Hannah. In total, talked for nearly an hour—an outrageous amount of time for someone like me. Pleasant, we laughed a lot, yet I still couldn't sleep. Days may not move quickly for a dying man, but the night moves slowly, too, for a man who lives alone and who is starting to ask himself, *Is it time?*

That's why I was restless and I finally admitted it.

Like it or not, a formal date with someone like

Hannah Smith implied a commitment, however minor, that caused a claustrophobic twinge. But Hannah wasn't the cause. By three a.m. I'd convinced myself it was true so celebrated by pulling on running shorts and shoes, then jogging to the beach while my brain thought it through.

What I felt was more accurately linked to a combination of recent events and elements, I decided: the haunted look in Angel Sampedro's face, dried flowers in the family album, the *POP-POP* of a silencer, the resonance of human bone beneath my own mortal feet.

Is it time to . . . make a change?

Unfortunately, I'd made the mistake of asking Tomlinson that question on the long boat trip home from Lostman's River.

"First off, Doc, your entire premise is totally bullshit! Same with the question 'What time is it?' Try this: start counting in your head, one-two-three-four-five, and keep counting until your attention swerves to something else. Something *interesting,* man, and there's your answer! Why? Because time stops the *instant* we release the bullshit concept that time actually exists. Understand? Let go of all the illusionary crap on the outside and we become timeless beings, man. *Inside,* you know? Where it counts."

There are those rare occasions when I envy Tomlinson's drug-buffered view of life, but I still could not let go of the question and it continued to pester me all day Thursday and into the night. Had I reached a period in my life when it was time to . . .

Do what? Be specific, for christ's sakes!

Okay. Time to settle down . . . buy a van for the kiddies, take up golf, attend functions, be home by ten, pay bills on time, discuss insurance policies, endure lunch dates, smile blandly at parties, vote the straight ticket, mow the lawn, wave cheerfully at a neighbor when, in fact, you want to stick that leaf blower right up said neighbor's ass.

That's what you're thinking about doing, Ford? Oh . . . then at least be honest and project ahead: might as well burn the false passports, the old logbooks, clean out the secret hidey-holes, and notify your overseas friends—via Facebook, maybe!—that your traveling days are over. Why? Because you have met a long-legged, independent woman who, while not wildly attractive by Hollywood standards, jabs a hole in your chest when you imagine how she might look stepping out of the shower or signaling to you from beneath the sheets. If that's your problem, remember what the Brazilian said about relationships: Impossible!

I was driving myself crazy.

"Crazier," Tomlinson informed me Friday morning when I sought out his wise counsel as a

Zen Buddhist master. Which sent me back to the lab, thinking:

Make a list, Ford, it's what you always do. Pros on one side, cons on the other. Then measure the list with a micrometer. Note the weight of every loaded word on the con side, compare those weights with loftier words in the pro column. Finally, subtract smallest number from largest number and then . . . and then divide the goddamn results by your total IQ of late, which shouldn't reduce the sum by one goddamn digit!

My cell phone chirped before I began this idiocy with a pen and legal pad. Hannah texting, *See you at 8?*

It was 6:30, almost dark outside. Thank god, she didn't add one of those idiotic smiley faces or I would have hurled the phone across the room, then booked the next flight for Cartagena.

Looking forward to it! I replied, then sat at the computer because I had thirty-five long minutes to kill before showering for our date. Fortunately, and surprisingly, there was an interesting e-mail awaiting to blot up the time. Dr. Arlis Milton of Atlanta writing with answers, as promised, but also to say things weren't going well with the retriever's reintroduction to civilization, although the man did his best to hide the truth among seven careful paragraphs.

The most interesting graph revealed much about the dog—Sam was the unfortunate name—and his late owner, Bill, no last name offered:

By now you've probably done your homework and discovered my wife's maiden name so know that my father-in-law was among the most respected field trial breeder/hobbyists in the country. Are you the biologist Marion Ford who has published in various Florida journals? If so, you may appreciate that Bill was also a noted geneticist and wealthy enough to fund his own research as well as his hobby. Bill had great hopes for Sam, and his sire who was a Grand National champion . . .

Geneticist? That was intriguing. So the owner had been William-something, Ph.D. who, the letter informed me, had died in an Alligator Alley car crash on his way to a field trial near Miami. Three paragraphs later, Dr. Milton got to his real reason for e-mailing:

Naturally, we assumed both dogs also died because of the fire. It is for this reason that our attorneys wrongly settled Bill's estate without addressing a codicil that required my wife to provide for his animals. This was more than a year ago . . .

One year? The physician was telling me that, legally, he and his wife had been spending money that shouldn't have been disbursed, but all I could think was, *Twelve months alone in the Everglades, but that damn dog survived!*

Sam had issues, though, the letter continued. He wasn't "showworthy" (*saleable,* I translated) because of physical injuries. But was still "very trainable" (*out of control,* was the inference) despite the "expected behavioral changes" required of a dog to survive in the wild—even one with "national champion bloodlines."

In short, by taking possession of the dog, Dr. Milton and his wife had touched a legal base, as required by their inheritance, and now the dog was for sale. I had done a good deed, so was being offered the right of first refusal, but the price—$1,500—was *probably* firm. If interested, call ASAP.

There was also a P.S. so saccharine sweet it made me wince: *Bill loved the movie Old Yeller and the sequel about Old Yeller's son. Savage Sam. Silly movie but thought his new owner might like to know!*

Funny. I was laughing as I skimmed through the letter again, picturing Dr. Milton's elegant Georgia home and the dog's swath of destruction that had surely motivated the letter. No time to reply, though, let alone call, because it was almost seven. Time to shower up, shave close, and get ready for my long anticipated date.

That's when I heard it. A strange *Hoo . . . Hoo . . . Hoo . . .* sound coming from outside. Reminded me of the hoot-owl call boys sometimes make by blowing through their hands. Whatever the source, it didn't belong on the walkway or in the mangroves where it was coming from. Had I been in South America, Indonesia, some far-flung place on an assignment—anywhere but in my own home—I would have taken the fifteen seconds required to grab a flashlight. Probably would had slipped a pistol into my pocket, too.

I didn't. Another mistake—and it might have killed me.

33

BAREFOOT, WEARING ONLY RUNNING shorts and a tank top, I walked out on the deck and heard it again: *Hoo . . . Hoo . . . Hoo . . .* Then my eyes followed my ears shoreward, where, in an instant, all seemed to be explained: someone had set a paper bag ablaze at the entrance of my walkway near the gate.

Idiots, I muttered. The oldest of adolescent pranks: scoop animal poop into a grocery bag, light said bag on fire, then laugh from the shadows while an outraged neighbor stomps the fire out, then has to clean excrement off his shoes.

I looked to my right: Friday night is party night at Dinkin's Bay. The marina's traditional Pig Roast and Beer Cotillion—acronym, PERBCOT, but is often referred to as PERV-COT because the hilarity sometimes gets out of hand. Music was thrumming, the docks crowded. Now, apparently, one or more of my playful neighbors were challenging my absence with an ingenious practical joke.

Through cupped hands, I called toward the mangroves, "Put it out before you set the dock on fire! I'm late for a date."

Hoo . . . Hoo . . . Hoo . . . was the reply.

"Goddamn it, I don't have time for this!"

Silence while the bag continued to burn, sparks thermaling starward.

I hollered, "*Tomlinson!* If it's you, I swear to god I'll . . ." but left the threat unfinished because now I could smell burning wood. My walkway has been braced and redecked in the patchwork tradition of most old docks and some of the planking is vintage Florida pine—highly combustible. If a plank caught fire, a stringer would go next. Time to act or I'd have a mess to deal with. Worse, I'd be late for my date!

Because I was barefoot, I couldn't kick the bag off the dock, so I looked for the first thing handy. The bamboo shaft I'd snatched from Bambi's hands was still leaning against the house where I'd left it. Above it, though, hanging from a beam, was an old gaff hook I seldom used but kept around because it was lashed to a fish billy that had once been my father's—a chunk of mahogany two feet long. Use the hook to yank the bag away or use the disposable bamboo?

I chose the gaff because I hadn't felt its heft for a while, then trotted down the steps, onto the walkway, the burning bag so bright it fired the lucidum eyes of something feeding in the shallows. I slowed to look—yep, a couple of big stingrays suctioned to the bottom—then had to wait while my eyes readjusted before I continued on. Which is why I didn't notice a man's mud black face protruding from the water nearby. Nor the red laser beam I tripped as I approached the walkway gate, which would have told me there was a camera nearby videoing the whole scene.

Instead of excrement, the bag contained only balled-up newspaper—not that I inspected it closely. I used the steel hook to fling the thing into the bay, turned to watch flames create steam . . . then froze, confused by what I was seeing:

White eye sockets blinked at me from a face of black marble, the statue of a man standing in water, ten paces away, his shoulders glistening as the statue pivoted—a throwing motion.

What the hell . . . ?

A shaft of light launched itself toward me, impossible to dodge it traveled so swiftly, a harmless trick of moon and shadows that split my chest with the impact of a sledgehammer and the crunch of splintering bone.

"I got him!"

A man's voice conveying a reality while a

primal voice—my voice—screamed, *"Goddamn it!"* Then I was on my back, perplexed by the crushing weight on my chest, a sensation levered by all that was above me, the weight of mangrove darkness and stars. No pain, but I couldn't breathe. Could I crawl? Yes . . . two feet of water helped float me to my knees. My glasses were around my neck on fishing line, lenses streaked but usable. Floating nearby was a frail shaft of wood: the spear that had hit me and broken away from my body.

"Got him in the heart, I think! Check him, Luke, check him!" Then a boyish howl: *"YES!"*

Sound of footsteps . . . a red bead of light was leading a man's silhouette toward me, then over me, the man wary, taking his time, as if approaching a snake. The red light blinking with mechanical precision as my brain linked the image with events and I realized Bambi was approaching, Luke Smith, a camera around his neck.

Jesus Christ . . . the lunatics are making a video.

Yes, they were. Bambi on the Sony while Deano, out on bail, but now standing in water, awaited a damage report from his coproducer. Something else: Deano had another spear in his hand, ready, while his cameraman kept rolling, getting it all down. Deano impatient, too, demanding, "Where'd I hit 'em, goddamn it?

Close to the heart? Knocked him right off the damn dock, you see it!"

Bambi, with his Boston accent, telling him, "Hold your horses!" Then asking me, "Are you okay?" without taking the camera away from his face.

Stupid question! Something, a sliver of bone, I guessed, was protruding from my sternum—embarrassing—so I covered the boney stub with my hands, safe from the lens, while I sucked in air so hot it burned my teeth.

"Help . . . me . . . up!" I managed to say. It was the voice of a stranger, but my lungs were gradually filling, my brain was eager to clear—if I could just get to my feet, I'd be okay!

No deal, not just yet, Bambi was busy. Zoom in tight on the fallen quarry: Marion D. Ford, the biologist who had damaged their failed careers. Focus . . . zoom closer, hold the camera steady. Night optics blur so easily! Suddenly, though, Bambi didn't like what he was seeing. Camera was lowered, allowed to hang from a neck strap, while he said, "Jesus Christ, Deano, he's bleeding."

"No *shit*. But did I get him in the heart?"

Bambi began to back away. "I mean, he's really *bleeding*. You didn't use a blunt tip? Goddamn it, you promised you'd use rubber!"

"No! I said I wouldn't use *metal!*"

"He's hurt bad, Dean. Shit, man, the point's sticking out of his fucking chest!"

"It was a clean hit and I didn't use metal!"

"His fucking chest, you hear me! I never agreed to this bullshit."

Bambi was ready to run, but I knew I couldn't let that happen. Leave me alone with the crazy spear hunter before I was able to move? My lungs were starting to function, my brain was rebooting, assembling details faster and faster, but that all had to remain a secret and hiding secrets is something else I'm good at. So I did my best to appear calm when I wheezed, "It was an . . . accident. I'll be okay."

Was that true? I believed I'd recover even if Bambi didn't. The sliver buried in my sternum couldn't have gone very deep, but if it had I was screwed. My heart lay against that boney plate. My lungs there, too, which explained the burning sensation. Or was I in shock, lying to myself?—minimizing the damage, which badly wounded men sometimes do? I'd witnessed that reaction on the other side of the Earth. Central America, South America, too. Men who'd groaned "We'll joke about this one day" while their life's blood was sumped into the jungle.

Bambi wanted to believe me, though, and he stopped backing away. *Good.* At least one of them had sense enough to know he would have to explain to police. Which he proved by explaining to me, "Seriously, Dr. Ford, I didn't think he'd pull a stunt like this! It's what we're calling a

Challenge Coup—a way to create drama between opponents. This wasn't supposed to happen, I swear!"

I reached a hand toward him. "I . . . believe you. Help me up."

Deano didn't like that. "No you don't, goddamn it! Get back on the camera, I'm not done."

Bambi had started toward me but stopped. "Probably shouldn't move you. You have any friends around? Someone should call an ambulance, I think." Then added in a rush, "Or I can do it. I've got my cell right here."

"The hell you will!" The slosh of a big man wading through water is a sound I know well. Deano, the Zulu pretender, was coming in for the kill. Allow him to get close enough, he'd put the other spear in me.

Fear . . . we all process it differently. In me, panic arrives as a neural chill . . . a chill soon replaced by a chemical surge, then a chemical burn that I feel in my brain. The transformation is abrupt. It narrows the senses like being shunted into a tunnel or looking through a sniper scope. When it happens, my world is drained of color and I am indifferent to the subtleties of black and white—and pain.

A common word for that chemical transformation: *Rage.*

The transformation happened now. I was on my knees on the east side of the dock, Deano on the other side but farther out, water to his waist, most of my body screened from his view. He couldn't see what I had already spotted: the floating handle of a mahogany club that had been knocked away when I fell. The club was dragging a gaff hook along the bottom as it drifted.

Something else I noticed: Bambi, a Sony digital hanging from his neck, was wearing a photographer's vest, the glint of a flashlight lens visible when his right leg moved. The leg moved now when I told him, "Grab my hand." Then raised my voice above Deano's heavy splashing to urge, "Don't worry about him. You want the police on your side or not?"

"You're missing good footage, you idiot!" Deano hollered, coming faster now while Bambi's jerky movements told me he was close to a meltdown.

I assured him, "It's not your fault—it's *his* fault," but got one foot under me just in case Bambi didn't come through. But he did, after one nervous glance at his partner . . . reached, grabbed my hand, and pulled.

I let it happen . . . used the momentum provided by Bambi's kindness to come up hard and smash the man's nose flat with the palm of my hand. If I hadn't caught him by the camera strap, he would have gone down. But I did catch him. Used the strap to choke the man into compliance, yelling, "Dial nine-one-one! Do it or I'll kill you right here!" When his frantic nodding had convinced me, I yanked the flashlight from his pocket, then shoved the cameraman toward shore. "Do it now!"

Deano saw it all and it stopped him, the spear at shoulder level ready to throw. He yelled, "Ford, that's not the way the game's supposed to go!" then took a step back when I tried to blind him with the flashlight. I had the wooden gaff in my hand, prepared to duck . . . was also fighting a sudden nausea because, for the first time, with the flashlight, I could see my bloody tank top and the object buried in my sternum.

Deano's attention, though, shifted to Bambi, who was crawling into the mangroves for protection, his nose a smear of black, but the phone already in his hand. It caused Deano to turn as if considering new quarry—and that's when everything changed. The flashlight I was holding became a stage light. The spear hunter became an electrified clown who screamed, *"Shit!"* . . . jumped as if he'd been cattle-prodded and threw his hands wildly into the air. Then bounced around on one good leg, the other leg paralyzed because of what he had just stepped on—only one explanation, as I knew from experience. I watched the big man stumble, fall, get up and fall again, while his larynx was tortured by a shriek so agonized it pierced the party music at the marina. Deano was lunging toward shore in a panic when I heard Mack's booming voice, "Hey! What's going on?" Then Tomlinson's voice, concerned, hollered, "Doc! You okay?"

No . . . I wasn't doing well at all. I'd seen what was stuck in my chest. Impossible to pull it out because the edges were serrated like a blade of boney sawgrass—not that I was dumb enough to try. Only two inches of the thing showing, but if even the tip had pierced my heart I would soon be dead. Nothing I could do to stop it from happening and no time to waste, so I walked methodically toward Deano, flashlight in one hand, wooden gaff in the other.

Like most snakes, he'll run unless you corner him, I had told Vargas Diemer.

The crazy brother-in-law couldn't run now, though—not with a leg paralyzed by pain and the primitive protein now pumping through his system. Even if he tried, I would summon whatever was needed to catch him. Thought about it as I slogged past Bambi, who was saying into the phone, "Yeah, an ambulance . . . *Christ* . . . I don't know how bad. *Bad!*"

Took two more steps before I stopped and told him, "Cancel that."

"What?"

"Tell them there's no rush."

"Jesus, man, I think you're in shock. You need to sit down."

"Stay out of this," I warned Bambi, then continued walking, my eyes seeing only the spear hunter—the man sitting now and moaning—while all the options played through my mind in stark black-and-white: *Gaff Deano under the jaw, drag him out and drown him fast. No . . . grab the son of a bitch by the ponytail, take him way, way out in the Gulf of Mexico, where . . .*

Where, if I didn't bleed to death in the next couple of minutes, there were all kinds of options.

The wooden walkway lay between me and Deano. It took some effort to climb over it, but I managed, hearing him say in the voice of a spoiled child, "Shit, I need a doctor! You guys do something *now!*"

Because I was behind him, only a couple of steps away, he was startled when I replied, "I plan to," and he spun around. Looked up into the flashlight's beam and shielded his eyes.

"Dude, you're blinding me—this is serious!"

"Couldn't agree more."

"Goddamn thing went clear through my foot! Pain's killing me, man!"

"Then I better hurry," I said and pointed the flashlight at the ground. That's when Deano saw the club I was carrying, plus the stainless gaff hook, then connected it all with the look in my eyes, the tone of my voice, and he scooched away from me.

"Don't," he whispered, "please don't," the child in him doing all the talking now.

Several seconds, I stood there and thought about it, staring at the rich boy with the damaged brain who had failed at everything: big, babyish face, mud-streaked with tears, cradling his swollen foot in both hands. Then looked from Deano to my stilt-house, where my eyes lingered on the pond shimmering beneath, the small pond that is Dinkin's Bay. Took a deep breath, my internal monitor aware that my lungs didn't gurgle with blood. So maybe I would live, and maybe it was time to be smart for a change. Time to . . . *what?*

Not befoul my own nest, for one thing. And also to stabilize my wound by not moving.

I sat heavily on the walkway, placed the gaff hook behind me, and said to Deano, "Hurts, doesn't it?" Then angled the flashlight toward the broken stingray spine protruding from my sternum. A thousand years ago, sacrificial victims of the Maya had, no doubt, felt the same numbing fear.

"Goddamn worst pain I've ever felt in my life," the spear hunter replied, then yelled, "Luke, where the hell's that ambulance?"

TWENTY MINUTES LATER, I was in the ambulance, on a gurney, growing increasingly unsettled by the concern of the EMT who had already strapped me immobile and was now on the phone with a trauma physician.

The stingray barb had moved in my chest, apparently, and I was listening to fragments of one-sided medicalspeak that confirmed I might be dying.

CT scan . . . depth of penetration "significant" . . . Yes, assess damage associated with a fractured sternum: mediastinal structures, pulmonary and myocardial contusions. Then came a long list of words that grated against the beep of the fluctuating heart monitor but might explain my plummeting blood pressure and why I would have to be rushed straight to surgery.

I was feeling hazy, too, a symptom of failing cranial hydraulics that spooked me. An odd realization: *Time—whatever the hell time is or was or isn't—I might be running low.* I couldn't see my watch, but knew it was after eight. *Date night!*

"Need to call someone," I told the EMT, my chest burning from the effort.

She shook her head, busy with a syringe. "Quiet! Later, when we get things figured out."

"Send a text?" I asked.

The woman looked at the monitors in a way that wasn't encouraging, which pissed me off— irrational and I knew it—then made it all better by allowing me to dictate a message.

Moments later, my phone chimed with Hannah

Smith's reply: *On my way, hold on. Please hold on!*

Moments later, I heard another chime, and a second message was held above my face to read privately: *Love always, Hannah.*

"Your wife?" the EMT asked, taking the phone away.

"Maybe so," I replied. "And I'm buying a dog, too."

Center Point Large Print
600 Brooks Road / PO Box 1
Thorndike ME 04986-0001 USA

(207) 568-3717

US & Canada:
1 800 929-9108
www.centerpointlargeprint.com